The Interpreter

OSS

D0878589

A.J. Sidransky

THE INTERPRETER

In the heat of wartime Manila, 23-year-old American GI Kurt Berlin is recruited by the OSS to return to Europe to aid in the interrogation of captured Nazis. A refugee from the Nazis himself, Berlin discovers the SS officer he's interpreting is responsible for much of the torment and misery he endured during his escape. And that very same Nazi may hold the key to finding the girl he left behind. Will the gravitational pull of revenge dislodge his moral compass?

From the terror of pre-war Vienna to the chaos of occupied Brussels, through Kurt's flight with his family through Nazi-occupied France, to the destruction of post-war Europe, The Interpreter follows Kurt's surreal escape and return. How much can his young mind absorb before it shatters?

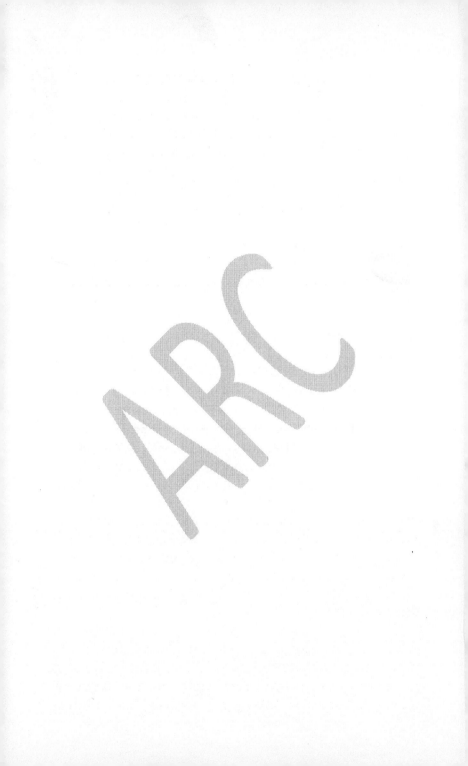

ACKNOWLEDGMENTS AND FORWARD

At the end of World War II, the American government, along with the armed forces, initiated a program to recruit former Nazis to work with them against the Soviet Union. One of these programs known as Operation Paperclip, was specifically directed at Nazi scientists. It brought former physicists and others to the United States to add their collective knowledge to ours during the cold war. The Soviets had a similar program known as Operation Osoaviakhim. In all, thousands of former Nazis and their families were granted not only relief from prosecution, but new lives in the United States.

Imagine if our government or military had in fact recruited former Nazis as spies to fight communism in the coming cold war? While there are no other named operations on the part of our government or military to overlook Nazi activity, actively solicit the help of former Nazis and reward them for their new loyalty, unquestionably thousands, perhaps tens of thousands of former Nazis and Nazi supporters escaped justice, came to the United States and began life anew in the land of their former enemies. That supposition is at the heart of The Interpreter. From this author's perspective, the question is whether the perception of national security should have outweighed the need for justice and closure to begin with. In the end we turned a blind eye to the fact that these former combatants condoned the actions of their government when they had the chance to resist.

This book is a work of fiction. It does though contain factual elements from the life of Kurt Berlin, the husband of my cousin, Susan Reichman. When I first heard the story of how Kurt's mother smuggled gold out of Nazi Germany in her corset, I was dumbstruck. When I approached Kurt, then in his 80's, to learn more about the circumstances of his escape with his parents from Vienna, he told me that I could use some of their experiences in a book, but that he didn't want a book written about him. He believed his story, while unique, was not exceptional. I agreed not to write a biography or memoir about him and his parents, but I disagree that the story isn't exceptional. It most certainly is.

Both Kurt and Susan were remarkable people. They exhibited the resilience that is so often the signature trait of survivors. What was so unique about them was that they were so young when they experienced the trauma of escape. Both born in 1927, they were 12 years old when the war broke out. Elements of both of their stories appear in The Interpreter.

I spent many hours over decades discussing those critical months in the year before the war began in 1939 with Susan to better understand why so many of our family didn't leave and ended up murdered at Sobibor and Auschwitz. Some 35 years ago, when I asked her why they didn't leave she asked me a question. Susan asked me if what happened there was happening here would I leave and when? My answer was I would leave when I knew it was time. She then said that by the time you know it is time to leave, it's too late.

I wrote this book during the election campaign of 2016, which was terrifying. Too many times what I heard on television news at the end of my writing day mirrored too closely what I had learned and was writing about. We need to open our eyes now to prevent fascism's return under the banner of the American flag and a red hat.

I would also like to say a word about the Kindertransports that saved the lives of thousands of German and Austrian Jewish children. Imagine how these children felt in those final moments looking back at their parents on train platforms all over the Reich never knowing if they would see their parents again. Many didn't. I asked Susan once why our relatives in Hungary and Slovakia didn't send their children alone, the way Kurt's parents had. She told me that was something unique to the character of the German and Austrian Jews. We Hungarians didn't have the force of character to stand smiling stone-faced while our children disappeared from before our eyes. This comment was made with love and admiration not malice. As a parent I'm not sure I could have done it myself.

I have many people to thank for their contributions to this book. First and foremost, Kurt Berlin and Susan Reichman Berlin. Kurt's parents, Hertz and Berta Berlin. Susan's parents Gyula Reichman and my dear, dear Aunt 'Ica', Ilona Rothman Reichman. My grandfather, Jack Greenfield, for all that he taught me about World War I, Austria-Hungary, its history, and the short-lived communist government of Hungary under Bela Kun. Both he and Hertz Berlin were caught up in that whirlwind in Budapest in 1919.

To my dear cousins, Kurt and Susan's daughters, Debbie Vas, Lisa Pion-Berlin, and Cindy Halberlin, for permitting me to use parts of their parents' stories in this novel. I don't have to tell any of you how much I adored your parents and how much they loved all of you and your children. Both you and your children are a living triumph over Hitler and his plans for our people every day. To Rachel,

Joslyn, Jeremy, Emma, Jesse and Adam, your grandparents were superheroes.

I would also like to thank my wife, Hope, and my son Jake, who encourage me to keep on writing and working despite the difficult path the world of publishing suffers from today. To Black Opal Books for offering me the opportunity to put this work out there for readers. To the Jewish Book Council, in particular to Naomi Firestone-Teeter and to Miryam Pomerantz-Dauber, for their constant support through a difficult and long writing period. To Erica Obey, my fellow author and friend, whose suggestions improved this book dramatically. To fellow author Annamaria Alfieri, for much guidance and encouragement. To friend and fellow author Julian Voloj, for proofing the German dialogue in this book. And to my best friend, William Cruz, for believing in me and reminding me that I can do it, every day. To Fern Schapiro the final beta-reader for her honest assessments of what worked and what didn't.

To all those I may have overlooked. Thanks. I hope you enjoy the story.

A J Sidransky,
New York City
December 22, 2018

OTHER WORKS BY A J SIDRANSKY

Forgiving Maximo Rothman
Forgiving Mariela Camacho
Stealing a Summer's Afternoon

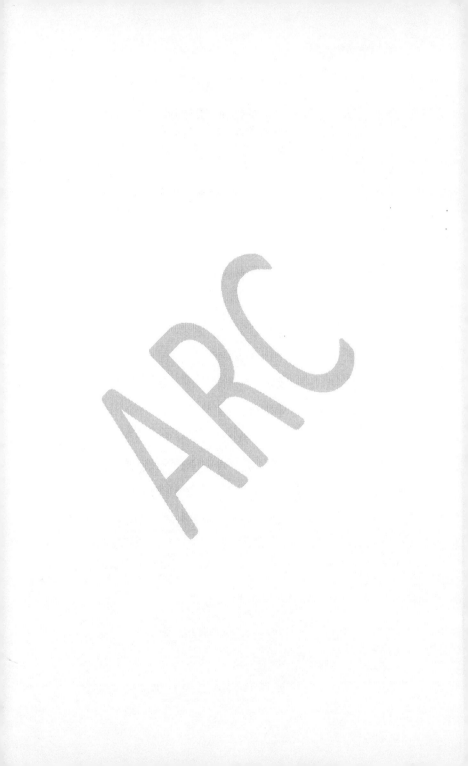

The
Interpreter

A J Sidransky

A Black Opal Books Publication

Black Opal Books

BECAUSE SOME STORIES JUST HAVE TO BE TOLD

GENRE: WAR

THE INTERPRETER
Copyright © 2019 by A J Sidransky
Cover Design by Transformational Concepts
Cover photos used with permission: Getty
All cover art copyright ©2019
All Rights Reserved
Print ISBN: 9781644372173

First Publication: March 2020

Published by Black Opal Books **http://www.blackopalbooks.com**

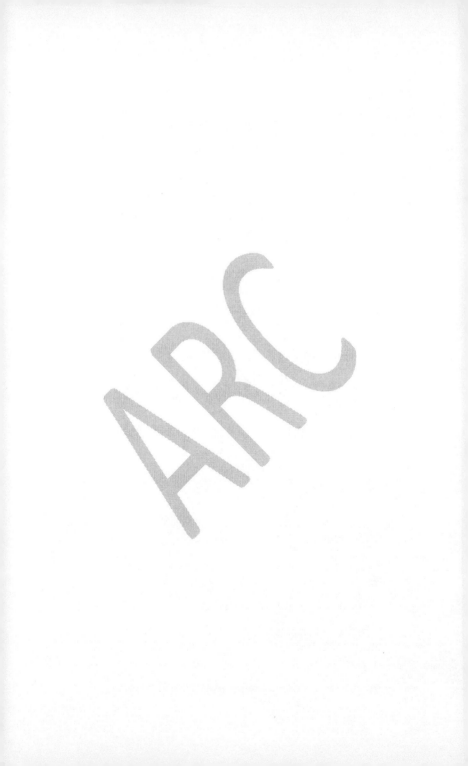

DEDICATION

For Kurt and Susan,

*and the millions of children whose lives were forever
changed by the Holocaust,*

and,

*for all the children today, whose lives are being thrown
into chaos by despots, dictators and war*

CHAPTER 1

Manila, The Philippines - March 1945

Kurt's eyes opened tentatively. He'd slept for the first time in days without dreaming of the corpse of the Japanese soldier he'd killed a week earlier on Manila's Baywalk. The body of the soldier, no older than himself, danced like a rag doll as Kurt's machine gun mowed him down. He was never prepared for how the act of taking another man's life would change him.

Kurt stood and stretched, dead tired and dead hungry. The heat was intense inside the musty, improvised barracks located in an old school behind a church. He grabbed a towel from atop his duffel and wiped the sweat from the back of his neck, head, and face. Regulations required helmets be worn at all times when outdoors and in all unsecured areas. Kurt slipped it on then took it off just as quickly, leaving the barracks bareheaded. He'd take his chances.

Blaring sunshine blinded him. As Kurt's eyes adjusted, two of his buddies waved at him from the shade of a dusty, scraggly, tree. "Where you going?" one called out.

"Mess."

"Yeah, that's what it is," the other shouted back.

Kurt didn't care how bad the food might be, he hadn't eaten in over a day. He needed something warm in his stomach. Three men approached him at a brisk pace. Two of whom, one short and one tall, he didn't recognize. It was clear neither had seen battle, their uniforms pressed and spotless. The third, his captain, called out to him. "Berlin."

Kurt stopped and saluted.

"Come with us," his Captain ordered.

Kurt's instinct was to ask why, but this was the U.S. Army, so he just followed, his stomach grumbling.

"You were born in Vienna, Corporal?" the short one asked.

"Yes," Kurt replied. "I believe that's in my file."

"No need to be a wiseass," his Captain said.

"Sorry, sir." Kurt suppressed a smirk. "Yes, I was born in Vienna…sir."

"No one would know it by your English. You sound like you were born and raised in Vienna, Virginia."

Kurt permitted himself a satisfied smile.

"I suppose your German is perfect too," the tall one said.

"Yes, sir." Kurt hadn't spoken a word of German in years. After arriving in the United States, he quickly perfected the English he had been studying since he was twelve. Within a few months, Kurt refused to speak German at all. The Nazis had made it abundantly clear. Kurt may have been born in Austria, but he wasn't Austrian, and he certainly wasn't welcome. "To be truthful sir, I don't speak German with anyone anymore."

"But you can still speak it?"

"I suppose," Kurt replied. He relaxed a bit, letting his shoulders drop. He wondered where all this was going. "I often dream in it."

"Good," the tall one replied, this time in German. Kurt was surprised. The officer's English was as natural as his own. "My name is Captain Johan Rosenthaller, and this is

Major Eric Winston. I was born in Germany, and I am also Jewish." He had the thick, formal accent typical of Berliners.

"How do you know I'm Jewish?" Kurt interrupted in English.

"It's in your file, corporal." Rosenthaller continued in German. "We would like to offer you the opportunity to do something unique for your new country."

"And that has something to do with my ability to speak German?" Kurt replied, again in English. He wasn't going to give Rosenthaller the satisfaction of hearing him speak German.

"Yes."

"If it requires me to speak German, I'm not interested."

Rosenthaller looked at Kurt's commanding officer. "Perhaps, we're done here."

"Berlin," the Captain said, "hear the man out."

Kurt, tired and hungry, figured the quickest way to a meal was to hear what Rosenthaller had to say. He leaned back in the chair, purposefully disrespectful of Rosenthaller's rank. "Okay, what do you have in mind?"

"We represent United States Army Intelligence. We've captured a lot of Nazi officers, Wehrmacht, SS, Gestapo. We need native German speakers as interpreters. Men like yourself, who understand the nuance and subtext of what these bastards are and aren't telling us."

Kurt's mind raced. He never wanted to hear a word of German or see the decaying grayness of Europe again. It held nothing for him save sorrow and loss. At the same time, a single face appeared before his eyes.

"You would be promoted to Lieutenant," Winston said.

Kurt's mind continued to float. He was somewhere else, so far away he could feel the cold tingle of a European winter on his skin even as sweat dripped from his scalp.

"Corporal Berlin are you interested?" Rosenthaller said, this time in English, breaking the spell of Kurt's memories. Rosenthaller switched again to German, knowing full well that only he and Kurt would understand. "It's not only a strike for your adopted country, it's a strike for our people, for the millions who have disappeared."

Rosenthaller's voice and words gained volume and clarity in Kurt's mind.

"Where would I be stationed?"

"Brussels"

Kurt's decision was made. "When do we leave?"

"1500"

试我

Brussels looked like a bruised boxer, though badly beaten up one could recognize its face. The streets, once orderly and clean, were dirty and filled with the detritus of war. There were rubble-filled gaps between the buildings and pockmarks from gunfire everywhere.

Kurt was both happy about and dreaded being in Brussels. It was his ground zero, the intersection where his past, present, and future collided. Brussels held the answers to Kurt's most piercing questions, whether those answers were miraculous or disastrous.

The first few interrogations Kurt interpreted were perfunctory, mostly lower rank Wehrmacht officers. Often not much older than he, these men were promoted to their ranks toward the end of the war. Hitler and his generals had run out of experienced officers. They had sacrificed most of a generation, perhaps a generation and a half. These men knew little about what their superiors had done or where they had fled to. They wanted to go home to their families, if they still had families. Kurt detached himself from his emotions, focusing instead on translation, and the nuance of language. He found the work more challenging than he had imagined. Rosenthaller told him the interrogators were impressed by him.

The reports and pictures from the camps were both frightening and numbing. Every time Kurt read them or looked at them, he knew he could well have ended up there, more likely dead than alive. His thoughts would drift to all the missing. Kurt began looking for his friend Saul and the Mandelbaum's a few days after arriving but found no trace of them. He continued searching for information through the Army and aid organizations, walking the streets on his off hours in the hope he would stumble upon someone, anyone.

And Elsa? Kurt went to the convent where he had left her the day after he arrived, but the convent was gone. It had taken a direct hit from something; bombs, tanks, grenades, who knew. Kurt was torn. He had to find Elsa, the pain of having left her was still searing. Kurt promised Elsa he would come back for her. Perhaps it was too late. He didn't know if he could face the truth when he found it. Every day Kurt planned to visit the churches to find out what had happened to the little convent. Every day he put it off until the next. Not knowing kept hope alive.

At his desk in his small, cramped office, Kurt pulled out the transcript of the interrogation from the day before. There were two copies, one in English and one in German. Typists worked all night transcribing them. Kurt had to compare them line by line to make sure the translation was correct.

There was very little of substance. The captured soldier was a Lieutenant in the Wehrmacht, stationed in Antwerp. His commanding officer died in the battle that liberated that city. The OSS wanted information on Belgian collaborators. The captured Lieutenant claimed to know nothing; his superior maintained all contact with De Vlag and the

Flemish National Union, himself. The interrogator didn't believe him, but there was no way to force the soldier to talk. They doubted he could supply any useful information anyway, so he was sent to a holding facility near the Dutch border.

Kurt peered out the window at the trees lining the street. The emerald brilliance of the young leaves was the same color as Elsa's eyes. Spring reminded him of Elsa, it was when they had met. Kurt had to find her. The ringing phone broke his concentration. "Berlin," he said.

"Kurt, come to my office," Rosenthaller commanded.

"Yes, sir. Be right there."

Kurt walked down the hall. The secretary sent him in directly. Rosenthaller sat behind his desk. Another man, in civilian clothes, stood by the window sucking on a pipe. Kurt saluted.

"At ease Lieutenant, please sit down. May I introduce Colonel Anderson McClain?"

The tall, thin, middle-aged man in a well-made, dark-grey suit turned from the window and nodded in Kurt's direction. He dragged on his pipe and let out a cloud of smoke. The scent of the tobacco reminded Kurt of his father. Kurt rose to offer his hand, but McClain turned back toward the window.

"The Colonel arrived yesterday from Washington. He's here on an important and sensitive mission."

McClain turned again toward Kurt and smiled. "How old are you, young man?" he said.

"Twenty-three, last month, sir."

"And I understand you were born in Vienna."

"Yes, sir."

"May I ask you a question?"

"Yes, sir. Of course."

"In your view, what is the greatest danger facing the United States today?"

Kurt hesitated. "I'm not sure what you mean, sir?"

McClain walked around Rosenthaller's desk and sat down. "You're young, Lieutenant Berlin, but from what we can tell you're very bright, or so Captain Rosenthaller tells me. Think about the past quarter century. What force has represented the greatest threat to our way of life?"

Kurt glanced at Rosenthaller. His face was a blank. "I'm sorry sir, perhaps I misunderstood your question."

McClain smiled. "I didn't expect an answer. Mostly, I was noting how you would respond, if you would remain calm and impartial. We need that for this project. You passed with flying colors."

Kurt wasn't sure what McClain was getting at. He had acted respectfully, as his parents had taught him. That's all.

McClain leaned on the edge of Rosenthaller's desk. He drew on this pipe and sent another cloud of smoke into the room. "Would you like the answer?"

"Yes."

"Communism. The Soviets are the biggest threat to our future and always have been. Even more than Hitler was."

Kurt was taken aback but maintained his composure. Nothing was worse than Hitler and the Nazis. He knew that firsthand. "But the Soviets are our allies, sir."

"They've been our allies out of common cause," McClain replied. "Their system is contradictory to ours. The war is not over, only this part. The next phase is about to begin. Fascism, in many ways, served us well. It acted as a buffer against communism and the ability of the Soviet Union to export revolution. Remember, it stopped communist expansion in Germany, Hungary, and Austria in the '20's." McClain gestured to the window. "Had Hitler stayed within his borders none of this would have happened. We might even have become allies. We had common cause against the Soviets."

Kurt was shocked. How could this man think of Hitler

as an ally? He searched Rosenthaller's face for a reaction. There was none.

"Colonel McClain is forming a unit to determine which of these senior officers we've captured might be useful to us in the coming fight. I've recommended you to him as our best interpreter."

Kurt hesitated. "Thank you, sir." He wanted no part of this McClain, he didn't trust him instinctively, but he didn't want to be insubordinate either.

"Well, Berlin? Are you in or out?" Rosenthaller said.

"Whatever I can do for our country, sir."

试我

The late afternoon light cast a beautiful golden hue over the park across the street from Kurt's office. Kurt sat down on a bench under a broad, leafy tree. An ice cream vendor filled waffle cones at a stand across the way. Ice cream always reminded Kurt of Elsa. He remembered that first Saturday after they arrived in Brussels, in the small park near the Mandelbaums' apartment. They had gone for a walk and shared some. Her French was so perfect. She was so perfect, in her spring dress and white gloves.

Kurt had tried to forget, especially after finding the convent destroyed. His heart broke then and there. Elsa was dead. Kurt knew it. Yet, he had to be sure. He pulled a small piece of paper from his inside pocket. The address was only a few blocks away.

The Church of our Holy Savior was reached by a long, steep flight of steps. It was much larger than the church on the little side street where Elsa used to go to feel closer to her past. The doors were open. Pews had been removed from the rear part of the church, now occupied by beds and other furniture. Children played quietly in one of the small, recessed private chapels that lined its sides. Light streamed in through stained-glass windows that soared above him. A service was underway at the front of the church in the remaining pews near the altar. The scent of incense tickled his nose.

Kurt removed his cap and walked slowly and quietly to the front. He sat down in the last pew on the last seat and waited for the service to end. The sound of the priest's chanting comforted him in a detached way. It wouldn't have mattered if he were in a synagogue or a church, or one of the Buddhist temples or mosques he had come across in the Philippines. Kurt didn't believe in God anymore, but the serenity of the space eased his mind. Kurt couldn't reconcile the idea of God with what he had seen. Images of dead children in Philippine villages and German death camps haunted him. He envied these people here in the church their faith.

A priest held up the wafer, prayed in Latin. The faithful rose from their seats and filed past, kneeling and accepting the body and blood of Christ. If only, Kurt thought, it was that easy. He recalled the great comfort Elsa took from her faith, and Mandelbaum from his. Where were they now?

The morning's meeting with McClain and Rosenthaller weighed on him. He didn't like McClain, and he was troubled by Rosenthaller's lack of response to what McClain had said. McClain's statements hadn't surprised him. Kurt learned quickly after arriving in the United States that many Americans felt an affinity for Hitler. They didn't give a crap what Hitler said or did with regard to the Jews. They respected his quest for orderliness and power.

When Kurt arrived in Washington D.C., and then later when he entered the army and was sent to Georgia for training, he came to understand why Americans were ambivalent about the Nazis. It was because Nazi Germany already existed in the American South, only it was the Negroes who were the Jews.

The service ended. Worshipers filed out quickly and quietly, many smiling. Salvation was theirs. The priest, a man in his fifties with graying hair, noticed Kurt in the pews and approached him.

"May I help you, monsieur?" the priest said in broken English.

"Mai oui," Kurt replied. "I'm looking for someone."

The priest smiled. "You speak French?"

"Oui,"

"May I join you?" The priest pulled up his cassock at the knees as he sat down.

"Of course," replied Kurt.

"And you believe we can help you to find this person...," he looked at Kurt's insignia, but was unable to decipher his rank.

"Lieutenant..." said Kurt

"Oui...Lieutenant."

"I am looking for a nun and a young woman. The young woman would be twenty-two." Kurt pulled out a photograph of Elsa, grasping it tightly.

The priest looked at the photo and shook his head. "No, I've never seen her. Perdon, monsieur, may I ask a question?"

"Yes?"

"You're American, yet you speak French with a German accent."

"I was born in Vienna. I came to Brussels in 1939."

"I see. I am Father Marcel." The priest rubbed his hands over his thighs to clean them. "You are Jewish?"

"Yes," Kurt replied.

"And the young woman you seek? She is also Jewish?"

"In a fashion." Kurt smiled. "That might depend on whose definition we are using."

The priest nodded almost unperceptively, his expression becoming more serious. "And how is it she would be with one of our sisters?"

"When I left Brussels in October of 1940, she was living with the Sisters of Charity."

Father Marcel averted his eyes. His response was quick. "That convent was destroyed. The Germans blew it up."

Kurt's stiffened. "Do you know why?"

"For hiding Jews." The Priest continued to avoid Kurt's gaze.

"What happened to the sisters?"

Now Father Marcel looked directly at Kurt. The pain in his eyes was evident. "They were blown up with it, along with the Jews they were hiding."

The statement hit Kurt like a thunderbolt, his worst fears confirmed. "Did anyone escape? Survive?" Kurt asked, guilty at leaving Elsa.

"No one survived, and no one escaped, but two sisters were absent at the time of the attack," Father Marcel said. "They were saved by provenance."

"Or luck." Kurt rubbed his eyes. He felt exhausted. "Where are they now?"

"One died last year in Louvain during the liberation. The other is here in Brussels. She lives in a convent on the other side of the city."

"Can I see her?"

The priest hesitated. "She lives as a recluse. She rarely speaks since that day. She prays to the Virgin continuously as penance for surviving her sisters in Christ."

"Can I see her?" Kurt repeated, rising from the pew.

The priest looked up at Kurt. "I will see what I can do. Come back in a few days."

CHAPTER 2

Vienna, Austria - March 1939

Hertz suppressed a shudder as he read the morning paper. Hitler had taken Czechoslovakia. As if for verification, the live crowds on the radio cheered along. "This, changes everything," he said, tapping his finger on the newspaper.

Berta brought him his coffee, the color perfect, as always. She sat down opposite him, her hands clasped in front of her.

Hertz took several sips from his cup. "We have to get Kurt out of here," he said. "We have to reconsider the Kindertransport."

Berta looked out the window. She didn't want Hertz to see the fear in her eyes. "I don't know if I can do that, send him away, alone."

Hertz finished his coffee, let out a long, slow breath. "He'll be safer there than here."

Berta walked to the sink with Hertz's empty cup. She washed it then wiped her hands on her apron. "Then I would prefer he go to Brussels, rather than London. Your brother is there."

Hertz shook his head. "My brother is single and lives in a rooming house. Kurt can't live with Sam."

"But Sam can keep an eye on him. I would worry less." She hesitated for a moment, before returning to the table. "And us?"

"We stay until we liquidate everything we have left. We need money to travel. The visas take months. Kurt has to go now."

"And where does he go from there?"

Hertz placed his hands over Berta's. "To America with us, I hope, if your sister can move our case up, otherwise…England, when they have a spot for him."

Berta took her hands from under Hertz's. "My sister is doing everything she can."

Hertz sensed her irritation. He rubbed his eyes. The stress was palpable. "How much longer do you think we have here? They know about my past. I'm sure about that. How long do you think it will be before they come for me, a Jew and a communist?"

Berta returned to the sink, her back to Hertz. She picked up a dishrag and wiped the silverware in the drain board. "That was fifteen years ago, you were young and foolish."

Hertz came up behind Berta and put his hands on her hips. "Nevertheless, they know. Kurt's life is in danger, all our lives are in danger."

试戋

Kurt lay on his bed daydreaming. A warm breeze came through the window rustling the heavy drapes, an early sign of spring. He longed for the chance to stretch his arms and legs, perhaps to play football as he did with his school friends before all this started.

His school friends. Kurt wondered how he had thought of them as friends at all. After the Anschluss, most of them shunned him. Then they called him a dirty Jew, forced him to sit alone on a bench at the back of the room. They excluded him from playing sports. Only Hans Gunter stood by him. When the other boys attacked Hans, calling him a Jew lover, Kurt came to his aid and that was the end of that. Kurt's parents agreed with the Headmaster, it would be better if he were tutored at home. Since then he had lived in a kind of a prison, each day a little worse, every day some new decree as to what Jews couldn't do. As to his Jewish friends, they were in the same situation as him. They couldn't see each other. It was too dangerous to chance the streets.

They were Jewish. Of course, Kurt knew that, but it had never seemed to matter before. They gathered with the family to celebrate the ancient festivals, they would visit with friends on the Sabbath, but they were hardly religious. They ate ham in the house, used electricity on the Sabbath. Some of the relatives had married Gentiles. Many celebrated Christmas. His father. said he was a citizen of the world, not the subject of a long list of rules extrapolated by men who lived in walled-in ghettoes long ago. The Jews had come out of the ghetto physically, now they needed to free themselves mentally.

Nor was it like Kurt never felt the sting of hate. His parents had educated him. There would always be people like Frau Krauss who lived upstairs. They hated Jews for the sake of hating them. "It makes them feel superior," his father said. "They're ignorant. Look around at Vienna, the greatest city in the world. Why? Because of the Jews, and everything we have given this city, and the Empire before it."

He heard the key in the lock of the front door. A moment later his father appeared in his doorway. "Shouldn't you be studying?" Hertz said.

Kurt hated when his father did that. It seemed to Kurt that little mattered to him other than Kurt's studies. He wished his father understood how profoundly this isolation was affecting him.

"Come into the living room," Hertz said, before speeding down the hallway.

Kurt slipped on his shoes and followed his father. Berta was seated on the couch, her posture straight and perfect as always. Her dark blond hair was pulled back, revealing fair skin and blue eyes. She looked more Aryan than Frau Krauss.

"Sit down next to your mother, please" Hertz said. "I have some news." He took a cigar from the box on the little table next to the chair, clipped the end, ran it under his nose then lit it, savoring the first puff.

Kurt suspected the news was excellent. His father didn't waste cigars on a casual matter. "Are we going to America?' he asked.

Berta took Kurt's hand in hers. "Not quite yet, my darling."

Hertz puffed on the cigar then released the smoke. Its heavy, acrid scent filled the room. The breeze entering through the window moved the smoke about, sunshine falling in dusty streaks through the partially opened drapes.

Hertz leaned forward in his chair. "You'll be leaving for Brussels in a few days."

"What about you and mother?" Kurt searched his father's face for any hint of obfuscation.

"We will follow shortly and then we'll leave for America together, or you will go to England and we will follow later."

Kurt released his mother's hand and stood up. "No, I don't want to go alone. I won't leave you." He felt a lump forming in his throat. Kurt wanted to cry, but knew he couldn't, the same way he'd wanted to cry but didn't so many times in the past year. Kurt's life was stolen from him. He had lost everything, his friends, his freedom, his self-respect. The only thing he had now was his parents. He couldn't lose them as well.

"Kurt, son, listen to me…"

"…No, I won't! I don't want to hear this!" Kurt felt his mother's hands on his shoulders. He shrugged them off and stood stiffly in front of the mantle opposite his father's chair. The cigar continued to burn slowly in its ashtray as Hertz placed a series of papers on the mahogany coffee table. "Here, let me explain."

Hertz's coolness confounded Kurt. He pointed to the largest pile at the left of the table. "These are the orders we have received from the government relative to the forced liquidation of our property required before we can leave." Hertz pointed to the next, much smaller pile. "These are the receipts for the proof I must furnish for each order. Have I made much progress?"

Kurt remained silent.

"You see this third pile?"

"There is no third pile, father."

"Exactly. That's where our exit papers would be." He pulled another set of documents from inside his coat. As he stretched his arm to place them on the table where the third pile would be, Kurt noticed a small tear in the fabric of Hertz's coat. His father was fastidious. Before all this started, he wouldn't have left the house in an item of clothing that was in any way frayed. "These papers are your ticket out. You have been accepted for a Kinder-transport leaving Wednesday. In two days, you will be out of this hell, and I might sleep a whole night."

Kurt searched his father's face. Hertz's resolve was firm, but Kurt discerned the slightest tremble at the corner of his mouth. Kurt turned to his mother. Berta's expression was like that of an angel. Kurt knew instantly how much she loved him by her smile, which hid her breaking heart. Kurt was terrified. He took a breath to steady himself. "Of course, father," he said, straightening his posture. "We will be together in Brussels before long."

Kurt embraced his mother. A moment later he felt his father's arms around them both, an almost inaudible whisper in his ear. "We love you," Hertz said.

试戈

The cavernous hall of Westbahnhoff station was a reminder of the glory of the vast Empire that built it, the Empire Hertz had fought for. It shattered to pieces at the end of the Great War, leaving central Europe a mosaic of new states defined by boundaries drawn with little attention to the realities of culture and race. That was the unique thing about Austria-Hungary, it was an umbrella, like the towering ceiling above them. Under that umbrella sat a dozen nations speaking more than fifteen languages and practicing more than five faiths. The polar opposite of the Hitler's Aryan paradise.

Families crowded alongside the train that would take their children out of the Reich. The locomotive was decorated with a Swastika. Even here, the Nazis pressed their position of control. Armed guards patrolled the platform as if these children were dangerous criminals.

The children milling about the platform ranged in age from three to seventeen, some visibly frightened and crying, others calm. The older children clearly understood the façade their parents were presenting, and in true Austrian fashion, maintained their own façades as well.

Hertz considered them lucky to have gotten Kurt on this

transport. This group would be housed in Belgium and funneled to Britain as sponsors became available.

"You have everything?" Hertz asked.

"Yes, father," Kurt replied. He smiled for his parents' sake.

"As soon as you're settled you will contact your Uncle," Berta said. She pushed back Kurt's hair from his forehead.

"Of course. When will you be coming?" Kurt didn't really expect an answer. Berta glanced at Hertz.

"As soon as possible," Hertz said. "In the meantime, you'll be safer away from all this."

Kurt heard someone calling his name. A boy waved farther down the platform.

"Do you know him?" Berta asked.

"Yes, his name is Heinz. He was in my grade at school."

"Go, say hello."

Hertz put his hand on the small of Berta's back, as much to steady himself as to calm her. A whistle signaled boarding time. Kurt ran back to them. "I will be fine. I promise." He said, fighting back his tears. "Come soon, please."

"We will," Hertz said. "Kiss your mother."

Kurt wrapped his arms tightly around Berta. He breathed in the scent of her perfume, a scent he had known since earliest memory. "Thank you, mother."

"There is nothing to thank me for." Berta placed her white-gloved hand on one cheek and kissed Kurt gently on the other.

"There is. More than you know."

Berta stepped back and held Kurt by his arms. He had grown in the past few months, taller than her now. She wanted this image of him to stay with her, so grown up in his best suit and tie.

Embracing Kurt, Hertz thought his legs might collapse. There was little more he wanted than to see his son become a man. Hertz cared little for all the things he had amassed in the nearly two decades since he arrived in Vienna, a young, cerebral communist. Kurt was the truest thing Hertz had ever known, this young life that he was willing to let go, if it meant the young life would continue. "Till we see each other again," Hertz said. "In the meantime, go, and never look back."

Kurt kissed Berta again then picked up his suitcases and

walked toward the train. Hertz watched him, and recalled a similar moment long ago in 1914, when his parents took him to a train in a small town in southern Poland, what they then called Austrian Galicia, to fight a war for his country, a country that no longer wanted him, his wife or his son. Hertz watched as Kurt took a step up onto the train then turned to look back one last time.

Hertz smiled. "I told him, never look back."

"Thank god he did," Berta said.

Kurt saw them there, his father's arm around his mother's waist. They were smiling. That was the way he would think of them.

Inside the train was chaos. There were over 100 children. The younger ones were crying, the older ones, like Kurt, sat or stood solemnly. They had an idea of what was happening. The rest, in the middle, behaved as if they were on their way to a great adventure. The noise was deafening, and the few attendants sent by the Kultusgemeinde to escort the children were incapable of controlling them.

Kurt made his way through the first car toward the second. Heinz waved to him. "Come sit with us," he said, pointing to their compartment. Kurt peered in. It was crowded, three other boys, one about his age, and two younger. Their bags were strewn about making the compartment seem ever tighter.

"Thanks, but I think I'll move to the next car. Perhaps there'll be a little more room. He swung one suitcase in front of him, the other behind, struggling through the aisle to the end. In the last compartment sat two girls of about his age.

"May I share this compartment?" he asked.

"Yes," the young woman nearer the window said, continuing to stare out of it.

"Thank you," Kurt replied. He placed his bags in the small closet to the right of the door and sat down. "My name is Kurt Berlin," offering his hand.

"Elsa Graz," said the girl by the window, extending a white-gloved hand.

"Margot Morgenstein," said the other.

Another girl appeared in the doorway. "Margot?" she said.

"Trudi, I didn't see you on the platform."

"Nor I, you. Wilma is here as well. Come join us. We're sitting in the next car."

Margot opened the closet to retrieve her bag.

"Let me help you with that," Kurt said.

"It's that one there."

Kurt placed the bag outside the door.

"Thank you," Margot said then disappeared down the corridor.

Kurt glanced at Elsa. Blond and fair, she looked very Austrian, like his mother.

"I don't know how these girls can act so giddy, as if they are leaving for a summer in the mountains," Elsa said, continuing to stare out the window.

Kurt felt the same way. He was desperately sad, confused, and frightened. He had to retain his composure though. Kurt wouldn't embarrass himself for his parents' sake, if for nothing else. Peering outside, he found them standing in the same spot where he left them. Kurt followed Elsa's gaze through the window. "Are those your parents there, the man in the brown fedora and the woman in the yellow dress?"

"Yes," Elsa replied.

"Those are mine," Kurt said, pointing to Hertz and Berta. "Let's open the window."

"Is it permitted?"

"Who knows? Does it really matter anymore?" Kurt stood and pulled up the lower portion of the window. Elsa slid over. She hesitated for a moment. "I don't know. I'm not sure I can say goodbye, again."

Kurt waved to his parents. They were talking, his father shaking his head, his mother disagreeing. Berta walked toward Kurt's window alone.

"This train will depart in two minutes," came an announcement followed by a whistle.

Elsa stood and leaned out. "Mama, Papa," she called." Her parents waved back. She leaned a bit farther out. "I love you." She pulled herself back into the car, tears on her cheeks.

Berta reached the window as the train began rolling forward.

Kurt reached for her hand. Their fingertips touched. "I love you both," Kurt called out.

The image of his mother become smaller and smaller as the train pulled away. When the car passed the huge arches that led to the open tracks, Kurt lost sight of her altogether. Elsa was crying silently. Kurt moved next to her. Finally, he cried too.

The train became quiet shortly after leaving Vienna. The vista changed from city to countryside. In the distance, one could see mountains. The sight of huge red flags with the swastika in black within a white circle marred the tranquility of the scene, hanging from every barn and farmhouse. That flag chilled Kurt no matter how many times he saw it. Mostly, it prompted him to ask himself the same question over and over, how was it that these people, his countrymen, had hidden their true feelings so well for so long.

Kurt busied himself with a book and some lessons but couldn't concentrate. Berta's image remained in his head. He tried to talk with Elsa, but she cried silently for the first hour after they left Vienna. She was asleep now, her head resting in the corner between the back cushion of the seat and the window.

Kurt needed to stretch his legs. He would visit with Heinz. As Kurt walked back through the car, he noticed the faces of the younger children filled with fear. He could tell which children had a sibling, as they hung to them or held them by the hand.

Kurt never thought about being an only child before. He always kind of liked it, never having to share his parents' attention. Now he felt very alone. At least these children had each other. Kurt had little idea of what lay ahead for him, other than that he would be alone in the home of strangers. He peeked his head into Heinz's compartment.

Heinz put a finger over his mouth. "I just got Pauli to sleep," he whispered, tipping his head toward his younger brother.

"Come stretch your legs," Kurt whispered.

"May Karl come too?" Heinz asked, nodding to the other boy in the compartment.

"Of course."

They walked toward the rear of the car near the door to the

next.

"I should introduce you," Heinz said.

"You did earlier," Kurt replied

"Of course," said Heinz, "With all the chaos, I forgot."

Kurt extended a hand to Karl. "Nice to meet you, again,"

"Likewise," said Karl accepting Kurt's hand. "When did you find out you were leaving?"

"Two days ago," Kurt said. "And you, Heinz?"

"They told me about two weeks ago, but they didn't tell my brother until earlier this week. He's had a very bad time of it. Some boys caught him in the street about a month ago and beat him. He wouldn't leave the house after that."

"Is that when they decided to send you out?" Kurt asked.

"I'm not sure. They've been talking about it for some time."

"My parents told us last week," Karl said, "but they didn't tell us that they weren't going with us until this morning. They went so far as to pack bags for themselves, so we wouldn't suspect anything. They put on a strong face, but I can see how frightened they are. My mother disappears into the bathroom and when she comes out her eyes are red. I know she's been crying."

"I don't know if my father will leave," said Heinz. He's worried about my grandparents. I heard him tell my mother last night that he will send her next and he'll stay till he can get his parents out with him."

"My father says he has a plan," said Kurt. "He's smart, smarter than the Nazis I think, but they keep changing the rules every day."

"How did this happen?" Karl asked.

"I don't know," said Kurt. He thought of Frau Krauss. At least she was honest about her hate. "I guess you never really know what's in someone's heart."

Elsa was awake when Kurt returned. He smiled. Elsa smiled back, averting her eyes from his. Kurt opened his bag and took out the cookies his mother made. "Would you like one?" he said and held them out to Elsa.

"Yes, thank you," Elsa replied. She took one and tasted it,

the white gloves on her tiny hands now dusted with chocolate crumbs. "Delicious." Elsa cleared her throat. "I would like to apologize for my behavior. I have been very rude."

"Not at all," Kurt said. "This has been very difficult."

"More difficult than I could ever have imagined anything." Elsa stopped for a moment, straightening her posture. "For me it came as somewhat of a surprise."

"When did they tell you that you were leaving?"

"Four days ago." Elsa sighed. She dabbed at her eyes with a white, lacy handkerchief. "You see, it wasn't just that, but also finding out that I'm Jewish."

Kurt felt the flush rise into his cheeks. "Excuse me?"

"I was raised Catholic. About two months ago my parents told me that I could no longer continue at my school. I couldn't imagine why. They had to explain. They had told me all my life that my father was an orphan and an only child. It turns out he was Jewish, my mother isn't. His family rejected him when he married my mother."

"I thought Mischlings could remain in school?"

"My father is a prominent artist, modern art. What the Nazis call degenerate art. They wanted to make an example of him, and hence me. The teachers in school were merciless. My parents decided it was better for me not to be at school, and finally not to be in Vienna at all. I just don't feel like I belong here."

CHAPTER 3

Brussels, Belgium - May 1945

Kurt walked down the steps of the Church of Our Holy Savior into the evening light. Dusk came late this time of year. He couldn't accept the implications of what Father Marcel said. If he did, it meant Elsa was dead. The Nazis, looking for Jews, had blown her to bits. Kurt headed back toward his old neighborhood to walk the streets again, looking for anything or anyone that could connect him to his past, and Elsa.

The tram came quickly. Kurt boarded without paying. Nobody questioned uniformed Americans, ever. He rode for a few minutes, every block, every store, reminding him of something, some moment related to Elsa. After a few stops he got off and walked.

Much of the neighborhood was in ruins. The Germans hadn't surrendered an inch easily. Kurt turned into the little street where he lived with the Mandelbaum's. It was deserted. He stopped in front of their building and considered ringing the bell. What was the point, though? Another family lived there now.

A few days after arriving, Kurt came here to search for them. The front door was ajar. Kurt climbed the stairs to their apartment and knocked. A woman answered.

"Are the Mandelbaum's here?" Kurt asked, knowing full well they weren't.

"Who?" she replied, shaking her head, her red hair wrapped in a kerchief. She didn't know anyone by that name. She, her husband, and children, had lived here since the fall of 1943.

"May I come in?" Kurt asked. "I used to live here before the war."

The red-haired woman nodded and stepped aside then gestured for him to enter. Kurt looked around. Some of the Mandelbaums' furniture was still there, the dining room table, the breakfront in the living room. The silver pieces that caught the sunlight through the cracks in the drapes and reflected it back into the room were gone. Kurt held his cap in his hand and fought back tears.

"Terrible what happened to them." The red-haired woman said. She crossed herself. "You are a Jew?"

Kurt turned to face her. "Yes."

Confusion spread across her face. "But you are American? How could you know them?"

"I was a refugee, they protected me. I escaped in 1940."

The woman turned away from Kurt. "I see. It's very sad, but we didn't know. It was hard for us too."

Kurt had heard this too many times. The need to explain, the need to tell everyone and anyone that there was no way they could have shielded their neighbors. "Can I ask you something?" Kurt said, twisting his cap in his hands.

"Of course," the woman replied. She reached for a pack of cigarettes from the windowsill and offered him one.

"No, thank you," he said. "Perhaps it wouldn't be a bother if from time to time I come by to see if they've returned? Here's my card. If they do, please give it to them."

The woman took the card politely and placed it into the pocket of her apron. "Yes, that's fine." She walked to the door and opened it. As Kurt walked past her, she touched his arm. "You know the truth. No one is coming back."

诶找

Kurt checked his pocket to see how much cash he had with him. He didn't want to go back to the hotel that served as their barracks for dinner. Instead, he would stop at a little restaurant he remembered on the other side of the park, a few doors down from the shop where his mother had worked. Kurt knew it had survived the war; he'd seen the 'open' sign in the window from the tram. He needed to be alone, or rather away from the army, for a little while.

Kurt walked the few blocks back to the restaurant. A young couple sat at a table in the rear holding hands. The proprietress, not the same from before the war, sat Kurt at a small table in the window.

"Merci," Kurt said.

She smiled and asked him if he spoke French.

"Mai oui," he said.

She smiled and reached for a menu. "I haven't much. Getting provisions is hard. I cook what I get. Today I got some chicken. The waterzooi is delicious. I just made it."

"Tres bien," Kurt said again. "And a small salad?"

"Is frisee all right?"

"That would be fine. Do you have any white wine?"

"I think I can find you a glass."

Kurt looked out the window. A young man in tattered clothing and a cap bent over a pile of debris picking through it. The scene wasn't unusual these days. People were desperate for anything they could find. The young man pulled a large piece of wood from the middle of the pile and stood up. He looked toward Kurt. Inadvertently, their eyes met.

Kurt wasn't sure at first. The man had a beard and was painfully thin. He jumped up from his seat and ran out of the restaurant. The man stood in front of him holding up the piece of wood like a bat, ready to strike Kurt.

"Saul?" Kurt said, barely above a whisper.

The man stood there transfixed. He couldn't take his eyes off Kurt. Finally, after what seemed like an eternity he said, "How can this be?"

"Saul?" Kurt repeated, this time more loudly.

"Yes, yes."

Kurt opened his arms. Saul dropped the wooden scrap and fell into them, weeping. They embraced so tightly Kurt thought his ribs would break. "You're alive." Kurt said, his voice breaking through his tears.

"Yes," Saul wept. "I refused to die."

The proprietress looked suspiciously at Saul. He was dirty and disheveled. Kurt pulled her to the side. "He's an old friend. I spotted him through the window. Please, let me give him a meal. He's had a very bad time of it."

She glanced at the couple in the rear of the otherwise empty restaurant then looked at Kurt askance. He didn't wait for her response. Kurt pulled $10 from his pocket and put it in her hand. It was a fortune for her, twenty times what his meal would cost. "Please," Kurt said. She slipped the bill into her pocket and retreated to the kitchen.

Saul's face was different than Kurt remembered. Though they were the same age, Saul looked much older. He had deep lines on his forehead, his hair had thinned, his cheeks were sunken. Kurt wasn't sure what to say. He wanted to ask so many questions but thought it would be better to let Saul open up when he was ready. Saul smiled weakly, revealing yellowed teeth. Despite what he saw, Kurt found the friend he once knew in Saul's smile, the friend he used to play football with, talk about girls with, plan on killing Nazis with.

"Thank you," Saul said.

"For what?" Kurt asked.

"For this." Saul looked around the restaurant. "You have no idea how hungry I am."

"There is nothing to thank me for. You would do the same for me."

Saul stared at him. "What is your rank?"

"Lieutenant," Kurt replied. He took a sip of his wine.

"What are you doing here?" Saul asked.

Kurt started to tell Saul his story. "I was fighting in the Pacific…"

"You saw action?"

"Yes." Kurt hadn't expected to be interrogated. He let it continue, sensing that it would be easier for Saul to ask Kurt questions than to answer his own. There would be time for that.

"When did you arrive in America?"

"June 1941. The day Hitler invaded the Soviet Union."

Saul receded into himself for a moment. He looked out of the window, remembering. "We knew it was over that day."

"So, did we."

"There was no way Hitler could have beaten them. We were rejoicing, silently. They watched our every move, everything we did. It wasn't long after that, things began to get worse."

Kurt was about to ask him the first of his many questions when the proprietress arrived with the salads and Saul's wine. Saul picked up his fork and touched it to the poached egg resting on top of the bitter greens. He pierced it, the creamy yolk escaping and coating the greens and the bacon lardoons.

"Do you know how long it has been since I had a poached egg?"

Kurt said nothing. Saul lifted a piece of frisee and lardoons to his mouth. He chewed it slowly, savoring it. Saul took a second bite, this time with the crouton and some of the white of the egg. His eyes closed, as if in ecstasy.

"You eat bacon now?" Kurt said, taking a sip of his wine.

Saul smiled. "I eat anything I can get my hands on."

They both laughed, but a moment later Saul began to cry. Kurt moved his chair around the table next to Saul and put his arm around him. Saul's head rested on Kurt's shoulder. "I have too much to tell you, but I can't, not right now."

"Go ahead my brother, cry. Don't worry, it will make us both feel better." Kurt felt the wetness of his tears on his own cheeks.

CHAPTER 4

Brussels, Belgium - March 1939

K urt and Elsa waited patiently in the rear of a large passenger hall at Brussels-South Station. Three men and a woman sat at a table processing the children. They took the youngest who were alone first, then those with older siblings. One of the men approached them. He looked at the sheet of paper in his hand and then at Elsa.

"Fraulein Graz?" he asked.

"Yes," Elsa replied.

The young man looked at Kurt, his face puzzled. "There's no mention of a brother in your file."

Elsa's face reddened. "Oh no, no, he's not my brother."

"We met on the train," Kurt said, extending his hand. "Kurt Berlin."

The young man cleared his throat. "I'm sure your parents would insist on a chaperone."

Elsa blushed again. "Kurt was being nice. I'm alone. So is he. He kept me company." She glanced at Kurt. "He's made this much less difficult."

Now Kurt felt the blush rise into his face. "It was nothing."

"Well, regardless, I'm afraid we have a small though by no means an insurmountable problem. Fraulein Graz, the family that was to host you had a sudden emergency, a sick parent who has come to live with them. They won't be able to take you. But, as it happens, we have another family that offered to host two teenagers. We assigned them only one. By coincidence, that happens to be young Herr Berlin here."

Elsa smiled. "That would be fine, as long as I wouldn't be an added burden."

"No, no they would be delighted," the young man assured her. "Well then, why don't you both follow me." A smile came up around the corner of Kurt's mouth. He felt a little less alone.

The Mandelbaums were older than either Kurt's or Elsa's parents, closer to the age of their grandparents. And by their appearance it was clear they were orthodox. Mandelbaum wore the sober, dark, old-fashioned suit favored by observant Jews. His wife kept her hair covered by what was clearly a wig.

"Herr and Frau Mandelbaum, may I introduce Herr Kurt Berlin and Frauline Elsa Graz."

The Mandelbaums smiled broadly. "We are so happy to meet you," Frau Mandelbaum said.

"Though I'm sure we would all have preferred to meet under different circumstances," added Herr Mandelbaum.

"In any event, we thank you for your hospitality," Elsa said.

The young official handed Kurt's and Elsa's documents to Herr Mandelbaum. "Do you have transportation?"

"Yes," said Mandelbaum.

A hired car took them back to the Mandelbaums' apartment. The five-story building was old, and Kurt doubted there was a lift. He considered the situation. "Herr Mandelbaum, what floor do you live on?"

"Three."

Kurt heard his father's voice in his head. He couldn't permit Mandelbaum, much less his wife, to carry the bags, nor could Elsa. It wouldn't be proper. "I can make it in two trips," he said.

"That won't be necessary, though I thank you," Mandelbaum said. "The driver will help us." Mandelbaum picked up one small suitcase and the driver another, leaving the larger two for Kurt. He followed them up the winding stairway to the apartment.

On the right post of the door was a large mezuzah, more prominently displayed than the one Kurt's family had on their doorpost before the arrival of the Nazis. Both Mandelbaum and his wife touched it then kissed their fingers before entering.

Kurt placed the suitcases to the right of the door inside the apartment and walked down the hallway to the living room. The apartment was in the back of the building. The windows looked out on an interior courtyard. The room was dark, the heavy drapes reducing the limited light even further.

The furniture was equally dark and heavy. To the left of the sofa was a large breakfront. Inside were many silver pieces, candelabrum, platters, and plates. The breeze that fluttered the drapes would momentarily increase the light level in the room as steaks of light glimmered off the silver.

"Welcome to our home," Frau Mandelbaum said. She motioned toward the sofa as she walked to the kitchen. "Please, make yourselves comfortable."

Kurt and Elsa sat down on the deep green, velvet couch. Mandelbaum entered from the front hallway as his wife returned with a tray carrying a silver tea set and plates with cookies, which she placed on the mahogany coffee table in front of the sofa.

"We will have some refreshments, and then we will get settled," Mandelbaum said.

"May I pour your cup?" Frau Mandelbaum asked Elsa.

"Please."

Frau Mandelbaum held up a small cup on a saucer. Elsa reached for a sugar cube with a small silver tong and placed it in the cup, along with a thin slice of lemon. Frau Mandelbaum hovered a silver strainer over the cup and poured the rich, clear, amber liquid through it.

"Danke," said Elsa. She reached for a cookie with the ornate silver tong, a checkerboard of vanilla and chocolate, and placed it gently on the rim of the saucer.

Frau Mandelbaum repeated the process for Kurt, Herr Mandelbaum, and herself. "Please, before it gets cold, enjoy," she said, sitting down opposite Elsa.

Kurt took a sip of the tea and a bite of the cookie. "This is delicious, thank you."

"You're welcome," Frau Mandelbaum replied.

"As you will see, my wife is an excellent cook. I should tell you a few things though, so that we don't have any problems from the outset."

"Of course," said Elsa, "I, we, don't want to be any trouble."

"Of course not," Frau Mandelbaum said.

Mandelbaum took a sip of his tea. "Our home is kosher. I don't know if your parents were observant, but we are, and if you aren't familiar with kashruth, Frau Mandelbaum will teach you."

Kurt glanced discreetly at Elsa. He knew little of the Jewish dietary laws himself. He surmised Elsa knew even less.

"Also," Mandelbaum continued, "we are strictly observant of the Sabbath. I don't expect you to attend prayer with us unless you so desire, but we will require that you respect the Sabbath laws in the house. I will review that with you before our first Sabbath together."

Kurt watched Elsa out of the corner of his eye. She put down the cup and saucer and clasped her gloved hands in her lap. "Of course," she said. Her lips closed and curved upward into a pleasant smile.

"Now, as to your lodging," Mandelbaum said. "This is a two-bedroom apartment, so we think it best that Elsa stay in the small bedroom next to ours. You, young man, will stay in my study." Mandelbaum pointed toward an alcove lined with bookcases behind French doors adjacent to the living room. "We will set up a day bed for you there. I'm sure we will all be comfortable."

Kurt looked toward the study. It would only be for a little while. Till his parents arrived.

试试

Kurt woke with a start, his pajama top soaked with sweat. He'd had the dream again. He was standing on the platform in the U-Bahn station near their apartment in Vienna, waiting for his parents, he spots them on the opposite platform. Kurt waves, then calls to them, "you're going in the wrong direction." The train arrives, they board without seeing him, and the train pulls away. One didn't need to know much about Freud's theories to understand the dream.

Kurt heard Mandelbaum's footsteps before he saw him. A moment later, the tall, thin man appeared before him, wrapped in a dark, heavy, night-robe with a matching sleeping hat.

"Good Shabbos," Mandelbaum said.

"Good Shabbos," Kurt replied.

"I'll be leaving for shul in a little while if you'd like to join me."

Kurt hesitated. "If you would like," he said. He knew his parents would expect him to be a good guest. "You know, I don't have much experience with this."

Mandelbaum smiled. "Every Jew has a place in HaShem's house. Please remember what I told you about today's restrictions."

"Of course."

Mandelbaum walked off then stopped. "Do you think Fraulein Elsa would like to join us? Frau Mandelbaum would be delighted to bring her."

Kurt swallowed hard. He didn't want to insult his host. "May I speak frankly, Herr Mandelbaum?"

"Of course,"

"This is very new to her. Her life in Vienna was very different. Give her a little time to get used to it."

Mandelbaum smiled. "Thank you, young man. I will take your advice on this matter."

As they entered the dark, small, cluttered synagogue, Kurt recalled the dramatic dome in his family's synagogue in Vienna. It was filled with light streaming through soaring, stained-glass windows. His family attended services on the High Holy Days of the Jewish New Year. The men, many of them in formal clothes with high hats, accompanied their elegantly dressed wives and daughters to wooden pews lined with velvet cushions, their sons following close behind. A choir and an enormous organ sat off to the left of the podium, from where the Rabbi would lead the congregation in a service conducted in perfect German. Then he remembered the flames that shot up into the night sky a few months ago when the dome of their synagogue collapsed after the mob set it afire on Kristallnacht.

Kurt shivered.

This synagogue was the complete opposite. There were two doors on opposite sides of the old, squat, building. One marked for men, the other for women. The anteroom was cramped, with piles of prayer books on tables and a rack of prayer shawls to one side. There were small windows set into the sidewalls at a height higher than most of the men were tall. Some light filtered in through the dirty glass. Bare bulbs hanging from the ceiling provided the rest.

A curtain on the right side separated the room. It was clear to Kurt that the women sat on the other side. They could listen to the service but weren't permitted to see it. He thanked himself for speaking up to Mandelbaum about Elsa. This experience would have been too much for her, five days out of her former life.

Mandelbaum handed Kurt a skullcap and mimed to him to place it on his head, then introduced him to several of the men standing nearby. The introductions were in a mixture of French, German, Flemish, and Yiddish. One of the men introduced his son. He was around Kurt's age, tall and thin with a scraggly beard.

"Nice to meet you," Kurt said.

"Ah, you speak French," the young man replied, taking both Kurt's hands into his. "Welcome, my name is Saul."

"Mine is Kurt, and I should apologize for my French now."

"No need to worry, I speak Yiddish, it's very similar to German. We will make it work."

The Rabbi, an ancient, bearded man wrapped in a prayer shawl too large for him, entered the room from a door to the side of the Torah Ark. Everyone stood. The Rabbi cleared his throat.

"We can speak after the service," Saul said.

Mandelbaum handed an open prayer book to Kurt. He pointed to the print. "Can you read Hebrew?"

Kurt smiled.

"I didn't think so," said Mandelbaum. "Just watch me and follow my example."

Kurt felt lost through most of the long, cacophonous service.

It seemed as if all the men were reciting the same thing at different speeds and with differing accents at the same time. Occasionally, one or another would have a moment of intense passion, their chants rising in both volume and intensity, nearly to the level of pleading.

Kurt glanced over at Saul observing him at prayer, his eyes often closed, his lips moving quickly, his connection to the experience obvious. Kurt wondered if he could ever feel that connection to this mysterious God who seemed so different from the impersonal, detached, abstract concept that modern Austrian Reform Judaism presented.

The only prayer he recognized was the Shema, which was also the only prayer said in Hebrew by the congregation in his synagogue. He jumped into the chanting a second late upon recognizing it. It felt good to have something in common with these people, his people, though they looked and sounded very different from any Jews he had ever known.

Mandelbaum whispered in his ear. "What is your Hebrew name, and that of your father? We intend to honor you with an aliyah."

Kurt looked at him, completely lost.

"You'll be called to the Torah. You're our guest, and it's an honor for both you and us."

"I don't have one that I know of. My father's name is Hertz."

Mandelbaum smiled. "No matter, we will call you Chaim, life. And your father's name is a good Yiddish name, Hirsch." Mandelbaum shuffled to the end of the narrow aisle and whispered into the ear of a man wrapped in a heavy blue and white prayer shawl, then returned to his seat. "When he calls your name, you will go up to the Torah. I will go with you."

Kurt watched as the first two men were called up. "You're next," said Mandelbaum. A middle-aged man with thick glasses standing next to the Torah reader called out loudly, "Chaim ben Hirsch!" Mandelbaum put his hand gently under Kurt's arm and led him to the pulpit. The men at the pulpit picked up a large prayer shawl and placed it over Kurt's shoulders. A chill ran down his spine.

"Repeat after me," Mandelbaum said.

Kurt listened to the words as Mandelbaum spoke them three or four at a time. "Barchu et Adonai Hamvorach."

He repeated them haltingly, "Bar-chu A-do-nai Ha Mi-vo-ra."

"Good enough," Mandelbaum said, then continued.

Kurt followed him as best he could. Smiles crept up the stern faces of these men, so dedicated to the exact execution of their dedications to their god. After Kurt repeated the final line, Mandelbaum took the fringes of the prayer shawl and put them between Kurt's fingers. "Touch them to the Torah here, where the reader is pointing, then to your lips."

Kurt did as Mandelbaum instructed. He listened as the reader chanted without understanding one word. Somehow, suddenly though, Kurt felt a connection to this thing. For the past year he hated this part of himself, being Jewish. It had brought Kurt nothing but unhappiness. He sent out a plea to God. Please let me see my parents again. With that, Kurt's tears dropped to the fringes of the prayer shawl. When the reader finished, he instructed Kurt to touch the scroll again. Kurt did, then looked up. The men around him offered their hands. "Yasher ko'ach," they shouted. Kurt turned to Mandelbaum. "Welcome young man. May this be only the first of your blessings."

After Shabbos lunch, Kurt found Mandelbaum in his study. "Excuse me," he said. Mandelbaum looked up. He was scrutinizing a passage of Talmud. "We would like to go out for a walk."

"Yes, it's beautiful, the first real spring day," Elsa said, standing behind Kurt.

Mandelbaum considered their request. "You would need a chaperone." He glanced at his wife, sitting on the couch in the living room.

Rebecca Mandelbaum raised an eyebrow. "I think it's fine, Yehuda."

Mandelbaum hesitated. "All right, but remember, it's Shabbos, no handbag Elsa."

"Of course," Elsa replied. "I'll just get my hat and gloves."

They strolled to a small park a few blocks from their apartment. Kurt thought to offer his arm to Elsa, the way his father always did to his mother, then thought better of it. It wouldn't be proper.

"What a beautiful day," Elsa said.

"Yes," Kurt replied, removing his hat. "And it feels good, the sun on my face."

Elsa smiled. As they entered the park, she slid her hand into the crick of Kurt's arm. His lips turned up into a smile. "What a lovely spot," Kurt said. "I wish I had a few Francs. I would offer you an ice cream."

Elsa stopped. She reached her gloved fingers into the small pocket on the left side of her dress and withdrew a two Franc coin. "Do you think this will be enough?"

Kurt smiled. "I hope." He considered the situation for a moment. "I would prefer if you let me pay you back when we get home."

"As you wish," Elsa replied. She smiled, "but after Shabbos of course." She placed the coin in Kurt's hand and retook his arm as they strolled to the ice cream vendor.

"Bon jour," the vendor greeted them. "Je Vous aidee?"

"Two cones please," Elsa replied in French. She turned to Kurt. "Vanilla?"

"Oui."

"Vanilla, si vous plait."

"Mai oui." The vendor took two thin waffles and placed them on top of a warm brazier to soften them. After a moment, he curled them on a metal tube to form a cone, then removed the cones and placed a large scoop of vanilla ice cream in each. "Ici," he said, handing them the delicious treats.

Kurt handed the coin to the vendor. "I hope this is enough," he said, in halting French.

"More than enough. Enjoy." The vendor gave some coins back to Kurt.

They strolled to a bench under a broad, leafy tree arm in arm. Kurt felt normal for the first time in over a year. "How about here?" he asked.

"Sure." Elsa sat down on the wood bench. She tasted the pale, yellowish-white ice cream. "Delicious."

"Yes, it is," Kurt agreed. They sat silently for several minutes, neither quite sure what to say. "We used to have ice cream at the Prater every Sunday," Kurt said, finally breaking the awkward quiet. "It was near my Grandparents' apartment."

"We used to go there too," Elsa said. She relaxed her shoulders a bit, slipping into the bench more comfortably. "My father loved it. He would paint there sometimes." Elsa looked off toward the small playground and tensed up again just as suddenly as she relaxed. "Then they banned us from the parks. Father was devastated when they took his paints. He cried. I'd never seen him cry before. He said he couldn't live without them. To him painting is like breathing." Elsa turned to Kurt, her face gray and somber. "I wonder if he feels like that about me, now that I'm gone as well." Elsa licked at her cone absentmindedly. "I think that was the moment I became an adult."

A pang of sadness passed through Kurt, bringing him back to reality. "I understand. I feel different now too, like I'm not a child anymore, almost like I'm an orphan."

Elsa reached her hand to Kurt and placed it on top of his. "Do you think we will ever go home?"

"I don't know."

"Promise me."

"Promise what?"

"That you will be with me, that you won't abandon me. I can't stand the loneliness."

Kurt hesitated for a tiny moment then said, "I promise."

They finished their ice creams in silence.

CHAPTER 5

Brussels, Belgium - May 1945

Kurt followed Colonel McClain into the interrogation room. The stenographer, seated in the corner, saluted. A large tape recorder was situated on a table behind him. The stenographer would take down the English testimony in shorthand. The German portions would be recorded, transcripts produced overnight. Kurt would compare them the next morning.

"Have a seat," McClain said. He pointed to a chair at the far end of the table. "I will sit here, opposite you. The prisoner will be between us. As we discussed previously, I will ask him a question, then you will translate the question. You will instruct him to answer slowly then you will translate his answer."

"Of course, sir."

"And if you have any questions or comments just raise your hand, and we will stop for a moment."

"Yes, sir."

"Ready?"

Kurt nodded.

McClain picked up the handset of the telephone on the table in the center of the room and dialed. "Bring him in," he said. A moment later the door opened. Two military police entered with the prisoner, a huge man, easily 6'5" and very muscular. His hands were enormous, his clothes in the style of a factory worker. His blond hair was long and unruly, his reddish beard unkempt. His blue eyes were the color of ice, and just as cold.

McClain directed the prisoner to sit in the chair between the table and the rear wall of the room. The prisoner's hands were cuffed behind his back. He sat awkwardly. leaning forward, attempting to stretch his long legs under the table to keep from slipping off the chair.

"Take off, please," he said in broken English, wiggling his fingers.

McClain remained standing. "Ask him what it is he wants," he said, smiling, clearly enjoying the prisoner's discomfort.

"Was willst du?" Kurt asked.

"Bitte nehmen Sie mir die Handschellen ab," the prisoner replied.

"He would like us to remove the cuffs."

McClain walked around the table to face the prisoner. "Why?"

"Warum," Kurt translated.

The prisoner looked up at McClain. A smile crept up around the prisoner's mouth. "Da eine Brezel nicht sprechen kann."

"Because a pretzel can't speak," Kurt translated. There was that typical, superior, cynical, Teutonic attitude.

"Uncuff him!" McClain ordered the MPs. One moved across the room and removed the cuffs. The prisoner pushed himself back into the chair and rubbed his wrists. "Tenks you," he said.

McClain signaled to the stenographer to turn off the tape recorder. "Tell him to stay seated. If he so much as tries to stand up I will have the MP shoot him for attempted escape."

Kurt thought for a moment. He translated in his head then interpreted clearly to express the speaker's intent. This was no easy task. It required that he concentrate on both meaning and nuance. Kurt was merely a messenger delivering McClain's orders.

The prisoner stared directly at Kurt; his icy stare diabolical. Kurt tried to squash his conflicting emotions. He had feared these people for years. They were his tormentors, now they were prisoners at the mercy of the Allied forces, and that included him. Kurt recalled the very moment after the Nazis took Brussels when he realized that his German was his greatest weapon. It gave Kurt a secret power over them, he understood every word they said when they had no idea he was listening. It was the same now. Kurt had control over this man. His words were at Kurt's mercy.

"Please tell your Colonel that I have no intention of trying to escape. I am too much of a coward," the Nazi said.

Kurt translated.

McClain turned to the MP's. "One of you may leave." McClain gestured to the stenographer to turn the recorder back on. "Let's get started."

"I am Colonel Anderson McClain. State your name."

Kurt translated, focusing completely on the words. Everything else in the room, all his other senses, receded.

"Joachim von Hauptmann."

"Your rank and division of service."

"Schutzstaffel, Captain."

"Where were you born?"

"Vienna."

"What year?"

"1896."

"You are a member of the Nazi Party?"

"Yes."

"What brought you to the party?"

"My beliefs."

"What beliefs?"

"To destroy the communists and the Jews before they destroyed us."

Kurt's flinched on hearing the word Juden.

"I fought against them in Budapest in 1919 and 1920 and also in Munich in 1920?"

"Repeat those years," Kurt said.

"What did you ask him, Berlin?" said McClain.

"Sorry sir, I asked him to repeat the years, I want to make sure I get them right."

McClain listened intently as Kurt translated, his eyes closed, nodding almost imperceptibly. Kurt waited for McClain to give him the next question, glad to have a moment to clear his mind. He expected McClain to say something about the prisoner's anti-Jewish remarks, but nothing came from him. McClain paced in front of the table. He rubbed his chin with his left hand.

"What were you doing in Budapest in 1919?" he asked.

Kurt focused on von Hauptmann. "Was haben Sie 1919 in Budapest getan?"

Von Hauptmann stretched his long arms and legs. He wove the fingers of his right hand into his left and cracked his knuckles, looked at Kurt and smiled. "Gegen die Kommunisten und die Juden gekämpft."

This time Kurt nearly froze. For a moment, he wasn't sure he could continue. He summoned his determination, looked at McClain and said. "Fighting the communists and the Jews."

"Ask him how it was that he came to be in Budapest at that time, rather than in Germany?"

Kurt translated. Von Hauptmann answered.

"I was in the Austro-Hungarian Army. At the end of the war I was stationed in Transylvania. My unit was evacuated westward. I was in Budapest when the Armistice was declared. I had no money and wasn't able to return home, so I stayed there to find work. I also met a woman."

McClain watched von Hauptmann's face as Kurt translated. A smile crept up around the corner of the Nazi's mouth. "You understand some English."

"A few word, I learn."

"Why and when did you study English?"

Von Hauptmann listened to Kurt's translation and chuckled. "You have exposed me, Colonel. I am mercenary. When your forces landed successfully at Normandy, I knew the war was lost. There would be no negotiated peace. I began studying English from a textbook I found at an abandoned school here in Brussels, secretly. I only regret I didn't recognize it earlier. Otherwise, I might be able to converse with you now, without your young assistant here." He turned his head to Kurt, staring at his uniform. "You have an interesting family name, Lieutenant. Are you German?"

Kurt translated von Hauptmann's answer without responding to his question.

"What did he ask you directly, Lieutenant?" McClain asked.

Kurt kept his eyes fixed on von Hauptmann. "He asked me about my last name and if I'm German."

McClain smiled and began pacing again. "How long did you stay in Budapest?"

"On and off until 1927."

"Why did you leave and where did you go?"

"I went where I was needed. To Munich, to Vienna, to Berlin, back to Budapest and so forth."

"Why?"

"Party work."

"When did you leave Budapest for good?"

"In the winter of 1927, I received a telegram from my uncle in Vienna informing me that my mother was quite ill. She requested that I return. She had sizeable holdings there."

"Your father was dead?"

"Yes. My mother died a few months later."

"You didn't return to Budapest after that?"

"No. I inherited my mother's home and became more active in the party."

"Did you participate in the July revolt?"

"Against the socialists? Yes, of course."

"And your girlfriend in Budapest? You left her there?"

"Yes. The relationship had run its course. The party needed me. Women are an afterthought for me, Colonel. My honor and the honor of my people come first. The Jews and the communists were defeated in Hungary. Horthy's government was strong. The party was on the rise in Germany. I was needed in Vienna."

This time Kurt let the word Juden slip through his mind. It was just a word, like any other.

"What was your responsibility in the party from the time of your return to Vienna in 1927 till the Anschluss in 1938?"

"I had many."

"What were they?"

"Recruiting active members in secret and preparing for the day when we would take power."

Kurt recalled the weeks just after the Anschluss in March 1938. The Nazis came out into the streets like they had been waiting for the moment for years. Now he knew for certain they had. Bile rose in his stomach. He swallowed hard, his eyes on

McClain, waiting for the next question.

"You said many. What else?"

"I was also involved with organizing our anti-communist activities."

"Did your work change after Hitler took power in Germany in 1933?"

Kurt translated. Von Hauptmann considered the question. "That depends on your view. I became more involved with anti-communist activities, which were necessary to prepare for our eventual assumption of power, less involved in recruiting."

McClain smiled. "You are something of an expert then, concerning communists?"

"Yes, and Jews too."

Kurt's took a breath. He translated von Hauptmann's answer then studied the Nazi's face. It was the picture of hubris.

试试

A few days after finding Saul, Kurt found him a room. The landlady demanded far more than the room was worth, but Kurt agreed. He paid for six months up front. It was the incentive she needed to take Saul in. Then he bought him some clothes and the other necessities he needed to begin to feel human again, simple items like a toothbrush, a razor, and a watch.

That evening after von Hauptmann's first interrogation, Kurt met Saul for dinner at the same restaurant where they found each other. Kurt arrived a few minutes early. Though his years in the army had toughened his hide when it came to anti-Semitism, he was preoccupied with the interrogation from earlier that day. Von Hauptmann was unfiltered with his hatred, and McClain didn't seem to care.

Kurt recalled his days in basic training. Several other soldiers taunted him about being Jewish. "They're just hazing you, private," his commanding officer said. "You gotta toughen up, Izzy," using a derogatory term for Jews.

Kurt did toughen up. The next time he bloodied his tormentor's face so badly the boy needed stitches and had a permanent gap in his smile. Fighting back made Kurt feel powerful. Von

Hauptmann's unrepentant viciousness toward Jews disturbed him, though. It dragged him back to a place of powerlessness. Kurt expected limits, which McClain hadn't set.

Saul waved from the doorway. Kurt watched as the proprietress greeted him, visibly happy that he was clean and shaven. He wouldn't frighten away any customers today, not that there were many to be had.

Kurt let Saul lead the conversation. He was anxious to ask him what had happened to everyone they knew, what he knew of Elsa, but he didn't want to push him. Instead, Saul asked Kurt about himself, about his escape, about America.

Over bowls of beef stewed in Belgian ale with carrots and parsnips, Kurt told Saul about America. "It's a marvel," he said. "Everything and everyone is young. It's completely different than here. There's energy, vitality, and there's nothing they don't believe they cannot do." Kurt relaxed a bit. Five years of war retreated from its permanent position in front of his eyes.

"And how is it for the Jews there?" Saul asked.

The question jerked Kurt back to reality. He didn't want to tell Saul the truth. What was the point? Though Kurt had experienced the undercurrent of anti-Semitism and mistrust that many Americans had for Jews firsthand, he knew that no matter what he had experienced it would appear as a bug bite against the gaping wound Saul and every other Jew in Europe had. "It's good," he said. "We are free to do whatever we want."

The proprietress brought dessert, apple tart with fresh whipped cream and strong coffee. Saul devoured it in silence. He looked directly at Kurt, "Thank you," he said.

"For what? Dinner? I enjoy your company."

"No," Saul replied. "For not asking me."

"I figured you would tell me when you're ready."

"I owe you that much," said Saul. He pushed the last bite of his tart and whipped cream onto his spoon, popped it in his mouth, then savored it.

Kurt took a forkful of his. The warm apples melted in his mouth. "This reminds me of my mother," Kurt said. For Kurt, apple tart was the ultimate memory, the taste and scent that brought him back to his childhood.

"I feel guilty enjoying it," Saul said.

Saul's face transformed. Kurt changed the subject before Saul broke down again, overwhelmed by his own survival. "You don't owe me anything," Kurt said. "If anyone owes anything, it's me. I got out of here."

Saul breathed deeply and looked away. "I don't know if I can tell you yet."

Kurt signaled to the proprietress for the check. "Whenever you're ready." He sipped at his coffee.

Saul took the last bite of the tart. "I'll never be ready, but we need to start."

Kurt put down his coffee. "Do you think anyone is alive?"

"I don't know. Let's go somewhere else to discuss this. Somewhere less…bright. I may break down. It's all too fresh. I remember a place. It's not far from here."

Three old men sat at the bar smoking and drinking beer. American swing played on the radio. The bartender was drying glasses. He looked hard at Kurt in his American uniform. Saul walked toward the booths at the back. Kurt asked for a bottle of cognac. The bartender laughed. "If only I had one, I would be sure to overcharge you for it."

"What do you have then?"

The bartender scrounged around. He pulled out a bottle of brandy about two-thirds full and held it up.

"That will do," Kurt said. The bartender handed it to Kurt with two freshly dried glasses. Kurt gave him some Francs and receded into the semi-darkness at the rear of the bar.

They settled into a booth with torn, brown leather seats. Kurt poured the dark amber liquid into the glasses. He held his up to Saul's and whispered, "L'chaim."

Saul touched his glass to Kurt's and replied, "I suppose, yes."

Kurt took a sip. The brandy was of poor quality and burned his throat.

"Where do you want me to start?" Saul asked.

"Wherever you want."

"I know what's on your mind. I should start by telling you I doubt she's alive."

Kurt took a long slug on the brandy and swallowed hard. It was out there on the table now. Saul knew him too well. "I've been looking for her. I've got a lead. But I need to know what you know."

Saul's expression revealed his fragile state. His face appeared to crumble. Even this darkness wasn't enough to disguise his emotions. "I shouldn't have listened to them," Saul began.

"To who?" Kurt asked.

"My parents. They sent me away. That's why I survived. I wasn't with them when they were taken."

"Where were you?"

"On a farm near Mechelen. My father paid a farmer to take me in to work for him. I was like a slave. They gave me a place to sleep in the barn, and food. I worked for nothing. After my parents were taken, I ran away into the forest and found the resistance. Finally, I felt like I was fighting back."

"And your sister?"

"They kept her with them in Brussels. My father was afraid to send her away. She couldn't come with me, it would have to have been to somewhere else, and he was afraid she would be raped if she were alone, so she stayed with them." Saul wiped a tear from his left eye. "She was very beautiful."

"I remember." Kurt sipped at the brandy. "Do you know what happened to them?'

Saul nodded. "The same thing that happened to everyone else. They were sent first to a transit camp. It wasn't far from the farm where I was hiding. From there they were sent to Auschwitz." Saul began to cry, silently. He closed his eyes and took a deep breath then continued.

"The farmer wanted more money. He sent a message to my father in Brussels. The messenger came back and told him they had been taken away. The farmer had some connections through the garrison in the village. He found out where they were sent."

"He told you this?"

"Yes. He knew there was no more money, so he told me I would have to provide my own food going forward. He would hide me, it was the Christian thing to do, he said, but he couldn't be expected to feed me too."

"What did you do?"

"I left that night. I stole some things, clothing, a blanket, food for a few days. I knew the resistance was operating in the forest, so I went to find them. I went by way of Mechelen."

Kurt's mouth went dry. He wasn't sure he could speak. He thought of himself and his parents. He didn't know what he would have done in Saul's situation.

"It was madness there, thousands of people milling around the camp, which was little more than an open field. Trains pulled in while I was watching. They deposited even more people."

"Did they know where they were going?"

Saul shook his head. "No, not at that point. I had a few gold coins. My father gave them to me for an emergency when I went to the farm, so I decided it was time to use one. I got the attention of one of the prisoners, a man, just an ordinary man, and I told him who I was looking for. He told me to hide behind the trees a few meters from the fence. A short time later my father appeared. I ran to him, and through the fence I took his hand. He cried. He told me to be a good boy, a brave man, to live for him and my mother and my sister. Somehow he knew."

Saul stopped speaking. Tears flowed down his cheeks. Kurt put his hand over Saul's. Saul grasped it tightly, squeezing it. "Are you able to do this?" Kurt asked.

Saul took a deep breath. He pulled a handkerchief from his pocket and wiped his eyes and face. "My father took a small bag from his pocket. It contained ten diamonds. "Take this," he said. "It will help you."

Kurt felt as if he would vomit. He thought of his own father's endless flow of small, blue-black, velvet bags filled with gemstones, the currency that saved lives.

"I took the diamonds. I shouldn't have. I should have given him the gold coins I had, and perhaps the gold and the diamonds together could have saved them. Perhaps they could have escaped. Instead, I survived."

"Nothing could have saved them, brother," Kurt said. He

took Saul's other hand as well over the table. Saul held on so tightly it hurt. 'That's enough for now," Kurt said.

Saul stared directly at Kurt, but Kurt knew Saul didn't see him or hear him. He simply continued without missing a beat. "My father told me to live a good life, to remain a Jew, to find a good woman and have children, and to fear God." Suddenly Saul's eyes changed again. He let go of Kurt's hands. Saul was back in the booth. "I don't fear God," Saul said. "I don't fear anything now."

CHAPTER 6

Vienna, Austria - March 1939

Hertz leaned against the arm of the brocade couch, peeking out of the window through the drapes in Frau Bauer's apartment. He had been there three days. Their neighbor, Otto Bauer, had come to alert them in the middle of the night that he was to be arrested the following day. Bauer's mother was away for several weeks visiting her daughter in Innsbruck. Otto insisted Hertz hide there.

Hertz played the radio continuously for the first day or so. New regulations for Jews were issued constantly to curtail every regular activity, shopping, travel, banking. This morning he had turned it off. It made the small, cluttered apartment even more claustrophobic, shrinking the world outside a little more each day.

Bauer's information was correct, their precinct was swept for Jewish men twice in as many days. Bauer's mother was due back in three days more. Hertz would have to be out of her apartment in two, so that Bauer's wife had time to clean, erasing any evidence of his presence.

Hertz heard a key in the front door. Otto and Berta appeared from the hallway. Hertz embraced Berta. Otto turned his head to give them the most minimal amount of privacy. Berta was, as always, elegantly dressed and coifed, despite the prohibitions against a visit to a beauty salon. She wore a Nazi armband over her coat. "Have you any news about Kurt?"

Berta smiled. "Yes. I received a call from the Kultusgemeinde. He arrived safely and is settled with a family. I have the address. We can write to him."

Hertz felt both relieved and sad. He had taken his son for granted over the years. Now Hertz wanted nothing more than for all of them to be together. He noticed Otto's look. "Something is wrong?"

"Yes," Otto said.

"Konrad called this morning," Berta added. "The Gestapo has been by the shop twice. They're looking for you. They want to question you about your connection to the communists in Budapest in 1919 and the uprising here in 1927."

"I told you," Hertz said. "It was only a matter of time. What did Konrad say to them?"

"He told them he hadn't seen you in several days. We need to get you out of here," Berta said.

Hertz thought for a moment. "Contact this man. I will tell you his name and where you can find him. Don't write anything down."

Upon arriving home Berta went directly to the bedroom, took off her coat and tossed it carelessly onto the bed. She surprised herself. Neatness and orderliness were her nature and routine. Her life though, was no longer routine.

Hertz's instructions raced through her mind, over and over. Open the armoire, on the bottom on the left side were some small drawers. Pull out the top right drawer where he kept some cufflinks. Push against the back of the drawer. The panel gave way as Hertz said it would.

She slid her index and middle fingers into the gap, felt the velvet bag he said would be there, and pulled it out. Inside were three diamonds of about a carat each. Hertz claimed to have gotten them as repayment from a man he lent some money to some years ago. He was saving them for their 20th anniversary. They would have made earrings and a pendant. Berta grinned. Hertz was a terrible liar. He rarely remembered her birthday, let alone their anniversary.

Berta spied Otto as he turned the corner. She nodded in the direction of the shoemaker's store farther down the street. As he passed, she waited a moment then followed him into the shop.

"May I help you?" asked a balding, middle-aged man sitting on a stool, a sole-less shoe propped up on the worktable in front of him. A portrait of Hitler hung high on the wall.

"Yes," Berta said. "I hope so. I was referred by an old friend."

The cobbler peered at her over his half-glasses. His face conveyed neither trust nor distrust. "Who?"

"Hertz Berlin."

With that, the cobbler returned to his work. After a long moment, he said, "I don't know anyone by that name."

Berta stepped closer to the counter, clutching her hat in both hands. "He said to tell you he has a shipment that must leave in the next twenty-four hours."

"I'm afraid I don't know what or who you're talking about." The cobbler reiterated.

Berta maintained her composure. Hertz said the cobbler might appear cautious, or even hostile. "He suggested I remind you of your last meeting with him in July of 1927."

The cobbler put down his tools. "That was another lifetime." He pointed toward the portrait of the Fuehrer. "You see where my sympathies lie now. We are united, one Reich, one people. I can't help you."

Berta stepped to the counter and put her hands down on the top. She leaned into the space between them and pleaded. "Please, my husband needs your help."

The cobbler got up from his chair. He glared at Otto. "And who is this man?"

"A friend."

"Turn that to closed." He pointed to the sign hanging on a nail in the window. Otto flipped the sign. The cobbler stared at Berta intently, examining her expression. "Where was your husband born?"

"Tarnau, in Galicia."

"Where did he serve in the war?"

"The Romanian front, Transylvania." Berta took a breath to calm herself. Perhaps the cobbler would help them. She raised her eyes to Hitler's portrait. Perhaps not. Who could know these days? Perhaps, she thought, she should leave now before she fell into a trap.

"Where was he in 1919, after the war?"

"Budapest," Berta continued. She detected a change in the cobbler's expression. His mouth began to curl upward.

"For which side did he fight?" he asked, lowering his voice and softening his tone.

Berta hesitated. "Bela Kuhn."

The cobbler's shoulder's relaxed. He smiled. "You're clearly his wife. All right then." He extended his hand. "I am Hans Fredrisch, my apologies for my behavior." Hans pointed toward the portrait of Hitler again. "One must be very careful these days. His eyes are everywhere. Your husband once saved my life. How can I help you?"

"Hertz has to leave the country. Immediately."

试戋

Hertz tried to quell the nausea that plagued him since the beginning of the ride hidden in the back of Hans' car. He'd felt the road change from pavement to gravel. "Are we here?" he asked.

"Yes," Hans replied. "You can sit up now."

Hertz struggled to right himself in the tight back seat of the Volkswagen. He gagged, nausea nearly overcoming him. The outlines of three figures standing next to a barn, two men and a woman, were visible in the shadows. The car slowed to a stop. Hertz got out. Even in the semi-darkness, he recognized Berta's expression. She smiled, but her terror was evident.

"These are the men who will take you to Switzerland," Hans said. "Coleman and Berg."

Hertz shook hands with both quickly. He embraced Berta, breathed in her perfume, wanting to remember it forever. "I'm sorry," he said.

"For what?"

"We should have left sooner, a year ago, when my brother did."

"There's no benefit in that now," Berta said, stroking his

cheek, her hand soft and warm.

Hertz reached into his pocket and handed the envelope to Berta. She lifted its flap.

"No, not here," he said. He looked back. Hans was waving, pointing to the lorry parked nearby, its engine purring. "I have to go. Know that I love you. I always have. I always will." Hertz leaned into Berta; their lips touched. For a moment he hesitated, the feeling of others watching him as he kissed Berta making him uncomfortable. Then reality overtook Hertz. He pressed into her, held her tightly and kissed her passionately. She responded in kind. As Hertz released her, Berta slipped the small velvet pouch and a piece of cloth into his hand.

"What's this?"

"The diamonds. Hans refused them."

Hertz slipped the pouch into his pants pocket. "And this?" He looked at the cloth, realizing it was the Nazi armband he wore after the Anschluss to walk around the streets unmolested.

"You may need it," Berta said. He stuffed it into his pocket as well.

"Auf vieder seien, my darling," Hertz said, kissing Berta one last time.

"Don't look back," Berta said.

Hertz walked to the lorry. He placed his foot on the back and stepped up and in. As he did, he turned for one last glance of Berta. What strength she had, this quiet, demure woman whom he had made his wife. He thought of Kurt at the railway station a few days earlier. They were more alike than either of them knew.

Hertz wedged himself in between the wooden cases that lined the sides of the covered lorry. He took the blanket that Hans had left for him and laid it out. It provided both a little comfort and a little warmth. He leaned his head against the panel that separated the cab from the rear. "Don't chat with the drivers," Hans told him. "It's better for everyone if we all remain strangers, less chance of accidental betrayal later."

The rocking rhythm of the truck induced Hertz to close his eyes. He was tired from both the late hour and the stress of the last few days. Hertz recalled his arrival in Vienna in 1919. It was not unlike his exit, hidden in the back of a lorry under a haystack, with little more than the worn clothes on his back and a few things in his army rucksack. So, this is how it ends? Hertz lived a lifetime in those twenty years. The crown of that life was Berta and the jewel in the crown, Kurt.

讹戋

The truck stopped with a start, waking Hertz. Mumbling came from up front, but Hertz couldn't quite make it out. Edging closer to the small window between the cab and himself, he slowly slid it open.

"The tire is gone. We need to change it," said Coleman.

"I told you to slow down," Berg replied.

"I didn't see that large hole in the road. I was trying to get us there as fast as this old piece of shit would take us. I don't like this kind of work, transporting Jews."

"He's an old friend of Hans. And what are you anyway, some kind of Nazi? Who cares if he's a Jew? He's a comrade."

"A comrade? Not by the looks of him in his fancy jacket and tie."

"Hans says he saved his life in '27'."

"Never mind, we have to get to Lustenau by morning. The guards change at 8:00 AM."

"The spare is in the back."

"Perhaps our guest would like to help out. A comrade should know how to change a tire."

Coleman pulled back the tarp that covered the rear of the lorry. "Excuse me, sorry to disturb you."

"I'd be happy to help," Hertz said.

Coleman appeared embarrassed. "So, you heard us."

"Yes."

"Just as well. The spare is there behind that box. If you wouldn't mind?"

"No, not at all," Hertz replied. He took off his coat and tie and pulled the two boxes sitting in front of the tire out of the way.

Coleman climbed into the cabin. "Roll it to me. You'll find

the jack and the tools in a sack just behind there."

Hertz grabbed the sack in one hand and the jack in the other, swung the bag over his shoulder and climbed down out of the truck. He'd changed plenty of tires in the war. "May I?" he said and placed the jack into position. "How did that happen?"

"The Fuehrer hasn't ordered the repair of this roadway yet," joked Berg. "Our comrade here forgot his glasses. He didn't see the enormous hole a few meters back."

Hertz pumped the jack. When the tire was off the ground, he loosened the lug nuts and removed them. "Could you please pull that off so that I may put on the spare?" he said.

Coleman removed the old tire. "My apology," he said.

"For what?"

"For what I said before, I imagine you heard me."

"Which part, about my clothes or about me being a Jew?"

"Both."

"Your apology is accepted."

Hertz lifted the spare and placed it on the axel.

"Shit," Berg said.

Hertz turned. In the distance were lights from another vehicle approaching them at a healthy speed. "What time is it?" he asked.

"2:30," Berg said. "We better hope that's not the local patrol."

"Get back into the truck," Coleman said.

"It's too late for that," Hertz replied. He reached into his pocket and pulled out the pouch Berta gave him earlier. He hadn't planned on using the diamonds this way, but he might not have a choice. As he emptied the contents of the pouch into his palm, the approaching car slowed and stopped. Hertz looked down into his hand, the headlights of the vehicle illuminating its contents. These weren't the three stones Berta had retrieved from his armoire, but instead her engagement ring and her diamond stud earrings. She had hidden them when the Nazis demanded that the Jews sell all their gold and jewels. She could part with anything else, but not these, the first things Hertz had given her.

"Heil Hitler," two men said as they got out of their car, a

large, black Mercedes.

"Heil Hitler," Hertz, Coleman, and Berg responded, arms raised in the Nazi salute.

"Gentlemen, a gutten aben, or should I say nacht. I am the Gauleiter of this district. It's quite late. What are you doing out here?"

"Changing a tire," Coleman said, gesturing toward the wheel well. "I stupidly missed that hole back there."

The Gauleiter, a rotund man in a long, black leather coat, too small for his girth, paced in front of them. "There is a curfew. Where are you going?"

"We have a transport of goods to Switzerland," said Berg. "They have to be there by 8:00 AM. We were delayed by an engine problem in Vienna."

"And what is in this transport?"

"These," Hertz said. He pulled the Nazi armband out of his pants pocket and handed it to the Gauleiter. Coleman and Berg stared at Hertz.

The Gauleiter examined the armband and quickly shoved it into his pocket. "For our brothers in Switzerland?"

Hertz nodded.

"Very good."

"They need them for a rally tomorrow night," Hertz added. "We don't want to disappoint them."

"Of course not," said the Gauleiter. "Forgive me for inter- rupting you gentlemen, but you know we can't be careful enough these days, what with all the Jews trying to escape." He turned to Hertz and smiled. "Carry on then," he said, he and his driver returning to their car.

"I thought we were finished," said Coleman, breathing heavi- ly.

"So, did I," said Berg, his hands on his forehead. "Where did you get that armband?"

"I carried it with me in the streets just in case I needed to blend in. My wife brought it for safety. Turns out she was right." Hertz then opened his palm exposing the remaining earring and ring. "I slipped him one of these with the armband. Even the most dedicated Nazi prefers diamonds to Jews."

Both Coleman and Berg were silent.

"Shall we finish?" Hertz said. He thanked God for Berta. She had saved his life once again.

试试

"It's 7:15, you have forty-five minutes. Get your bag and come out," said Coleman. "This is as far as we go."

Hertz climbed down. He checked the inside pocket of his coat. The Swiss Francs were tucked down into its bottom. He picked up his suitcase. "How far is it?"

"About a kilometer to the border crossing."

"There's a path along the road just on the other side of those hedges. Follow that," said Berg. "You'll hear the crossing before you see it. When you get close enough, you'll see the path turn off to the left. Follow that path along till you see the fence. You have a watch?"

"Yes,"

"Keep track of time. About 200 meters down from where you first see the fence you will see a spot covered with leaves. It's a small trench. You remove the leaves and slip under the fence."

"How will I recognize it?"

Coleman pulled a small photograph from his pocket. "This man will be waiting there. He's a border guard. He's not one of ours, but easily bought. He's been paid half already. You pay him the rest after. Remember, after he pulls you through to the other side, not before. You have the money?"

"Yes, it's right here," Hertz said, patting the outside of his jacket.

"He gets off his shift at 8:00 exactly. These Swiss are very prompt. If you arrive at the rendezvous point early, hide in the bushes. Be careful, they have occasional patrols with dogs on this side. Good luck to you. Don't give him the money till he pulls you through."

Hertz walked stealthily through the brush. The forest didn't provide much cover as the spring growth was late in the mountains, the trees and bushes still bare. He was conscious of every sound. Hertz checked his watch, 7:40. He wasn't sure how far he had come.

As Berg told him he would, Hertz heard the border crossing before he saw it. The guards on his side were shouting. "Stop, stop him!" Hertz panicked and jumped back into the bare bushes. He thought they had seen him. No one appeared. In the distance, there were sounds of men running, dogs barking and gunshots, then a scream of pain. Hertz froze. There was more shouting.

"Take this man out of here!"

"Yes, sir!"

"Look for more, that way, to the north side!" shouted the same voice.

Hertz couldn't move. He looked at his watch again, 7:45. After a few moments Hertz willed himself to regain his composure. Perhaps this unexpected event could work to his advantage. The guards on this side would be occupied. He propelled himself forward, his legs shaking.

Hertz followed the path to the left. Eventually, he came to the border fence. After a few more minutes walking, he noticed a spot where the fence seemed a bit cluttered with leaves. He rechecked his watch, 7:56, then ducked behind some bushes and waited, hoping he was in the right place.

The shouting continued, this time too far away to understand what was said. Hertz remained silent, his stomach in knots. He thought he might vomit. Hertz gave one dry heave then held back another, forcing himself to calm down. The shouting seemed to be moving away. It was then that Hertz thought he heard footsteps and froze. A guard was at the fence along with a Rottweiler. The guard pushed the leaves that covered the hole out of the way, scanning the bushes.

Hertz emerged from behind the trees. The guard waved to him then placed a finger to his lips. Hertz grabbed the handle of his bag and walked quickly and quietly toward the fence. The dog growled as he approached. The guard placed his hand on the top of the dog's head to calm it. Typically, Hertz would have frozen at the sight of a growling Rottweiler, instead he slid his suitcase under the fence.

"Where's the money," the guard said.

"When I cross," Hertz replied.

"Let me see it," said the guard.

Hertz hesitated then reached into his pocket to take it out. There were more gunshots. "There's no time," Hertz said. "You want your money, help me through, now."

The guard grabbed the suitcase, pulled it through then tossed it aside. He got down on his stomach and extended a hand under the fence. "Now come, before we get caught."

Hertz grabbed the guard's hand and pushed himself through with his legs. When he got to his feet, a pistol was pointed at his head. "The money, now," demanded the guard.

Hertz reached into his coat and took out the billfold. The guard counted it quickly and placed it in his pants pocket, the gun still pointed at Hertz. "You see the little building over there, behind you?"

Hertz turned. "Yes."

"Start running,"

"What?"

"Hmm," the guard said chuckling. "They didn't tell you? They never do."

Hertz reached for his bag.

"No, leave that. We'll retrieve it later. Go."

Hertz knew he had no choice. He turned and started at a trot toward the little hut. After about twenty meters the guard blew his whistle. He shouted, "Illegal crossing!" and let the dog loose. It charged after Hertz. Hertz tried to outrun the animal, but it was much too fast. Teeth grabbed the tail of Hertz's coat and pulled him down. As suddenly as it began, it ended. The guard was standing over him, his gun pointed at Hertz's head. The dog growled, showing his teeth.

"I've got him!" the guard called out.

Hertz had escaped the Reich, but he wasn't sure to what.

CHAPTER 7

Brussels, Belgium - May 1945

McClain chose to sit today. It was clear to Kurt that despite their lack of a common language, a synergy was developing between McClain and von Hauptmann. McClain was less confrontational, he even smiled at von Hauptmann when the MPs brought him in. Kurt's was sickened by his position as their conduit.

"Tell Captain von Hauptmann I want to discuss his early history in the Nazi party."

Kurt took a breath. Interpreting von Hauptmann's interrogation was affecting his mental state and he knew it. Nevertheless, he continued. That was his job. "Sagen Sie ihm, dass ich seine Vergangenheit in der NSDAP besprechen will."

"Naturlich," von Hauptmann, replied smiling.

"Of course," Kurt said. He waited for McClain's next question.

"When did you officially join the party?"

Kurt translated.

"I joined the German Worker's Party in April 1919, in Munich. It later became the Nazi Party."

McClain struck a match and lit his pipe. "You said previously, that you were in Budapest in 1919."

"I was in Budapest until March of 1919." Von Hauptmann corrected. He stretched his legs under the table.

"Do you speak Hungarian?"

"Egen," replied von Hauptmann. "Es te? Beszels magyarul?"

McClain looked at Kurt and smiled. "I guess that means yes."

"It does," von Hauptmann replied in German. "I asked him if he speaks Hungarian." Von Hauptmann smiled broadly, very pleased with himself.

McClain relaxed, exhaling a plume of smoke. "He has a sense of wit about him, our friend. Don't translate that."

Kurt remained silent. Von Hauptmann wasn't his friend.

"Why did you leave?"

"The communists took over. I was a member of the Arrow Cross. I was arrested. My girlfriend bribed the guards to get me out of prison. I had to leave the country immediately."

McClain nodded and puffed on his pipe. "Did she go with you?"

"No."

"Why?"

Von Hauptmann became circumspect. "Her mother was dead, and she cared for her father and younger siblings. Her duty, I would say."

"Why Munich? Why didn't you go back to Vienna, or to Berlin?"

"Because the communists had declared a free state in Bavaria. The Friecorps were organizing a counterattack. I wanted to fight."

"Tell me about Munich," McClain said, now looking directly into von Hauptmann's eyes.

Von Hauptmann leaned forward. He licked his lips. "It was wonderful. We slaughtered them. I killed them with my bare hands." Von Hauptmann mimicked choking a man. "It was over in two days."

Kurt hesitated, disgusted. He wasn't sure what disgusted him more, what von Hauptmann said, or the easy rapport he was facilitating between the two men.

"Berlin, what did he say?"

Kurt caught von Hauptmann's gaze. He translated von Hauptmann's last statement, stressing how much he enjoyed the act of murder. McClain seemed impressed.

"Did you go to Vienna afterward?" McClain asked.

"No."

"What did you do?"

Von Hauptmann thought about the question for a moment after Kurt's translation, as if weighing the best answer. Kurt was never sure whether von Hauptmann's response was true to fact or custom tailored to what he thought McClain was after. He never doubted von Hauptmann's shrewdness.

"I received a secret message from my girlfriend that the anti-communist forces in Budapest were organizing to overthrow that filthy Jew communist, Bela Kun. I went back to help them finish the job."

McClain sat up. "You were in Budapest then when Kun's government was overthrown?"

"Yes. I was well acquainted with several of their leaders from my days in the Austro-Hungarian army and was delighted to hunt them down and bring them to justice. I was personally responsible for the death of one of their top deputies."

"Who?" McClain asked.

"Baron Petar Karoly. He was a traitor to his class and his people. He was seduced into socialism by his Jewish wife and her intellectual friends."

When he heard "Judische" again, Kurt nearly froze. It was the hook that snagged him every time.

"I take it you don't much care for the Jews, Captain." McClain said.

Kurt's guts churned. He thought he noticed a smile creep up around the edges of McClain's mouth. McClain knew Kurt was Jewish, yet he went down this path of questioning. He suspected McClain enjoyed watching his reaction.

Kurt took a deep breath before continuing. He was exacting in his correctness and icy cold in his delivery. There was no doubt in Kurt's mind that von Hauptmann was a first-class anti-Semite. He was beginning to think McClain was one too.

"Nein," von Hauptmann said. "They are a plague. Do you not agree?"

Kurt translated von Hauptmann's answer as coolly as he had McClain's question. Now McClain smirked and looked directly at Kurt. "Ask him if that's why he became involved with the

Nazis."

Kurt steeled himself, stared at the wall and translated, then waited for von Hauptmann's answer.

"Yes. I found them, the Nazis, when I went back to Munich after we defeated Kun, the early autumn of 1919. They were exactly what I was looking for, and I was exactly what they were seeking."

"What do you believe they were seeking?"

"Dedication and loyalty."

"Would you say you have those traits?"

Von Hauptmann smirked. "What do you think, Colonel?"

"Colonel," Kurt interrupted. "He didn't answer the question."

"What did he say?"

"He asked if you think he has those traits."

McClain smiled this time. "Tell him I would have thought so, but then, why is he cooperating with us?"

Kurt translated McClain's last statement.

Von Hauptmann leaned his elbows on the table, his chin resting on his clasped hands. "Ich brauche einen neuen Master."

"He said, he needs a new master."

McClain nodded and continued. "What was your party number?"

Kurt wondered what relevance that had?

"595"

"That's impressive," said McClain. "You were one of the original 100 members."

"He said 595, sir? Did I misspeak?"

"No, lieutenant. They started their numbering at 500 to make the party seem larger to their enemies."

"Yes." Von Hauptmann replied, his expression one of self-satisfaction.

"That's how you met Hitler?"

"Yes. I knew he was our leader from the first time I heard him speak."

McClain stopped for a moment and considered his next question. "Did you participate in the Beer Hall Putsch in November of 1923?"

"Yes." Von Hauptmann grinned.

"Were you arrested?"

"No, I escaped, again."

"You were fortunate."

"Yes."

The questions and answers picked up pace. For the first time Kurt had trouble keeping up. He didn't want to tell McClain. He wanted the session to end, the sooner the better.

"Where did you go?"

"Back to Budapest."

"How long did you stay there that time?"

"Until 1927 as I told you, off and on."

"Where did you go off and on?"

"To Germany mostly, to help to build the party."

"And otherwise? What work did you do in Budapest?"

"I worked for Horthy's men. They often needed to make people disappear."

"I see," said McClain. He looked at his watch and yawned. "I think that's where we will end for now. Guard, bring the prisoner back at 2:00."

试找

Kurt re-took his position in the interrogation room, Von Hauptmann already seated at the table. He was a few minutes late and still mentally tired from the earlier session.

"Shall we begin?" McClain said.

"I'm ready, sir" Kurt replied.

McClain signaled for the technician to start the tape recorder. "This afternoon I would like to cover Captain von Hauptmann's activities in Austria through the Anschluss and until the beginning of hostilities.

Kurt translated.

"My pleasure," von Hauptmann said.

Kurt found McClain addressing von Hauptmann as Captain particularly egregious. This merciless, unrepentant Nazi was undeserving of that sign of respect. Kurt considered reporting it to Rosenthaller but thought better of it. He didn't want to make waves.

"When did you join the SS, Captain?" McClain asked.

"Wann sind Sie der SS beigetreten?" Kurt asked.

"In 1936 and 1937, secretly. I went to Berlin for training then went back to Vienna. I was ready to serve when our people arrived in Vienna in March 1938."

Though translating rapidly, Kurt was finding it increasingly hard to concentrate.

"What was your responsibility within the SS after the Anschluss?" McClain asked.

"I worked in several areas simultaneously, one overtly and two covertly."

"What was your overt responsibility?

"I was responsible for separating the Jews from their wealth."

"Were you also involved with the direct actions against the Jewish population?"

"Generally, not at that time," von Hauptmann replied, "though I was involved with major operations, like the action of November 9 & 10, 1938."

Kurt's mind was in disarray. That night, Kristallnacht, played back in his head, the screaming mobs, the flames, the sound of shattering glass, the menacing men in uniform and out.

"So, what were your responsibilities? Describe them."

"Primarily, accounting for Reich property."

"What exactly does that mean?"

"At that time, we were simply interested in getting the Jews to leave. At the same time, they had amassed a great deal of wealth, which belonged to the German people. They stole this wealth from us through international business and communism. They were rich. We wanted them to leave, but without their wealth."

It was as if a heavy drape was drawn back in Kurt's mind. It was more than just hate, it was jealousy. He recalled how their neighbor, Frau Krauss, glared at his mother whenever she was dressed for a special occasion, her fine clothing and jewelry obvious to anyone who saw her.

"Why were you chosen for this?"

"Because I am fastidious. When given a task I complete it to the letter of my charge. It was basically an accounting project. We stripped the Jews of their wealth. Their businesses were taken almost immediately after the Anschluss. Their bank accounts were frozen at that time as well. Other assets, real estate, stocks, etc., were stripped shortly thereafter. Artwork and jewelry were taken shortly after that. It was a crime for Jews to own gold or diamonds. They were under strict regulations regarding what they could take with them when they left the Reich."

Kurt recalled his father gathering up every piece of jewelry and packing it into a leather bag to be taken to a government office for 'repatriation,' as the Nazis called it. Hertz left Kurt his gold watch and told him to keep it in his pocket, not on his wrist. He remembered when the Nazi guards came to their apartment and took their artwork and his mother's piano. The tall skinny leader to the group was wearing a monocle. He checked off items from a list on a clipboard, as sturdier men removed them from the apartment. A wave of nausea rolled over Kurt.

"Lieutenant!" shouted McClain, "I'm waiting!"

"Sorry, sir." Kurt pulled himself back to the present and translated McClain's question.

"They would be required to submit certain papers and were permitted only a very limited amount of cash with which to leave the country," said von Hauptmann. "My job was to make sure the papers were in order and that there was no smuggling."

Kurt fought the rancor rising in him. Von Hauptmann was talking about them, his family, without even knowing it. He thought of his mother trying to leave the Reich. How terrifying it must have been for her, alone and desperate.

"When you say your job was to make sure their papers were in order what does that mean?"

"I was often at the railway stations to inspect their papers upon exit. If they lacked a specific form or a receipt for exit taxes or whatever, I would confiscate their passport and papers and they couldn't leave."

McClain took his pipe and put it between his lips. He sat down on the edge of the interrogation table. "Didn't that defy the basic policy of the Reich, which was to get rid of the Jews?"

Von Hauptmann chuckled. "Colonel, with all due respect, that is the difference between executing policy and orders. Our orders were to force the Jews to leave. Our policy was to make sure they left with nothing. If they tried to smuggle something and we caught them, we would confiscate the contraband and send them to a camp."

"What happened to them once they went to a camp?"

Von Hauptmann smirked. "That wasn't my area."

Kurt's irritation increased. He felt as if the walls were closing in on him. He tried to control his heartbeat with his breathing, but without anyone noticing. Luckily, McClain was completely focused on the Nazi, unaware of Kurt's emotional discomfort.

McClain looked directly at von Hauptmann. "Captain, did you ever enrich yourself from the contraband you found?"

Von Hauptmann straightened in the chair. "We only took what was rightfully ours. Occasionally, I took a commission."

Images ricocheted around Kurt's mind so quickly he nearly missed his cue. He blurted out the translation of von Hauptmann's answer.

McClain pursed his lips and nodded slightly. He looked at Kurt, smiled broadly then continued. "So, you were an accountant by day, and a spy by night."

Von Hauptmann smiled at Kurt's translation.

CHAPTER 8

Detention Camp, Switzerland - April 1939

Hertz sat on the edge of the narrow bed waiting for his lawyer. He reread the cable from Sam:

Details in place STOP Money required cabled to Bank Bern STOP Attorney will arrange release from camp soon as all docs in place STOP I will handle Belgian visas STOP By end of May you will be in Brussels STOP Kurt fine stop worrying STOP

Hertz smiled, his younger brother's wit never escaped him. But it was Berta he was most worried about now, not Kurt.

Hertz looked around the room. There were perhaps fifty gray metal beds in this barracks alone, a wood building with no heat and no insulation. The facility, an old Swiss Army training center, had been slated for demolition. With the large number of illegal refugees streaming over the border from the Reich, most of them men, the Swiss had nowhere else to put them. They couldn't be walking around the neat, clean streets of Bern or Geneva or Zurich, these dirty, disheveled Jews. A tired looking man of about his age with several days stubble on his face entered the barracks.

"Excuse me," he said.

"Yes," Hertz replied.

"You are Berlin?"

Hertz recognized the man's distinctive Viennese accent. "Yes."

"I thought so, I remember you from your store. I bought coffee there occasionally."

Hertz stood up and offered his hand. "I'm sorry to meet you again under such circumstances."

"Me too."

Hertz touched his hand to his chin realizing he too was unshaven. He would never have walked about in public like this before. "I'm sorry, I don't recall your name."

"Offenberg. My mother-in-law lived in your district. She loved your shop."

"What is her name?"

"Denberg, Ida Denberg"

Hertz smiled. "I remember her. I hope she's well."

"She's with my wife, still in Vienna."

"As is mine."

A long awkward moment followed before Offenberg broke the silence. "You have a visitor at the gate. When they called out your name, I knew it was you I had spotted yesterday, so I offered to fetch you."

"Thank you." They shook hands again, for longer this time and more firmly. Hertz put his left hand over Offenberg's right, already in his grasp. "Think positively, everything will turn out all right."

Offenberg pursed his lips. "I hope so. You know it never meant much to me, this Jewish thing, but apparently, it means a great deal to our former countryman."

"Sadly," said Hertz. He looked at his watch. "I must go. Perhaps a coffee after dinner?"

Offenberg laughed. "Sure, if you can call what they give us here coffee."

By the time Hertz arrived at the gate, the lawyer was inside. A small, thin man with receding blond hair in his mid-forties, he was brushing dust off his double-breasted, blue suit with his fingertips. "Herr Langer?" Hertz said. Langer looked up at him absently before limply taking Hertz's hand.

"Yes." Langer looked Hertz up and down. "You are Berlin?"

"Yes."

"The guard said we could meet over there." Langer pointed to a small room off to the left of the waiting area. My apologies, I don't have much time."

Hertz followed the lawyer into the room. There was a window in the wall separating it from the central waiting area. Langer sat down on the far side of a wood table. "Herr Berlin, I will be brief. I don't much like doing this kind of work, but your brother has paid us handsomely, so here I am."

"What do you have for me?"

"Not much as of yet. The first order of business is to obtain your asylum papers." He placed a small stack of documents in two piles on the table. "These are originals and carbon copies of the affidavits necessary to apply for asylum. Please sign both copies and initial the various pages where I have attached a small clip."

Hertz signed as instructed. Langer took up the papers and put them back in his black leather briefcase. He placed another document on the table.

"And this?" Hertz asked.

"Authorization for payment of our fees from your account at Union Bank."

Hertz read the document. "I would prefer to pay you half now and half after you've obtained my Swiss asylum papers and my visas."

Langer smirked and cleared his throat. He straightened his posture. "Sometimes, you people make it easy to understand why the Germans are, shall we say, uncomfortable with you. Herr Berlin, I don't much care what you would prefer. We find this business to be distasteful to begin with, but then that's what we do here in Switzerland, we conduct business. If you want us to represent you, please authorize the payment."

Hertz picked up the pen and signed. He had no choice but to work with this bastard. Langer picked up the signed authorization of payment and placed it in his briefcase preparing to leave. "I will contact you through the authorities here at the refugee center when your asylum is granted."

"How long do you expect that to take?"

"That depends?"

"On?"

"Which officials we have to contact and whether they are inclined to your cause or to that of your enemies. But then, everyone has a price."

Hertz slipped his hands into his pockets. "Clearly."

The attorney turned toward the exit. "I'm already late."

"One moment, Langer," Hertz said.

Langer's body stiffened. "Yes"

"Yes…Herr Berlin," Hertz said.

Langer cringed. "Yes, Herr Berlin, how can I help you?"

"We need to discuss the matter of my wife's access to my numbered accounts at Union Bank."

"I'm afraid we are still working on that. German banking laws don't permit Jews to hold bank accounts, even at foreign banks."

"I believe I have an alternative,"

Langer chuckled. "And that would be?"

"Add the name of my Aryan partner's wife to the account. We will obtain an identity card with her name and with my wife's picture."

Langer laughed again. "As you wish. Good luck with that. What is the name of your partner's wife?"

"Greta Winkler. And one more thing."

"Yes."

Hertz pulled an envelope from his pocket. "Please send this message to Konrad Winkler through the daily pouch to your firm's offices in Vienna."

"Herr Berlin, that pouch is often searched, and the sealed envelopes opened."

"No need to worry Herr Langer, the envelope is unsealed, and the note will appear innocuous. It's written in code. As the Nazis suggest, we Jews are very duplicitous."

CHAPTER 9

Brussels, Belgium - May 1945

Kurt jumped to his feet and saluted.

"At ease, Berlin," said McClain. "Captain Rosenthaller will be joining us today."

"That's excellent, sir," Kurt replied, speculating about Rosenthaller's presence. Was he here to observe von Hauptmann, or perhaps Kurt?

"Sit down," McClain said. "Before I have them bring in the prisoner, I want to speak to you."

"About what, sir?" McClain's statement confirmed Kurt's suspicions. Rosenthaller's presence was about him.

"As I've mentioned to Captain Rosenthaller, your translation skills are exceptional in both speed and accuracy."

"Thank you, sir." Kurt controlled his breathing. He didn't want to appear rattled by either Rosenthaller's presence or McClain's pronouncements.

"At times you seem to be affected by the content of the prisoner's responses."

Kurt maintained his silence. He hadn't realized McClain had noticed his response to von Hauptmann's anti-Semitic remarks. McClain glanced at Rosenthaller. Kurt thought he detected the slightest nod of Rosenthaller's head. "Concentrate on the task and not on the prisoner's biases or comments." McClain came closer. "You best serve your country by executing your duties. Are we understood, Lieutenant?"

Kurt felt the blush rising to his face. "Yes, sir."

"Bring in von Hauptman!" McClain called to the guard.

Von Hauptmann sauntered into the room, his hands behind his back. "Guten morgen," he said.

McClain nodded his head and gestured to the chair behind the interrogation table. Von Hauptmann looked over at Rosenthaller. He squinted his eyes to read Rosenthaller's name on the flap of his jacket pocket. "Sie sind deutscher Kapitän?" he said.

Rosenthaller ignored him.

"What did he say, Berlin?" McClain asked, before Kurt could get the translation out of his mouth.

"He asked if Captain Rosenthaller is German." Kurt realized the game had intensified.

"Tell him Captain Rosenthaller is of no interest to him."

"Kapitän Rosenthaller hat Sie nicht zu interessieren," Kurt translated.

"You mentioned in our previous conversation that you had covert as well as overt responsibilities. I'd like to turn to your covert responsibilities," McClain said. "What were they?"

Von Hauptmann considered McClain's question. Kurt found the prisoner's penchant for retrospective during his interrogation both astonishing and maddening. He behaved as if he were being interviewed for a memoir, waxing nostalgically about his storied past.

Von Hauptmann leaned slightly forward in his chair then took a sip of the water from a glass to his right. "Infiltration," he said.

"Of who? Of what?" The tone between McClain and von Hauptmann continued to become friendlier, the questioning more like a journalist's interview than an interrogation.

"The communists. I was assigned to a unit with the task of flushing out communists and socialists, exposing them and arresting them. Vienna, Red Vienna as it was known, was particularly infiltrated with this scum, as it has always been a center of socialist activity. When we took power in March of 1938, we weren't entirely sure of the extent of socialist and communist presence in the country, or in Vienna itself. We had some party lists, but those were incomplete. The communists and the socialists weren't stupid. They knew what we did in Germany from 1933 onward and expected that sooner or later we would take power in Austria."

Kurt put his hand up to stop von Hauptmann.

"What's the problem, Berlin?" McClain asked.

"I would like to translate that before he continues, for the sake of accuracy."

"Of course," McClain said.

"Warten Sie!" Kurt barked at von Hauptmann, hoping to show his resolve to McCain and remind von Hauptmann who was in charge. In fact, he was stalling for time to calm himself. Rosenthaller's presence was spooking him. When he regained his composure, Kurt translated the statement then turned back to von Hauptmann, "In kurzen Sätzen weitermachen."

"What did you say to him? McClain interrupted.

"I asked him to continue in shorter segments."

McClain was visibly irritated. "Don't give him instructions without asking me first,"

"Yes, sir." Kurt faced on von Hauptmann. "Weitermachen," he said.

"As I said, the communists expected that we might seize power at some point, so they prepared themselves. They set up a clandestine organization to help their members escape if need be and to infiltrate our own organization, to spy on us from the inside, as we did with them."

Kurt held up his hand again and translated.

"What was your cover?" McClain asked.

"Because of my background I spoke Hungarian like a native, so I assumed the identity of a Hungarian communist who had escaped Horthy's regime."

"Very compelling. How is it that you spoke Hungarian so well?" McClain asked. "You said you were from Vienna, originally. Hungarian is nearly impossible to learn like a native speaker."

"I confess, I grew up in both Vienna and Budapest. I am half Hungarian."

McClain picked up von Hauptmann's file. He thumbed through it. "That's odd. There's no mention of that in any of the documents we found on you at SS headquarters."

Von Hauptmann laughed. "Racial purity was a very

important component of our movement. I made sure my files reflected that."

"So then, Captain, your mother was Hungarian?"

"Actually, as I suppose it's no longer a matter of life and death, I will be honest. My father was Hungarian. His name was Molnar. He was a commoner. It was with his name and pedigree that I infiltrated the communists. My mother was the daughter of an Austrian Baron. I took her name and her pedigree after the Great War. By 1920, I knew where my destiny lay."

"Resourceful," said McClain.

"Should I translate that, sir?"

"Of course,"

"Einfallsreich."

Von Hauptmann smiled and tipped his head to McClain. "That I am sir, otherwise I doubt I would be sitting here alive today."

"Continue," McClain said, smiling, as if he had just won a prize.

Kurt glanced at Rosenthaller, who exhibited a similar expression to McClain's. Clearly, they were pleased with how the interrogation was going. "Fahren Sie fort," Kurt said.

"By infiltrating the secret communist underground in Vienna, we knew who our enemies were, and we knew who their infiltrators were. We kept this information; we didn't act on it for some time. If we had, they would have known we had infiltrated their organization."

"Excellent point, good strategy," commented McClain. "When did you finally act on your intelligence?"

"In the spring of 1939. We knew war was coming, it was time to flush them out. The communists had set up a network to smuggle their people out of the Reich, and we wanted to end that. Often those who escaped carried secret information. Most importantly, we didn't want a possible fifth column within the Reich after the real war began. We needed to capture or kill these men and their cells."

Kurt, listening intently, was both absorbed and repelled by what he heard. He began to understand the deep and dangerous undercurrents of the world he had lived in. Kurt recalled the circumstances of his father's escape from Vienna. He could well have been caught up in von Hauptmann's dragnet. Kurt again directed his mind to the words and their counterparts in English, so as to maintain control over his emotions. He would mull over their implications later.

"What did you do with those you caught?" asked McClain.

Von Hauptmann smiled. "Officially, they were sent to Dachau or Mauthausen."

"Unofficially?"

Von Hauptmann smiled. He slid a finger across his neck like a knife slicing through it.

Kurt found it insufferable that this man could be so casual about a lifetime of murder and deadly intrigue. His felt as if his head might explode. He needed someone to talk to, to advise him. He thought about Sam.

试读

Kurt sat silently at the table in McClain's office with McClain and Rosenthaller. Their lunch was served on delicate white china accompanied by ornate silver flatware and beautiful crystal stemware. Brussels was in ruins, but Colonel Anderson McClain of the OSS was dining in style.

"Fascinating interrogation this morning," Rosenthaller said. "I think we've hit the jackpot with this one." He cut a large slice off his steak and popped it in his mouth.

"I think so," McClain said. "Wouldn't you agree, Berlin?"

Kurt smiled and swallowed. "Of course, sir." He took a sip of his wine, a deep, rich Burgundy.

"He's exactly what we're looking for," McClain said. "A dedicated anti-communist with intelligence training. He also speaks Hungarian, which might be a real asset depending on what ultimately happens there."

"What do you think will happen there?" Rosenthaller chuckled. "You know we've already agreed that Hungary will be within the Soviet sphere of influence. He's doubly valuable." Rosenthaller took a long, healthy, slog of wine to wash down the steak and the fried potatoes that accompanied it.

"Excellent." He raised the glass to the light and examined the wine's color. "Where did you get this?"

"A counterpart of mine in Paris," replied McClain. "He knows how much I appreciate it. He sent a couple cases. I'm not done with von Hauptmann though. I still have questions."

"It appears he's a killing machine," Rosenthaller said, continuing to sip at his wine. "No compunction at all at the thought of picking up a gun and eliminating the enemy at close range."

Kurt kept eating, listening. The conversation was surreal. Von Hauptmann was a murderer and deserved punishment, not recruitment into American intelligence.

"None at all," McClain continued. "He's admitted to more than one execution, and I'm sure there are many more."

"I think he's an excellent candidate for this program, perhaps the best we've come across so far," Rosenthaller said. He took another swig of his wine. "Perhaps you could have your friend send me a case of this? You know these men who survived the trenches in the first war, they're made of steel. My father fought for the Kaiser on the eastern front. He never flinches at anything. If not for him, we would never have gotten out of Germany."

"I agree," said McClain, "von Hauptmann is exactly what we're looking for. My guess is he's done some terrible stuff here in Brussels though. I'll have to question him about that. We need to recruit him before the British or the French ask to interrogate him."

"I'd suggest you do that quickly, Colonel. I'm getting daily inquiries about him and a dozen others we're holding. The picture emerging about what the Nazi's did to the Jews is getting increasingly ugly very quickly. There will be a need to settle scores."

Kurt was stunned by Rosenthaller's cavalier attitude toward and personal detachment from his own people. How he referred to them as them, never us. As a Jew, Kurt expected Rosenthaller to want to see justice done.

"I have no intention of letting anyone try von Hauptmann," McClain said. He speared the last piece of his meat, "regardless of what he's done. He's too valuable a tool in the coming fight."

Kurt nearly choked on a small piece of steak.

诔戋

"Bring in the prisoner," McClain said to the guard.

A moment later von Hauptman entered the interrogation room without handcuffs. He nodded to both McClain and Rosenthaller and resumed his position. "Ich hoffe, Sie haben ihre Mittagspause genossen?" he said. Von Hauptmann continued to focus on Rosenthaller. Rosenthaller's expression remained stone-like.

Kurt didn't wait for McClain. "He wants to know if you enjoyed your lunch."

"Ja," McClain replied with a smile. He sorted through some papers preparing for the interrogation.

"Vielleicht werden Sie mich irgendwann einmal einladen." von Hauptmann said, a half-cocked smile on his face.

"Perhaps you will invite me sometime" Kurt translated.

"Perhaps." McClain looked up. "Let's begin." McClain looked directly at von Hauptmann. "I want to pick up where we left off. We were discussing what happened to the communists you captured in Vienna." McClain picked up the transcript from the previous interrogation and read out loud in poorly pronounced German. "What did you do with those you caught?" I asked. You answered. "Officially they were sent to Mauthausen." McClain mimicked the same gesture Von Hauptmann had used that morning, sliding a finger across his neck. "And unofficially?"

Kurt translated.

Von Hauptmann smiled. "What specifically do you want to know? I think I have been quite forthcoming with my answers."

"We would like to know how that process worked."

Von Hauptman nodded his head and smiled. "Sie haben Angst vor Ihren sowjetischen Verbündeten, nicht wahr?"

Kurt looked at Rosenthaller from the corner of his eye to see his reaction. Rosenthaller hadn't flinched. He still had no intention of letting the Nazi know he understood his every word. Von Hauptmann's statement was insubordinate, a challenge to the authority of his captors. Kurt translated. "You are quite frightened of your Soviet allies, aren't you, Colonel?"

McClain smiled. "Please remind Captain von Hauptmann that I ask the questions and he answers them, then ask him why he thinks that?"

Kurt translated as instructed.

Von Hauptmann took a sip from the water glass to his right. "I want to phrase this correctly," he replied. "I don't want to anger the Colonel with my questions. I thought that by now we would be discussing my involvement with the disposition of the Jew problem here in Brussels, rather than my part in the dispatching of political enemies before the war. Isn't that the information you're after?"

Kurt translated slowly and precisely. He knew Rosenthaller wouldn't correct him in front of von Hauptmann to keep his cover, but nonetheless, Rosenthaller could correct him later for any inaccuracies, which Kurt didn't want.

McClain thought for a moment before responding. He cupped his chin with his hand. "We will arrive at that soon enough. Let's get back to my question. How did the process work? Were the prisoners sent to Mauthausen, or were they executed?"

Von Hauptmann listened intently to Kurt but kept one eye on Rosenthaller as if he suspected Rosenthaller understood him without translation. He replied. "It depended on the circumstances. If the prisoner was of use, say for instance, that additional information through interrogation could lead us to others, we sent him to camp. If not, we executed them summarily and disposed of the bodies. There was no need to feed them and guard them if they had outlived their usefulness."

McClain waited for Kurt to finish his translation before making a note in his book. "Can you give us an example of when someone was useful to you?"

"Of course," replied von Hauptmann. He thought for a moment. "As I mentioned, we were interested in their escape apparatus. Often, they smuggled their people out of the Reich just before we could arrest them."

Kurt held up his hand then translated. He signaled to von

Hauptmann to continue.

"We knew there was a cell in Vienna that had infiltrated us. Their agent was alerting them just before we were set to make arrests. I, in my guise as a Hungarian communist, volunteered to smuggle one of their people to the Swiss border. This led me to the mole in our organization as well as their organizer."

Kurt translated. McClain nodded.

"I went along on the lorry to the Swiss border. I learned the identity of the informant, the driver and some of the corrupt Swiss guards. I also met the organizer."

"How were they disposed of?"

"I shot the informant who had infiltrated us, the driver, and the fugitive on the spot. They were clearly of no more use to us. We knew who their handler was. I burned the truck with their bodies in it. The next day I arrested their handler in his cobbler shop."

Von Hauptmann paused and chuckled giving Kurt a moment to translate what he said. "Imagine, he had a portrait of the Fuehrer hanging over his workbench. He was also a Nazi party member. We sent him to Mauthausen. He was persuaded to lead us to his superiors. These communists are soft, they break easily."

McClain nodded again. "You have no problem then, taking a man's life?"

Kurt translated.

Von Hauptmann smiled. "No."

McClain looked at Rosenthaller. Their eyes met for the tiniest moment. Kurt thought he detected smiles at the corners of each of their mouths before McClain turned back to von Hauptmann. "What other contact with the communists did you have?" he asked.

Kurt translated. Von Hauptmann leaned over the table and clasped his hands. "I was sent to Moscow in June 1939. My formal assignment was as a member of our diplomatic staff to work with Ribbentrop on the negotiation of our non-aggression pact with the Soviet Union. I was secretly there to gather information on those Soviet officers and diplomats we were working with, to infiltrate the upper echelons of their diplomatic service, to collect information on their people." He winked at McClain. "You know Colonel, kompromat, as your Soviet allies call it."

"How long did this assignment last?" McClain asked, keeping his eyes focused laser-like on von Hauptmann.

"About a year. We thought we had mollified the Soviets. I had obtained the information we sought, and my services were needed elsewhere."

"Where were you sent?"

"Here, to Brussels, to deal with other problems."

"Such as?"

Von Hauptmann smiled. "The Jews."

"I think that's all for today," McClain said. "Guard, take Captain von Hauptmann back to his cell."

CHAPTER 10

Vienna, Third Reich - April 1939

Berta smelled coffee before she opened the door to the shop. Rosenblum & Berlin had been roasting coffee for over 100 years. Her father made Kurt a partner as a wedding gift. Now the gold script on the door said Winkler Family Coffee Roasters, the faint remains of her family names still visible under the new lettering. A tinkling bell announced Berta's arrival. Konrad Winkler, dressed in a light gray suit and bow tie, smiled. "Berta, how nice to see you."

"You as well," Berta said.

Konrad kissed Berta on both cheeks. "Please come back to my…um, the office." He turned to the two women behind the counter. "I'm not to be disturbed,"

"Yes, Herr Winkler," they replied.

Berta followed Konrad back through the narrow hallway that led to the storage areas. The aroma of coffee beans in their burlap sacks was even more intense here than in the front of the shop. Berta desperately wanted a cup of coffee.

Konrad held the door for her. "Bitte, come in and sit down."

"Thank you." Berta hesitated. "Those girls? They can be trusted?"

"Yes, my sister's daughters. The one that lives in Salzburg. We needed help after the Jewish employees were dismissed. I figured I could trust my nieces more than strangers. If I'm wrong, I will be in prison by tonight."

Berta placed her handbag on a narrow table near the door. "And me with you."

"Would you like a cup?" Konrad pointed to the china coffee set on the small table to the left of his desk. In Berta's family for decades, it displayed the business' crest. Berta had taken her first cup in it as a young girl. "It's the classic Viennese roast," said Konrad, "I remember that was always your favorite."

"Yes, thank you." Berta reached for the pot to pour the coffee.

"No, please, Berta, sit down, you are my guest." Despite the decades they had known each other, and the trust Hertz placed in Konrad, Berta felt more like an intruder than a guest. Konrad picked up a cup on its saucer from the tray atop the little table. He poured the cup slightly over halfway. "Sugar? Cream?"

"Yes, please," Berta replied. "Two sugars and a good bit of cream. Light and sweet," she smiled, "Hungarian style."

Konrad laughed. Berta let herself relax a bit. Konrad placed the sugar cubes in the cup and poured some cream. "Is the color correct?"

"Yes, exactly as I take it, thank you." She sipped the warm, thick coffee. It was delicious. It was also impossible for her to get. Jews weren't permitted coffee. She looked around at the many framed awards her family had won for their products lining the walls. Would the Nazis make her family's history and artistry disappear?

Konrad poured a cup for himself and sat down on the chair next to Berta. "Not to rush, but we have much to do."

"Yes." Berta sipped at the coffee. It was extremely satisfying. She felt like an addict reintroduced to her drugs. "I received a letter from Hertz the day before yesterday. It said little other than to come see you."

Konrad placed his cup back on its saucer. He folded his hands in his lap. "Let me begin by telling you what we have already done."

Berta nodded.

Konrad cleared his throat. "We began making arrangements before the Anschluss. Hertz transferred the ownership of the shop to me shortly after Kristallnacht. There are two sets of documents. One for the Nazis, and a second drawn up privately and executed by both of us, that details the real disposition of the business."

"I see," Berta said, placing her cup in its saucer.

"According to the official documents, my wife and I own all interest in this business." Konrad leaned in closer to Berta. "But in actuality, Hertz gave me the money to buy it from him."

"So, in other words, he bought the business from himself?"

"Exactly. Privately, he promised me half the business in perpetuity. I will act as caretaker. In the event you leave and never return, the entire business will pass to my children upon my death. Each month I write profit checks to both Greta and me. She withdraws funds from her account, ostensibly for our home and upkeep. In actuality, I have been passing that cash to Hertz for your family to live on."

Berta smiled. She felt more at ease knowing she had a real ally. "Now things make more sense. I kept wondering where he was finding money."

"I have some more cash for you." Konrad handed a sealed envelope to Berta. She smiled and thanked him, slipping it into her handbag.

"Over the years," Konrad continued, "Hertz acquired other assets as well, real estate, stock, artwork."

"But the Nazis took our artwork along with my piano, just shortly after the Anschluss."

"Hertz sold me those pieces. The Nazis collected them and were to deliver them to me. Truthfully, not everything ultimately made it to my possession. I am sorry, but I don't know what became of the piano."

"And the real estate and stocks?"

"I have the stock certificates. They don't throw off any income. But the two small apartment buildings do. I deposit the rents into an operating account from which I pay their bills. Each month I skim off a portion of the profits, which I then deposit into a numbered account at a Swiss bank, along with the cash I skim from this business. Sam can access that in Brussels."

Berta's stomach twisted. She was relieved to know Hertz's arrangements, but still had no idea of his whereabouts.

"I also have good news for you. Hertz is in a refugee camp in Switzerland. I received a coded message through the Swiss law firm representing him yesterday."

"Thank God," she whispered, choking back tears.

Konrad reached across the table and put his hand over Berta's. "Keep your composure, old friend. We are almost there."

"I'm trying."

"It's very hard, I know."

"How many years have we known each other, Konrad?"

"Too many to count. I came to work for your father in the warehouse when I was fifteen. That was in 1912."

Berta dabbed a handkerchief to her eyes. "Who could have foreseen this?"

"No one. It's madness."

"Apparently it wasn't far below the surface."

"I am ashamed," Konrad said.

Berta took both Konrad's hands in hers. "Don't be, you've been a good friend. I don't want to leave, but what choice is there? I've never known anywhere else."

"You'll be back. This madness can't last forever."

"Even if it doesn't, I don't think I can ever trust my country, or my countrymen, again."

Konrad reached into the inside pocket in his jacket. He pulled out an envelope and handed it to Berta. She opened it and removed a single piece of paper and a card. Berta looked at the card, then turned it over in her hands. It was an official Kennkarte, a state identity-card with her picture on it. "How did you get this?"

"It's for you."

She looked at the name. "I can't let you and Greta take a chance like this. I can't use her name."

"It's alright Berta. She knows, and she wants to help. It's only for a short time, till we can get you out of here."

Berta sighed. "Where did you get this photo?"

"Hertz gave it to me months ago." He pulled a letter from his inside pocket. "Read this, please."

Berta scanned the letter. "I am to visit the man he's mentioned here. I have to find his address. Give me a moment."

Berta took Hertz's address book from her bag. "Here it is."

"Do you know him?"

"No. I know of him. He's a jeweler."

"What do you think Hertz has in mind?"

"I don't know." Berta closed the address book and placed it on her lap. "Would you come with me?"

"Of course."

Berta felt both liberated and fearful boarding the tram with her new Aryan identification in her bag. She walked in silence with Konrad, glad to be in the open air. Once at their destination, Berta looked at the list of tenants, searching for Hermann Frye. He was in apartment 4. She pushed open the door, Konrad following her inside. They climbed the wrought iron stairs to the second floor. Apartment 4 was in the rear. Berta knocked on the door. "Eine moment," she heard. The door opened. An overweight, aging man in a silk smoking jacket and pajamas stood before them. "May I help you?"

"I'm seeking Hermann Frye."

"I am Hermann Frye. And you are?"

"Berta Berlin."

Frye smiled. "I've been expecting you. And who is this?"

"Konrad Winkler, my husband's business partner."

"Please come in." Frye's apartment was dark and cluttered. He kept the drapes drawn. "Follow me please."

Berta and Konrad maneuvered around the mess. A harsh, bright bulb hung from the kitchen ceiling, which made the walls seem even dirtier.

"Please have a seat," Frye said. He disappeared into the butler's pantry. When Frye returned, he placed a leather bag on the table. "Hertz came to see me about a year ago. We've known each other for many years." Frye pointed to the bag. "He said that at some point either you or he would come for it."

Berta unzipped the top and peered inside. "Oh, my lord."

"What is it?" Konrad asked.

"It's my jewelry. I thought Hertz sold all this last spring when the Nazis ordered us to." She took two pieces out of the bag, a bracelet and a necklace. She held them tightly in her hands, then touched them to her cheek.

"He brought it here, for safe keeping," Frye chuckled. "I sold most of these pieces to him to begin with. It's better than money for what you have to do now."

"He thought of all this, and he never told me," Berta said.

"Sometimes it's better if we don't know," replied Frye.

Berta sat in the living room, the contents of the leather bag on the coffee table. The pieces of jewelry were like a coded re-counting of her life, birthdays, anniversaries, the birth of a child, the celebration of a success. Only she and Hertz knew what each piece meant; a silent secret shared between them.

The day Hertz packed these pieces into a box to take them to the Reich Tax Offices for "repatriation," Berta controlled her-self until he left the apartment. Then she went into the bedroom, closed the door, and wept. It wasn't their worth, but rather their value that was taken from her. The Nazis were determined to rob them of everything, including their memories, and then to erase them, as if they never existed at all.

Berta picked up a small gold brooch and held it in her palm. It was in the shape of a rose in full bloom, its petals an example of the finest, thinnest gold filigree. In the center of the rose was a cluster of tiny garnets. Hertz gave it to her on the occasion of their sixth anniversary. Berta touched the delicate petals. The brooch had another meaning that was secret between them. It was just after the July Revolt of 1927. Hertz had abandoned the communist movement for good. He was committed to their life together. His struggle was over.

Frye told Berta to sew the pieces into her clothing. The best hiding place was the lining of a heavy coat. Berta had heard too many stories of Jews who had done precisely that and gotten caught. Besides, it was spring, and the Nazis would be suspect of anyone wearing a heavy coat in warm weather. With the re-strictions on luggage, Berta couldn't pack a large item like a coat in her suitcase either. She would have to find an alternative.

A wave of exhaustion swept over Berta as she arrived home. The constant, endless stress of life under the Nazis was taking its toll, especially with Hertz and Kurt gone. The loneliness was overwhelming. Berta checked the front door and wedged the chair that now stayed permanently in the hallway under the doorknob. She went into the bedroom to undress. As Berta bent to remove her stockings, the metal rod from her girdle jabbed her in her ribcage.

Berta took Konrad's hand as she stepped down from the tram. Konrad carried the leather bag. Both wore Nazi armbands. They looked to all the world like one more happy, Austrian couple, strolling slowly, smiling in the warm, spring sunshine.

Arriving at Frye's building, Berta pressed the buzzer. They climbed the stairs to Frye's apartment. This time he was waiting at the door waving them to come in quickly, a finger over his closed lips.

The apartment was as dank as the previous visit. Frye led them into the kitchen. Konrad placed the leather bag on the table.

"Why did you bring this back?" Frye asked.

Berta reached into the bag and took out a long, steel girdle rod. "I want you to convert this jewelry to gold and then have the gold melted down and cast into rods like this."

Frye smiled broadly. "Brilliant," he said, running his fingers along the length of the rod. "Berta, I must commend you. Sheer genius."

Dressed formally in a grey suit and white blouse, Berta waited at the lingerie counter at M. Neumann Department Store. A hat with a lace front partially covered her eyes. On her left arm was a Swastika armband. She wore it always now.

Berta considered how artificial the Nazi system was. With her blond hair and blue eyes, no one ever suspected she was Jewish. That only made her life more surreal. But at least she could get around now without harassment.

"How can I help you, madam?" the counter clerk, a well-appointed woman of perhaps thirty, asked.

"I am in need of some corsets for myself, and also for my mother and sister."

"Of course. Do you know your size?"

"Yes. I am a size 26. My sister and mother are a bit larger than me. I would say my sister is a 32 and my mother a 36."

"Is there any chance they could come into the store to be

measured? We don't take returns on these items."

"I'm afraid not. They have left for the summer to the Tyrol and won't return until September."

"Of course. Will you be seeking full or half corsets?"

"Full."

"How many will you need?"

Berta felt her stomach flutter. "I think six each will be fine."

"Very well then. Please wait here. I'll be back momentarily."

Berta let out a long breath as the saleswoman retreated through the door into the storeroom. That had gone well enough. The total would be eighteen. Berta would need twice that number. Tomorrow she would go to Gerngross Kaufhaus across town and repeat the charade.

The clerk returned with the corsets wrapped in brown paper. She placed them in a large box. "I hope this package won't be too much for you to carry?"

Berta lifted the box off the counter. "No, no, not at all. My driver is waiting. Thank you so much."

"Thank you, Frau…."

"Winkler, Greta," she replied.

The saleswoman handed her the bill. Berta took out her wallet and extracted the correct amount, counting it out.

"Thank you for shopping with us, Frau Winkler," the saleswoman said.

"My pleasure."

Berta felt a touch from behind and heard her name. Her heart nearly jumped from her chest. She hoped the counter clerk hadn't heard it. A handsome, impeccably dressed man stood in front of her. Berta tried to calm herself before speaking. "Fritzy, how nice to see you."

Berta fumbled her package purposely, forcing herself a few steps forward, away from the counter. Fritzy grabbed the box and steadied Berta with his other hand. "Why don't we go over there and chat for a while," he said, pointing to two chairs situated in a corner of the lingerie department.

Berta walked slowly toward them. She hadn't seen Fritzy since shortly after the Anschluss. He was the husband of her childhood friend, Amalia. Though he never showed any dislike for Jews, Fritzy was more than a bit enthusiastic about the arrival of the Nazis, and he and Amalia quickly cut off contact with her and Hertz. Berta received a note from Amalia, polite but to the point, that though she kept a deep fondness for Berta, they could no longer see each other. The letter cut through Berta's heart. Had their friendship been so superficial? It was only the first of too many to slice at her.

"I thought you would have left months ago," Fritzy said, placing the box on Berta's lap. Berta followed his eyes to her armband.

"I have no choice. It's too dangerous to go out otherwise."

"You know, I could denounce you for that."

She slipped her gloved hand over the swastika. "Fritzy, please."

"Berta, for old time's sake if nothing else, I'm suggesting that this is likely to get worse. You have to leave Germany."

"Would that I could." Berta chuckled. If only it was that easy, she wouldn't be perpetrating this charade.

"You know, we, Amalia and I, we never had anything against you or Hertz personally, but as a group the Jews brought down our country. The Fuehrer is right. You need to leave. Find your own place."

"And where would that be?" Berta snapped back. "And with what money should we go? You've stripped us of pretty much everything."

Fritzy looked around then sighed. "I told you, I'm not going to denounce you. But you must give me that armband. I'm working for the party now. I can't suffer that you walk around impersonating an Aryan. I hope you, and Hertz, and your son, find refuge. The Reich has no place for you."

Refuge, she thought. If I can get these corsets home that might happen. "Fine." Berta slipped the band off her arm discretely and crumpled it into Fritzy's hand.

"I will tell Amalia that I saw you and that you are well."

"Please, don't," Berta replied.

Berta sat quietly on the couch; the curtains drawn. She took a sip of schnapps, the last bit left in the bottle she had poured into a small, etched glass from a set that once belonged to her grandparents. She ran her finger around the rim. If things went well this was the last time she would drink from them.

For a moment Berta was desperately sad. She would leave all her possessions here, every one of which had meaning to her. But what were they really? Just things. Berta knew she had to accept this. Her life would continue long after the Nazis destroyed her possessions or gave them away to someone they considered more deserving by virtue of race. But the future would happen only if Berta could cut herself from the umbilical cord connecting her to her past.

After running into Fritzy, Berta realized how artificial her Aryan disguise was, and how dangerous her life had become. She had to get out of here. If only she would hear from Hertz. She waited daily for Konrad to come by or call to tell her he had a message. It was too dangerous to contact Konrad herself.

There was a tap at the door. For a moment terror consumed Berta, then she realized it wasn't the Gestapo. They wouldn't tap. Berta walked down the long hallway and removed the chair from under the doorknob. "Yes?"

"It's Otto."

Berta opened the door. Otto Bauer stood with a plate in his hand covered with a dishtowel. "May I come in?"

"Of course."

"Rosalie asked me to bring you this. She knows they're your favorite."

Berta took the plate from Otto and peeked under the towel. She choked up. Some people still cared. "Thank you, Otto, butter crescents, they are my favorite. Please come in. Sit down for a few minutes."

"Sadly, I can't. We have to go to a neighborhood meeting. Attendance is required now."

"I understand."

"We wanted to know how you are, and Hertz and young Kurt."

Berta leaned against the wall. "They are safe. I can't tell you more than that."

"I know this must be impossible and horrifying for you."

"It is." Berta fought back the tears. "Thank you and Rosalie for your kindness. I will tell you the truth. I hope to join them soon."

"I hope so." Otto touched Berta's hand.

"When the time comes, I will leave this plate by your door. Come quickly when you see it. I will leave the door unlocked. Take something to remind you of us, always."

"I couldn't." Otto averted his eyes.

"You must. You have been a fine and dear friend."

Otto wavered. "I promise. We will never forget you."

Berta embraced him. "Go now and keep yourselves safe."

Berta closed the door behind Otto, took one of the sugared crescent cookies and bit into it. The sweetness warmed her heart.

CHAPTER 11

Brussels, Belgium - May 1945

Kurt stared out the window from the edge of his bed. He was drenched in sweat. It was Saturday, no work. He'd slept terribly the previous night. He'd had the dreams again, one after the other, over and over. The first, the same dream he had when he was a boy in Vienna after the Anschluss. He spies his parents across the platform at the U-bahn station. They abandon him. Only now he wasn't a 16-year-old boy in the dream, he was a man. He hadn't had the dream since before the war started. Now it came every night, over and over again.

The second was of the Japanese soldier he'd killed on the Baywalk in Manila, his body riddled with machine gun bullets. The soldier rose from his death and turned his gun on Kurt. But before he took aim at Kurt, he shrieked murderer. A massive burst from the barrel of the Japanese soldier's gun ended the dream.

Kurt took a drink from the glass of water on the night table. He wiped his forehead and face with a hand towel. Hauptmann's interrogation played out in his head again. Kurt considered his options. Complaining about McClain to Rosenthaller would result in reassignment. That might be better for him psychologically, but at the same time, Rosenthaller might disqualify Kurt from the unit entirely. He could be sent to another city or back to the States. Kurt needed a little more time; at least till he could speak to the Sister who had witnessed the attack on the convent.

Kurt checked his watch, the one his grandparents gave him for his Bar Mitzvah, a lifetime ago in Vienna. He thought of them for a moment but could barely remember their faces. The memory of their voices was gone completely. Kurt shuddered. He couldn't let the past control him.

It was 8:00 AM. He would wash and eat something, then fetch Saul. They would go to Leopold Park to the sport fields, to find a football game. Perhaps then, he could think more clearly. He walked over to the sink outside the tiny bathroom, picked up the soap from the porcelain dish, and lathered his hands into a thick foam. Cleanliness had become an obsession since returning to Brussels. It was as if there was something in the air he was trying to wash off.

Kurt rinsed his face. The tepid water felt good. Despite his lack of sleep, Kurt was alert. Grabbing the towel on the rack to his right, he dried himself then looked in the mirror. Another face appeared in the reflection with his. Kurt turned to ascertain if it was real. "Sam!" he shouted.

"My God in heaven," Sam replied. "You're so happy to see me?"

"I thought you were in Vienna."

Sam took hold of Kurt's shoulders. "I was. I got back last night. Now, let me look at you." Sam inspected Kurt. "You continue to get taller."

Kurt laughed. "And you continue to get grayer."

Sam touched his finger to his temple. "In Vienna, we used to say it added a bit of sophistication to a man."

"Sit down, Uncle," Kurt said, pointing to the blue velvet chairs against the wall to the left side of the bed. "Did you find anyone in Vienna?" Kurt touched his watch absently.

Sam hesitated. "Yes, and no."

After a long moment, Kurt asked. "Lisle?"

"She's alive."

Kurt wasn't exactly sure what to say.

"When she saw me, she looked as if she had seen a ghost," Sam added.

Kurt searched Sam's face before asking more questions. He seemed all right. "Where did you find her?"

"In their apartment." Sam took a pack of cigarettes from his coat pocket. "Do you mind?"

"No, no. Go ahead. There's an ashtray there." Kurt pointed to the small table by the chair. "And her parents?"

"Her mother is dead, some long illness. Her father is alive." Sam took a long drag.

"What did she say?"

"It was very strange. First, she smiled. Then she ran to me and wrapped her arms around me. She held me tightly for a moment, then slapped me across the face. Then she ran to her bedroom. She slammed the door and locked it. Her father was sitting at the dining table. He was silent as I begged her to open the door. I turned to him and asked him to speak to her. He laughed at me. 'She expected you to send her a ticket to come to you,' he said, then laughed again. 'But you Jews, you're all the same. Out for yourselves. You used her and left her. What man would want her after that? She was a race defiler.'"

Kurt felt the anger rise in his chest. He hadn't known that Lisle's father was an anti-Semite. Kurt was sixteen when Sam left Vienna. It wasn't a subject his parent's and his uncle would have discussed in front of him a year before the Anschluss.

Sam dragged heavily on the cigarette again. "Finally, she opened the door and came out. She apologized in a way. It was very awkward. I considered confronting her father for what he said, but decided an old man wasn't worth it. He hated me before the war. He hated his daughter for loving me." Sam took another cigarette and lit it off the first.

"Did she say anything more?" Kurt asked.

"She asked me for money." Sam laughed. "Imagine."

"What did you do?"

"I gave her ten pounds and left. I'm not sure how I loved someone who came from so much hate."

Kurt hesitated. He touched his watch again. "Is anyone else alive?"

"I found Konrad. Greta is dead, along with one of their daughters."

Kurt felt the weight of Sam's answers. He knew this day would come, eventually. This war had destroyed everything in its path. "How? What happened?"

"Konrad sent them to a relative in Dresden. He thought they

would be safer there."

Kurt choked up. He remembered Konrad and Greta and their daughters so clearly. Kurt and his parents would spend Christmas with them every year. There was always a stocking with Kurt's name on it filled with candies and small toy soldiers. Kurt had heard about the bombings in Dresden. Tens of thousands died. "Which daughter?"

"Ann Marie, the younger one."

"And Helga?"

"She's with him. She survived the bombing then returned to Vienna. She walked a good part of it. They're living in the back of the shop. Their apartment was destroyed in the fighting."

Kurt got up from the chair. He turned to the wall, focusing on the flowered pattern in the wallpaper. His breath caught in his throat. "And my grandparents, are they dead?"

Sam sighed. "They're not in Vienna. I don't know for certain, but I can surmise."

Kurt trembled. "Did Konrad know?"

Sam sighed. "Konrad watched over them through the summer of 1943. On several occasions before that, they were ordered to report for resettlement. He paid the officials to take them off the lists. By that summer he had run very low on cash, and the person in charge wasn't quite corrupt enough. That official agreed to take them off the transport going directly to Auschwitz and sent them instead to Theresienstadt."

Kurt leaned against the headboard of the bed. He tried to remember their faces as he held back the tears. He was exhausted, his mind filled with death, whether awake or asleep. "What is Theresienstadt?

It was a camp for the wealthy and the old, for people who might be missed if they disappeared. Mostly, it was a stopover before Auschwitz."

That word instantly turned Kurt's stomach. He had seen the pictures. His mind raced. An image of Saul's parents and his sister on the transports from Mechelen, days and nights standing in a cattle car without food, water or bathrooms, only to arrive at Auschwitz, its chimneys belching black smoke. The image of his grandparents, old and tired in their always formal dress joined that of Saul's family climbing down the ramp from the cattle train. They appeared disoriented and confused, his grandmother holding his grandfather's arm, his grandfather standing ramrod stiff, chin up, his cane in his right hand.

"Were they sent to Auschwitz?"

"I don't know."

"Do you think they survived somehow?"

"I would doubt that." Sam sat down next to Kurt on the bed. He put his arm over Kurt's shoulders. "Let's not make any assumptions. We still don't know. There's still hope."

Kurt nodded and reached for Sam, holding him tight. "At least we're here together."

"Yes. Now tell me, how is your assignment?"

"Very difficult." Kurt didn't want to burden Sam with his concerns about von Hauptmann. Besides, the interrogations were classified and if he told Sam he would put both of them in a compromising position. "I can't say more than that."

Sam nodded his head. "I understand."

"How is Marianne?" Kurt asked.

Sam's face turned up into a smile, lightening the gloom that had settled over them. "She's very well. She's pregnant."

Kurt jumped up from the bed and grabbed Sam's arm, pulling him up and hugging him. "That's marvelous Uncle. When is the baby coming?"

"September."

Kurt hesitated for a moment. "Have you found out anything about your father-in-law?"

"No," Sam replied, "which is why I decided to come back now. Marianne and my mother-in-law need to know what happened to him."

"Sometimes there's a miracle Uncle. I had one a couple weeks ago. I found Saul." Kurt told Sam some of Saul's story. Sam's eyes widened. "That is a miracle. We're beginning to account for the missing, and the numbers are staggering. Is he with his family?"

"No, they're missing. He believes they were sent to Auschwitz."

"I understand. If he'd gone with them, he'd have met the

same fate."

"I owe Saul help, Uncle. That could have been us. I can't say much now, but I've decided that when this interrogation is over, I'm requesting a transfer. It's too much. It brings back too much. I want to bring Saul with me back to the States. He has no one."

"I understand, nephew." Sam hesitated a moment. "And Elsa?"

Kurt took a deep breath. He averted Sam's eyes. "I went to the convent where she was living when we left. It was destroyed. I found a priest who knew what happened there. He's trying to arrange for me to speak with the only survivor. I have no idea if she's alive, but I doubt it."

"Perhaps you'll have another miracle."

"I hope so."

"What are your plans for today?"

"I was going to fetch Saul and head to Leopold Park to find a football game. Now I don't much feel like it."

"It's a beautiful day, nephew. Go fetch Saul. Kick some balls around. I'll meet you later for dinner. Bring him."

Kurt and Saul strolled through Leopold Park. They were sweaty and tired after finding a pickup game with some teenagers on a patchy field in the heart of the park. Kurt remembered a day he spent there with Elsa, a day when they told each other they loved each other and wanted to spend their lives together.

"You played well today, brother," Kurt said.

"Thanks," Saul replied. He stopped walking. "There were times in the past few years when I thought I wouldn't live to play again. Sometimes when I was at the worst points, I would think of those games we played with your schoolmates. How I would have to hide my dirty clothes from my father. I wish I still had to hide my dusty pants from him today."

"I know how much you miss them," Kurt said. He felt the same way.

"I know that," Saul said.

"You're not alone. I won't let you be."

Saul put his hand on Kurt's shoulder. He smiled; the tears evident in his eyes. "Thank you, brother."

Kurt pulled Saul to him. "Those were happier times, though we didn't know it then. There will be good times again." Kurt released his hold on Saul, but kept his hands on Saul's shoulders. "I have some news. Sam is here. Come to dinner with us tonight."

"Of course! I would love to see him." They continued down the path toward the large lake in the middle of the park. "You hungry?" Saul asked.

"Yeah, starving, why?"

"Look over there."

Kurt followed the line of Saul's arm. Down the paved path was a crepe vendor. She had set up a small kitchen with a wood-burning stove under a huge elm tree. "You got any money?"

Saul smiled. "No, I figured you did."

Kurt swiped at Saul's head playfully. Saul put up his fists and jabbed back, laughing. He ran toward the crepe seller, Kurt following. In the weeks since they had found each other Saul had put on weight and increased his strength and stamina, in no small way the result of Kurt's generosity and vigilance. These moments of lightness were the ones that kept Kurt going.

"I'll pay you back, someday!" Saul shouted back to Kurt. He ordered two chocolate crepes from the woman and waited with Kurt, both of them panting from the run. "Let's go over there by the lake to eat them."

They walked around the curve in the path to the tranquil waters at the heart of the park. Children played on the lawn in front of it. "How about there?" Saul said pointing to a shady area under a large tree.

"Sure," Kurt said.

They ate the crepes slowly and in silence. Kurt peered out over the lake. "You know, they used to rent rowboats over there," he said, pointing to a small dock on the west side of the lake."

"I didn't," Saul said.

"I took Elsa here once for a picnic."

Saul smiled. "I remember that day. You asked me to come and I told you that you were an idiot. You couldn't see how much she loved you."

Kurt felt himself blush a little. It was the day he told Elsa he knew her secret, that she went to church. "We played a game. We made believe we were in Vienna at the Prater, that there was no war. We talked about the future. She told me she wanted to teach art to children."

"Did she ask you what you wanted for your future?" Saul asked, after a long while.

"Of course," Kurt chuckled.

"What did you say?"

"I told her I wanted to be a soldier."

They finished their crepes in silence.

CHAPTER 12

Brussels, Belgium - April 1939

E lsa took Kurt's arm as they walked to the little park. Kurt loved when she did that. "How long has it been since you last saw your uncle?" Elsa asked.

"Sam left just before the Anschluss, so it's a little more than a year. He lived with us for a short time when he came to Vienna. I was little then. Sam was fun to have around."

"I imagine. Auntie's and uncles are like that. They encourage you to do what your parents won't allow."

Kurt laughed. "This one did anyway."

"I had an auntie like that, my mother's sister. She studies art at the University. That made my grandparents very unhappy." Elsa pulled Kurt a little closer as they stopped at the corner across from the little park. She hesitated for a moment. "Have you heard from your parents yet?"

"No, but I expect we'll hear from them soon."

"I hope so. I'm very worried about them, especially father."

Kurt took Elsa's hand in his. "I'm sure they're fine."

"Enjoy your visit with your Uncle." Elsa kissed Kurt's cheek then smiled. "See you later."

Kurt crossed the street to the park. He turned and watched as Elsa, hips swinging gently from side to side, disappeared around the next intersection. Kurt spotted his uncle. Sam hadn't changed much in the year since Kurt had last seen him. He was perhaps a bit thinner, but otherwise looked exactly the same, a younger version of Kurt's father. Kurt waved. "Uncle," he called across the lawn.

Sam walked toward him. "I thought I would have seen you a little sooner," he said. "How are you doing?"

"I'm doing well, I guess," replied Kurt. They sat down on a wooden bench under a large walnut tree. "I hate to admit this, but as much as I miss my parents, I'm feeling much better here than in Vienna."

"I'm not surprised."

A dam burst inside Kurt. "There, you're afraid all the time. Always tense. You never know who might be at the door or watching you, or what might happen if you leave the house. Here I can breathe, but I feel terrible about my parents, and I feel guilty to have left them." Kurt's entire body melted into the bench, exhausted.

"I understand," Sam replied. He let Kurt catch up with himself. "How is the place where you're staying?"

Kurt grimaced. "It's all right, but it's not home."

"Of course not." Sam offered Kurt a piece of chewing gum. "What are they like?"

"You know how my mother feels about gum." Kurt took it and popped it into his mouth, laughing. "They're an old couple, their name is Mandelbaum, quite religious."

Sam twisted his face. "That's difficult."

Kurt chuckled. "You have no idea."

"Yes, I do," Sam said. "You forget, my parents were religious. Does he wear side locks?" Sam asked, imitating the way Chasidic Jews wrap their curls around their ears.

"No, just a long beard, and there's lots of rules on the Sabbath."

They were quiet for a moment. Kurt felt more comfortable than he had since arriving. He wished he had seen Sam sooner.

"Are you alone with them?" Sam inquired.

"No, that's a bit complicated too. A girl around my age, also from Vienna, she's staying there as well, so I'm sleeping on a daybed in the study. It's too short for me."

Sam put his arm around Kurt's shoulder. "Well, we Berlins were never short."

"It's all right though, she's very pretty. I think I'm falling in love with her a little."

Sam squeezed Kurt's shoulder, hiding his smile. "Ah, be careful young man. This is neither the right time nor place to fall in love. And you're too young, anyway."

Kurt blushed. "I think she likes me too, a little."

"And how would you know that."

Kurt felt the blush rise from his neck to his cheeks. "I can tell."

Sam laughed. "Of course, you can. Just be careful, as I told you." Sam took his arm from Kurt's shoulder and became very serious. "Nephew, I have some news for you."

"What?"

"Your father escaped. He's in Switzerland."

Kurt tensed. "Where is my mother?"

Sam drew in a breath. "Still in Vienna."

Kurt felt the panic rise in his chest. Again, his world changed in an instant. This roller coaster ride was too quick and too steep. Kurt jumped up from the bench. "I thought they would come out together. How could he leave her there?"

"He had no choice. Your neighbor, Bauer, found out the Nazi's were coming for your father. He had to leave immediately."

"Is mother all right?"

"As far as we know. I got a telegram from your father in Switzerland."

Kurt felt faint. He stumbled back to the bench. The image of his mother alone in Vienna terrified him. "You don't understand Uncle. She's in terrible danger."

"We know, be calm," said Sam. "We have a plan."

Elsa explored the neighborhood a little, before going back to the Mandelbaum's apartment. She needed to think, to clear her head. School was fine, at least there was little emphasis on anything Jewish. They studied the same subjects as she had at home, literature, mathematics, poetry, science, some history and then English. Nevertheless, Elsa felt uncomfortable, she didn't fit in.

She stopped in front of a shop selling women's clothing and admired the silk scarves in the window. One was particularly beautiful, featuring a modern, geometrical design in blues and yellows. Elsa pictured it around her neck clasped with her mother's turquoise broach. In the storefront glass, she noticed the reflection of a small church across the street. Elsa crossed and stood by its steps for a moment. Slowly, she climbed to the portico. Next to the door was a bronze plaque which read, the Church of the Sisters of Charity.

Entering, she took a small, lace doily from the wooden box next to the door, covered her head and dropped a few centimes into the charity box. She took a taper from the table against the wall and lit a candle, curtsying deeply then walked to the front and sat at the edge of the third pew. Two old women sat across the aisle deep in prayer. The church was otherwise empty.

Elsa kneeled and prayed, almost inaudibly. "I hope you can still hear me, even though I'm now Jewish. Please Holy Mother, bring my parents here to me safely. Please." Tears escaped her eyes. As Elsa wiped the tears away, she felt a hand rest gently on her shoulder.

"Good afternoon, my child," a nun said in French. Elsa looked up. The Sister had the weathered face of an old woman, but the eyes of a young girl. Elsa buried her face in the nun's habit and cried. "What troubles you?" the Sister asked. She stroked Elsa's hair.

"I am alone," Elsa said, first in German and then in French.

"No, you're not, my child."

"I am. You don't understand." Elsa told the nun her story.

"I am Sister Jeanine Joseph. What is your name?"

"Elsa Graz."

The Sister dried Elsa's tears with the cuff of her habit. "You are never alone, dear child. The Lord is always there, if you seek him."

"Even if I am Jewish now?"

"Always, and for anyone and everyone. Whenever you need to feel his comfort and grace come here, come to me."

"Sister, thank you. This has been so hard. I have never known anything but the church. These new customs, they're strange to me, harsh. I miss my parents. I used to go to church with my grandmother. It always made me feel safe. That's why

I came in."

"You are always welcome here."

"Thank you," Elsa said. She hugged Sister Jeanine tightly, drew in a deep breath, then shuddered. She felt safe for the first time since she left her parents.

Kurt headed back to the Mandelbaums. He was over-whelmed by what Sam told him. Scared to death for his parents, Kurt knew he was powerless to help them. The possibility ex-isted that he might never see either of them again.

Sam had begged him to calm down. Kurt did everything he could not to break down completely right there on the park bench. His two weeks of relative safety were gone. He could think of nothing but his parents till he saw them again. As Kurt turned into a small street to take a short-cut, he saw a young woman descend the steps from a church halfway down the block. When she turned her head to check the traffic, he saw her face.

CHAPTER 13

Brussels, Belgium - May 1945

"C aptain," said McClain, "you mentioned that you had an-
other area of covert responsibilities."
"Yes," von Hauptmann replied.
"What was that?"

"To locate and neutralize enemies still within the Reich.
Fifth Columnists. And it wasn't completely covert. You might
say I developed a reputation among those who resisted us."

Kurt saw relief in the changing line of questioning, no Jews
and nothing that would relate to his family. He jumped on von
Hauptmann's answer.

McClain glanced at Rosenthaller. "Please, tell us more."

"We had eliminated most if not all of the communists. We
were looking for other dissidents, artists, clergy, journalists.
The kind who could command attention from their supporters
abroad and cast us in a bad light."

"And your methods for dealing with them?"

"Shall we say…persuasion?"

"Details?"

"Usually, it began with house arrest. Then we would
threaten their families; wives, children, parents."

An image of Elsa's parents conjured in Kurt's mind. His moment of relief dissolved instantly.

"What were they threatened with?"

"Incarceration at home at first. If the subject continued to
speak out or to send negative propaganda outside the Reich, we
would punish them, eventually leading to their incarceration at

a camp."

"Why not just send them to a camp, to begin with?"

"The situation was different with these types than with Jews or communists. There were prominent people outside the Reich who would speak out for them, and that cast us in a bad light. Also, we didn't want to let them leave and continue to malign us."

"What did you do with them?"

"We whittled them down. Eventually they would be sent to a camp. They were eliminated when they attempted to escape."

"And they always attempted to escape?"

Von Hauptmann smiled. "Of course."

Kurt listened even more intently, recalling the circumstances of Elsa's parents' deaths.

"How did you feel about this work? Did you view it as less important than what you had done previously?"

"No, not at all. My heart and soul were dedicated to the Fuehrer, the party, and the Reich. I viewed these dissidents as scum. In some ways, they were worse than Jews. They were Aryans who defiled their race."

"Where did you execute your duties in this area?"

"In Vienna. Until I was sent to the Soviet Union in June of 1939."

"Yes," replied McClain. "For espionage. But you mentioned you were recalled. When and why?

Von Hauptmann took a deep breath. "In March 1940. For planning and training."

"Training in what?"

"Handling of large populations."

McClain shot a glance at Rosenthaller. "What exactly does that mean?"

Von Hauptmann leaned forward, his arms resting on the table. "Ay, you Americans. Sometimes I wonder if you are as naïve as your questions."

Kurt translated. He hoped both McClain and Rosenthaller would recognize the comment as insubordinate and react accordingly.

McClain considered his response. "Please ask the prisoner if he thinks I am naïve, coy or stupid."

Kurt looked at Rosenthaller searching for emotion in his face. There was none.

"Why are you hesitating Berlin?"

"I don't want to be disrespectful, Colonel."

"Then translate."

Kurt looked at von Hauptmann. "Denken Sie, ich bin naiv oder dumm?"

Looking directly at McClain, von Hauptman said no in English. "I want make more fast."

McClain sat down opposite von Hauptmann. "Fine then, let's speed this up. Tell us about your training."

Kurt realized it was hopeless that McClain and Rosenthaller would see this murderer for what he was.

"At that time," von Hauptmann began, "we realized that we would have a problem. We intended to bring all of Europe under our control. This was just before the hot war began in the west. Up until then, we had attempted to force the Jews out of the Reich. Many left but stayed in Europe. We realized we were destined to get them back and inherit millions more as we extended our control over the continent. We needed to develop a plan to manage such a large population. We settled on a dual approach. One might call it security and intimidation."

Kurt steeled himself. The moment had finally come. He needed to remain calm and he knew it.

"Who developed this plan?"

"Mostly, Heydrich and Eichmann."

"What did the plan consist of?"

"The first component was to account for the population, the second to control it. We would approach both the remnants of the former national governments and the leaders of the Jewish community to provide us with an accounting, a census of sorts. Then we had an idea of numbers. At the same time, we told the Jews this was for their own protection, to keep them safe. We also handled them roughly in front of the non-Jewish population whenever possible, to intimidate the locals as well. They would understand what could happen to them if they tried to intervene."

McClain listened intently to Kurt's translation. Kurt felt himself begin to sweat. Those first months after the German invasion of Belgium played back in Kurt's mind, the endless fear, the powerlessness. His mouth went dry. He reached for his water.

"It seems then that the plans were in place before the war to handle the Jewish problem?" McClain asked.

Kurt glanced at Rosenthaller to see his reaction to the term, 'Jewish problem.' There was none. Kurt froze his mind and continued.

Von Hauptmann sat up. "An initial plan. Not what ultimately was chosen to solve it. Of course, as I've told you before, we always had the intention of executing our policies. Our management of those policies had to evolve as the Reich grew."

"And your position in Brussels?"

"The disposition of the Jews."

CHAPTER 14

Brussels, Belgium – May 1939

Sam waited anxiously on the platform. The engineer gave off a sharp whistle as he coasted the locomotive into the station. He searched the windows for Hertz as the train slowed. Steam rose from under it. Through the steam, Sam saw an older, stockier version of himself. He waved and shouted. "Hertz, over here!"

Hertz spotted Sam. He was wearing a light blue sport jacket and a straw hat. Sam had that same mischievous smile he'd had since childhood. He picked up his pace and ran towards him. They collided. Hertz's bags, still held tightly in his hands, crashed into Sam's back.

"Ouch!" Sam shouted. Hertz dropped the bags and hugged Sam again, both of them laughing. "Where's Kurt?"

"I thought it would be better not to tell him until you arrived," Sam said, "just in case something went wrong."

Hertz considered Sam's statement. "You're right. What if something had gone wrong?"

Sam stepped back and smiled. "But it didn't. You're here." He grabbed Hertz and pulled him close, again.

"Yes, thank God."

"God?" said Sam. "From the atheist."

"Maybe not so much anymore. Take me to my son."

Sam picked up Hertz's bags and led them out of the station.

"I don't have any coin for the tram," Hertz said.

"No tram today. I've got a car."

Hertz stopped. "A car? You're must be doing very well. And

when did you learn to drive?"

Sam stopped in front of a gray Citroen. "It's not mine, it's Marianne's, my girlfriend. Or her father's, actually. And I'm doing pretty well." He opened the trunk. "Put the bags in there and jump in. Marianne taught me last summer."

Hertz opened the front door on the passenger's side. He ran his fingers over the leather seat and the dashboard woodwork. "What does her father do?"

"He's a doctor, the doctor who's going to get Berta out of Vienna."

Hertz smiled. "And this girlfriend. Is she Jewish?"

"Jewish enough. Half."

"Which half?"

"The wrong half. But nevertheless, she loves me."

Hertz smiled. "And do you love her?"

"I think so. Her parents like me too. Her father even found me a job."

"Really? What happened to acting?"

"My French is terrible. My Flemish even worse."

"And what kind of job is this?"

"I work for his brother. He's a diamond dealer. I've learned to cut stones."

Hertz put a hand on Sam's shoulder. "My little brother has grown up."

"Did I have a choice?" Sam looked away. He hesitated. "Did you see her before you left?"

"No brother, I'm sorry. I went into hiding very suddenly. Konrad took your last letter to her."

"Is she well?"

"As far as I know."

Sam hesitated, then started the car. "She has to go on with her life. As do I. We live in different worlds now."

"Sadly, yes."

Sam touched his right hand to his eyes, wiping away a tear. He pressed down on the clutch and gas and pulled out into the road. A change in subject would lighten the mood. "Brother, I have something to tell you before we go to fetch Kurt."

"And what is that?"

"He's in love."

They both laughed.

"Soon my little boy will be a man too."

"Yes. His classes continue till 3:00. Let's get you a decent meal. You know, no one eats badly in Belgium. Though it's not kosher."

Hertz laughed. "As if that's ever mattered."

Hertz sliced into the steak sitting next to a mound of pommes frites. He hadn't tasted beef, real beef, not the scraps that appeared in soup at the camp, in months. He scooped it up on his fork with some of the potatoes and savored it. Chewing slowly and languorously, Hertz was beginning to realize the effect both dietary deprivation and stress had had on him. "That is perfect."

"Yes, pretty good."

"Tell me, how are we progressing?"

"Things are moving along. Now that you're here, Marianne's father will approach his friend at the health ministry to issue us the documents we need to send to Berta."

"And this friend can be trusted?"

"Yes, for the right price."

"We know that price?"

"10,000 Francs"

"He doesn't come cheap."

"Nothing does. Then it's up to the Nazis to approve her temporary exit visa."

"And this has been done successfully before?"

"So, I am told. Do you have an alternate plan?"

"Yes, a very bad one."

"Which is?"

"Berta has a forged Kennkarte in the name of Greta Winkler."

"Konrad's wife?"

"Yes. She would leave under that name."

"That's very dangerous for everyone. If Berta gets caught, all of them would be thrown into prison or worse. When do you want to begin this process?"

Hertz finished his last slice of steak. "Tomorrow. I have to get Berta out of there. Now let's go see my son."

Sam looked at his watch. "It's still early. Have a coffee."

"Hmm," Hertz mumbled. "Real coffee?"

"Yes, and Tarte au Pommes with fresh whipped cream."

Hertz stood behind the trunk of a tree a few meters down the block and across the street from Kurt's school. Sam stood near the front entrance. At 3:00, students began streaming through the front door, books in hand. Kurt spotted Sam and ran over to him. He had grown in the months since Hertz had seen him. Sam pointed to where Hertz was standing. Hertz stepped out from behind the tree. Kurt's expression changed. He ran to Hertz and embraced him. "Father," Kurt sobbed. "Father."

"I've missed you too, son." Hertz tried to hold back his own sobs, but they came, nonetheless.

Kurt's knees wobbled. "I've worried about you and mother day and night." He attempted to control himself but broke down again. Sam and Hertz led him to a bench on the street. "Where's mother?" he asked.

Hertz's heart pounded. "She's still in Vienna. She will join us soon. I'll explain everything, first calm down a little. It's so good to see you." Hertz had never been a particularly demonstrative parent, which was the Austrian way. Now, something burst out of him, a passion and need to show his affection in a way that reminded him of his own parents and grandparents in that little Polish shtetl. He drew Kurt to him again. "We will all be together soon."

Kurt hugged his father tightly, the way he did when he was a little boy. Slowly he calmed himself. "How did you get here? What happened in Switzerland?"

"Slow down, I will tell you everything."

Kurt hesitated and turned back toward the school. He scanned the street for Elsa.

"What are you looking for?" Hertz asked.

"Umm, someone, my friend. She's gone. We were to walk home together. I want you to meet her."

Hertz glanced at Sam. They exchanged grins. He put his hand on Kurt's shoulder. "We will have plenty of time for that."

Elsa shaded her eyes against the sun. She looked around for Kurt, then saw him across the street with Sam. Sam pointed to something. Kurt stood up, hesitated, then ran towards a tall man standing next to a large elm tree. Elsa squinted her eyes, then recognized the man from that day at the train station in Vienna. Kurt's father.

Elsa panicked. If Kurt's parents where here, he would leave the Mandelbaums. She would be alone. Elsa felt her lunch creep up into her mouth. She walked away as quickly as possible, her head down. As she turned the corner, Elsa heard Kurt call her name but kept walking in the direction of the church. Her pace quickened to a run. She grabbed the metal rail and pulled herself up the church's steps, stopping for a moment on the portico to calm herself, sobs wracking her body. How much more could she bear? She was so alone.

Elsa pushed open the door to the church and slipped inside. The dark coolness of the room enveloped her, calmed her. She walked slowly to the candles, took a taper, knelt and lit one. "Please Mother Mary, help me," Elsa whispered, "help me to find strength." She rose and walked to the pews and sat in front, near the altar. She took the rosary Sister Jeanine Joseph gave her from her bag and mumbled the words of the Hail Mary.

The gentle pleading of the prayer comforted Elsa. She wiped her eyes on the sleeve of her dress and sat upright in the pew. From across the church, she saw Sister Jeanine Joseph come towards her.

"I wasn't expecting you today, child."

Elsa looked up at her, smiling weakly.

"You've been crying. What's happened? Have you heard something from your parents?"

"No. It's not that."

"What's wrong then?"

"I've committed a terrible sin."

Sister Jeanine took Elsa's hand. "Would you like me to fetch Father Pierre?"

"No, no."

"Would you like to tell me?"

Elsa breathed deeply. "I don't know. I am terribly

embarrassed."

"By what?"

Elsa sighed. "I have been jealous of someone else's happiness."

"And what was this...jealousy?"

"Kurt's father is here. I saw him on the street in front of the school."

"And you are afraid?"

Elsa began to cry again. "Yes, sister. I am afraid, both for my parents and for me."

"For your parents I understand, but why are you afraid for yourself?"

Elsa's crying turned to weeping. "I am afraid Kurt will go to live with him. He will leave me and forget me. I will be alone." Elsa took her handkerchief and wiped her eyes and cheeks.

Sister Jeanine Joseph put her arm around Elsa as she had done many times since her first visit. "There, there, child, don't be angry with yourself. What you feel is normal. We all fear loneliness. You have many around you though, who love you. And from what you have told me about Kurt, he will not abandon you."

"What if they leave for America?" Elsa sniffled and wiped her eyes again.

"Trust in God, my child. Things will be all right."

Elsa sighed. "Sister, it's worse," she said. "I know I'm only sixteen, but I think I've fallen in love with him."

"Your French has improved, son."

"Merci, mon pere. Elsa helps me with it and also my friend Saul. How do you like the ice cream?"

Hertz smiled. "I hate to say it, but it's better than what we get in Vienna."

"Like I told you, brother," said Sam, "Nobody eats badly in Belgium."

They laughed. "Did you want another, Kurt?"

"No, now please tell me about mother."

"All right," Hertz said. "I heard from her a few days ago. She has done everything we needed to do, and now that I'm here we can bring her out."

"Is she going to escape as you did, to Switzerland?"

"No, no. Please don't worry. Your uncle and I have a plan."

Kurt stiffened his back. He needed to know. He wasn't a child. "Father, please tell me. I worry about her day and night."

Hertz looked at Sam. Sam nodded his head almost imperceptibly.

"Yes, you have a right to know," said Hertz. "You have met your Uncle's girlfriend?"

"Marianne? Yes." Kurt blushed a bit. "She's very pretty."

"Her father is getting us documents to bring your mother here on the rouse that you're dying of measles."

Kurt's heart pounded. "And you think they will let a Jewish woman out of Germany for a dying child?" He jumped up from the bench. He didn't know where to look. Kurt wanted to scream. How could his father have left her there? How could he believe this crazy plan would work? "Father, you know how they operate!" Kurt shouted in German. "They'll never let her out for that! They'll laugh at her, happy that they can torture a woman whose child is dying!"

Both Sam and Hertz got up and reached for Kurt.

"Calm down!" Hertz pleaded.

"Let us explain!" Sam demanded.

Kurt shook off their hands and sat down. "If they don't let her out, I'm going back!"

"Kurt, just listen!" Hertz was desperate to make Kurt understand. "Marianne's father has done this before. He secures documents stating that the mother is needed for a donation of blood for a transfusion and that the medical authorities will return her to the Reich in two weeks. She has to register with the German embassy here. And do you think they care if a single Jew escapes after they think they've taken everything they can from that Jew? That's their goal!"

Kurt put his head in his hands. "This is insanity."

"It's the only option we have," Hertz said, his hand on his son's back.

CHAPTER 18

Brussels, Belgium – May 1945

McClain puffed thoughtfully on his pipe staring out of the window of Rosenthaller's office. Rosenthaller chatted with an officer from the British High Command on his phone. McClain listened intently to one half of the conversation. Rosenthaller's responses consisted mostly of "Of course," and "certainly," and "we're on the same page." McClain, knowing full well what the conversation was about, was impressed with Rosenthaller's commitment to their shared goals for the project, and his willingness to be duplicitous to reach that goal.

McClain turned to face Rosenthaller when he heard, "no, Colonel, we haven't seen him, but we are looking for him, and if we do, we will certainly bring your people in for the interrogation. Yes, it appears he is guilty of mass murder, and as such has to be apprehended and punished." Rosenthaller winked at McClain. "I will, Colonel, and good to speak to you too."

Rosenthaller hung up the phone and smiled. "Do you think he bought that?"

"Absolutely," replied McClain. "All that British comrades-in-arms shit."

Rosenthaller chuckled. "Jolly good!" he shouted attempting a British accent.

McClain took a seat across from Rosenthaller. "Well Captain, how do you propose we proceed?"

"Carefully. We have stumbled upon exactly what we're looking for. Von Hauptmann is a committed anti-communist…"

"…That's clear…"

"…experience in undercover work, speaks not only German, but Hungarian. He has a working understanding of Russian as well. He can be used in more than one environment. He even has espionage experience directly in Moscow."

McClain nodded. "I do have some minor concerns about that."

"What?"

"How well known was he there? His value inside the Soviet Union diminishes significantly if he's recognizable to anyone who may have survived the war and Stalin's whims, and might still be there."

"According to what he told us he was only there for a short time. How well known could he have been. We should try to confirm what he's told us at some point with other high-ranking Nazi's we're holding, but that might give away the fact we have him to the British or the French if we're asking about him. They may be reading the transcripts."

"You're correct. There would be a record of any interrogation. He knew Molotov, though. Molotov is pretty high up in the command now, Foreign Minister. Question is if he would even remember von Hauptmann."

"There's always disguise if we ultimately have to go that route," said Rosenthaller.

"Yes, good point."

"And good spy craft. And for what he'll be doing he'll need to be a master of disguise," added Rosenthaller.

McClain laughed. "So, I guess that means we're going to recruit him. That's going to take some, shall we say, alterations."

"Yes," Rosenthaller replied. "I realize that."

"Do you think the young man will cooperate?"

Rosenthaller raised an eyebrow. "I'm not sure. That depends on what we ask him to do, or how we ask him to do it."

"Von Hauptmann's statements about Jews and his part in their persecution has to disappear. I can convince my superiors to overlook that truth if it isn't on paper, in sworn testimony.

Frankly, they're already impressed by what I've told them about his background. I've been thinking that he may be useful in other ways too."

"In what way Colonel?"

"There are a lot of so-called refugees who've entered the States since '39 from Germany, Austria, Hungary, and Czechoslovakia. We suspect many of them are communists and have ties to the USSR, and in particular the NKVD. He may be useful is ferreting them out."

"You think there are active cells operating in the States now?"

McClain smiled. "Of course. No question about it. We're already meeting privately with Members of Congress and others in the government to look into the problem. We can't let our guard down, particularly now."

"Oh, I agree," said Rosenthaller. "I never told anyone this, but before Hitler came to power my father actually voiced support for him because of his anti-communist position, despite his anti-Semitism. My father and his brothers owned a newspaper in Berlin. They inherited it from my grandfather. The fate of private businesses under the Bolsheviks in Russia terrified them. The Reds were gaining power in Germany after the Great War. They and their friends believed the Jews could work something out with Herr Hitler after he came to power to quiet his rhetoric."

McClain tamped down fresh tobacco in his pipe. He lit it, puffing vigorously, sweet-smelling smoke filling the room again. "Clearly they were wrong about that." McClain chuckled. "It's a shame though. If he had let the Jews alone, we might have taken a completely different path. I believe the American government would have worked out an arrangement with him, along with the Brits."

"Probably true," said Rosenthaller, nodding. "But then, had that happened, I wouldn't be sitting here with you."

"Do you plan on going back to Berlin after this is all over. Reclaim your family's business?"

"No," Rosenthaller replied, to quickly for it to be a lie. "My father is a typical German. He's too proud to admit to what actually happened, that we ran away in the middle of the night. He likes to tell people that he and my uncles sold the paper and left before the reality of Hitler's policies became evident. He claims he had opportunities here in the United States, which he was already seeking to take advantage of. The truth is he had assets outside the country when Hitler came to power, more than enough to re-establish himself. They so feared a communist takeover that he used British banks exclusively for almost all his long-term deposits and investments after 1921. And the paper wasn't doing all that well anyway."

"Interesting. He had a bit of foresight and some luck. Where are they now?"

Rosenthaller smiled. "Sunny, southern California."

McClain perked up. "Really. That's where the future of the country is, you know. What kind of business are they in?"

"They bought a failing movie studio in 1938. Then they got a government contract in 1940 to make propaganda films in both English and German. Roosevelt was hedging his bets that we would be entering the war sooner or later on the British side."

"Very smart."

Rosenthaller nodded. "Yes, thank you. Now as to our problem, Colonel McClain. Here's what I propose to do about Lieutenant Berlin."

话找

Rosenthaller waved Kurt into his office and gestured to the sofa across from his desk. Kurt took a seat in the far corner. On the coffee table in front of him was a bound volume titled, "The Coming Conflict with Communism." The author was none other than one Colonel Anderson McClain. Despite his desire to pick up the report and read it, he didn't dare. An infraction of protocol like that wouldn't sit well with Rosenthaller, and he suspected the Captain wasn't pleased with him to begin with, which is why he had been summoned. The cordial though formal relationship that existed between Rosenthaller and him had deteriorated in the weeks since he had gone to work exclusively for McClain. Kurt suspected McClain was the cause of the problem.

Rosenthaller hung up the phone with a quick, "of course Major," and stepped around the desk. He moved one of the chairs from in front of his desk and flipped it around and sat down opposite Kurt. Rosenthaller then took a silver cigarette case from his jacket pocket and offered one to Kurt.

"No, thank you, sir," Kurt said.

"Do you mind if I do?"

"Not at all, sir."

Rosenthaller lit his cigarette and took a deep drag, exhaling slowly. "Lieutenant, I asked you to come see me today because I have something quite serious to discuss with you."

Kurt's heart beat rapidly. Despite how much he disliked working with McClain and interpreting von Hauptmann, he didn't want to be moved or dismissed at this time. That could lead to his leaving Brussels, and now was not the time for him to go. He still hadn't found out what happened Elsa, and until he could meet with the sister who had survived the convent's destruction he needed to be here. And then there was the matter of Saul. He couldn't leave him either. Kurt needed time and help to bring Saul with him wherever he went next, which perhaps his army connections could provide.

"Sir," Kurt said, interrupting Rosenthaller, "I know why you've called me here, and please, let me assure you, I'm doing my best. I admit, there are times when some of the things the prisoner says can be jarring, but I've not let it affect my work."

Rosenthaller smiled, he flicked the ashes growing on the end of his cigarette into the porcelain ashtray on the coffee table that separated him from Kurt. "Lieutenant…Kurt, if I may, that's not at all why I've called you here. We, Colonel McClain and I, are very happy with your work, both in the interrogation room and in terms of the final transcripts you've provided us with."

Kurt was caught completely off guard. Perhaps he was imagining the looks of irritation McClain exhibited if he was the slightest bit late in his translation of the prisoner's testimony or if he sensed McClain recognized his personal revulsion to von Hauptmann's anti-Semitic statements. He was sure

Rosenthaller himself had picked up on it when he observed von Hauptmann's interrogation. Now he was even more apprehensive. Rosenthaller didn't ask junior officers to come by for a chat for no reason. "Then excuse me sir, but what was it you wanted to see me about?"

Rosenthaller lit another cigarette off the first. "As I said Kurt, we are very happy with your execution of your duties. We need to consider though certain other factors in terms of what we are trying to accomplish here and so, Colonel McClain thought it a good idea for me to meet with you and further illuminate our plans to you while he's visiting Paris."

"Of course, sir," Kurt replied. "I'm here to serve."

Rosenthaller smiled. "Good," he said. "As you've mentioned von Hauptmann's clearly an anti-Semite, both Colonel McClain and I are aware. It hasn't gone unnoticed. But to be clear, he is a Nazi, and that was to be expected. Nevertheless, I have to tell you that he appears to be the most compelling prisoner we have. He's invaluable for what we are attempting to do. OSS needs men like him."

Kurt felt his body tense up. He did everything he could to control it. He knew what he was getting into when he accepted the assignment. What he didn't know was how much the Army was willing to overlook for the sake of this 'war' with the Soviets they were so sure was coming. "Captain," he said, "with all due respect sir, I understand our mission, but despite the prisoner's unusual personal experience with undercover intelligence, the man is an admitted murderer. And not only on the battlefield. He's a murderer, sir. And he clearly enjoys the act of killing"

Rosenthaller leaned forward. He lowered his voice. "Lieutenant, to some extent we all are. People die in wars, there's collateral damage. We were both soldiers. Aren't we both guilty of that too, to some extent?"

Kurt was disturbed by Rosenthaller's suggestion that in some way, any way, he and von Hauptmann were equivalent. Yes, Kurt knew what he'd done in battle. He knew what happened when American forces recovered a village and found Japanese soldiers or sympathizers, but he himself had never participated in revenge, and certainly had never killed for sport as von Hauptmann had. He knew better than to be insubordinate though, despite Rosenthaller's friendly tone. Kurt didn't respond.

"We have a small issue, Lieutenant, and we need your help."

"In what way sir?" asked Kurt.

"It relates to the final records and report on Captain von Hauptmann. Colonel McClain and I recognize how beneficial and complete his experience is for our program, but we are faced with a problem relative to some of what he has said as it applies to Jews, and how regulations view those actions vis a vis his recruitment."

Kurt was shocked, yet knew he had to respond in some way. "How does that relate to me, sir?"

"We need to make certain changes to your transcripts from his interrogations."

"I'm sorry sir, I don't think I understand what you're asking of me."

Rosenthaller leaned in again. "Kurt, he's the most valuable asset we've come across short of a nuclear physicist. He has both knowledge and experience with the communists in Europe and inside the Soviet Union. He also knows every one of his Nazi peers who may end up in the service of the Russians. We need him for our side regardless of what else he's done."

Kurt remained silent as Rosenthaller took a sip of water from the glass on his desk in back of him.

"We need you to remove all but the most general references to Jews from his transcripts. He has to appear to be anti-communist, not a rabid anti-Semite. Our superiors expect some level of anti-Semitism from all of these men. Evidence of that isn't a game breaker, but by agreement with our allies, involvement in actual actions against the Jewish or other local populations is."

Kurt was dumbfounded. How could Rosenthaller, himself a Jew, ask him to cover for a murderer? Kurt's stomach knotted up. He fought his revulsion before it rose into his throat.

"Kurt, do you understand? We need to fix the transcripts to get approval of his recruitment from higher up. Otherwise, we would have a problem with the Brits and French on the committee that approves our recruitments. Can we depend on you?"

Kurt's mind was in disarray. He couldn't do this, wouldn't do this. Von Hauptmann deserved prison at the least. He looked at Rosenthaller. "Sir," he shook his head. "I'm sorry, I don't think I can…"

Rosenthaller's expression hardened. "Lieutenant, we will make this worth your while."

Kurt remained silent. The idea that his superior officer was going to bribe him to commit a crime reverberated around his brain. "I…don't think…"

"Kurt, if you do this for us," Rosenthaller was standing over him now, "we will secure citizenship for your parents, immediately."

Kurt nodded. "I see," he said. He thought he would vomit. They would make him an accessory to their crime. He would help a Nazi murderer go free. But his parents would be rewarded for his complicity. What would his father say?

CHAPTER 16

Vienna, Austria - June 1939

Berta slipped the last of the gold rods into the slits of the corset. The muslin cloth hid the glistening result of her plan to smuggle the jewelry she had melted down out of the Reich. Berta wrapped the last of the corsets around her waist, then concealed it under her blouse.

Konrad delivered Hertz's coded letter to Berta the prior week. Three days later the documents summoning Berta to Brussels on account of Kurt's "failing health," arrived as well, although in a much more formal and officious manner. That was part of the game. The Nazi's were nothing if not officious. Berta went immediately to obtain a temporary exit visa. She signed a document forfeiting what little they still appeared to have in the event she didn't return within two weeks and also had to pay for the visa. Of course, the clerk required a bribe as well.

"Where did a Jew get such a large sum of money?" the clerk asked with a sick smirk.

"My very generous relatives in America were kind enough to send it," Berta lied.

"Generous Jews? How odd," the effete, effeminate, overly manicured official replied, holding on to Berta's visa till she extended her cupped hand in his direction. He took the money discretely and stamped her visa loudly. "Remember," the official barked. "You must return to the Reich within two weeks, or your passport will be revoked."

Berta looked at the passport with a large "J," stamped in red over her photo. She would be delighted on the day that she could tear it to shreds. "Yes, I understand. Thank you."

"Heil Hitler," the official shouted, jumping out of his seat and saluting.

Slipping the documents into her bag, Berta walked out slowly and with her head up. This degradation would soon be over. Either she would get to Belgium or be caught smuggling and sent to Mauthausen.

Berta took the first of two suitcases and placed it on the kitchen table. She undid the straps and popped open the bag, then ran her hand along the bottom until she reached the small groove Hans Fredrisch had made on one side, slipped in her nail and gently undid the false bottom. The piece detached easily. She took half the corsets and put them in the suitcase then refitted the false bottom making sure it was secure, placing her clothing on top. Berta repeated the process with the second bag, then placed the suitcases by the front door, along with the plate for the Bauers. As she turned back into the long hallway, she stopped and looked at the framed photographs on the walls.

Berta ran to the credenza in the dining room and opened the bottom drawer. Despite Hertz's instructions not to take anything that would indicate she wasn't returning, she took their leather-bound photo album. She opened the second suitcase and removed her clothing, popped the false bottom again and slipped the album in with the corsets. They could steal her life, but they couldn't steal her memories.

Konrad arrived at 8:00 AM. They would drive to West-bahnhoff Station. He would wait in the Great Hall while she passed through the visa station. Hopefully, there wouldn't be a problem. If there were, Konrad would know what had happened. He could tell Hertz. Berta wouldn't disappear, untraceable.

Berta put a light coat over her shoulders and opened the door. Konrad took one suitcase, she the other. In her free hand, Berta held Bauer's plate. She looked back into the apartment. Her parent's portrait caught her eye. Berta choked back tears. She wouldn't be able to say goodbye. She sensed she would never see them again. Konrad would visit them later today, if she boarded the train, to tell them she was gone.

For a moment, Berta's strength and resolve almost failed her. She nearly broke down then and there, but instead stood up straight and took in a deep breath. When she turned and closed the door, Berta saw Konrad's tears.

"I am so ashamed," he muttered.

"Don't be," Berta replied. "Your honor alone has washed away the dishonor of your countryman."

"Thank you."

Berta kissed Konrad on the cheek. "No, thank you, for everything."

Konrad nodded his head, picked up both suitcases and walked to the stairs. He would return later to take the photographs from the long hallway for safekeeping and lock the door. As she passed the Bauer's apartment, she gently placed the small plate in front of it.

Berta stood in front of a uniformed SS officer, a large and intimidating man. "May I see your papers?" he growled, extending his black-gloved hand.

Berta handed him her passport along with the letters and papers Hertz sent from Brussels. He examined them quite thoroughly.

"You have been summoned to Brussels as your son is quite ill?" the SS officer said, a scowling smile on his face.

"Yes," Berta replied. "He may die." She kept her head down, not wanting to make eye contact.

"I suppose even you Jews will do anything to keep your children alive. Though I'm not sure why?" He laughed.

Berta wanted to scream, to slap his face, but she knew her future depended on this moment.

"Why did you send him to Brussels, to begin with? Wouldn't you rather have your son with you?"

Berta stammered. "For school, Herr Kommendant."

"Is that the only reason?"

"Of course, sir." Berta kept her head down. She felt beads of perspiration begin to form under the rim of her hat.

"And where is your husband?"

"He's in Brussels with my son."

"And his blood is not sufficient for this procedure?"

"He's not the boy's real father," Berta lied. "His natural father is dead. Their blood types aren't compatible." She raised her eyes to the Nazi's. "Ours are."

The SS Captain looked through the papers again. "But yet they have the same name?"

"He adopted him when we married."

The Nazi slammed his fist down on the table. "That adoption certificate should be here!"

"Please, Herr Kommendant, I have all these papers. I must go to Brussels. My ticket is for today."

The SS officer lowered his voice. "I see that, Jewess." He leaned toward Berta. His hate was palpable. "You understand," he snarled, "you must return within two weeks, or your passport will be revoked. You will be stateless. If you try to re-enter the Reich without your papers, you will be sent directly to camp."

A chill ran down Berta's spine despite the warm Spring weather. "Yes sir, I understand."

The SS officer looked her over. "Take off your coat."

Berta removed it and handed it to him.

"All too often, you people try to smuggle the rightful property of the Reich out of our country." He ran his fingers over the coat looking for bulges under the lining and evidence of new stitching. Berta felt as if her knees might buckle. She concentrated her energies to calm herself. Everything depended on this.

"Now, let me see those suitcases."

Berta picked up both suitcases individually with great effort. The SS officer offered no help, thankfully, as their weight might have made him suspicious. She placed them on the table between the Nazi and herself. He unstrapped the first bag and opened it, rummaging through the clothing, lingering on her under things, rubbing the fabric through his fingers. The thought of this animal's hands on her clothing made Berta sick. She would have to wash everything before she could wear it again, if she had the chance to wear it again.

The SS Captain put his hand on the outside of the second suitcase. "Perhaps this requires closer examination."

Berta thought her chest would explode. "Please sir, my train leaves in a few minutes."

"Kommandant!" a younger officer shouted from a table farther down the line.

"Ja!" the SS officer shouted back, removing his hands from Berta's luggage.

"Could you pick up the phone, please? I think we have a problem."

Berta watched as the Nazi picked up the phone on the table behind him then ran down the aisle and behind a curtain. A few moments later he returned. "You Jews," he chuckled, "always up to something. Imagine one of your brethren trying to smuggle an infant onto the train in a suitcase. No exit visa for the child? The child stays!"

The SS officer took one more look through Berta's papers. "You've taken enough of my time today, Jewess." He waved at a matron standing several feet away. "You. Take this Jewess and search her."

The matron approached Berta. A heavy, middle-aged woman in an unflattering grey uniform, she growled at Berta. "Follow me." Berta's heart pounded in her chest. Her mouth went dry. She gazed toward the entrance to the Great Hall to see if Konrad was watching but couldn't see him through the crowd.

Berta followed the matron into a windowless room. "Place your bags there and remove your clothes," the matron said, tapping her crop against her leg absently.

"But my train…"

"No talking," said the matron.

Berta undressed. The matron walked around her, poking Berta with the crop. She stopped in front of Berta and ran her hands along the sides of her body. "What's this?" she asked, pointing to the tip of one of the girdle rods.

Berta thought she might vomit. "What is what?" she replied, as calmly as possible.

"This," the matron repeated, this time touching the exposed tip of the gold rod.

"The girdle's stays," Berta said.

"The matron smiled. "You Jews, always devious. Take off the corset."

"Why?" Berta asked, her voice quivering.

"Do as I say, or I will call the Captain."

Berta untied the corset and handed it to the matron. She covered herself with her arms as the matron examined it. A chill wracked Berta's body. She thought her teeth might begin to clatter.

The matron put her crop down and removed her leather gloves. She grabbed the tip of the girdle rod and pulled it slowly from inside the corset, the gold glistening. "My, oh my."

Berta avoided the matron's eyes. She began to shake. Her life was over. She would never see Hertz or Kurt again.

"Shall I call the Captain?" the matron said. She ran the gold rod along Berta's arm.

"No, please," Berta whimpered. "I beg you."

"You beg me? I'm not sure begging will help you."

"Please, I will give you whatever you want. Please, let me go. I've done nothing to you."

The matron chuckled. "If you have this, you have more."

Berta moved into the corner of the room and leaned against the two walls to steady herself. "Take the whole corset. All the rods are gold."

"Is that all you have? Nothing in our coat? Your bags?"

Berta looked at matron, "No, I swear. Please, let me go to my son and my husband."

The matron picked up one of the suitcases. "It seems very heavy."

"It's just my clothes. Please, please, let me go. My train is about to leave."

The matron blocked Berta in the corner. "What else do you have."

Berta pressed her teeth against her lower lip. She had to give the woman more. "Let me show you."

The matron backed up. Berta opened one of the suitcases and pulled out a pair of socks. She reached inside the balled sock and pulled out the gold pin with the garnets, the one piece she had saved for herself. "Here, they're rubies." Berta doubted the matron would know the difference between rubies and garnets.

The matron took it along with the corset. "Get dressed. Go."

Berta slipped on her blouse quickly, grabbed her suitcases and ran from the room.

"Go! We'll see you again soon enough," the matron called after her, laughing.

Berta headed toward the train, praying her legs wouldn't give way till she got into her seat.

CHAPTER 17

Brussels, Belgium - June 1945

S am and Kurt waited in the telephone communications room at the British High Command. The overseas operator was sitting in the next room, visible through a large window in the wall. She signaled for them to pick up the handsets of the phones in front of them. "Go ahead," the operator said. Regulations required she remain on the line.

"Halo?" came Hertz's voice from the other side of the Atlantic, the voice hollow and distant, as if from a well.

"Father?"

"Yes. Kurt, how are you?"

"I'm well. Sam is with me."

"Wonderful," Hertz replied.

"Where is mother? "

Berta's voice came through the crackle of the line. "I'm here, my darling. How are you?"

"Happy to hear your voice. I miss you, both of you."

"We miss you as well," Hertz said. "How are you, Sam?"

"I'm well, brother. I have some news for you."

"What?"

"Marianne is pregnant."

"That's wonderful!" shouted Berta, Hertz laughing in the background. "When is the baby due?"

"September."

"Marianne and her mother must be very excited. We will have to find a way to get to London."

Kurt thought for a moment about what McClain had said.

These Nazis would be given citizenship and clean records for cooperation with the Americans. His parents were still waiting for theirs. They wouldn't be able to travel out of the country till they obtained it. He could change that.

"Perhaps we will come to America," Sam said through the crackling line.

"Sam, have you learned anything about your father-in-law?" Hertz asked, his tone now somber.

"No. I'm doing what I can to find him."

"Of course," replied Hertz. "How is your work, son?"

"It's good, father," Kurt lied. "My superiors are very impressed with my translation abilities." Kurt sensed a moment of hesitation from his parents. "Is everything all right there?"

"Yes, yes," Hertz said. "We were wondering, we didn't want to bother you. What is it like there? Is it much changed?"

Kurt looked over at Sam. They both knew that wasn't at all what Hertz was asking. Tell him about Saul, Sam mouthed to Kurt.

"We found Saul, father."

"Thank God in heaven," Berta said.

"And his parents? And the Mandelbaum's?" Hertz hesitated again. "Wolfson?"

Sam shook his head.

"We don't know anything yet. Saul is looking for them. We're helping."

"And Elsa?"

Kurt's throat tightened. "Nothing yet. I'm searching for her."

"Sam," Hertz said. "Did you go to Vienna?"

Finally, the question.

"Yes. I got back a few days ago," replied Sam.

There was a deafening silence on the line. If not for the static, Kurt would have thought the line had disconnected.

"Is anyone alive?" asked Berta.

Sam hesitated a moment. "I have much to tell you, but none of it good. Some of it, Kurt already knows."

"Please, brother," said Hertz. "At this point, any news is better than not knowing."

Sam looked at Kurt. Kurt nodded. "I found Konrad," said Sam. "He's alive, as is his younger daughter. His wife and older daughter are dead."

"I am so sorry," Hertz said. "How did it happen."

Sam recounted what he told Kurt a few days earlier.

"How has he taken it?" Berta asked.

"Not well. He's broken. He blames himself. Konrad thought the deeper into Germany they were, the safer they would be."

"What is his physical state?" Hertz asked.

"Very poor. He's like an old man. Broken."

Kurt recalled Konrad, always chipper and confident, always dressed impeccably with a perfectly tied bowtie standing behind the counter in the shop.

"Did you go to the store?" Hertz asked

"It's badly damaged. That's where Konrad is living, in the back. His apartment was destroyed in the fighting."

"And our apartment?" asked Berta. Kurt could tell she was crying.

Sam spit out the facts in a monotone. "Someone is living there."

There was a momentary pause. "Curse them!" Hertz shouted. "What's mine is mine! I paid a fortune for that apartment!"

"Hertz calm down! This isn't the time," Berta snapped through tears. "And the Bauers?"

"No trace of them."

"And Lisle?"

Sam hesitated, "I saw her. She and her father survived."

Kurt shook his head. Don't, he mouthed.

"What's past is past. I gave her some money," said Sam.

"Did you find my parents?" Berta asked, finally, almost inaudibly.

"Berta, I'm sorry," Sam said. Kurt watched Sam's face drain of color. He knew how much Sam feared this moment. His grandparents took Sam in when he arrived from Poland. He was a member of their family. And he loved them.

Berta's weeping worsened noticeably, despite the terrible connection. "Somehow, I knew," she said. "Tell me, please."

Sam took a deep breath. "Konrad protected them for as long as possible." He looked at Kurt. Kurt turned his head, his right hand on the watch that sat on his left wrist. "He paid off the Nazis as long as he could, even after the money we left for them ran out. In the summer of 1943, they were to be sent to Auschwitz. He bought them off that transport. Instead, they went to Theresienstadt."

Berta wept openly into the phone. "I left them. My parents, I left them to die, alone."

"What is this Theresienstadt?" Hertz asked.

"It was a camp for certain types, people who couldn't just disappear, the wealthy, the well-known, the elderly. They are not among the survivors found there, I'm sorry." Sam's voice broke. "Our Vienna is finished. There's nothing there and no one left. Everything is gone. Our whole lives."

Kurt felt tears flow down his own cheeks. He knew the world they had lived in had exploded, but until this moment Kurt hadn't realized it was gone forever.

"Thank you, Sam," Berta said, composing herself. thank you for going and finding out for me. When you go back, you must take care of Konrad and thank him. He did as much for them as was possible. He has been like a brother to me my whole life." With that she put down the phone.

Kurt couldn't take any more. He too put the handset back on his phone, put his head in his hands and cried. Sam put his free hand on Kurt's shoulder. "Hertz, are you still there?"

"Yes," Hertz said. "And our mother? Our sisters?"

"It doesn't bode well. The worst of the slaughter was in Poland. There is always a chance, but it's doubtful."

"One last thing. Your father-in-law?"

"Nothing, I'm searching for anything."

"This might help you. The bastard who sold him his papers was named von Hauptmann."

Sam was caught off guard. "How do you know that?"

"He sold me mine as well."

Sam swallowed hard. "Thank you, brother. Till we speak again."

"No, till we see each other again, brother. Kiss my son for

me and tell him to be strong."

Sam hung up the line and signaled to the operator to discon-
nect. Her eyes were red too, and her face wet with tears.

CHAPTER 18

Brussels, Belgium - September 1939

Mandelbaum blessed the wine. He recited the beautiful prayer in a melody reserved especially for the holiday. At the end, he raised his glass, "Le'chaim, and may HaShem grant us a good year, a year of peace."

"I would like to make a toast as well, if I may," Hertz said, standing up.

"Of course," said Mandelbaum.

"To our hosts, Yehuda and Rebecca Mandelbaum and to Yaakov Seidleman and his family. Thank you, Yehuda and Rebecca for taking care of our son and Elsa, and to Yaakov for providing us with a home, our new apartment in his building around the corner. Thank you all for your help, generosity, and hospitality."

"You are more than welcome," both Mandelbaum and Seidleman said.

Mandelbaum continued and blessed the Challah. He broke off a piece and passed the loaf around on a beautiful, shining, silver tray.

Hertz, sitting to his right, tore off a piece and passed the platter to Berta. "Yehuda, this has been a very interesting day," Hertz said. "I feel like I'm back in my father's house again, but twenty-five years later."

"I would have to consider that to be a compliment," replied Mandelbaum, tasting the challah."

"Not necessarily," said Sam, sitting a few seats down the table. "You didn't know our father."

Both Sam and Hertz laughed. Berta leered at them, raising an eyebrow. She had warned them earlier about such comments.

"By your participation in shul today, it's clear you were raised in a traditional way," said Yaakov Seidleman.

"You participated in the service today?" said Sam, taking a bite of his challah. A smile crawled up around his lips.

"Yes, I did, I was honored with an aliyah," Hertz replied. "Perhaps you would like to join us for Yom Kippur."

"Perhaps," Sam said, his smile growing even broader.

"You would be welcome," added Mandelbaum.

"Was your family observant?" Seidleman asked Berta.

Berta hesitated a moment before answering, a bit intimidated by the question. "No," she replied. "But we always celebrated the Jewish New Year as a family."

"It was always a big day, a big party at my grandparents' apartment," Kurt added.

"And you, Elsa?" Seidleman said.

Elsa had been quiet all afternoon. She helped Frau Mandelbaum prepare the many dishes for the holiday. When Frau Mandelbaum went to the synagogue, Elsa told her she would rest and read a bit. Then Elsa snuck out and went to church, as she did every day, to light a candle for her parents. "We didn't observe holidays," Elsa said, her eyes averted from Seidleman's gaze. "This is my first time."

"Here comes the soup," called Rebecca from the kitchen, breaking the tension building around the table. She carried a large porcelain tureen with both hands. It was blue and white with a pattern of windmills on both sides.

"What a beautiful piece," Rachel Seidleman said.

"Thank you, it was a gift from my grandmother for our wedding. It came all the way from Delft." Rebecca glanced at her husband and smiled. "She said every Jewish woman needed a beautiful tureen to compliment her matzo ball soup."

Rebecca placed the tureen in the center of the table. "Please, pass me your plates." She ladled the clear, golden soup into the bowls with two perfectly shaped matzo balls each and passed them to her guests. "I should tell you all that Elsa made most of these. Having her here is like having my daughter home again."

"Where is your daughter?" Rachel asked.

"In Paris, she's married to a Frenchman," Rebecca called out, returning to the kitchen.

"She married a Jew who lives in France," Mandelbaum corrected.

"Do you not believe that one can be a citizen of a modern state and a Jew?" Sam said.

Hertz looked at his younger brother, his eyebrows raised. He had spoken to him earlier, told him to keep the conversation apolitical and areligious.

"That's a complicated question, young man," Seidleman said. "I've discussed it with my son and my daughter many times," he said, nodding his head toward Saul and his sister.

"And I agree with you, Sam," Saul said. "My father, on the other hand, does not. I was born in Belgium, and especially now, I believe we have a duty to protect our country. We all know what's coming."

"I don't believe the Germans will repeat the mistakes they made in the last war," said Mandelbaum. "They will respect our neutrality,"

"I couldn't disagree more," retorted Seidleman. "They will roll over us as they did the first time."

"Which is why we must prevent that," said Sam. "We share common cause with our neighbors.

"Our gentile neighbors?" Seidleman asked. He chuckled, then wiped his mouth with his linen napkin.

"This soup is excellent, and the matzo balls so light," Berta said, hoping to change the subject. "Elsa, what a marvelous job."

"Yes, it's excellent," said Kurt. He glanced at Elsa from the corner of his eye. Her expression and pallor had changed from calm and bright to uncomfortable and gray.

"Yes," Sam said, "our gentile neighbors," picking up where he'd left off. "The government has announced that they will be forming a self-defense force. I intend to join up."

Hertz dropped his spoon into his soup, some of the golden liquid spilling onto the white tablecloth. "What?"

"Yes, brother, I meant to tell you. I haven't had a chance. I can't stand by and watch this. Not after they forced me to leave Vienna. I have to fight it."

Hertz hesitated. Sam often picked the worst times to tell him something. "We are guests here. We can discuss this later."

Seidleman smiled and cleared his throat. "And I see how well your common cause with your gentile neighbors worked out for you in Vienna. Gentlemen, we have no friends but ourselves. How many Jews served and died in the Kaiser's army in the Great War? How is it for the Jews in Germany today? You think the Belgians will support us against the Nazis?"

"Father," Saul said. "Please."

"No," replied Sam. "I should tell you that none of us would be sitting here today without the help of our gentile friends and neighbors. We could not have escaped without them. And you won't either?"

"And how much did you have to pay them for that help?" Seidleman asked.

An uncomfortable silence descended on the room. Hertz glanced first at Sam, then at Berta, then back to Sam. He shook his head almost imperceptibly. No matter how much Sam wanted to confront Seidleman, Hertz wanted him to back off.

"Why is it so quiet in here?" Rebecca Mandelbaum said, returning from the kitchen carrying a tray of kugel.

Sam looked up at her and flashed his most charming smile. "We have been slain into silence by your matzah balls, Madame."

诶戋

Sam had his hands in his pockets as he and Hertz walked to the tram a few days later on their way to work.

"Something is bothering you," Hertz said.

The tram stop was empty. Sam shifted his gaze from his feet to Hertz. "Why do you say that?"

"Because you've got that same troubled look you had when you were a little boy and you wanted to admit to something you'd already lied about."

Sam pursed his lips and nodded. "I've made a decision."

Hertz shook his head. "Ay, not that again. I thought we'd settled that."

"I'm going to join up. Next week. I can't wait any longer."

Hertz put his hand on Sam's shoulder. "Brother, please, we should have our papers soon."

"Should, should," Sam said, taking a step back. Hertz's hand slipped off Sam's shoulder. A woman and a child arrived at the tram stop.

"Once I get to the United States, I can bring you," Hertz said, moving closer to Sam, switching to German and lowering his voice. "If you join the Belgian Army, I won't be able to get you out of here."

Sam put his hand on Hertz's shoulder. He smiled. "I know brother. Let's be honest with each other. We both know that could take years."

Hertz knew Sam was right. Desperation led him to continue. "We can speed it up."

Sam smiled. "Like the way Lena should have had your papers six months ago, a year ago. Look, we both know the Germans aren't stopping in Poland. Sooner or later they will attack in the west."

"Yes, I agree but in France, not here. They won't make the same mistake they made in the last war."

Sam was unconvinced. "I wish you were right. Even the Belgian government is certain it's only a matter of time, probably next summer. I have to do something." Sam's emotions began to get the best of him. He raised his voice. The woman with the child was joined by two men. They were looking at Sam and Hertz now. It was unlikely though, that they understood what Sam and Hertz were saying as they were speaking German. "Marianne is here, I want a life with her."

Hertz tightened the space between them again and controlled his voice. "You could bring her to America. Marry her, and I can bring you together."

Sam shook his head. "No, I'm not going to America and leaving her, the way I ran from Vienna and left Lisle. Her family has been here for generations. Her mother is Christian. We want a life together, here."

Hertz knew the argument was lost. He put his arm over his brother's shoulder. "You were always very stubborn, you know."

Sam laughed. "And you, easy to convince? Right."

"I suppose not. If this is what you want, I understand. Have you proposed yet?"

Sam smiled. He pulled a small box from his pocket and opened it. Inside was a ring with a one-karat stone. "Tonight. I cut it myself."

Hertz examined it. "Very nice work."

"Brother. Do one thing for me?"

"Of course, what's that?"

"Give me your blessing."

Hertz felt a pang of sadness. "I'm not your father." He felt remorseful for both Sam and their father. Neither could know what each had lost. Hertz remembered how Sam cried when their father scolded him or struck him because he had done poorly in cheder or was caught making mischief. How foolish his father had been not to have seen what a fine man that little boy would become.

"You're more of a father to me than he ever was."

"Of course," said Hertz. Hertz pulled Sam to him and embraced him. "You have my blessing. May you have nothing but happiness all of your lives," Hertz whispered in Sam's ear.

The tram stop had become crowded. Hertz felt the eyes of the waiting passengers on his back. The tram arrived. The crowd boarded. Hertz and Sam remained behind.

试试

Sam and Marianne stood together under the chupah. The setting sun streamed in from the windows behind them. Pink flowers ringed the white linen chupah, filling the living room of the Halevy's elegant townhouse with sweet fragrances.

Hertz was delighted for Sam, but terrified at the same time. In a few days, Sam would leave for his military training. War would come soon enough; they all knew that. In the meantime, Sam's life with Marianne would be crammed into a few days at the seashore, near Oostende. Thankfully, the weather was unusually warm for October.

Hertz was surprised when Sam told him he wanted to be married by a rabbi. It was the least he could do for their mother, and it was no small task to find one. Eventually, through Isaac Wolfson, the headmaster at Kurt's school, Hertz found a German refugee with a rabbinical education liberal enough to marry Sam and Marianne.

"Mazel tov!" shouted the assembled guests to the sound of breaking glass. Sam kissed Marianne, her petite body wrapped in an exquisite white satin dress. Sam towered over her, tall and thin.

Hertz insisted Sam let him buy his wedding clothes. They went to Marianne's father's tailor. He fashioned a double-breasted suit in a deep navy-blue. The cut of the suit accentuated Sam's slim waist and broad shoulders. Hertz glanced at Kurt a few seats away. Elsa sat next to him, her hand on her knee next to his, their pinkies touching. Kurt looked exactly as Sam had at his age, and for a moment Hertz imagined Kurt under the chupah. He prayed he would live to see that day.

"My friends and relatives, thank you for coming," said Jacques Halevy, Marianne's father. "Please come into the dining room for a dance and something to eat."

"She's perfect for him," Berta said, taking Hertz's hand.

"Yes," Hertz replied, looking over at Kurt and Elsa.

"Then why do you look so miserable?"

"Because I know what he's facing. You remember 1914."

Berta raised Hertz's hand to her cheek. "I do. Don't tell them, at least not yet. Let them have a few days."

"I'm not going to tell him. It wouldn't make a difference anyway." Hertz kissed Berta gently on the lips. "Thank you, my darling."

"For what?"

"For everything," he said. Hertz turned to Kurt and Elsa, "come, let's celebrate!"

The large mahogany dining table sat under the window. It was laid out with a buffet; cold meats, breads, cheeses, with hot dishes placed in between the cold platters. Servers stood by with small plates and large serving utensils.

On the opposite side of the room was a small bar with two barmen pouring champagne. Chairs were set along the walls. A quintet played in the study, which was open to the living room. The music wasn't Mozart or Brahms or Strauss, as it would have been in Vienna. It was Jazz, American Jazz, the love of which brought Sam and Marianne together.

Their friends danced on the herringbone parquet floor, revealed when the Persian carpets and the furniture were removed. Flowers filled vases in every corner and along the windows. Hertz had no idea where Jacques had gotten them or how he could afford them. Money was becoming increasingly dear, but then this was his only daughter, and he was a wealthy man with connections.

"Brother!" Sam shouted, raising his glass. "I think it's high time you made a toast to us!"

Hertz smiled to himself. His baby brother was a bit drunk. The shots of schnapps they drank in the dressing room before the service had set in. "Of course!" Hertz shouted back. He picked up a champagne glass and signaled to the band to stop playing.

"Dear friends!" Hertz shouted over the conversations and laughter, tapping on the crystal with a fork. "I believe the time has come for me to toast my brother and his charming and devastatingly beautiful bride." There was laughter and shouts of 'bravo.' Hertz cleared his throat. He looked toward Berta, Kurt and Elsa standing next to the buffet and smiled. "Let me start by welcoming Marianne and her parents to our family, and to thank them for this superb party."

Jacques Halevy and his wife raised their glasses.

"Even in these difficult times," Hertz continued, "we must find occasion to be happy and to celebrate. I should tell you that my brother wasn't always the dashing young man you see here today. The Sam I remember was a skinny country boy in a small village in Poland. He used to tug at my shirt when I was studying. Sam would sit on my lap and fall asleep on the porch of our father's house. He was four years old when I left to fight the last war, and the thing I had hoped for him, for my son, for all young men, would be that you would never know the misery of war."

Hertz choked up for a moment. He cleared his throat again.

"In a few days, my brother will leave his new wife to join the Belgian Defense Force to defend this nation that has been so generous to accept us." Light applause broke out, along with some cheers. "My advice to you is this. In the difficult times ahead, remember how happy you are at this moment. Remember how much you love each other. Politics is fleeting. Your love is forever. It will nurture and protect you. In the meantime, dance, sing, eat and enjoy each other. And as our mother used to say, may you have one hundred twenty years of happiness." Hertz raised his glass high. "Mazel tov and L'chaim! Kiss your bride, you fool!"

Sam raised his glass and downed the pale, sparkling liquid. He kissed Marianne deeply and passionately then put down his glass, walked to Hertz, and embraced him. "Thank you, brother," Sam whispered in Hertz's ear. "I can never thank you enough for what you did for us today."

"You can thank me," Hertz whispered, "by staying alive."

"When do you think you will be leaving for the United States?" Jacques Halevy asked Hertz, sipping champagne, the band playing. Couples danced on the crowded floor.

"Honestly, we thought we would have been gone by now, but there is a problem with my documents."

"May I ask?"

"Of course," Hertz replied. "There is some question as to what national quota I fall under."

Halevy raised his eyebrow. "You're Austrian."

Hertz grimaced. "Not so simple."

"But your Belgian asylum papers…"

"The Americans don't care. I was born in Austrian Galicia, and I lived in Vienna, but my place of birth is in what was until recently, Poland. Since the Americans don't recognize the German occupation of Poland, I am Polish by birth and must apply under the Polish quota."

"How are you handling this?"

"We've hired a lawyer in Washington."

"That will get you nowhere." Halevy said. He offered Hertz a cigarette.

"No, thanks"

Halevy lit his cigarette with a gold lighter embossed with his initials. "May I introduce you to someone?"

"Of course."

Halevy turned and waved to an elegantly dressed man of about fifty standing by the bar. Halevy motioned for him to join them. "This is my friend, Pierre Rousseau. Monsieur Rousseau, Herr Hertz Berlin. Monsieur Rousseau works for the Foreign Ministry. Herr Berlin has a small problem. Perhaps you can help him. In the meantime, I have to check on my wife and the caterer. It's nearly time for dessert. I will leave you two to chat."

Rousseau extended his hand. "My pleasure. What can I do to help?"

Hertz was cautious. He didn't like discussing his business with strangers. His time under the Nazi regime taught him to be suspicious of everyone. "It's nothing, really."

Halevy lifted an eyebrow. "Jacques wouldn't have called me over if he thought it was nothing."

Hertz took a chance. "I'm having a problem with my American visa application. There are some questions about my place of birth. According to the Americans, I am Polish, not Austrian, and they won't approve my application under the Austrian or German quota."

"I see," Rousseau said, nodding. "I might be able to help you."

Hertz finished the last of the pale, sparkling, liquid in his flute. "I'm not sure I would impose upon you."

Rousseau became deadly serious. "You should. You need all the help you can get." Then he smiled and offered Hertz his card. "And it's not an imposition."

Hertz took Rousseau's card. He wondered what this help would cost. "What do you have in mind?"

"I could issue you a naturalized Belgian passport. That would put you on the Belgian quota."

"I would imagine that list is equally as long."

"I have a friend at the American Embassy. He would handle your case. Let me know." Rousseau bowed. "It was a pleasure meeting you. That was a beautiful toast you made."

"Thank you."

"I trust you had enough time to discuss your business?" Halevy said returning from the kitchen. He handed Hertz another flute of champagne.

"Yes, thank you. May I ask Jacques, what are your plans?"

Halevy cleared his throat. "I haven't told my wife and daughter yet, though Sam knows. I wanted to wait till after the wedding. I am sending them to London. Pierre has obtained the necessary travel documents for them. Not emigration visas, just tourist visas. They will overstay their welcome."

"And you?"

"For the time being, I have to stay here. Tie up loose ends."

"I understand."

"Do one thing for me, Hertz?"

"What's that?"

"When you get to America bring Sam and Marianne as soon as possible. Please. Even London won't be safe once this thing explodes."

CHAPTER 19

Brussels, Belgium - June 1945

Kurt waited for Sam in the hotel lobby. Von Hauptmann's interrogation was becoming more than he could handle. He needed to speak to someone.

Sam waved from the double doors at the front of the lobby. "Come," he called. Sam's jeep was waiting, his driver at the wheel. "Jump in. I thought we would take a ride. I have to go check on something at the camp where we're keeping the captured officers."

"Sure," Kurt replied. Where is it?"

Sam climbed into the back with Kurt. "Mechelen. I have some business with the commander there. I thought we could talk on the way."

The mention of Mechelen sent a chill down Kurt's spine. "The Germans' transit camp for deporting Jews?"

"Yes, appropriate, don't you think?"

Kurt imagined himself and his parents in the back of a lorry crammed in with other desperate, terrified Jews, on their way to the beginning of their end.

"What was it you wanted to talk about?" Sam said. "You don't sound well, nephew."

Kurt cleared his throat. "Uncle, I don't know if I can continue this work."

"What's the problem?"

Kurt motioned his head toward the driver. "Is it safe to speak in front of him?"

The jeep moved onto the open road as they reached the

outskirts of Brussels. It was littered with garbage and debris.

"No windows." Sam gestured to both sides of the jeep. "He can't hear much up there. I have to shout when we're moving. I'll move closer, and we'll speak German."

"Uncle," Kurt began with some trepidation, "do you know anything about a program to enlist former Nazi officials in service to American Intelligence?"

"Why?"

"That's the program in which I'm working."

Sam's face became deadly serious. "You know, speaking to me about this is a breach of your clearance."

"I know," replied Kurt, letting out a long sigh. "I have to talk to someone. The officer we're interrogating is a murderer. He should be tried. I thought I could confide in you." Kurt waited a moment for Sam's response. There was none. Perhaps confiding in Sam was a bad idea, after all. "Am I compromising you by speaking about this?" Kurt asked.

Sam nodded his head in the affirmative. "I think you already know that. What is it you want to know?"

Kurt felt the agitation rise in his gut. "For starters, why are they doing this?"

"Who is they?"

"Army intelligence. The American government."

Sam thought for a moment before responding. "What have they told you?"

"They say they need these monsters to fight what they claim is the next phase of this war, against the Soviets."

Sam sighed. He was tired of the paranoia and suspicion that accompanied every day now that the fighting was over and the jockeying for position for the future had begun. Sam saw only death, destruction, and survivors, but it seemed everyone else, particularly the Americans, saw only a power struggle for whatever would come next. "Simply said, that's what they believe."

"Are the British doing the same?"

Sam nodded. "To a lesser extent. Remember, London and much of England was bombed by the Nazis. The British want revenge. The Americans didn't experience the same, save for Pearl Harbor. They wouldn't be so nonchalant about these bastards if New York or Washington had been leveled by their bombs."

"Do you agree with this?" Kurt asked, desperately hoping to hear that Sam didn't.

Sam contemplated Kurt's question. "It's not whether I agree. It's really a question of degrees. Some are worse than others. Some should be summarily executed, regardless of what they know or how useful they might be. Mass murder must be punished."

"But?"

Sam looked at Kurt's face. He knew what Kurt wanted him to say. Sam also knew that in the reality of what the world had become, Kurt's innocence, the innocence of youth, expected justice, despite the terror Kurt had seen and experienced. Sam decided to tell Kurt the ugly truth. "Some have so much knowledge of events and persons involved, we need to know what they know. The only way to get that is to make them believe they won't be hanged."

Kurt put his hands over his eyes. "Should they be given new identities and citizenship?

"What!" Sam snapped.

"That's what they're doing."

"I didn't know about that. I'm pretty high up and I can say with some certainty that the British government isn't offering that."

"That's what they've told me they're prepared to do with this prisoner. They want to recruit him as a spy. He walks away free. New name, new life, new everything."

Sam filled with anger. Were these men blind to what had happened around them? He struggled to control himself in front of Kurt. "I'm going to ask you some questions. I don't want to compromise either of us any more than we already have. Be careful with your answers."

Kurt nodded. "I understand."

"Did this prisoner admit to murder."

"Yes."

"Were these murders directed against civilians."

"Yes."

"Did he commit them willfully?"

"Yes."

"He confessed to them?"

"With relish?"

"How do you know your commanding officers want to make this offer to him?"

"They told me so." Kurt stopped short of telling Sam they had asked him to falsify the transcripts in exchange for his parents' citizenship.

"Did they mention the British High Command at all?"

"Yes."

"In what capacity."

"They said they wanted to finish their interrogation and recruit him before the British or French could question him."

"Why?"

"Because they know he's a war criminal."

Sam hesitated for a moment. He threw caution to the wind. "What is his name?"

Kurt hesitated. "Uncle, do you really think I should tell you?"

"Kurt, you came to me with this!"

"His name is Joachim von Hauptmann."

"Is there anything else?" Sam asked. "I can tell by the look on your face."

Kurt knew the moment of truth had come. "Yes, they asked me to edit his transcripts to remove mention of his actions against Jews."

试诶

Kurt walked around the grounds at Mechelen in a fog. Sam had a meeting with the commanding officer. He said he would be no more than half an hour. The barracks, if you could describe the shacks that housed the prisoners as that, were filthy and overcrowded. The prisoners ranged in age from their early twenties into their fifties. They were to the last man, dirty, disheveled and angry.

The prisoners complained in low grumbling voices about

their defeat. In his American uniform, they assumed Kurt could-
n't understand a word they were saying. Kurt listened, intently.
Some blamed the German High Command, some Hitler, but
most blamed the Jews. Somehow, they had convinced themselves that the Jews, dead and turned to ashes, were responsible
for Germany's defeat. It was as it always was, the valiant Aryan
race was the victim of a Jewish conspiracy to destroy it.

Kurt felt no empathy for these men. They were his enemies
and would remain so, always. Kurt walked among them with
his hand on his pistol. His uniform inspired fear in them, the
same way their uniforms had inspired fear in him in what had
come to feel like another lifetime. He liked that feeling.

Kurt considered his conversation with Sam. The breach of
military protocol and security was enough to get them both
courts marshaled. However, Kurt knew von Hauptmann belonged here, in this camp, or worse, in a maximum-security
prison, awaiting a death sentence. Kurt had heard reports of
what the Soviets had done in their zones. They didn't wait for
justice, or trials, they summarily executed every Nazi officer,
Wehrmacht, SS or Gestapo they came upon. Millions of Russians had died at the hands of these men, and the Soviets weren't
wasting time with legalities.

Kurt approached the perimeter fence. He narrowed his eyes,
envisioning Saul standing on the other side looking for his parents. Kurt turned and looked back at the large, grassless, open
field between the fence and the barracks and imagined it filled
with people, his people, Jews. They were dressed in whatever
they were wearing when they were rounded up, perhaps carrying a suitcase or holding the hand of a small child. Kurt saw the
fear on their faces.

Kurt squatted down and looked at the fence again, imagining
Saul there with his father. He became nauseous. Kurt remembered Monsieur Seidleman. He was tall and thin with a short
dark beard, kept immaculately trimmed. He dressed modestly
and always had a smile when he saw you. When you asked him
how he was, Seidleman would always respond, "very well, ba-
ruch haShem."

Kurt imagined Seidleman at the fence, holding Saul's hand,

imploring him to live, tears running down his face. In a tiny moment, the image in Kurt's mind changed. It was Kurt on the other side of the fence and Hertz on this side pleading with him to live, to survive. Kurt's nausea worsened. He hadn't eaten since early that morning. It was now early evening. He felt himself dry heave. Between paroxysms, Kurt promised himself that von Hauptmann would never go free.

试戋

Sam finished his meeting with the officers at the camp and asked the Commander to stay behind.

"Certainly Colonel. Is there something else?"

Sam closed the door to the commander's office and summoned his thickest upper-class British accent. "I need to ask you something off the record."

"Of course."

"Have you come across an SS Captain by the name of Joachim von Hauptmann?"

The commander thought for a moment then pulled out a folder from the bottom drawer of his desk. He pulled out a sheet of paper and ran his finger down the list of names on the right side. "Yes. I thought it sounded familiar. Here he is."

"What is that?"

"This is a list of SS officers who were directly responsible for the deportations of the local Jewish population. He's right at the top."

"How did you assemble this list?"

"Various sources, intelligence, interrogation of captured junior officers. Local witnesses."

"Was he ever a prisoner here?"

"No. And the note here says he's a top-valued asset. We want to interrogate him. We've been looking for him."

"Have you made inquiries to the Americans?"

"I'm sure we have. Let me check." The Commander pulled out another folder and thumbed through several pages till he found what he was seeking. "They claim they haven't seen him. Do you have information on him?"

Sam shook his head. "No, old chap. But I'm looking for him too."

CHAPTER 20

Brussels, Belgium - November 1939

C ome in, please," Mandelbaum said to Hertz and Berta.
"Thank you," Hertz replied. Crying came from the direction of the bedrooms. Isaac Wolfson, the director of Kurt's school was seated on the couch in the living room "What's happened?"

"I think you'd better join us. There's been some trouble."

"Where's Kurt?" asked Berta, looking around Mandelbaum's living room, her eyes darting from corner to corner.

"He's here. He's with Elsa in her room. Rebecca is with them." Mandelbaum looked tired. He sat down in the large club chair opposite the couch.

"Elsa's father was arrested and taken to Mauthausen," said Wolfson.

"When did this happen?" asked a shocked Hertz. Berta took his arm.

"A few days ago," said Wolfson."

"Where is her mother?" Berta asked.

"Still in Vienna…"

"Is she safe?" Hertz asked.

"At the moment, but there's more. He's badly injured," Wolfson continued. "It's all most bizarre. Graz attempted to enter the Kunstmuseum to protest the removal and destruction of his works. He was stopped by the guards. The Gestapo arrested him. They beat him severely. He was taken to the hospital and patched up, then sent directly to Mauthausen."

The sounds of Elsa's weeping coming from the bedroom

worsened.

"Frau Graz was ordered to the hospital to identify him," Mandelbaum said. "Graz was unconscious. It's undetermined if he will survive."

"And Frau Graz?" Berta enquired.

"The Nazi's are demanding she denounce and divorce Graz," said Wolfson. "Otherwise, she will be sent to Mauthausen as well."

"Father, mother," Kurt said from the entrance to the living room. The shadows cast by the drapes made Kurt's entry difficult to detect.

"We've heard what's happened," Hertz said.

"Father, you have to help them."

Did his son think he was some kind of superman? "We will do what we can son. Go back into Elsa's room. Comfort her." Hertz looked at Wolfson, whose glasses sat on the tip of his nose. Their black rims accentuating the grayness of his goatee. Wolfson pulled out a pack of Galois and offered one to Hertz.

"No, thank you," Hertz said.

A large, glass ashtray sat on top of the coffee table, filled with cigarette butts. The Mandelbaums didn't smoke. Wolfson sighed. "I'm afraid it's a terrible habit that's only gotten worse since I became director of this school."

"I understand completely," Hertz said.

Wolfson struck a match and lit the cigarette. He inhaled deeply. The pale, blue-grey smoke formed a cloud that hovered over the room.

"Can you tell us more specifically what the situation is?"

Wolfson reached for another cigarette. He lit it off the last one. "It's a challenging and complicated case. You understand her father is a Jew, and her mother is not."

"Yes."

"Her parents approached us in Vienna in '38. At first, we said no. Elsa's a Mischling. The rules are different for them. Elsa didn't appear to be in danger at that point. We suggested that mother and daughter leave the country and that we would refer her husband to other, should we say, more shadowy organizations to help him escape."

"I'm very familiar with them," Hertz replied.

"Too familiar," said Berta.

"I'm sure." Wolfson took another drag on his cigarette. "Elsa's mother came back to us some months later and told us that her husband refused to leave illegally. He insisted on demanding his rights, to fight the regime. He believed in the goodness of the people."

Hertz raised an eyebrow. "Really? He's got nerve. Perhaps I will take that cigarette now."

"Please." Wolfson handed him the pack. "As I was saying, he tried to obtain permission to leave legally, but was denied. The regime wants to make an example of him as he's been too vocal, and his case has been publicized throughout Europe."

"He's a very prominent artist, I understand."

"He wanted his work transferred to him or sent out of the country. The Nazis pressured Elsa's mother to denounce and divorce him. At that point, we agreed to take the child."

"Kurt told me her parents said they would join her here."

"Well, that's the catch. The problem has been the same all along. Her mother won't leave without her father. Frau Graz is convinced if she leaves, they'll kill Graz, and she's probably right. As I said, after this most recent public demonstration, Graz was beaten and sent to Mauthausen."

"Is there any chance Frau Graz can be persuaded to leave?"

"I'm not sure. And then there is the question of paying for her exit. They've been stripped of everything. We cannot afford to pay her way. Our funds are to be used exclusively for Jewish children."

Hertz took a drag. The smoke caught in his throat. "Herr Director, if the money were available, could Frau Graz be persuaded to leave?"

"I don't know."

"Try. I will pay for it." Hertz pulled a small velvet bag from his jacket pocket and opened it. Two diamonds tumbled out onto the table. "Here's a down payment."

试读

A week later Hertz's received a note from Wolfson, it's
meaning clear. Hertz must come to his office immediately.
Hertz wasted no time. He was there in less than thirty minutes.
He knocked on Wolfson's door, turning the knob simultaneously. "What's happened?"

Wolfson's face was gray. "Graz is dead."

Hertz sat down in the hardwood chair opposite Wolfson's
desk. He didn't take off his coat or hat. "How?"

Wolfson shook his head from side to side. "Would you believe it if I told you they shot him while trying to escape from
Mauthausen."

Hertz reached for Wolfson's pack of cigarettes. "I would believe anything you tell me about the Nazis."

Wolfson leaned back in his chair. "Graz could barely walk,
let alone escape." Wolfson took a deep drag on his cigarette.
The smoke swirled around him.

"How did you find out?"

"That Dutch group with which we are working on his be-
half."

"I take it you haven't told the child?"

"Not yet."

"Can you get Frau Graz out?"

"Yes, she has agreed to come. We can have her documents
ready in a week or so, but we need more help."

"How much more?"

"About the same as what you gave us before."

"Done," replied Hertz. "You will have it this afternoon."

诶战

Hertz felt like he was experiencing déjà vu when he opened
yet another hand-delivered note from Wolfson six days later.
Again, he was needed immediately. Wolfson wrote to enter
from the rear door in the basement. He didn't want anyone to
see Hertz arrive.

"What's happened?" Hertz said as he opened the door to
Wolfson's office.

"There appears to be a problem at Aachen. Veronica Graz

has been detained at the border."

"Why?"

"We don't know. I would go to Aachen myself, but we don't have access to a car."

"May I use your phone?"

"Of course, why?"

"My brother's father-in-law has a car. Given the circumstances, I'm sure he would let us take it."

The drive to Aachen took a little more than two hours. The Chauffeur slowed the Mercedes to a crawl as they approached the border checkpoint. Armed soldiers in pairs patrolled the grounds. They signaled to roll down the windows. "What's your business here?" the soldier asked, his gun at ease across his chest. His breath was misty in the cold winter air.

"We are meeting a representative of the Dutch Federation for Refugee Artists," said Hertz.

"What's his name?" the soldier asked.

"Van Faber, Karl. I believe he's inside the Customs House."

"Please, wait here."

"Certainly. May we get out of the car? It's been a long ride."

"Of course."

A man in a long grey coat waved in their direction from the front of the Customs House.

"That's van Faber!" shouted Wolfson, waving back at him.

"Wait, wait!" shouted Hertz after the soldier. Hertz ran toward the soldier to catch up. Another soldier ran after Hertz and grabbed him. Hertz shouted, "That's him, that's van Faber. Let me go!"

"Patrice!" called out the second soldier. "They say that's who they're looking for!"

"Tell them to come here and fast!"

Hertz and Wolfson ran to the first soldier. He was moving at a trot. By the time they reached Van Faber, they were out of breath.

"Are you all right, Isaac?" van Faber asked.

Wolfson bent over, trying to catch his breath. "Yes, yes, too much smoking," he said finally. "This is Hertz Berlin."

Van Faber extended his hand. "It's good to meet you. Thank you for your generosity. Please come inside, it's very cold."

Hertz and Wolfson followed van Faber into the Customs Building, then down the hall to a small room overlooking the crossing between Belgium and Germany. Wolfson sat on a brown wooden chair against the wall opposite the window. "What happened? Where is she?"

Van Faber let out a long sigh. He sat with his hat in his hand, his head hanging between slumped shoulders. "I arrived about a half hour before the train. I didn't want to be late, you know. I checked in with the commanding officer and waited across from the checkpoint to watch as she progressed through. I recognized Madame Graz as she exited the train. I had an old photo from a newspaper article about her husband. She was very nervous, crying a bit."

Van Faber took a breath. He appeared visibly shaken. "Madame Graz stepped up to the table. The clerk examined her papers and was about to stamp them when an SS officer took them. You understand, I couldn't hear anything, but I could tell he was shouting. She began to cry. She was pleading with him. Then the SS officer grabbed her by her upper arm and dragged her away."

"Oh, my God," said Wolfson. Wolfson placed his hands on the sides of his head.

"How long ago was that?" Hertz asked.

"About four hours, maybe a little more. I spoke with the commander here. He sent an inquiry across to the Germans. Then I called you. I haven't heard anything since."

"What would you propose?" Hertz asked.

"I think we need to ask the Belgian commander what's happening," replied Wolfson.

Hertz looked at his watch. It was nearly 4 o'clock. They had been waiting for almost two hours. The Belgian commander sent a second inquiry to the German Commandant on the other side. He would send another at 5:00, if they still hadn't heard back.

Hertz stared across the border. He'd felt a profound chill

since arriving, and it wasn't the winter weather. Looking back at the Reich was something Hertz swore he would never do. He spied a very tall, very muscular man in the black uniform of the SS, pacing on the other side of the border, a black baton in his hands. His hat was pushed back revealing his face. This face looked vaguely familiar to Hertz, but he thought nothing of it. They all looked alike, these Nazi supermen in their uniforms. "Is that the SS officer who dragged off Veronica Graz?" he asked van Faber.

Van Faber looked out the window across the barbed wire and anti-tank barriers. "Yes, I believe so."

"Excuse me," they heard from behind them. The Belgian commander stood in the doorway.

"Have you heard anything?" van Faber asked.

"Yes, if you would all please have a seat."

Hertz looked from Wolfson to van Faber, neither moved.

"I'm afraid I have very bad news."

The three looked at each other. "Go ahead," said Hertz.

"Veronica Graz is dead."

Wolfson dropped into the chair behind him. He put his hands over his face. "How could that happen?"

"I will read you the official German statement," the Belgian said.

"How could that happen!" Wolfson screamed. "She had official papers to enter Belgium! You let this happen!"

"Monsieur, I assure you…"

Wolfson jumped out of the chair and charged the commander. "Murderer!" he screamed. Hertz and van Faber restrained him.

"Isaac, calm down!" van Faber pleaded as they pulled Wolfson back to a chair.

"Commander, please, read us their statement," Hertz said.

The Belgian pulled the piece of paper from his pocket, unfolded it and began:

"With regards to your earlier inquiries as to the status of a certain Veronica Graz, formerly a citizen of the Greater Reich, she was taken for questioning upon arrival at the Aachen border crossing by the Schutzstaffel for irregularities in her papers and currency restrictions. During the interview, she attempted to attack the officer in charge of the interrogation with a concealed weapon. A scuffle ensued, and in subduing Frau Graz, she fell and suffered a concussion, which resulted in a massive head injury leading to her death a short while later."

"A scuffle! A concealed weapon!" van Faber shouted. "She was tiny! The officer who dragged her away was enormous! I saw the whole thing!"

"I'm sorry, gentlemen. There is nothing more I can do, save to ask for the body."

Hertz looked back out through the window. That same SS officer he spied earlier looked directly at them. He was smiling.

诚找

Hertz found Berta sitting in the living room. "Where's Kurt?"

"In his room, studying," Berta replied. "What's happened."

Hertz sat down on the couch. "Veronica Graz is dead," he whispered.

Berta put her hand to her mouth. "God in heaven, what happened?"

"An SS Captain pulled her off the customs line and took her for interrogation. They claim she tried to attack him. He was twice her size. They say she fell, hit her head and suffered a severe concussion which led to bleeding in the brain."

"What?" said Kurt standing in the doorway. "What's happened?" he said.

Hertz opted for the truth. "Elsa's mother was murdered by an SS Captain thirty meters from the border."

Kurt put his head in his hands and started to cry. Berta moved to him. She put her hand on his shoulder.

"This will never end until they kill us all. That's what they want," he sobbed.

Hertz felt his stomach turn. In his heart, he knew Kurt was right. Too wise for his years, he had seen too much. Hertz needed to get all of them out of here. Nowhere was safe with the Nazis a two-hour drive to the east.

"Have you told Elsa?" Kurt asked, composing himself.

"Not yet."

"And what about her father?"

Hertz looked at Berta.

"I told you that was a bad idea," Berta said.

"What was a bad idea?" Kurt asked.

Hertz moved to where Kurt stood. "Herr Graz was murdered at Mauthausen almost two weeks ago. We thought it would be better for Elsa if her mother told her."

Kurt looked at Hertz. He loved his father deeply, he believed he could do anything, solve any problem, but at this moment Kurt wanted to strike him. "So, now you can tell Elsa both her parents are dead?"

"I'm sorry, son."

Kurt pushed Hertz's hand off his shoulder. "Don't apologize to me. Do you know what this has been like for her, for me?" Kurt got up from the club chair. "Do you know what it was like for me that day in the train station, to leave you standing there, never knowing if we would ever see each other again? I was lucky."

Berta reached for him. "Kurt, please…"

Kurt backed away chuckling through his tears. "Tell me, both of you, what do you plan to do?"

"Why are you laughing?" Berta asked.

"There's something you need to know. And you might want to contact this person before you tell Elsa. She has a friend, a nun. She goes to church. She feels safe there. This nun befriended her, comforts her. Elsa confides in her."

"Why?" Hertz said. "Why would Elsa do that?"

Kurt stood firm, his fists clenched. "Because that's who she is. She was never a part of this. Elsa was raised a Catholic. Her Jewish father's family rejected him when he married Elsa's mother. All this means nothing to her, other than that it destroyed her life and her family. You might want this nun there when you tell Elsa."

Hertz paced about the room for several minutes. "I'm not sure how the Mandelbaum's are going to react to that."

"Who cares. It's not theirs to judge," said Kurt.

Hertz and Wolfson waited quietly inside the church. The interior was dimly lit and empty, save for a man at the front near the altar, tidying up. Mandelbaum refused to enter the building.

"It's very calming, the same feeling one gets in a synagogue, don't you think?" said Hertz.

"I can see what you're saying, but I don't find it calming at all. It makes me nervous, actually."

"Really, why?"

Wolfson thought for a moment. "Too many bad associations, these people, the church, they've never been our friends. Too many Jews have been murdered in their name."

"Yet I wouldn't be standing here if Christians hadn't helped me."

Wolfson chuckled. "It's a matter of personal experience I suspect..."

"...which is why Mandelbaum is waiting outside."

"No," Wolfson replied. "Mandelbaum is waiting outside because he believes it's a sin to enter a place of idolatry."

Hertz heard footsteps approaching on the stone floor. A nun in full habit walked toward them, rosary beads in her hand. "I am Sister Jeanine Joseph," she said, her voice quiet and melodic. "How can I help you?"

"Sister," Hertz said. "Do you know a young girl named Elsa Graz?"

"Yes, I do. Has something happened to her?"

"May we explain?"

Elsa sat on the edge of the bed, extremely uneasy. She looked at her watch again. It was past 10:00 in the evening. Mandelbaum had promised her he would be back with her parents hours ago.

Elsa heard the front door. "Herr Mandelbaum?" she called out and ran to the living room. Mandelbaum stood there with Wolfson and Hertz. "Where are my parents?" she asked.

"Elsa, please sit down," Wolfson said. "We have something to tell you."

Elsa took a step back. She put her arms around herself as if trying to keep herself warm. "Where are my parents?" she demanded.

Rebecca Mandelbaum came up behind her and put her hands on Elsa's shoulders. "Please child, come here and sit next to me," she said, pulling Elsa toward the couch.

Wolfson removed his hat and coat. He breathed fretfully. "My darling child, there has been a great tragedy."

Elsa felt like something struck her in the chest. She wanted to shake Rebecca's arm off her shoulder, run to her room and lock the door.

"Elsa, you must know that your parents loved you," Wolfson said.

The word "nein" escaped Elsa's lips, barely above a whisper. She couldn't focus. The tears welled up in her eyes, chaos further obscuring her mind. This couldn't be happening. They had promised her. She had been so happy that finally they were coming.

"I'm so sorry, Elsa," Wolfson said. His voice sounded far away like it was coming from another place. "They're dead. I'm sorry."

"Nein!" Elsa shouted. "I don't believe you!" She tried to wiggle out of Rebecca's embrace. Wolfson reached out and took Elsa's hand. Elsa pushed Wolfson's hand away then screamed, "Don't say a thing like that!" She balled her fist and lashed out, striking Wolfson in the face.

Hertz rushed forward and tried to grab Elsa's arms. Elsa jumped up from the couch knocking Hertz backward with a force impossible for her tiny body. "Yehuda, bring in the Sister!" Hertz called out.

Mandelbaum rushed to the door and opened it. Sister Jeanine Joseph stood in the hallway.

"I can't go on this way!" Elsa screamed. "I don't want to live here! I want to be with my parents!" She ran into the kitchen. They followed her. Elsa grabbed the knife she spotted on the counter by the sink. "I want to be with them! If they're dead, then so will I be dead! No more of this!"

"Child stop!" Sister Jeanine Josef pleaded, reaching for her.

"Don't do this!" She lowered her voice and approached Elsa. "We love you. I love you."

Elsa stopped for a moment, the sharp blade of the knife at her wrist. She looked at Sister Jeanine Joseph and smiled. "I love you too, Sister." With that, she pressed the knife hard. She felt the blade cut deep and saw the dark red blood gush forth onto the floor.

CHAPTER 21

Brussels, Belgium - June 1945

A breeze rustled the curtains, moving the warm air around Kurt's room. "You understand how difficult this is for me," Saul said. He stopped pacing and looked directly at Kurt. "I feel responsible. I feel like I ran away."

Kurt did understand. The feeling that he had abandoned Elsa never left him. "We both know you didn't. Your father sent you away."

Saul settled into the chair across from the bed. "That's not entirely true." Saul hesitated. "I asked to go. I was terrified."

Kurt was no stranger to terrified, now or in the past. He searched for some way to help Saul. "Would it be easier if I asked you questions, rather than for you to tell me the whole story from the beginning?"

Saul considered Kurt's suggestion. He nodded his head. "Yes, that might help. I get overwhelmed when I try to remember everything."

"All right then," Kurt said. "Let's try. Are you ready?"

"Yes."

Kurt thought about how the interrogators in his unit approached a new interview. Calmness, almost to the point of nonchalance, seemed to foster trust. Kurt tried it. "When did the deportations start?"

Saul thought for a moment. "July of 1943, the second half of the month. There was an order that all Jews be resettled for labor in the east. My parents were frantic. We heard the rumors of what was happening in Poland. But the Queen interceded. She convinced Hitler to take only non-Belgian Jews."

A chill ran down Kurt's spine despite the warm day. That would have included Kurt, his parents, and Elsa. "How did the Germans know who was Belgian and who wasn't?"

"They had had two years to hound us, categorize us." Saul cogitated. "They had very complete records." Saul paused again, remembering. "Wolfson came to see my father. It was shocking. He had a black eye and a swollen chin. The SS had visited him. Somehow, they had obtained a list of the children he brought to Brussels before the war started. They wanted him to account for all of them. Wolfson told them he had sent them all out to England. They didn't believe him."

Kurt knew his name would have been on that list. The reality of the lives of everyone Kurt left behind was becoming clearer to him with every passing moment.

"They didn't beat Wolfson too badly that first time," Saul continued, his eyes gazing into a past he'd just as soon forget. "Just a taste, enough to scare him. Wolfson was frantic. He came to our apartment with a copy of the master list of the children with their whereabouts. You know he didn't have children of his own and he felt responsible for each one of them, like a father. Wolfson hid the original of that list in the wall behind his desk. He said that if he disappeared, which he believed was likely, someone needed to have a copy. He came to us because my father was on the Judenrat. After Halevy disappeared the Germans forced him to take Halevy's place." Saul took a deep breath.

"Are you able to continue?" Kurt asked, his voice still calm and modulated, despite his racing heart.

"Yes," Saul replied. "I remember that my mother was listening from the other side of the door of my father's study. She became hysterical. My father and Wolfson heard her. Father opened the door. My mother told them there was no way Wolfson could leave that list with us. If the Germans ever came across it, they would kill us."

"She was probably right," said Kurt. "What did your father do?

"My father said he had to think about it. Wolfson begged

him. He told Wolfson he needed a day. My parents fought all night. My sister was hysterical as well. By that time, wearing the star had become compulsory. Every time my sister went out, young men and soldiers harassed her. She was afraid to leave the apartment. She would be afraid to stay inside with that list there. She begged my father not to help Wolfson. My father couldn't live with himself if he didn't." With that Saul's voice broke. The tears welled up and spilled over onto his face.

"Do you want to stop?" Kurt asked. An image of Saul's sister appeared in Kurt's mind, like a ghost. She was a dark-haired beauty, kind and gentle.

Saul pulled a handkerchief from his rear pocket and wiped away his tears. "No, I have to do this." He breathed deeply to calm himself. Kurt's heart broke for Saul, and for himself.

"The next morning my father went to Wolfson's office to tell him he would take the list and find some way to hide it, and to make sure there was someone else who knew of its whereabouts." Saul chuckled. "They were concerned with a list. That assumed the children would survive what was coming in the first place."

Suddenly, Saul stopped speaking. His expression changed in an instant. He choked up again momentarily but regained his self-control swiftly. Saul reached for a cigarette, but didn't offer one to Kurt, as if he wasn't there.

"When my father returned from Wolfson's office, he was ashen and shaking. He sat down on the couch and asked my mother to bring him a shot of whiskey. He had a bottle hidden for the worst moments. Jews couldn't buy spirits. He took two shots in rapid succession."

"My mother asked him what had happened. He said Wolfson was dead. He found him beat to a pulp on the floor of his office. There was a hole in the wall where Wolfson hid the strong box with the list and other information about the children. The box and the list were gone. There was blood everywhere."

Kurt's skin crawled, feeling the terror as if it were happening at that very moment. He struggled to maintain his composure. "But the Nazi's didn't know your father was involved, did they?"

"We didn't know for sure. We didn't know what Wolfson might have revealed. My father said then and there that he would have to send us away. At first, we refused. He backed off the subject for the time being. In the meantime, we had to notify those families we knew who had any of these children. He went to his desk and made a list. We knew maybe ten families. Then he sent me to tell them. It took a few days. We were being watched constantly and could be stopped on the street for any reason." Saul took a last, long drag on the cigarette, took another from the pack, and lit it off the first.

Kurt reached for the pack then reached around Saul for his lighter. Saul didn't make a move. Instead, Saul breathed slowly and stared dead in front of him, looking right through Kurt. He remained silent for several minutes, then began speaking again.

"After about a week nothing happened. We thought perhaps the crisis was over. My mother sent me to the Mandelbaums to bring them some sugar. My father had bought some on the black market. We would share things when we got them. When I got to their apartment, the door was open. There was a SS officer, a huge man, screaming at them. I looked into the apartment but kept walking up the stairs to the next flight. One of his soldiers tried to stop me. The sugar nearly slipped out from my pack. I would have been arrested for that. I told them I lived on the next floor and begged them to let me continue. When I got to the top I hid in the shadow of the stairwell and listened. The SS Captain kept screaming at them. He wanted to know where Elsa was."

Kurt's stomach wrenched into a knot. He looked directly into Saul's eyes, unable to speak. Saul took another cigarette and lit it.

"This SS officer seemed to have a special hatred for her. He kept ranting about her father, that he was a special enemy of the Reich, that he had ridiculed Hitler, and that his daughter would meet the same fate as her parents. I kept asking myself how he knew what had happened to her parents? Then he laughed, howled, like a hyena."

Kurt was transfixed. "What did Mandelbaum tell him?"

"Nothing at first. He was very brave. He kept repeating that he didn't know where she was. He kept saying that she ran away.

The Nazi didn't believe him. I listened as best I could. I thought my heart would burst out of my chest. I had known Mandelbaum since childhood. He was my teacher in the cheder. I wanted to help him, but I knew if I did anything, they would kill me and him." Saul began to weep.

"Maybe that's enough for now," Kurt said, his heart pounding. For the first time, he wasn't sure he wanted to know the truth he'd sought so intensely.

"No, no! You have to know!" Saul screamed through his tears. "I am the only one who can tell you! I am so ashamed. I was a coward."

"No, you weren't," said Kurt. Kurt moved in front of Saul and knelt on one knee. He put a hand on top of Saul's. "A coward would tell me he knew nothing."

"I should have fought them! Helped Mandelbaum!" Saul balled his hands into fists.

"With what!" Kurt shouted.

Saul held up his fists. "With these!" After a few minutes Saul's weeping stopped. "I carried a knife, strapped here." He touched his leg. "I should have stabbed them, the two guards and the SS man."

"They would have killed you, brother."

Saul inhaled deeply then sat back in the club chair. Kurt hurt for Saul, and himself. He swore to himself he would never abandon Saul as he had Elsa. "I think we should stop. This is no good for you."

"I promised you," Saul's breathing evened as he focused again on the past. "They punched Mandelbaum a couple of times. I could hear the blows land, and the screaming of his wife and daughter. My stomach turned. His granddaughter was crying. She was perhaps four years old. He refused to tell them anything. I'm not sure how badly they beat him, I couldn't see from where I was. Then they grabbed Frau Mandelbaum. From what I could tell they forced her down on her knees by her hair. She kept screaming, 'let go of my hair!' "

"By this time Mandelbaum was crying. He was begging them to let her alone. I heard a thud, then a terrible scream. They hit her in the face with something, which must have broken her jaw. Both Mandelbaum and their daughter were screaming about her face, her jaw. Still, she said nothing. She was so strong. Then the SS captain had had enough. He told them he was running out of patience. He told one of the guards to grab the child."

Kurt's stomach was churning. He couldn't look at Saul. If anyone was a coward, it was him, for leaving.

Saul heaved. He placed his hand over his mouth then jumped out of the chair and catapulted across the room to the sink outside the bathroom. He vomited what little was in his stomach. Kurt led him back to the bed. Saul's face was grey. Kurt realized Saul's memories had become reality again. He was reliving his nightmare awake.

Saul looked up at Kurt. "They started to scream even worse than before. The child was screeching. I slipped down the stairs to see what was happening. The SS Captain held the child upside down by her legs." Saul stretched his arm out in front of him, his hand closed as if holding something. He looked directly into Kurt's eyes again, the fear in Saul's eyes terrifying Kurt.

"The man was so big, and the baby so small." Saul's voice lowered to a whisper. "She was screaming and squirming. He held his revolver in his other hand." Suddenly the volume of Saul's voice exploded. "…either tell me where she is, or I will shoot the child!" he screamed. Mandelbaum dropped to his knees. He whined like a dog. He begged the Nazi to spare her. Mandelbaum looked up at the Nazi, his face swollen. He cried like a baby, 'please, please. All right, all right, I will tell you. She is at the convent of the Sisters of Charity. Now please,' he begged for her through his tears, 'give me my granddaughter.'"

"The Nazi threw the child at him. The screaming was even worse than before. Mandelbaum looked up at the Nazi and said, 'thank you.'" Saul stood up, his hands on the side of his head like he was trying to press the memory out of it. "He said thank you!" Saul wept. "How could he say thank you! Then the Nazi raised his arm and brought the butt of the pistol down on Mandelbaum's head."

Saul sat down again on the edge of the bed and breathed deeply. "I don't know if I made a noise, if they heard me or why, but the Nazi turned around. I saw the delight on his face. He shouted to the guards, 'get that boy!' I sprang up the stairs as quickly as I could, and you know I'm fast. I went out the door to the roof and over the buildings till they stopped chasing me. When I got home, I told my father what happened. I was terrified. I begged him, please send me away." Saul began weeping again. "Perhaps if I had stayed things might be different."

Kurt sat down next to Saul on the bed. Saul buried his head in Kurt's chest, as he did that evening in the restaurant, his body shaking, repeating over and over, "If I ever see that bastard again, I will kill him."

CHAPTER 20

Brussels, Belgium - March 1940

Hertz and Berta walked into the office of Deputy Consul Wellington Thomas at the American Embassy Visa Section hand in hand, hoping their latest appeal would yield a positive result. Deputy Consul Thomas didn't rise to greet them. He gestured toward the chairs in front of his desk addressing them in German. "I understand you have new documents for your case?"

"Yes," Berta replied, handing an envelope to him.

Thomas reviewed the documents for several minutes. He stopped briefly to take a cigarette case from his inner jacket pocket, removed a cigarette from the case, and light it with a silver lighter having a mother of pearl grip. Thomas didn't offer Hertz a cigarette. He finished both the papers and his cigarette before speaking.

"Herr Berlin, Madame Berlin, I understand the seriousness of your situation," Thomas said, looking directly at Hertz and Berta, but somehow looking through them as well. "I am afraid, at least in my opinion, and I will refer this higher up for a final judgment, that the attorney your sister employed in Washington seems to miss the problem."

"Mr. Thomas, please…"

"Herr Berlin do not interrupt me. We have been through this before. You are stateless. You have refugee status in Belgium. You left Germany illegally. When you did, your German citizenship, which was the successor to your Austrian citizenship, was revoked."

Hertz fought hard to control both his voice and his emotions. Berta put her hand on his leg to calm him. "Deputy Thomas, I was never a citizen of the Reich, Germany as you call it. We were all stripped of our citizenship."

"I'm afraid from our standpoint that's not how we see it. You may have been 'second-class' citizens, but you were still citizens. Your Austrian citizenship passed to Germany upon unification."

Hertz put his hand to his forehead. "We were stripped of everything."

"Let me continue. Our government must sort out tens of thousands of cases like yours. An unprecedented number of people are seeking entry to the United States. We can't accommodate everyone. We have to abide by regulations. Your citizenship was revoked. Therefore, we determine your current citizenship for immigration by your place of birth according to the borders established by the Versailles Conference. You are Polish. That creates a quota problem."

"But my wife and child have also been stripped of their citizenship."

"They were both born in Vienna and left the country legally, yet they can't return. The United States views them as stateless. You, on the other hand are a refugee with legal refugee status granted by Belgium."

Hertz's carefully crafted plan had hit a wall. He picked himself up to leave. Berta took his hand and pulled him down back into the chair. "Deputy Thomas what would you suggest we do?" she asked.

"I would suggest you and your son go to the United States immediately. Your cases are approved, and if you don't act within ninety days your visas will expire. You will have to start the process over again. When you get there, you can petition for your husband. Spouses are treated with more urgency than say siblings, or siblings-in-law. He should be able to come in about a year's time."

Hertz put his hand into his coat pocket and pulled out a small velvet bag. He placed it on his knee. "Is there some way we can convince you to help us?"

Thomas looked at the bag, now in the palm of Hertz's hand. "I don't know what that is Herr Berlin, or what you mean, but if I were you, I would put that back in my pocket." Thomas stood up, his face reddening. "That's the problem with you people, you think you can buy your way into anywhere." He placed the papers back into their envelope. "Please contact me in writing to let me know if you want the visas for your wife and son issued. Good day." Thomas left the room before Hertz had a chance to stand up.

Berta stared out of the window of the small café. She barely heard the words coming from Hertz's mouth, but his tone was clear. It was that same tone of desperation he used whenever he was trying to convince her to do something she didn't want to do.

Hertz touched her hand. "Have you heard anything I've said?" he asked.

"I have, and I've heard it before. The answer is no. I won't go." She picked up the tiny china cup and sipped at the last of her espresso.

"Why?"

"Because I can't go through this alone. I haven't told you about everything that happened in Vienna after you left. It's too disturbing. And I don't think Kurt can take the separation. And lastly, because I love you and I won't leave you, or let you leave me again. Whatever happens to us happens together." She put her hand on his. "Perhaps you should contact that friend of Halevy."

试戏

Hertz waited for Rousseau impatiently on the same bench in front of the foreign ministry as he had two weeks earlier. The Belgian was forty minutes late. Hertz received a message from him the day before. The message contained neither good nor bad news, just a summons to appear at a specific time and place with instructions to bring another diamond of approximately the same size as the last.

"Don't turn around," came Rousseau's voice from behind him. "After I leave, exit the park and turn left. Walk two blocks. You will see a small restaurant across the street, L'Occidental. Sit at the end of the bar. When the bartender asks you if you want a drink, order a pastis. He will ask you what brand. Tell him you will take whatever M. Rousseau takes. He will return with the drink and a small package. Take the package and leave the stone. Your Belgian citizenship documents will be there, along with the name of the consular officer at the American Embassy you need to contact. The American is away until after Christmas. Don't leave here for five minutes."

"Understood," said Hertz. Five minutes passed feeling like five hours. Hertz turned though he knew Rousseau was gone. He followed Rousseau's directions to L'Occidental and took a seat at the bar. It was past 3:00 and the place was empty.

"May I get you something?" the bartender asked.

"A pastis, please."

The barman smiled. "What brand."

"I'll take whatever M. Rousseau takes," Hertz said.

"Very well."

The bartender disappeared into the kitchen. Hertz looked around at the room. It was a classic Belgian bistro. Dark, cluttered, tables covered in lace. The smell of the evening's offerings wafted in from the kitchen. Hertz put his hand into his coat pocket and clutched the small velvet bag holding the stone. The barman returned, a drink in one hand, his arm held tightly to his side to conceal an envelope. He placed the drink on the table. "As per M. Rousseau."

"Merci," Hertz said. He placed the small bag on the bar, his hand still covering it. Hertz lifted his hand and pushed the bag forward with his fingers. The barman removed the bag discreetly and slid the envelope into Hertz's waiting grasp.

"Good luck, Monsieur."

"Thank you." Hertz slipped the envelope into his pocket then got up to leave.

"Why don't you stay and finish your drink?" the barman said. "It's on Rousseau's tab."

Hertz smiled. "No, thank you, I have too much to do." For

the first time since boarding the train in Switzerland a year earlier, Hertz felt free.

诶我

Kurt stood tentatively at the door of the convent, his knapsack slipping from his shoulder. Elsa went there directly from the hospital after her suicide attempt. The Mandelbaums didn't know how to handle her after all that had happened. Hertz convinced everyone, including the parish's priest, that it would be best for her to be somewhere she felt safe. It hadn't hurt that Hertz provided money to the parish for Elsa's maintenance.

Kurt put off telling Elsa of their imminent departure for over a week, though he visited her every couple of days. He knocked gently on the heavy wood door. A moment later it opened, a tiny nun in a full habit stared up at him.

"Kurt, how nice to see you again. Come in." The sister walked slowly into the shadows in the entry foyer. Kurt followed her. Nearly 100, she carried a broom, which she used as a cane. A rosary hung from her wrist. "Elsa is in the garden. You know the way?"

"Yes," Kurt replied.

The nun took Kurt's hands in hers, mumbling a prayer. "May God bless both of you." The nun's gentle, aged, smile reminded Kurt of his grandmother. "Elsa would not have recovered without you."

"Thank you, sister."

Kurt walked through the hallway to the cloistered garden in the rear of the convent. Elsa wore a long dress with a pattern of tiny, pink flowers against a white background. She knelt in front of a statue of the Virgin, transplanting flowers from a pot into a floral bed. Kurt watched her for a moment, Elsa unaware that he was there. He marveled at how much more beautiful she became each time he saw her. And she appeared at peace.

Kurt knew they were too young for the feelings they had for each other, but felt circumstance compensated for their age. The love they felt was real. He was filled with her as he watched her. Elsa pressed the dark earth around the stem of a seedling, then straightened and stretched. As she caught sight of him, a smile lit her face.

"How long have you been there?"

Kurt helped Elsa to her feet. "A few minutes. I was watching you." He took her in his arms and kissed her gently on the lips. "I love you," he whispered.

"I love you, too," Elsa replied. She laid her head on his chest.

Kurt led her to a stone bench in the corner of the cloister. "I'm sorry I haven't been by in a few days. Things have been hectic."

"That's all right."

Kurt's chest tightened knowing what he had to do. In ten days, he would be on a train to Paris.

"How are your parents?"

"Fine."

Elsa touched his cheek. "I've missed you."

"Me too." Kurt kissed Elsa again, this time more passionately.

Elsa looked around the garden to make sure none of the sisters were watching. She kissed Kurt back, deeply. They sat together for a while, silent, Kurt's arm around her, her head resting on his chest. "Have you heard anything about your visas?" she said, finally.

Kurt's pulse quickened. "Yes."

Elsa moved away. "I suspected." She rose from the little stone bench.

"What do you mean?"

"That's why you haven't come by."

Kurt reached for her hand. Elsa stopped him. "When?"

"Ten days."

Elsa turned and faced the wall at the rear of the garden, her arms wrapped around herself. She shivered despite the warm afternoon. Kurt came up behind her and put his arms around her waist. Elsa trembled. Kurt nestled his face into her hair. "I'm sorry."

Elsa remained silent.

"I know, I promised," Kurt said. "There is nothing I can do. I have to go with them."

Elsa took his hands from her waist and turned, taking another step back. There were tears on her cheeks. "I understand," she said.

"Tell me to stay."

"I won't. I can't." Elsa picked up the small shovel she used to dig the hole for the seedling and put it in the watering bucket. "I'll be all right here with the Sisters."

Kurt reached for her, but she pulled back again. "I'll come back for you. I'll find a way when all this is over. I promise."

Kurt moved toward her. Elsa held out her hand to stop him. "No, it's better if you go now."

"You're angry."

"No, I'm not. I just need to be alone right now."

Kurt reached out one more time. Elsa took another step back. Kurt turned and ran out of the cloister, not stopping till he reached the Boulevard.

钱戋

"That was five days ago?" Saul asked. He cleaned the mud off his football shoes.

"Yes," Kurt said. He did the same, then wiped his hands on the small towel he pulled from his sport bag.

"And you didn't tell me till now? What's wrong with you?"

Kurt stared at the grass under his shadow. "I couldn't talk about it."

Saul thought for a moment. "You can't leave it like this."

"No, I can't. Will you do something for me?"

"What?"

Kurt pulled an envelope from the leather bag. "Take this to her."

Saul looked at Kurt's hand. "Where would I have to deliver this?" he asked.

"To the convent."

Saul hesitated. "Entering a church?" He shook his head in near disbelief. "I've come a long way since eating that first non-kosher ice cream cone."

Kurt laughed and pointed to Saul's uniform. "Yes, you

have."

Saul swiped at Kurt with his towel. "Of course, I will."

Kurt grabbed Saul by the shoulder, pulled him close and embraced him. "You are the brother I never had."

"And you mine."

"You have to promise me we will survive," Kurt said.

"I will. Now you tell me the same."

"I will too. And I promise I will find you when this is over."

They embraced again. Saul put the letter into his pocket and walked off in the direction of the convent disappearing down the street, his tzitzit dancing behind him through his soccer shirt.

Kurt waited impatiently by the door of the apartment among the suitcases packed for their journey. In three more days, they would be gone.

Saul had delivered his note. He waited till Elsa read it, and for her answer. Elsa cried a little and said no. Saul begged her for Kurt's sake to see him one last time. Finally, Elsa relented. Kurt asked that she meet him at his apartment at 3:00 that afternoon when his parents would be out.

Kurt checked his watch. It was 3:05. If the Viennese were anything, they were prompt. Leaning against the door, Kurt sighed. He was sure Elsa had changed her mind. He waited by the door another five minutes then walked to the kitchen and poured a glass of water, gulping it down quickly. Walking back toward the front foyer on the way to his room, Kurt stopped. He opened the door out of desperation and found Elsa there. She looked away from him.

"How long have you been standing here?"

"Since 3:00. I couldn't decide if this was the right thing to do."

He took her hand and led her inside. "Of course, it is."

Elsa sat down on the edge of the corner of the couch and looked around at the many boxes. "Are you taking all this with you?"

"No. Most of it is rented or borrowed. A few boxes are being shipped to Lisbon." Kurt looked at Elsa from across the room. She wore a pale, yellow dress with a matching hat and white gloves. "I will always love you."

"And I, you," Elsa replied. She bowed her head slightly, strands of her blond hair falling over her face.

"I will come back for you."

Elsa smiled and brushed back her hair, exposing her face and smile. "You say that now, but you won't. You'll never come back."

Kurt moved across the room and knelt in front of Elsa. "I promise you, when this is over, I will come for you. I will marry you and bring you to America."

Elsa caressed Kurt's hair, then his cheek. "You're so sweet; innocent and genuine. I know you think you mean this, but who knows how long this will go on, or what will happen to us. You must go. Start a new life."

Kurt got up from the floor. He lifted Elsa from the couch and took her in his arms. "I have to go, I have no choice, I know that, but I also know that I love you and that you love me, and that we are meant to be together. What was it the Mandelbaums called that? That Yiddish word? Beshert?"

Elsa looked up at Kurt and smiled. "Yes, beshert, meant to be."

Kurt looked into her eyes then closed his and leaned forward. Her lips met his. They kissed deeply and passionately. "I will love you forever," he said.

CHAPTER 23

Brussels, Belgium - June 1945

Kurt followed Father Marcel into the convent in the Maalbeek district on the outskirts of Brussels. The interior of the building was both spotless and Spartan, the whitewashed walls empty of decoration save for crucifixes centered on each. Nuns in habits scurried in silence through the hallways.

Kurt stood silently behind Father Marcel in the vestibule. A heavyset nun approached the priest and spoke to him in a low voice, barely above a whisper. Father Marcel whispered his response in her ear. She nodded and glanced at Kurt. "Follow me," she said.

They walked down a long hallway to a tiny chapel at the rear of the convent that opened onto a tiny garden awash with the colors of spring flowers and the gentle sound of running water. Kurt looked for the fountain that produced the sound but couldn't locate it. In the corner next to a statue of the Virgin sat a small figure, the rosary wrapped around her right hand, her head down. She slipped the beads one by one through her fingers, mumbling one prayer after another.

The nun who led them to the garden touched the shoulder of her praying Sister. "Forgive me Sister Marion for interrupting your devotions. The men you agreed to speak with are here."

Sister Marion looked up at Kurt and Father Marcel. Her expression was one of inconsolable sadness. She nodded and rose from her kneeling position in front of the statue of the Virgin and cleared her throat.

"Thank you for agreeing to see us," Father Marcel said, bowing slightly to the praying Sister. Kurt followed his lead. Sister Marion nodded her head and gestured toward the stone bench in front of them.

"Only if you will sit with us," Father Marcel said.

Sister Marion nodded again and sat down on the edge of the bench tentatively; her lips still moving in silent devotion, the beads continuing to slip through her fingers. After a long moment, she stopped and said in a shallow, raspy voice. "I haven't spoken in some time. It is my penance. I have agreed to speak with you only so that I might help to put the souls of my sisters at rest. Afterward, I will never speak again."

Father Marcel looked at Kurt and nodded.

"Thank you, Sister," Kurt said. "I am trying to find someone." He took the photograph of Elsa from his jacket pocket and handed it to her. "Do you recognize her?"

A tear slipped from Sister Marion's eye and slid slowly down her cheek. "Yes, of course, she was our angel. Elsa Graz. Sister Jeanine Josef brought her to us. She was to become a novice."

Kurt felt a sense of betrayal upon learning that Elsa planned to become a nun. They had promised themselves to each other. "Do you know what happened to her?" he asked.

"No," Sister Marion answered.

Kurt was confused by the sister's answer. "Was Elsa there that day, the day the Germans blew up the convent?"

"Yes."

"Please sister, I don't understand. You said you don't know what happened to her, but she was there. What happened that day?" Kurt looked into the nun's eyes. Sister Marion had the same look in hers as Saul had in his, the day before. It was as if her memory was alive. She spoke haltingly. The other Sister placed her hands on Sister Marion's shoulders. Father Marcel took her hand in his.

"I was in the cloister at the back of the convent, hidden from view," Sister Marion began. "I was making devotions to the Virgin, as I do every day. There was shouting from a bullhorn. I was terrified. I hid behind the hedges, against the back of the garden. I could hear what was happening, but I couldn't see much."

Kurt recalled the lovely, little cloister.

"There were soldiers, many of them. They were shouting to come out with our hands up. The Sisters were running around trying to hide our Jews." Sister Marion looked at Father Marcel, then touched his cheek. "We were protecting them. We had more than twenty hiding in the basement. During the day, they would come up a few at a time for some sunlight, usually in the morning. When the Nazis came, the Reverend Mother went to the doors and tried to prevent them from entering, at least until we could get everyone back into the basement."

Sister Marion stopped and took a deep breath. Her fragile body heaved. She mumbled a short prayer and slipped a rosary bead through her fingers. "The leader of these men pushed his way in. I saw him through the hedges. He was very tall and muscular. I was terrified. The Reverend Mother demanded that he stop, that he was invading a house of God. He laughed and raised his arm to strike her. My sisters rushed to her from behind and pulled her back before he could."

"Excuse me, Sister," interrupted Kurt. "Did the Nazis know that you were hiding Jews in the basement?"

"I don't think so."

"What happened next?" Father Marcel asked.

"Their leader, he wore the uniform of the SS, demanded to know if Elsa Graz was among us. No one said a word. He shouted again, 'Where is Elsa Graz?' He began destroying things, toppling statues, ripping crucifixes off the walls. He cursed God. He said Hitler was his God, the only true God. He threatened to kill us one by one, until we told him where Elsa was."

Sister Marion stopped again. She shuddered, mumbled a prayer and kissed her rosary. "Then he grabbed Sister Felice Maria and tore her habit from her head, pushed her to the ground, his gun pointed at her. 'I will start with this one,' he shouted. Sister Jeanine Josef stepped forward to help her. He struck Sister Jeanine. She fell to the floor." Sister Marion raised her arm and shouted, imitating the SS officer, "Do you think I am not serious!" The nun's eyes focused far off in the distance.

"I remained in the garden. I was too terrified to move. One of my sisters, may God rest her, Sister Veronica, knew I was there, and she kept her hand behind her signaling to me to stay there. That's when Elsa walked forward and revealed herself. 'I am Elsa Graz,' she said. She removed her habit." Sister Marion touched her hand to her own head. "She had shorn her hair, but her beauty, her radiant soul, shined through. 'Please leave my sisters alone. I will go with you,' Elsa said. 'Leave my sisters in peace.'"

"The SS man laughed again, this time even more hysterically. 'Take her!' he ordered his men. Sister Jeanine pushed herself up from the floor. She begged him to let her go with Elsa. The monster slapped her hard across her face with the back of his hand. She bled from her mouth. 'Fine, then you will share her fate!' he screamed. 'Take both of them!' he commanded his men. They pulled them out of the convent roughly. 'Round up the rest of them and tie them up in the main chapel! Lock the doors then level the building!' he ordered."

Sister Marion began to cry. "I didn't know what to do. I knew I couldn't help them. I thought to join them, but I was terrified. I escaped through the secret door in the wall at the back of the garden to the building behind the convent then through to the street. I came around to our street and hid toward the back of the crowd that had gathered. The soldiers aimed their tank at our convent, and they fired, and they fired, until it was nothing but rubble. With the first few shots, the screaming was terrible. Then I heard my sisters praying, singing. After a few more shots the singing stopped, but the firing continued."

The story devastated Kurt. He tried to refocus his mind, the images of what the Sister recounted for them playing out in his mind, the quiet sisters he had known, buried in the rubble of the convent." Finally, Kurt asked, "Elsa survived the bombing?"

"Yes, I believe so, but I don't know what became of her, or Sister Jeanine Josef," the Sister replied. "Now you understand why I don't speak. In my silence, in this silent place, I can hear their voices screaming and praying to our Lord, forever."

CHAPTER 24

Brussels, Belgium - May 10, 1940

K urt stared at the clock ticking gently beside his bed. 6:00 AM. It was the day of their departure. On his way to the bathroom, he stopped in the kitchen and took a slice of the Mandelbrot his mother made the day before. He bit into it, the almond flavor soothing, reminding him of his grandmother's kitchen. Kurt wondered how his grandparents were, if they were still in Vienna, then absentmindedly turned on the radio.

At first, he wasn't sure he heard the announcer on the radio correctly, so he turned up the volume. The Germans had crossed the Belgian border at several points. They had destroyed the Belgian Air Force on the ground. Kurt ran down the hall to his parent's bedroom.

"Mother, father!" he banged on the door. "Get up. The Nazi's are here!"

The door flung open, his father standing in front of him in bedclothes. "What!"

"The radio! Come listen!" screamed Kurt.

Hertz ran down the hallway, Berta close behind him. The announcer repeated the news. "We have to get out of here, immediately. Get dressed!" he shouted. "Kurt, call Halevy and tell him what's happened, if he doesn't already know. See if he can send his car, if he doesn't need it himself."

"I thought you arranged for a taxi!" Berta called out from the bedroom.

Hertz laughed. "Really, my darling, do you think he's

showing up?" Hertz turned to Kurt, "son, go now, get dressed."

"Yes," Kurt said.

"Berta, where are the diamonds?"

"In my bag."

"Bring them here. We need to sew them into your coat. A handbag isn't safe enough in this chaos."

"We don't have time for that."

"Then we need to split them up."

"Do you think that's wise?"

"We have no choice."

"What's Halevy's number?" Kurt shouted.

"It's in my address book next to the phone!" Hertz called back to Kurt, running back down the hallway.

Kurt picked up the small, black-leather bound notebook from the phone stand. He looked first under H then J for Halevy and Jacques but found nothing. Then Kurt looked under S for Sam and found Halevy's name and number under the subscript Marianne's father. He dialed and waited for the ringtone for what seemed like an eternity.

"Halo," came a voice roused out of a deep sleep.

"Monsieur Halevy, this is Kurt Berlin, Hertz Berlin's son."

"Who?"

"Your son-in-law, Sam, his nephew, Kurt."

"Oh sorry, yes, of course, excuse me, is something wrong?" Kurt heard the first distant siren of the day.

"Yes, I'm afraid there is," Kurt hesitated. "The Germans have invaded."

There was silence on the line for a moment then a crackling on the wires. "How do you know this?" Halevy asked.

"It's on the radio."

"Hold for a moment, please."

"Of course," Kurt said. He heard the radio at Halevy's house through the phone

"Thank you for letting me know."

"Wait, Monsieur Halevy, my father asked me to ask you something."

"Let me have the phone," Hertz said, entering the kitchen.

Kurt handed the phone to Hertz. "Halevy, are you all right?"

"Considering."

"I need to ask a favor."

"Yes, of course."

"Are you planning on fleeing today?"

"I don't suppose so. Not yet, anyway."

"We were to leave for Le Havre this morning. Can we borrow your car and driver to the station?"

"Of course, I'll call him and call you right back. What time do you need him?"

"Now."

"I will be right back to you."

Hertz replaced the handset on the receiver. He took a deep breath. "Son, we have a very large responsibility for you."

"What father?"

Hertz pulled several small velvet bags from his pockets. "These are our tickets out of this hell. Each of these bags is filled with diamonds." He opened one and poured its contents into his hand. The cut stones sparkled. Kurt stood with his mouth open.

"You will need to carry some of these bags in your clothing. We have to split these up, in case your mother or I are stopped and searched. Hide them deep in your pockets and don't look nervous about it. A thief gives himself away by his face."

"Yes, father."

The phone rang. Hertz ran to it. "Alors," he said

"It's Jacques. My driver will be at your building in thirty minutes. Wait by the window. You know my car, watch for it. Cable my daughter in London when you get to the United States. The driver has her address for you. Godspeed."

Kurt watched for Halevy's car as Hertz and Berta shifted things within their luggage. They each would take two suitcases. There were three more initially, but they would need to move quickly, and each had only two hands.

Kurt took the pair of white gloves Elsa gave him the day before, the pair she was wearing the day they met on the Kindertransport, from his pockets. He had shoved them there before his mother could see them. He put the small velvet bags containing the diamonds into them for good luck, two into each, then shoved them back into the bottom of his pockets. He slipped the photo Elsa gave him into the inside pocket of his coat, then scanned the street through the window. A long black Mercedes pulled up in front of the building. "I think he's here!" Kurt called to Hertz.

Hertz looked out the window. "Yes, that's him. Now grab your bags and let's go. And walk out on your right foot."

"Is this really the time for superstitions?" Berta said, taking two of the suitcases.

"Today, we need all the help we can get," Hertz responded, carefully stepping over the threshold right foot first.

Halevy's driver waited with doors and trunk open. He grabbed Berta's bags first and placed them in the trunk, then Kurt's, filling the space.

"Put these in the front with you," Hertz said. "I'll squeeze in back with them."

"Of course. Which station are you going to?" asked Maurice.

"Brussels South," replied Hertz.

"We need to hurry," added Berta.

"Of course, madam."

Hertz looked out of the window as they turned out of their street onto the main boulevard. Chaos was everywhere. People were running, not walking at their usual pace. In the distance, they heard sirens, many of them. There were police and uniformed gendarme with their guns drawn.

Kurt sat between Hertz and Berta, his face gray. Hertz put his hand on Kurt's knee. "You have to be strong now. Keep your wits about you. We will be away from here in a few hours."

Kurt hesitated a moment. "And if we're not?"

"We can't think like that."

Hertz gazed out of the window again. What if Kurt was right? As they proceeded down the Boulevard toward the center of Brussels, the number of people on the street carrying suitcases increased exponentially. Traffic began to build.

"What time is your train?" Maurice asked.

Hertz looked at his watch, 7:45, "11:00," he said

"We have plenty of time."

"Normally, yes," Hertz said. "I'm not taking chances today."

Maurice slammed the breaks. "Sorry," he said. "Are you all

right back there?"

"Yes," they replied.

"What happened?" Berta asked.

"A woman with a child ran in front of us."

Hertz looked at his watch again, 8:10, "perhaps, the side streets would be better."

"I don't think so, sir."

A few minutes later traffic began moving again. Then a couple of blocks later it slowed to a crawl. There were gendarmes on every corner. The driver opened the window and called out to one.

The officer approached them. "Yes?"

"What's the problem?" Maurice asked.

"Where are you going?" said the gendarme, peering into the car.

"Brussels South Station. My client has passage to Le Havre at 11:00."

The gendarme laughed. "Not today he doesn't. Most trains are canceled. They're being diverted to bring troops to the front. Also, there's a blockade two blocks up, and only official vehicles are permitted past there."

Hertz felt the panic rise in his throat. For Kurt and Berta's sake, he had to remain calm. "Perhaps, we should take the tram?"

"Do you think they're running?" Berta asked.

"Officer," Hertz said.

The gendarme ducked down to look in the window. "Yes?"

"Are the trams running?"

"Some of them,"

"Thank you."

"What are you thinking?" Maurice asked.

"We have to get to the station. The tram stop is two blocks ahead. Could you help us with the bags?"

The driver hesitated. "We could try to bribe the police at the checkpoint."

Hertz looked at Berta and Kurt. Kurt's face was white with fear.

"It's worth a try," Berta said.

"All right," Hertz said. "Pull the car to the side and let's see what we can't do." He reached into his coat pocket and took out one of the small velvet bags. Hertz poured the contents into his hand, selected three small diamonds of about a half-karat each and poured the balance of the stones back into the bag. "Take this," he said to Kurt, handing it to him.

"Be careful," Berta said.

Hertz walked the two blocks toward the security checkpoint slowly and deliberately, scrutinizing the three men there. All held guns. He needed to determine who was in charge. Hertz watched as one of the men called to another to speak with the driver of the car at the front of the line. The second man leaned into the car and took something from the driver. He straightened up, looked over some documents then gestured for the remaining gendarmes to move the sawhorses and let the car pass. He then waved the first soldier to the next car, took a cigarette out of his pocket and lit it. That was Hertz's mark. Hertz approached him slowly and with a smile. The gendarme looked up, no emotion registering on his face, his rifle in defensive position.

"Hello, good morning, Captain," Hertz called out, his arms visible, his palms open to the man in a gesture of surrender. The two small stones were in his pocket.

"Stop, stop there," the gendarme called back.

Hertz did as he was told. The gendarme approached him. He was shorter than Hertz, perhaps thirty years old. His eyes looked tired and he had stubble on his face. Hertz tried to decipher his rank from his uniform but couldn't. He knew nothing about Belgian military insignia.

"What is your business here, sir!" the gendarme barked. "Are you not aware that we are facing a national emergency!"

"Of course, Captain…" Hertz said, averting his gaze.

"That would be, Lieutenant." The young man stuck a cigarette in his mouth.

"Sorry…Lieutenant…"

"What's your business?" the Lieutenant said, interrupting Hertz.

Hertz modulated his voice to be as solicitous as possible. "I, my family, we need to get to the station. We have a train to Le Havre at 11:00."

The gendarme raised his eyebrows. "Do you really think that trains are leaving for pleasure this morning?" He struck a match and lit the cigarette dangling from his lips.

Hertz looked at his feet. "With all due respect sir, I am not sure, but we need to find out." Hertz raised his head and made eye contact. "We can only do that at the station."

The gendarme hesitated. "Let me see your tickets."

Hertz reached into his pocket and removed the large envelope containing his documents. The Lieutenant looked through the papers.

"You hold a Belgian passport. But I can tell by your accent, you're not Belgian." The Lieutenant inspected the tickets. "You're on the way to Le Havre to make your way to the United States, aren't you? Where are you from?"

"Vienna," Hertz replied, slipping his hand into his pocket and the removing two stones.

"Jews."

Hertz said nothing.

The Lieutenant moved closer. He stuck his finger in Hertz's face. "We saved your lives by accepting you as refugees, and at the first sign of trouble, you run."

"Lieutenant, please, my wife and son are in the car. He's only 17."

The gendarme took another step toward Hertz. He raised the butt of his rifle and pushed it into Hertz's chest. "He's old enough to fight, as are you."

"The Germans will kill us, we're Jews. Please, I can make it worth your while." Hertz opened his hand.

The soldier looked down at the stones, then stared menacingly into Hertz's eyes without saying a word.

"Please lieutenant, I know what this is like. I fought in the last war. Do you have children?"

The lieutenant stared at Hertz, his expression one of distrust. "No." He blew smoke into Hertz's face.

"Someday you may. Please let me give these to you and

please let us pass through. My son's life depends on it."

The Belgian took a last drag on his cigarette then crushed it with the toe of his boot. "Put them in my pocket."

Hertz dropped the two stones carefully into the side pocket of the soldier's jacket.

"Get back into your car. When you come to the head of the line tell the soldier that you are on government business and have him call me over."

It took nearly an hour to reach the front of the checkpoint. The guard shouted perfunctorily, "access to the center of the city is restricted, turn around! Turn here to the left and proceed to the next street then turn left again!"

"Excuse me," Hertz said.

"Didn't you hear me?" asked the guard.

"We are on government business. May I see the officer in charge please?"

The soldier looked into the car. "Government business? With your wife and this boy? And all this luggage? Hahaha, move along."

"What's this!" called out the Lieutenant.

"This fellow thinks he can fool me into letting him through."

"Let me see," said the Lieutenant. He walked around the car to the side where Hertz was sitting and signaled for him to roll down his window. "Give me your papers."

Hertz handed the papers to the Lieutenant. He looked them over haphazardly to impress the other guard, then stuck his head into the window. Hertz smelled alcohol on his breath. "I will let you go, but it will take another stone. Those two are small."

Hertz knew he had no choice. He reached into his pocket and removed the third stone and discretely placed it into the Lieutenant's hand as the Lieutenant handed him back their papers.

"Let this car through!" he shouted. Two guards moved the barrier. Halevy's driver put the car into first gear and rolled forward. Hertz felt like Moses at the Red Sea.

CHAPTER 25

Brussels, Belgium - June 1945

McClain resumed the interrogation where he left off the prior Friday, but this time without Rosenthaller. Kurt was glad Rosenthaller wasn't there after what he had asked him to do. He dreaded the thought of what was about to come. Kurt knew this was likely to be the most difficult interrogation for him to translate.

"What was your position with the SS here in Brussels?" McClain asked.

"Was war ihr SS Rang hier in Brüssel?" Kurt translated.

"I was Gauleiter in charge of logistics," von Hauptmann answered.

"What were your specific responsibilities?"

"I was in charge of ferreting out enemies of the Reich."

"Were you specifically charged with the handling of communists and socialists, as you were in Vienna?"

"No," von Hauptmann smiled. "I was promoted. I was in charge of handling Jews."

Kurt's spine stiffened. He willed his face to show no emotion. He had to be careful. McClain was von Hauptmann's ally now. Kurt would consider going above Rosenthaller to register a complaint about McClain and the interrogations later. He needed to witness the testimony without incident. Then he would do as Rosenthaller asked to get his parents' citizenship. Afterward, when the time was right, despite whatever consequences he might face for his participation in their plot, he would expose McClain and Rosenthaller.

"When did you arrive in Brussels?" McClain asked.

"Wann sind Sie in Brüssel angekommen?" Kurt translated.

"Im Juli 1940."

"What was your first responsibility?"

Von Hauptmann became more animated. He sat forward in his chair, his elbows on the table, using his hands to emphasize his words. "We forced the Jews to set up a Jewish Council. We used the Council to supply us with information, and to help us carry out our objectives."

"Did your experiences in Vienna, and the skills you developed there, help you to execute your responsibilities in Brussels?"

Kurt realized this was no longer an interrogation, but rather a job interview. He translated McClain's question.

"Oh yes, very much so. I was an expert at accounting. Whether it was artwork, or jewelry, or Jews, didn't matter. Except now we operated in the open. In Vienna we operated behind the scenes. Our methods of persuasion were based on the same principles we developed there though. Except here we kept the Jews calm by leading them to believe they could trust us."

McClain leaned forward over the table. The image disturbed Kurt. McClain and von Hauptmann looked like two buddies huddled over a football roster. "That's very interesting. It's not like they didn't know what your attitudes were toward them."

Kurt recalled the blindness with which Jews in Brussels viewed the Germans. Even after the crush of tens of thousands of refugees from Germany and Austria over six years, the news reports and newsreels, they couldn't bring themselves to see the truth. He translated calmly.

Von Hauptmann chuckled. "Colonel, I learned a critical lesson early on, back in the first war. No one wants to face the truth. In the trenches in 1916, soldiers would watch their comrades charge into no man's land to be mowed down by machine guns, yet ten minutes later they would do the same, somehow thinking they would survive."

McClain nodded. "I agree with you, Joachim." McClain's use of von Hauptmann's first name nearly derailed Kurt. He knew he wasn't imagining their comradery. "I saw it myself. I was in France in 1918."

Kurt fought with himself to continue. He had to do this, for Elsa, for Saul, for his parents, and in some way for himself. If he lost self-control von Hauptmann won. He couldn't allow that. "The Jews were no different," he translated. "Somehow, the Belgian Jews thought they wouldn't suffer the same fate as the German Jews or the French, and so on." Von Hauptmann sat back and smiled in satisfaction as Kurt translated his despicable thoughts.

"How did you develop this sense of trust?" asked McClain. He waited for Kurt's translation, his eyes on von Hauptmann.

"We approached them with lots of Mittleuropan charm. We assembled their leadership and told them they would become a self-governing authority. They would control their own destiny."

"Where did you draw the leadership pool from?"

"Prominent members of their community. Rabbis, educators, businessmen. The businessmen were particularly pliable. They were often more selfish than the others, and thought they could protect themselves, their families, and their holdings by cooperating. They were also generous with us. They had what to be generous with." Von Hauptmann chuckled. "Funny how they never realized, many not until the very end, that if we wanted something, we would just take it."

Kurt pleaded with his heart to slow down. It was as if von Hauptmann was a ghost spilling secrets about the world Kurt had lived in. He remembered how his father and mother spoke in muted tones when Jacques Halevy was commanded to serve on the Jewish Council. The Jews hated the council but pitied those forced to serve. When Halevy suddenly disappeared, the hushed gossip was that the Nazis had provided him with an exit visa to join his family in exchange for his mansion.

"Ask him if he hates the Jews," McClain ordered.

Kurt was caught completely off guard by McClain's question. The answer was obvious. Why would he even ask it? "What? I mean, yes, sir," Kurt blurted out. "Hassen Sie die Juden?"

"Natürlich waren sie wie Ungeziefer. Ein Krebsgeschür für das Reich und Europa."

Kurt swallowed hard, then translated von Hauptmann's invective. "Of course, they were a cancer on the Reich and Europe."

McClain smirked then asked his next question. "Were you responsible for organizing the deportations?" Kurt was sure McClain couldn't be more nonchalant. Perhaps it was because McClain thought this interrogation would never see the light of day.

"Yes," von Hauptmann said.

Kurt felt the bile rise in his throat. Von Hauptmann had just confessed to mass murder, yet McClain hadn't batted an eye. After what felt like an eternity, McClain resumed his questioning.

"Do you view your participation as a function of executing your duties or as a matter of conviction?"

With bitterness in both his mouth and his heart, Kurt translated. He concentrated on the statement so that he would remember it verbatim later. He wanted to use it as an example of McClain's moral disingenuousness later.

"Both. But it wasn't quite that simple," von Hauptman answered. He stopped for a moment and considered what he was trying to say. "I was responsible for executing policy. I didn't make the policy myself, though I agreed with and believed in our policy."

Von Hauptmann was being very specific. He wanted McClain to understand his motivations. "My charge was to execute policy, exactly as in Vienna. Whatever I was told to do, I did. If they told me to collect money from the Jews, I did. If they told me to do a census, I did. If they told me to deport them, I did."

"But you believed in and supported the policy?"

"Yes."

"You said in Vienna all the communists you caught were sent to Dachau or Mauthausen, officially. I think you and I both know what you meant. You killed them."

"Yes."

"So, you didn't execute your orders then, if they were sent to a camp?"

"I said I executed policy, not orders. Sometimes Colonel, orders and policy are not the same, and one must know when."

McClain nodded. "Was there ever a time when you executed policy, not orders in your capacity in Brussels?"

"There was, of course."

"Can you give me an example, please?"

Von Hauptmann thought for a moment. "Usually the two coincided. There is a situation though that comes to mind. It was in July of 1943. My orders were to round up all Jews who were not Belgian nationals for deportation east. They were to be sent to the east first. We had information on a large number of these people. This included children who left the Reich before the war began and were brought to Belgium awaiting emigration to Britain. We knew from Belgian visa records that not all these children had left for Britain. I needed to find any of these children who might still remain."

"You created a dragnet for children?" McClain asked in clarification.

"Yes, exactly."

Kurt's became lightheaded. He knew he would well have been the subject of that dragnet. Everything Kurt had learned in the past few days, from Saul, from Sister Marion, was flashing in his mind. He took a deep breath and translated what von Hauptmann said, slowly and with surgical accuracy.

"But you were executing your orders?" McClain said.

"Sie führt ihre Aufträge aus." Kurt translated.

"Yes."

"Then when were you executing policy?"

Von Hauptmann considered McClain's question slowly. "I was tracking down one particular child who we were quite certain was still in Brussels."

"What difference could one child make?"

Von Hauptmann raised his eyebrows, incredulous at the suggestion. "My orders were to account for all of them. I either had to find her or determine where she had gone. We found her in a convent not terribly far from here."

Kurt suppressed a gag. Truth was about to crash into him like a high-speed train.

"Our orders were to keep our hands off the convents and churches. The Fuehrer had promised the Pope he would respect the Church's property and position. Our policy was different. We would not tolerate anyone harboring of Jews."

Kurt held up his hand to stop von Hauptmann. "Warten Sie," he said. Kurt needed to compose himself. After stalling momentarily by jotting down some words on a pad to appear he was determining the proper and exact translation, Kurt calmed himself. It would be over soon. Even Rosenthaller couldn't condone this. Kurt translated for McClain.

"After I found the girl and accounted for her; she had to be accounted for," von Hauptmann said, punctuating his words by pounding his forefinger against the table—Kurt did the same—"I rounded up the nuns who perpetrated this crime against us, locked them in their chapel and bombarded the building with tank fire until it collapsed. They were hiding a Jewish child. That Colonel is the difference between executing orders and policy." As Kurt finished, Von Hauptman sat back, crossed his legs and rested his hands in his lap, a smug smile on his face.

Kurt looked into von Hauptmann's icy blue eyes and saw only evil. He had admitted to mass murder. Kurt realized ironically, that von Hauptmann didn't know Jews were hiding in the basement of the convent when he destroyed it. "Colonel McClain?"

"Yes, Berlin?"

"May I be excused for a moment?" Kurt asked. "I'm need to use the bathroom."

"Of course. We're done for now, anyway."

Kurt got up; his legs wobbly. He forced himself to walk proudly by sheer will slowly to the door, then picked up his pace to the bathroom. He went into the first stall and vomited his lunch into the toilet, sank to the floor and wept silently. Kurt had found his murderer. This changed everything.

CHAPTER 26

Brussels, Belgium - September 1940

Hertz, Berta and Kurt got as far as the train station that day in May. There was chaos everywhere. The government took most of the trains to transport men to the front. Anything moving in the direction of the French border was already packed, and only people with government documents were permitted to board. Hertz tried to bribe one of the officials and was nearly arrested. The official told him he had five minutes to disappear or he would arrest all three of them.

They left the station. Hertz tried to find a driver who would take them to the French border by car. Even his bags of diamonds couldn't convince anyone. What good were the diamonds if one was dead, or in a Nazi prison. They walked back to the tram and took it home and unpacked the boxes they'd left there. Who knew how long they would be stuck there now?

试试

Hertz waited patiently for Halevy outside his office as Halevy's huddled with his secretary. He thumbed through an old Belgian photo magazine from before the Nazi's arrival. He found the articles laughable. How naive life was just four months earlier.

"Hertz," Halevy said, his secretary leaving the room. "How are you, my friend?"

Hertz tossed the magazine onto the coffee table. "All is well, considering. What did you want to see me about?"

"I have something to tell you, top secret. Come into my office."

Hertz followed Halevy into the sunny room overlooking the private garden in the rear of the townhouse. He liked Jacques. Moreover, he found Jacques refreshing, a trait not widely encountered in Brussels these days. Even in the current situation, Halevy maintained both a sense of calmness and a positive attitude. "Tell me, then," Hertz said, settling into the black leather couch opposite Jacques' desk.

"I have secured myself an exit visa."

Hertz jumped to his feet and grabbed Jacques hand with both of his hands. "Congratulations! How? When?"

Jacques offered Hertz a cigarette and took one for himself. He lit both with an elegantly engraved silver lighter. "I leave for Casablanca by way of France, within the week. From Casablanca, I'll take a steamer to Dublin. From there I will make my way to London. Jacques leaned against the desk. He took a deep drag on his cigarette and exhaled slowly. "I will miss these though. No Galois in London these days."

Hertz considered whether to ask Halevy how he came to get his visa, but he didn't want to compromise him. Halevy finished his cigarette and stamped it out in a crystal ashtray on his desk. "I wanted to wait till I had all my papers to tell you. I'm hoping this information will help you."

"Please," Hertz said, grateful that Jacques offered this help.

"It seems one of our SS Captains is quite corrupt."

"I'm listening." Halevy settled into the soft, down filled couch.

"We, the Jewish Council, we meet with the Germans every week. They pressure us for information to tighten the noose around the community's neck, and to extort from us what little we still have. One day, about a month ago, one of the SS Captains sent his aides back to their headquarters and ordered the rest of the council to leave. He's quite presumptuous, this Captain. Some insignificant minor aristocrat. He wanted to speak to me privately."

"You agreed of course." Hertz chuckled.

"What choice did I have?" Jacques smiled. "I wondered

only, what it might cost me?"

"And what did it cost?"

"My house."

Hertz nodded his head. "Really."

Halevy smiled. "He can be quite charming this Nazi, in that clumsy manner minor nobility assumes." Jacques imitated the Nazi's gestures as he mocked him speaking. "He told me how much he loved my house, what a peaceful place it was, particularly the garden. Then he asked me where my family was. I told him that I was quite sure he knew. He asked me if I wanted to join them in London. I said yes, of course, but that was, as he knew, impossible, given the laws restricting Jewish travel and my position with the council. He said those problems could be circumvented."

Hertz was incredulous, but at the same time hopeful that he might benefit from Jacques' information. "What did he suggest?"

"That he could supply me with documents, for a price."

Hertz gestured around the room.

"Yes, and a substantial sum, in diamonds."

Hertz understood. "When are you leaving?"

"In a few days. I can't tell you more than that."

"I understand."

"Hertz, I told you this because we're family, and I believe this Nazi can get you out of here. He will do virtually anything for the right amount of money."

"I have to think about it. It's very dangerous. It's not just me, it's Berta and Kurt."

Jacques leaned closer to Hertz. "What other options do you have?"

"None, other than to make our way slowly to the Spanish border and try to slip over it."

"That's even more dangerous."

"You may be right." Hertz got up from the couch. He shook Halevy's hand. "Let me think about it."

"You have to let me know by tomorrow."

One week later, Hertz waited in the park opposite SS head-quarters. He saw a light go on in the window on the third floor at the west end of the building. He waited another moment for the window to open. That was the signal. Hertz looked at his watch, midnight exactly. If the Germans were anything, they were punctual. He slipped into the side entrance of the building as per Halevy's instructions and went directly up to the third floor. The door from the stairwell opened into a wide marble hallway with offices lining each side. The hallway was dark, save for night lighting. Hertz proceeded down the hall toward the light coming under the door of one office. He tapped on the door lightly.

"Heil Hitler," came a voice from inside.

Hertz was supposed to respond with Heil Hitler and the phrase, "I have a delivery for Captain von Hauptmann." He froze and thought about leaving but knew there was no choice. He had to do this. "Heil Hitler," he said. "I have a delivery for Captain von Hauptmann."

"Come in, the door is open."

Hertz turned the knob and swung the door inward, slowly, his heart in his mouth. Von Hauptmann was standing by the window behind his desk holding a lit cigarette. Von Hauptmann rested the cigarette in a crystal ashtray on top of the desk. Hertz recognized the ashtray. It had sat on Halevy's desk previously.

"Jacques sent me," Hertz said. He took two steps into the room and closed the door.

"How do you know Halevy?" von Hauptmann said, looking Hertz over.

"His daughter is married to my brother."

"And he told you what?"

"That you could provide documents for the right price."

Von Hauptmann walked around the desk. He leaned against it crossing his arms. Even in this position, he was taller than Hertz and imposing in both size and uniform. "Why should I help you, Jew?"

Hertz knew he had to choose his words very, very carefully.

"Because I can pay you handsomely for your services," Hertz replied. "No other reason. It's a business transaction."

"How do you propose to compensate me for my services?" Von Hauptmann picked up the remainder of the cigarette smoldering in the ashtray, took a long drag, the ash nearly reaching his lips, then snuffed out what remained. "Halevy had something I wanted. What do you have?"

Hertz swallowed hard. "I can compensate you well." Hertz reached into his pocket and pulled out another of the endless stream of black velvet bags that carried the only currency that could buy the attention of men like von Hauptmann. He opened it and poured the contents into his palm. Hertz held his palm out to von Hauptmann, the five small, elegantly cut stones catching the light from the fixture hanging above them.

"That's not nearly enough," von Hauptmann said.

"There's more if you will provide me with what I need."

"And what exactly is that?"

"Three Aryan passports and exit and entry documents from here to Lisbon."

Von Hauptmann laughed again. "And you think you will be safe there? How many times will you run from us? You Jews are so foolish. Don't you understand? You can't escape."

Something about von Hauptmann's voice was familiar, echoing back from deep inside Hertz's memory. He looked up slightly, searching von Hauptmann's face for familiarity. Behind the mask of middle age, was someone Hertz was sure he had once known. "From Lisbon, I can go to America."

Von Hauptmann looked directly into Hertz's eyes. He pointed to his desk. "Put the stones there. Come back in two days' time. Bring me twenty-five more like that, the finest quality. I intend to inspect them closely. Now get out of here Jew, before I change my mind."

Hertz slipped into their apartment quietly. He took off his shoes then checked on Berta and Kurt. Both were sleeping. Closing the doors to both bedrooms he moved stealthily down the hall to the living room, flicked on the lamp next to the credenza and slipped open the bottom drawer. Inside was the photo album Berta brought with her from Vienna, despite Hertz's instructions not to take anything that might make the Germans suspicious. If he found what he was looking for, the risk would have been worthwhile.

Hertz sat down on the floor, his back against the wooden doors of the credenza and leafed through the photo album. It was a collection of eerie images from his past. Hertz ran his hand over a slightly torn photo of his mother and his sisters. If he ever got to America, he would begin his search for them. He had to focus on what he needed to do now, get himself, his wife and his son out of Europe.

Hertz turned the page and saw the image he was seeking. He removed it from the album. It confirmed what he had suspected earlier.

试戈

Two nights later Hertz returned to SS headquarters, rechecking his pocket for the bag of diamonds. He reached the third floor and walked quickly down the empty hall toward von Hauptmann's office. He checked his watch, midnight on the nose. He tapped on the door.

"Enter," came the voice from inside.

Hertz took a deep breath and pushed open the door. Von Hauptman was sitting at his desk, smoking. "Let me see what you've got," the Nazi said, the smoke swirling around him as he exhaled.

"Let me see my papers first, the passports," Hertz demanded.

Von Hauptmann stared at Hertz for a moment. "You've got balls for a Jew. Usually, by now, the buyer is crying. Very well." Von Hauptmann pulled three official Reich passports from inside his desk. He held them up one by one. "All that's missing are the photos."

Hertz reached across the desk. Von Hauptmann pulled the passports back and slid them into an open draw. "Not so fast. Let me see the stones."

Hertz passed the bag with the stones to Von Hauptmann. The Nazi pulled a loupe from his pocket and examined them one by one. Hertz felt as if an eternity was passing. He didn't trust von Hauptmann. He could have someone waiting in the hallway to kill him, or outside the building to arrest him. Not even in the trenches in the Great War, with artillery landing every few moments while bullets whizzed by his head, had Hertz ever felt more helpless, more vulnerable.

Finally, von Hauptmann finished. He placed the loupe on the desk and rose from his chair. "Excellent job."

"Give me my documents," Hertz said, his legs weak from fear.

"Of course," von Hauptmann said and reached into the drawer. He pulled out a pistol. "You foolish Jew. Did you really think I would help you for this price? Bring me twenty-five more like this, and the documents are yours," he said. "Now, get out of here before I shoot you and end your miserable life, once and for all."

Hertz thought to charge him and grab the gun, but he knew he didn't have the strength to overpower von Hauptmann. He backed up toward the door and opened it, slipping out without turning his back on the SS man. Once in the hallway, Hertz turned and ran.

试戈

"This is too dangerous. You can't go back there." Berta said, nearly hysterical. "If anything, we need to go into hiding, now. How could you go to see him to begin with, and without telling me!"

Hertz demurred. "We have no other choice. There's no way out of here. We wouldn't make it as far as the French border without proper papers."

Berta wiped her eyes. "It's hopeless." She crumpled into the corner of the couch. "Please don't do this. I can handle almost anything, but I can't face this alone. You'll get yourself killed. Then he'll come for us. Hertz, please, I can't watch them kill my child in front of me." She wept into her hands.

Hertz moved toward her, reached for her hand. Berta slapped it. "Don't, no, not now. Tell me you won't do this."

He backed off. "I have a plan."

Berta smiled weakly through her tears. "I'm so sorry my

darling, but that's always the answer, I forbid you this time. There is no plan for something like this."

Hertz pulled an old photograph from inside his shirt pocket. "What is that?"

"Thank god it was in that photo album you hid in your suitcase when you left."

The photo was of five men in the uniform of the Austro-Hungarian army. In the center was Petar Karoly, their commander. On the far left was Hertz and on the far right was von Hauptmann. "Look at his uniform, the breast pocket, what name is there?"

Berta squinted at the photograph. "It looks like Molnar."

"Exactly, von Hauptman is Molnar."

"What are you talking about?"

Hertz pulled out a paper from his jacket pocket and unfolded it. "This letter denounces von Hauptmann as an imposter. He will be arrested if his commanding officers find out he's impersonating an Aryan. If I don't return with our papers, you will pass this along to Seidleman in a sealed envelope addressed to the German Commandant for Brussels. He's replaced Halevy on the Judenrat. I've already told Seidleman what to do if I disappear. He will pass it to the SS through an acquaintance on the council. You take the balance of the diamonds and go into hiding."

Berta shook her head. "This will never work." She began weeping again. "I can't run anymore. Please, I can't do this alone. Don't do this."

Hertz pulled a pistol from behind his jacket. "If necessary, I will kill him myself."

The next night Hertz stood in the little park across from SS headquarters. He checked his watch, 11:55 PM. He waited a few more minutes before entering the building, hurried up the stairs and proceeded down the hallway. He came to von Hauptmann's office and tapped on the door.

"Come in," von Hauptman called out.

Hertz took the gun he was carrying from its place under his jacket in the small of his back and opened the door quickly. Von

Hauptmann was seated at his desk. Hertz pointed his pistol directly at von Hauptmann's forehead, his hand trembling.

"I have to give you credit. You're brave, but stupid," von Hauptmann said. "Put that down."

"No, give me my passports and my documents."

"No." Von Hauptmann sat back calmly in his chair.

"I'll shoot you." Hertz growled.

"No, you won't."

Hertz played his hand. "I've got nothing to lose, Molnar. How long have you been parading around as an Austrian aristocrat?"

Von Hauptmann rose from his chair, stepped back and stared at Hertz. "What did you call me?"

"Molnar, your name, your real name." Hertz smiled.

"My name is von Hauptmann."

Hertz focused on von Hauptmann's face, clearly shocked. Hertz knew he had tripped him up. "No, it's not. We both know that. You are Jonas Molnar from Budapest."

Von Hauptmann flew across the room. He grabbed Hertz by the neck, knocking the gun from his hand and wrapping his enormous grip around Hertz's throat. He pressed against Hertz's Adam's apple so tightly that Hertz could barely breathe. "And how would you know that, you filthy Jew?" Who are you?" Von Hauptmann's face was an inch from Hertz's.

"Hersch Katz," Hertz squeaked out.

Von Hauptmann tightened his grip. "Hersch Katz? That Jew who licked Petar Karoly's ass every morning and evening?"

Hertz's could barely breathe. "The same."

"Impossible! I killed you myself!"

"Then how would I know you?" Hertz croaked, struggling to breathe.

Von Hauptmann removed his hand from Hertz's throat and stepped back. He examined Hertz's face. "It's been a lifetime, but I believe it's you. Perhaps I should finish the job now."

Hertz rolled off the desk and onto the floor grabbing the pistol. "Molnar, give me the papers and the passports."

Von Hauptmann moved carefully around the desk. "Go ahead, shoot me, then you'll have nothing."

Hertz followed him with the gun, both hands on it to steady himself. He didn't want to die here, but he knew killing von Hauptmann was a mistake. He could never dispose of the body, and someone might hear the shot. "Give me the papers, or I will kill you."

Von Hauptmann charged Hertz again. He grabbed the muzzle of the gun and pushed back Hertz's hand. The bones stretched to breaking, the pain excruciating as Hertz attempted to push back against von Hauptmann. He pressed as hard as he could, forcing von Hauptmann back a step. Hertz slid his foot behind von Hauptmann's ankle and kicked him off balance. Falling backward, von Hauptmann dropped to the floor crashing into the small table and the wood file cabinet against the wall behind him, his head hitting both. Blood seeped from the wound. Hertz kicked at his side. Von Hauptman didn't move.

Hertz put the gun down on the desk and opened the top drawer, searching for his passports and documents. Nothing. He opened the bottom drawer. There was a strong box at the back of it. Hertz pulled it out then took the gun and smashed its handle against the lock. At the third try, it cracked. He checked von Hauptmann, still out cold.

Hertz opened the lid to the box. Inside were numerous passports, official documents, and at the bottom under the papers, the bag of diamonds Hertz left days earlier. Hertz walked around the desk and kicked at von Hauptman again. Von Hauptmann's chest rose and fell in a shallow breath. Out cold.

Hertz returned to the box and found his passports. Next, he searched through the envelopes for his other documents. One envelope was marked Berlin. Hertz opened it and glanced at the papers. There were transit visas for Berta, Kurt, and him, all the way to Santo Domingo. Why Santo Domingo? Hertz stopped himself. What difference did it make? They had to get out of Europe. Hertz stuffed the passports into the large envelope and placed the envelope under his coat in the small of his back. He closed the top of the box and bent over to place it back in the drawer.

As Hertz closed the drawer, he felt a hand come around and grab him by the neck. The thumb and forefinger tightened around his Adam's apple again. At the same time, another hand slipped under his arm and pulled him up.

"You filthy Jew animal," growled von Hauptmann. His hand tightened. Blood dripped from a gash on his scalp. "I will kill you now!"

Hertz's mind was in chaos. He had to free himself, but von Hauptmann was too strong, even in his current injured and bleeding state."

"If you do," Hertz squeaked out through von Hauptmann's stranglehold, "you are finished." Von Hauptmann twisted Hertz's arm behind him so tightly, Hertz thought the bone might snap. "I'm growing tired of this," von Hauptmann snarled.

"I have left papers and a photo exposing you," Hertz growled, barely above a whisper. "If I don't return, those papers will find their way to your superiors."

Von Hauptmann yanked even harder at Hertz. "I don't believe you. You're bluffing."

"Look in my pocket, inside my coat." Hertz forced the words out with what little air he could muster through von Hauptmann's grip.

Von Hauptmann let Hertz's arm go while tightening his hold on his neck. He reached inside Hertz's coat and pulled out a sheet of paper. It was the carbon copy of a letter. He held it up to the light and read it then let go of Hertz. "You bastard, who has this?"

Hertz coughed and rubbed his neck then his arm. "It doesn't matter, there are several copies.

"Tell me, or I'll kill you now, and then your wife and son, within an hour."

"Stop, it doesn't matter. If you kill me, you'll be exposed. Just let me go. Keep the diamonds. Look, they're still there in the box. I didn't take them. We just want to get out of this hell."

Von Hauptmann released Hertz. He looked over the carbon again. "You stupid, conniving Jew. You think you'll get away?" Von Hauptmann laughed hysterically, like a madman. "Only if you're more cunning than I think you are. You want to leave? Now I'll tell you the terms of this deal to save your life, and the game we are going to play. But first, I want the original and the copies of this document delivered to me by sunrise. If not, I will finish you off myself. And Katz, don't think I did you any favors." Von Hauptmann laughed again like a madman, his eyes full of hate.

"Those papers will get you to Portugal, if you don't get caught first. They are diplomatic passports. You are to be the new cultural attaché to the German Embassy in Santo Domingo. You'll be traveling as a Nazi. Welcome to the party! Now, get yourself out of here, and this time I mean it! Have the copies of this letter and the original here by daylight. Remember, I know who you are and can stop you anywhere along the way with a phone call or telex."

CHAPTER 27

Brussels, Belgium - June 1945

It took Kurt some time to compose himself. After about fifteen minutes, he went back to his office to sort everything out and determine his next move. Perhaps he had misunderstood something. No, he knew emphatically, that wasn't the case. McClain didn't know what Kurt knew, and had his own agenda. He had to do something, fast. He couldn't let von Hauptmann walk away free. He would go to Rosenthaller and tell him everything. Rosenthaller was a Jew and a refugee himself. Rosenthaller would understand. Kurt would change his mind. He had to.

Kurt walked down the hall and peeked into Rosenthaller's office.

"Can I help you, Lieutenant?" Rosenthaller's secretary asked.

"Is he in?"

"Yes, would you like to speak with him?"

"Umm," Kurt said, steeling his resolve. "Yes."

The secretary picked up her phone. "Go ahead," she said gesturing to the door.

Rosenthaller was reading a report. He held up his hand and pointed to the chairs in front of his desk, indicating to Kurt not to speak and to take a seat. After a long moment, Rosenthaller closed the file and removed his glasses. "Yes, Lieutenant, how can I help you?"

Kurt felt his face flush. "Sir, I feel I need to inform you of what transpired today during the interrogation of Captain von

Hauptmann." His mouth went dry before he finished his sentence.

Rosenthaller sat back in his chair. "All right, Berlin. Speak."

"Captain, von Hauptmann is a war criminal. He's a murderer."

Rosenthaller's face remained expressionless, the same as it was the day he watched von Hauptmann's interrogation. "We know that," said Rosenthaller. "We've discussed this already. And I thought we had an understanding?"

"What he told us today changes everything sir, I'm sorry."

"What did he say?"

"He outright admitted that he massacred all the Sisters in a convent, and I have corroborating testimony from an eyewitness."

Rosenthaller sat up in his chair. He put his glasses back on and made a note on a blank pad on his desk. "Corroborating testimony?"

Kurt felt emboldened. "Yes, sir."

"How would you have that? Have you been investigating von Hauptmann on your own?"

"Well, not exactly, Captain. You know I lived here in Brussels before we escaped to the United States."

Rosenthaller leaned forward over his desk and clasped his hands. "I am aware of that, but that still doesn't explain how you would have any information or intelligence regarding von Hauptmann that we don't already have."

"I've been looking for someone…"

Rosenthaller removed his glasses. "You've been looking for someone? Who? A family member?"

"Not exactly. A young woman, someone I knew very well before we escaped."

"You know, this is highly irregular…"

"Yes."

"Who is this young woman to you?"

"We were on the same Kindertransport from Vienna. We lived together with the same host family."

"What is her name?"

"Elsa Graz."

Rosenthaller made a quick note. Kurt spied the pad. Rosenthaller had scribbled Elsa's name. "And you've located her? She has some evidence against von Hauptmann?"

"No, sir. I've been looking for her, and I found a nun who witnessed the event von Hauptmann confessed to today."

"And what event is that?"

"Von Hauptmann ordered the razing of a convent with the all of the Sisters locked into the chapel. Elsa lived in the convent." Kurt swallowed. His tongue felt as if it had swelled to twice its size. While he hoped for some expression of horror, some response indicating Rosenthaller's revulsion. He got none.

"Was this young woman in the convent when it was destroyed?"

"I believe von Hauptmann took her from the convent with him. That's what the witness said."

"So, let me see if I understand this correctly." Rosenthaller sat back in his chair, placed his forefingers together and pressed them to his pursed lips. "Von Hauptmann mentioned this incident during interrogation. You recognized the circumstances and believe he knows the whereabouts of this young woman you're searching for."

Rosenthaller's quick summary of the facts emboldened Kurt. He thought the Captain might be on his side, that Rosenthaller's measured reaction was simply his nature. Truthfully, in the months Kurt had known him, he had never seen Rosenthaller flinch. "There's more Captain. I believe he beat and tortured the couple we lived with."

Rosenthaller nodded. "And your basis for this accusation?"

"I stumbled upon a friend, my best friend from that time. He survived the war in hiding. He's a Jew, like us. His name is Saul. He saw the incident and described it to me. The description of events coincides. The couple he tortured, gave von Hauptmann the information that led him to the convent."

"And where is this young man now?"

"He's here in Brussels. I found him a room. I'm helping him."

"In what way?"

"With money." Kurt leaned forward. He was sure that Rosenthaller recognized the severity of von Hauptmann's offenses. "Captain, you have to intervene. Von Hauptmann is a war criminal, despite what we talked about. He may be valuable to us, but he was responsible for organizing the deportations from Brussels to the death camps. He admitted it today. You've seen the pictures. We all have. It could have been us, you or me. We can't let him get away, go to America, start a new life."

Rosenthaller sat up in his chair and placed his forefingers against his lips again. He remained silent for several minutes. Then he picked up the report he was reading when Kurt arrived and put it in front of Kurt. "Please read the title of this report for me, Lieutenant, and then turn to the last page and note the signatures."

Kurt picked up the bound folder and looked at the cover page. "Analysis of the Interrogation of Captain Joachim von Hauptmann. Prepared by Anderson McClain." He turned the report over and found the last page. There on the bottom were three signatures, Colonel Anderson McClain, Captain Johan Rosenthaller, and Lieutenant Kurt Berlin. Kurt put the report back on the desk and digested the implication of what he had just seen. "I never signed this, sir."

"We thought we'd save you the trouble, Lieutenant," said Rosenthaller. "I am aware of Captain von Hauptmann's various activities, criminal and otherwise. He is no saint, but then none of these men are…"

"Captain…"

Rosenthaller slammed his fist down on the desk. "Don't ever interrupt me!" he screamed.

Kurt slipped back into the chair and averted his gaze from Rosenthaller.

"While I understand your disgust, and your desire to exact revenge on these murderous monsters, you must understand certain very salient points about what we are doing here." Rosenthaller's voice returned to its normal, controlled monotone. "Colonel McClain is correct, in his analysis. The real enemy always was and continues to be the Soviets, the communists. If we are to win the next phase of this conflict, and we expect it will take decades, we need to enlist men who have direct experience with them, and how to deal with them. We need these men, regardless of what they may have done. And I might point out that in war men die, people die, there is collateral damage. Did you not feel regret when you fought in the Pacific? Do you think you hold no responsibility for the deaths of both soldiers and civilians there?"

The image of the Japanese soldier in Kurt's dream dangled in front of Kurt's eyes. Kurt pushed the ghost from his mind. "But Captain…"

Rosenthaller's face reddened, his voice rising again. "Lieutenant, you are to leave this alone. Colonel McClain has determined that Captain von Hauptmann is a valuable asset to us going forward. You are a member of an elite division of the United States Armed Forces. Your complete focus and loyalty are expected, despite what personal feelings you might have. Also, you will cease any activities searching for anyone you knew before, during, or after the war, and will not have contact with anyone outside of the service. You have a high security clearance, and I don't want to consider you a security risk. Have I made myself clear?"

"Yes, Captain."

"Colonel McClain will be away for a few days. I suggest you use that time to square yourself with our mission."

"Yes, Captain."

"And one more thing Lieutenant."

"Yes."

"Don't ever bring up our common ancestry again."

Kurt wandered the streets for hours after leaving Rosenthaller's office, distraught. McClain would be von Hauptmann's get-out-of-jail-free card. Von Hauptmann would be offered American citizenship if he agreed to work for the OSS.

Kurt walked to Saul's place and climbed the stairs to his apartment, eschewing the narrow, caged elevator. He knocked on the door.

"Yes?" Saul called out.

"It's Kurt. Get your coat. I need to speak to you, but not here."

Saul appeared a moment later. "What's wrong? You look terrible."

"I have something to tell you."

"So, come in."

"No, I need a drink."

"All right," said Saul.

They settled into the last booth at the back of the bar where Saul told Kurt what had happened to him and his family. "Two Stellas and two shots of whiskey," Kurt said to the barmaid.

"Well?" Saul said.

"After she brings the beers and the shots."

The barmaid returned a moment later and placed the drinks in front of them. Kurt threw back the shot then sipped at the beer's foamy top. "I know what happened to Elsa."

"How? What did the nun say?" Saul asked, his breath catching in his throat.

"That's only half the story." Kurt proceeded to tell Saul everything, what he learned from the Sister and what happened during the interrogation of von Hauptmann earlier that day.

Saul's hands were balled into fists. "This guy is responsible? You're sure?"

"I think so." Kurt pulled a photograph from inside his pocket. He handed it to Saul. "I took this from his file. Do you recognize him?"

Saul strained to see through the darkness. He pulled a match from his pocket and struck it against the table. The light illuminated the photo of von Hauptmann. Saul's breath caught in his throat. "Yes, that's him. I'm sure. I could never forget that face, or those eyes, blank and empty."

"He's as cold as ice."

"He has to be punished."

"Yes." Kurt fumed. "We have to do something because they're going to do nothing. They're going to give him a new life."

"That can't happen."

"But it will. And he knows what happened to Elsa. He knows if she's alive or dead. He's probably the only person alive who does."

Saul breathing became shallow. "I'll kill him with my bare hands."

"Not if I do first."

Saul finished his beer in one long gulp. "What do you want to do?"

"Deliver justice. But first, I want to find out what he knows about Elsa."

"How do you propose to do that?"

"I have a plan."

CHAPTER 28

Brussels, Belgium - October 1940

Hertz admired Berta's reflection in the mirror, ravishing in the blue ensemble she chose for the trip to Paris. But he knew her too well, her expression betrayed her true feelings. Berta was terrified. For Kurt's sake, both had to maintain the illusion of calmness.

"Are you ready for this?" Hertz asked.

"Do I have a choice?" She picked up a small Nazi Party pin and fastened it to Hertz's lapel. He did the same for her. "There, don't I make a fine-looking Nazi," Berta said.

A chill ran down Hertz's spine. The image of Nazi Berta was surreal. With her blond hair, fair complexion and blue eyes, she well could have passed. He touched his hand to her cheek. "You'd make a fine-looking anything." He kissed her gently on the lips.

A moment later Kurt entered the room. He stood in the doorway, his double-breasted, grey suit buttoned, accentuating his thin waist and broad shoulders. Hertz realized instantly that though Kurt's eighteen-year-old body looked older than the sixteen years on his passport, his face, thankfully, looked younger; convincingly enough to avoid suspicion.

"You look so handsome," Berta said. She straightened Kurt's jacket then fastened the Nazi emblem to his lapel. Kurt leaned over the dresser toward the mirror, revulsion obvious in his expression. "Is this really necessary?"

"Absolutely," Hertz said. "And remember everything else about your new identity. We are no longer Jews. We are dedicated Nazis on our way to Santo Domingo to represent the Fatherland."

"Yes, father."

"That's Heil Hitler."

Arranging a car to take them to Brussels Central Station was no small task. Jews couldn't take limousines or taxis. The address at which they lived was inappropriate for German officials. Anyone they encountered, even a taxi driver, could be a potential informant.

Luckily, Wolfson had a friend, a gentile active in the resistance, who worked as a concierge at a small but fancy hotel in central Brussels. He arranged a room for a night, a suite befitting a Nazi official, and a limousine to take them to the station early next morning. The Berlins appeared as any other well-healed German family.

The driver dropped them at the entrance to the station. Armed Nazi guards patrolled the area. Berta stepped out of the limousine. She placed her hand on the top of her hat to hold it in place against the breeze, the lace fluttering in front of her eyes.

The guard patrolling at the entrance came toward her. For a moment Berta trembled, then remembered, these men were no longer her pursuers, but rather once again, her countrymen. The soldier offered his hand as she stepped from the cobblestone curb to the sidewalk. "Danke schoen," she said.

The guard stared at the pin on the lapel of her jacket. "My pleasure, madam."

Hertz exited from the other side of the limousine and walked around it as the driver unloaded their bags, offering no assistance. His new social position prohibited it. He signaled to Kurt to do the same, nothing.

"Young man," Hertz said, gesturing toward the soldier who had helped Berta.

"Yes, sir,"

"Could you summon a porter?"

"Of course." The soldier called across the plaza to the guard at the entrance. A moment later a porter appeared with a long rolling cart. "There!" he shouted at the porter, directing him to the car.

Hertz reached into his pocket and pulled out a large wad of bills. He paid the driver and thanked him. "These are ours," he said to the porter in German pointing toward the bags stacked to his right.

"What class of service?" the porter asked in French.

Hertz looked at the porter as if he didn't understand one word. He turned to Berta. She smiled and translated then turned back to the porter and answered him in French. "First class. We're on our way to Paris."

"Schnell, schnell!" shouted the soldier. He bowed to Berta. "I'm sorry. They're very slow."

"That's fine young man, thank you for your help." Berta shot her arm into the air. "Heil Hitler." Hertz and Kurt followed her example. The soldier saluted back. "Heil Hitler. And a safe journey."

They followed the porter into the station to the boarding area. A young, serious looking SS officer, not much older than Kurt, approached them. "Heil Hitler," he said and saluted.

Hertz saluted back. "Heil Hitler."

"To where are you traveling?"

"Paris."

"May I see your documents, please?"

"Of course," Hertz pulled a leather document case from the inside pocket of his suit jacket.

As the young officer examined the papers, his expression changed. "Excuse me Deputy Consul Berlin, I had no idea," he said, fawning. "We weren't informed that a diplomat would be on the train this morning. I meant no offense by asking for your papers."

"None taken."

"How exciting to represent our Fuehrer and Fatherland. How long is your posting?"

"As you can see," Hertz pointed to the date on the document.

"I'm sure you will miss the Reich."

"We already do," replied Berta.

The young officer looked at Kurt. "When you return you will

be old enough to join us in the fight."

Kurt smiled. "That's exactly what I intend to do when I return. Join the fight."

The officer directed the porter to deposit the luggage by the first car. "Please, board there," he said to Hertz. "I will take care of the labeling of your bags personally. Have a safe journey, Heil Hitler!" he shouted, jumping to attention again.

"Heil Hitler!" they shouted back and saluted in unison.

Hertz brushed his hands along the sides of his jacket to reassure himself that the diamonds he had hidden there were still securely in place. He saw a figure lurking in the shadows. The figure stepped into the light deliberately, then withdrew again into darkness, confirming what Hertz had suspected. It was von Hauptmann. Hertz handed his tickets to the conductor, maintaining the same arrogant expression he had plastered on his face when he arrived at the station.

"Please walk to the left and down the corridor," the conductor said.

Hertz gestured to Berta and Kurt to board. He glanced back to where von Hauptmann stood. A sick smile crept up around von Hauptmann's mouth. As Hertz boarded, he prayed von Hauptmann was there merely to intimidate him.

The conductor stopped halfway up the car. "That is your compartment, number 6, Herr Berlin."

"Thank you." Hertz pulled some Reichmarks from his pocket and gave them to the conductor.

"And thank you, sir." The conductor bowed. "Enjoy your trip. We should be leaving in about ten minutes."

"I take it then that the trains run on time now?"

The conductor laughed. "Yes, they do, sir," he said.

Once alone inside the cabin, Hertz looked at Berta and Kurt. He sighed in relief. They had passed the day's first test. "Well done. Let's make ourselves comfortable." Hertz maintained his calm in front of them, not wanting them to know that their escape might end before it began. The five-minute departure whistle blew. Hertz took a deep breath and exhaled. He looked out the window again. His heart raced. Von Hauptmann had moved closer to the train, out into the open. He smiled broadly, his arms crossed over his chest, wide-rimmed fedora pushed back on his head revealing his hairline. The train whistle sounded again, and the cars began to roll. Hertz read von Hauptmann's lips. *Be careful Jew, I know who you are and where you're going.*

CHAPTER 29

Brussels, Belgium - June 1945

Kurt secured what was needed to execute his plan. He applied for three-days' leave, claiming he wanted to visit with Sam in Paris, use of a jeep from the motor pool to get himself there, and most importantly, an extra uniform to fit Saul. They had to look the part. The only real danger was Saul's inability to speak English. He taught him a couple of key phrases and hoped for luck.

The last piece of the puzzle was an order to move von Hauptmann. Kurt went to the office late in the evening, after he knew Rosenthaller and his secretary had both left. He took several copies of the form necessary to move a prisoner. Kurt typed the order on the secretary's typewriter with a carbon and signed Rosenthaller's name. He stamped the document with all the necessary seals. Von Hauptmann was his.

He left Rosenthaller's office and went to his own. He unlocked the bottom draw of his filing cabinet and removed the tapes and original transcripts of von Hauptmann's interrogations. He hadn't destroyed them as Rosenthaller instructed him. Kurt placed the papers and tapes into the leather brief case he kept under his desk and relocked the cabinet. He opened the door slowly and peered down the hallway in both directions. He had one more stop. He needed yesterday's interrogation as well.

Kurt moved stealthily down the hall to the stairs. He walked down the one flight to the next floor and checked out the hallway. Not a soul, but then it was almost 2:00 AM. He wasn't sure if there was a night patrol, so he had to be careful. He made his way down the hall to the office where the tapes and original shorthand notes of the interrogations were kept, slipped an army knife out of his pocket and jimmied the lock. The skills he'd learned during his time in the Philippines were invaluable. Kurt made his way to the holding bins in the rear of the office and picked that lock too. The tapes and shorthand books were kept by date and prisoner. He searched the prior day's work for von Hauptmann's file, but it wasn't there. He began to panic. Of course, he thought, Rosenthaller and McClain were intent on making that interrogation disappear. He would have to look elsewhere. Kurt slipped out of the office and headed back upstairs to McClain's office.

Once there Kurt began to doubt himself. Breaking into McClain's office was a serious offence. He nearly aborted the mission. Kurt considered again what his father would say. If he simply ended this now, his parents would still receive what Rosenthaller had promised him, citizenship. But he would let a murderer go free, and he would never find Elsa. He heard his father's voice and knelt in front of McClain's door. He slipped the tip of the army knife's blade into the door's lock and caught the latch. The door opened gently. Kurt pushed it open and closed it behind him carefully. He looked around the office and considered where McClain might have hidden the tapes and the shorthand notes. There was no obvious choice. Kurt thought for a moment about McClain's nature. He was very full of himself. McClain wouldn't have concerned himself with anyone stealing the tapes or the notes. He'd just put them in a convenient spot. Kurt looked through the draws in McClain's desk and then the two filing cabinets. Nothing. His eyes settled on the closet behind the entry door. Kurt turned the knob and looked around. A sport jacket and an overcoat hung lonely in the closet. On the floor was an open box with some papers in it. Kurt checked behind and under it. Nothing. When he stood up his eyes were level with the shelf above the coat rod. There was a small box. He removed it and there they were. Three tapes and two stenographer's notebooks. He checked the date on the notebooks. They were from yesterday. Kurt slipped them in his briefcase and slipped out of McClain's office. He relocked the door then walked quickly down the hall and the stairs. As he exited the stairwell on the first floor, he was caught by a light shining in his eyes.

"Lieutenant Berlin," a young soldier said. He looked at his watched. "What are you doing here so late in the evening?"

Kurt pulled the tapes he'd just taken from McClain's office from his briefcase. "Colonel Rosenthaller called me at my room a couple hours ago. They need this interrogation transcribed by 8:00 tomorrow morning. I'll be working all night."

"Don't you need a tape recorder for that?"

"I have one back at my room. This isn't the first time this has happened."

"Well, sorry I bothered you, sir."

"No bother. Good to see you're doing your job well. I'll be sure to tell Rosenthaller."

The young soldier saluted Kurt. Kurt saluted back then turned and walked slowly out of the building, praying his shaking legs wouldn't betray him.

The only question now was where they would take von Hauptmann. Saul had passed by the farm near Mechelen where he had hidden from the Nazis on his way back to Brussels. It was abandoned, the farmer and his family gone. After Kurt confronted von Hauptmann with what he knew, after von Hauptmann gave them answers they believed truthful, he and Saul would exact justice. Kurt no longer cared what would happen to him for what he was about to do. He couldn't live with himself if von Hauptmann went free. As Rosenthaller had said back in the Philippines, Kurt would strike a blow for his beleaguered people.

The next night, an unusually warm evening, as the sun dipped below the horizon, Kurt picked up the jeep at the motor pool. The soldier in charge wished him a great time. He told him to bring a couple of Parisian girls for the boys back here. Kurt laughed and said he'd hide them under the tarp.

Kurt drove the jeep to the building where Saul and his family lived before the war. Saul stepped out of the alley on the side of the building, dropped the butt of his cigarette onto the street, and hopped in. "Hello, brother," he said.

"Are you ready?"

"More than you can imagine."

Kurt drove back to his hotel. He parked a block away. "Follow me," he said to Saul. They walked through the lobby. Kurt waved at the duty officer. "You remember my friend?" he said.

"Of course. He going with you to Paris?"

"Yep."

"Lucky dogs."

Kurt and Saul climbed the two flights up to his floor rather than take the slow-moving lift. Kurt slipped the key into the door and ushered Saul in. "The uniform is in the closet."

Saul stripped off his clothes and put on the new uniform. Kurt smiled. Saul looked like an American GI. Two hours later, after practicing basic English phrases, they left by way of the rear stairs and exited the building through the kitchen.

It was past 11:00, the streets empty. They doubled back around the corner to the jeep and headed to the military holding facility to get von Hauptmann. Kurt flashed his ID to the duty guard and showed him his orders. The guard looked them over.

"Isn't it a little late in the evening for this?"

"The British command wants to interrogate him. I'm on my way to Paris for a few days. Rosenthaller asked me to transport him."

The guard looked over the papers again, then shook his head. "That's the US Army, always looking for a way to save a buck." He unlocked the heavy gate behind him. "Okay, go get him. He's in the last cell on the left."

Kurt gestured to Saul to get von Hauptmann, as per their plan. "I'll go get the jeep," Kurt said then turned to Saul and threw him a set of handcuffs. "Put these on him."

Kurt's heart was beating double-time. He pulled the jeep in front of the doors. Saul came out of the building, his rifle in von Hauptmann's back, pushing him into the rear seat. Saul pulled out a second set of cuffs and hooked them over the first and then to the jeep itself. He pulled a strip of cloth from his pocket, stealthily and speedily, and tied it around von Hauptmann's mouth, came around the car and jumped in.

Kurt put the jeep in drive and pulled away. One block later he stopped. The street was completely deserted, lit only by a single streetlamp directly above the vehicle. Kurt turned to von Hauptmann.

"Guten abend, Colonel." He pointed his revolver directly at von Hauptmann's forehead. "Don't make a sound." Kurt saw both surprise and hate in von Hauptmann's icy eyes.

The trip to the farmhouse took about an hour. "The barn is there," Saul said, "to the right, behind the farmhouse." Kurt parked next to it. He pulled the gag from von Hauptmann's mouth.

Von Hauptmann coughed then stretched his jaw, running his tongue across his lips to moisten them. "Young Berlin, are you willing to lose everything over me?" von Hauptmann said, in German. "I'm Colonel McClain's pet now. He will not be at all happy about this."

Kurt smiled. He placed the nozzle of his revolver between von Hauptmann's eyes. "Shut up, you piece of Nazi shit. I'd kill you right now, but my friend here wants at you, and I need to get a few questions answered, so you're not dead quite yet. You speak when you're spoken to. If you speak out of turn again, I'll punish you." Kurt pulled a dagger from inside his pant leg. "We'll start finger by finger. A little trick I learned in the Philippines."

Saul uncuffed von Hauptmann from the interior of the jeep but kept the Nazi's hands bound. "Get out," he said. Von Hauptmann stood next to the jeep, nearly dwarfing it. Saul's rifle was pointed at his chest.

Kurt opened the door to the barn and let his eyes adjust to the darkness, even thicker and silkier than outside. He reached down to his left. A lantern sat precisely where Saul said it would be. Kurt pulled a match from his shirt pocket and struck it against the handle of the door then lit the lantern. The glow illuminated the barn's interior. It smelled of old hay and horseshit. As he raised the lamp and surveyed the space, the light caught a rat's eyes, red and evil, scrambling for cover. How appropriate, Kurt thought. "Bring him in," he called to Saul.

Von Hauptmann stepped tentatively and awkwardly into the darkness, his hands still cuffed behind him. Saul prodded him, the nose of the rifle in the small of von Hauptmann's back. "Mach schnell!" Saul shouted.

"What do you intend to do with me?" von Hauptmann asked.

Rage rose like a volcano in Kurt's chest. He picked up an old piece of wood about a half meter long and heavy in his hand, and swung at von Hauptmann, striking him just above the waist on his left side. Von Hauptmann tumbled over, the expression of pain evident on his face.

"I told you, don't speak unless you are spoken to. That's our policy. You recall what you said about policy?"

Von Hauptmann was silent.

"I spoke to you, Captain," Kurt said. "I'm waiting for an answer."

"Yes," said von Hauptmann. "I do."

Euphoria swept over Kurt. He realized that this was the thing that had been missing since that first fight in the schoolyard after the Anschluss. Power. He towered over von Hauptmann now. Kurt controlled the Nazi's destiny, just as the Nazis had controlled his for so long.

"Shall we begin?" Saul asked.

Kurt thought for a moment. "Yes, let's soften him up a little first."

Saul laid his rifle on the ground, drew his pistol and aimed it at von Hauptmann as Kurt disappeared into the shadows. A few moments later Kurt returned with a wooden chair. "Where do they keep chord. I want to tie him up."

Saul considered Kurt's question. "The farmer used to leave heavy ropes behind that stall."

Kurt pulled his gun and pointed it at von Hauptmann's head again. "Get them, please."

"My pleasure," Saul said.

"Get up!" he ordered von Hauptmann.

Von Hauptmann struggled to his feet, his balance off with his hands cuffed behind his back. He moved toward the chair.

Kurt walked up to von Hauptmann. For a moment, he was intimidated by the German's sheer size. Kurt was both tall and muscular, but standing the Nazi towered over him. "Cover him," he called to Saul.

Kurt reached up and grabbed von Hauptmann's shirt with both hands and ripped it open, the remnants hanging from his cuffed wrists behind him. "Don't even think about escape, because you'll have to do it naked. He slid his hands to the sides of von Hauptmann's body, grabbed his pants and pulled them down below his knees then pushed him into the chair roughly.

"Tie him up now," Kurt growled.

Saul bound von Hauptmann to the chair tightly. When he was done Kurt pulled off von Hauptmann's shoes and then his pants and threw them into the corner. "We'll burn them later." Kurt laughed then shouted, "There is no escape!" This barn, this deserted farm, was perfect. No one could hear them. "I'm sure you've said that yourself to a few Jews."

Kurt pulled a piece of fabric from his pocket. It was the Nazi armband he wore in the street as a teenager in Vienna to disguise himself among his tormentors. He wasn't sure what had made him take it with him when he went back to Europe. Kurt shoved it into von Hauptmann's mouth. "Go ahead, Saul. You take the first shot."

Saul walked up to von Hauptmann. He looked at him for a long moment. "This is for my parents," Saul snarled. He punched von Hauptmann directly in the center of his face. The crack of bone was audible. A deep gurgle came from von Hauptmann's throat. Blood poured from his nose. His eyes slid back into his head.

"Your turn," Saul said.

Kurt approached von Hauptmann. He drew back his arms like a boxer, a skill he'd honed in the army, proving himself to other soldiers who taunted him for being Jewish. He pummeled von Hauptmann's ribs. "That was for the Mandelbaum's." Kurt laughed hysterically. He felt liberated. "Though I'm certain you have no idea who I'm talking about. You will before we're done."

Saul approached von Hauptmann again. "My turn. I had a sister. She was lovely and very shy. She was a kind person. She's gone. I know it in my heart that I will never see her again.

There was a particular day when I felt it, when I knew. She's gone, they all are, because you sent them. This is for her."

Saul took the small hammer they packed with other tools of persuasion and concentrated on the pinky of von Hauptmann's right hand. Von Hauptmann looked defiantly at Saul. Saul tapped the head of the hammer several times against the pinky then slammed it down crushing the middle joint. The pain radiated from von Hauptmann's finger into his eyes then transformed into his scream, muffled by the armband choking him.

Kurt pulled the gag from von Hauptmann's mouth. The Nazi moaned from deep inside, a long, slow, almost inaudible groan escaping his lips. "Remember what I told you," Kurt said. "Not one word."

Kurt backed off slightly. "We could kill you now, but we need answers to some very pressing questions. But I think you need to suffer first. I think you should sit here like this for a while." He pushed the gag back into von Hauptmann's mouth. "Stay like that, like a pig in its barn. Let the flies torture you for a while, and maybe the rats too."

试戈

Rosenthaller picked up the ringing phone. His secretary hadn't arrived yet. He hated the shrill sound. It went through his head like an ice pick. "Rosenthaller," he said into the mouthpiece.

"Captain, this is Mosely over at the holding pens."

"How can I help you?"

"I need some additional forms for last night's transfer."

"Last night's transfer? What are you talking about?"

"Von Hauptmann. You had him transferred to Paris."

"I did nothing of the sort!" Rosenthaller shouted into the phone.

"I'm sorry, sir. Lieutenant Berlin, he came by last evening, it's stamped here 23:06. He was with another soldier. He took von Hauptmann to Paris to be interrogated by the British. Your signature is here on the order, in duplicate. I need a triplicate."

"I'll be there shortly!" Rosenthaller screamed into the phone then slammed it down. He grabbed his coat and ran out of the office and into his secretary. "Get McClain on the phone, he's in Berlin. Tell him he has to get back here today. We have an emergency."

CHAPTER 30

Paris, Occupied France - October 1940

The Belle Epoch ceilings of the Gare du Nord soared above Hertz, Berta and Kurt, pigeons flying in and out of the cavernous station. Kurt breathed deeply and smiled. He whispered in Berta's ear, "So far, so good."

"Yes," she replied, looking around. Armed German soldiers patrolled the station, their rifles at the ready.

Hertz walked back toward them tickets in hand, a porter following with their bags. "Our train doesn't leave until tomorrow evening. Tonight's is fully booked." Hertz smirked. "Even my status as a German diplomat didn't help."

"I hope you didn't…" Berta whispered.

"No, no, of course not. The ticket agent did notice the pin and my title on our documents though. He was…deferential. I've arranged a hotel. Let's go to the street and hire a taxi."

"Please sir," a porter said in heavily accented, broken German, "wait here. I will arrange your transport. What hotel?"

Hertz looked at the receipt the ticket agent gave him. "Hotel Trillium. It's near the Arc d' Triomphe."

The porter bowed and ran off. Hertz sat down on a polished wood bench, Berta, and Kurt following his lead. He closed his eyes for a moment and sighed in momentary relief. Someone speaking in German broke the spell. "Excuse me. Are you Deputy Consul Berlin?"

Hertz looked up. A man of about thirty-five in a chauffeur's uniform stood in front of them, an SS pin affixed to his lapel.

"Yes," Hertz replied.

The chauffeur snapped to attention and saluted. "Heil Hitler!"

Hertz returned the salute. "And you are?"

The chauffeur stood straight as an arrow. "The embassy sent me. My name is Rolf Spiegle. Pleasse call me Rolf I will be your driver."

Hertz was uneasy. Anonymity was their surest protection. Was von Hauptmann responsible for this? Was it a trap?

"Monsieur," the porter called out, breaking the awkward silence that filled the space where Hertz's response to the driver should have been. "I have your transport arranged."

"That won't be necessary!" Rolf barked in French. "Wait there, by the door."

The porter stopped in his tracks. He removed his cap from his head and bowed. "Me oui," he mumbled and ran off, not waiting for Hertz to offer a tip.

"You didn't think we would come for you?" Rolf said, smiling.

"I didn't notify the embassy that we were coming. It was only for one night. I didn't want to bother them, what with all that's going on. The war effort comes first."

"You're no bother sir, none at all, rather our comrade. Let's get you to your hotel so you can freshen up. Then we will tour Paris. We have much to see and little time."

Rolf pulled an envelope from his pocket and handed it to Hertz. "The commandant asked me to deliver this." The chauffeur whistled; the porter reappeared. "Take these bags to my car. It's parked in front of the entrance. Schnell, schnell!" The porter scurried back to the luggage cart and pushed it hurriedly out toward the grand entrance. "This way, Herr Berlin."

Hertz opened the envelope as he walked. He read the short message written in elegant, cursive pen.

"Please honor us with the pleasure of your company, and that of your wife and son, this evening for dinner at my home at 9 PM."

Otto Abetz, Commandant of Paris.

试炼

Berta took the back seat behind Rolf. He'd abandoned the limo in which he'd dropped them off at the Hotel Trillium in favor of a convertible for their tour of Paris. "Would you prefer that I leave the top down?" the Nazi asked. "Sometimes the ladies worry for their hair."

Kurt looked at Berta. "Please, mother?"

"Leave it down," she replied.

"Herr Deputy Consul, would you prefer to sit in front with me or in the rear with your wife and son."

"In front, I think."

"Yes, it will be more comfortable. You are a tall man." Rolf held the door open for Hertz. "I thought we would take a ride around first, then you could stop for lunch and decide which landmarks you would like to see more closely."

Hertz smiled broadly. "Whatever you think best. You are our guide, after all."

Rolf pulled the big Mercedes into the street. "We should start here at the western end of the Champs Elysee and work our way back to Notre Dame."

"That's fine," Berta said.

Rolf turned the car into the rotary circling the Arc d' Triomphe. There was virtually no traffic, save for official vehicles.

"Young Kurt," Rolf said.

"Yes." Kurt could see Rolf's eyes in the rear-view mirror.

"The Arc was built to celebrate the French victory over the German states in the time of Napoleon!" Rolf shouted.

"I didn't know that."

"Perhaps we will destroy it when the war is over and put up a monument to our victory? Yes, yes! As the Fuehrer says, the Reich will last for 1,000 years!"

Kurt glanced at Berta. She touched his hand. "May the Fuehrer's words come to pass," she said, raising her voice and hoping to satisfy Rolf's patriotism.

"Heil Hitler!" replied Rolf. He turned to Hertz. "Have you been to Paris before?"

"No, but my wife has," Hertz said. "Many years ago."

"It's wonderful. But I prefer Berlin myself." Rolf kept up his chattering. "You have an interesting name, Herr Deputy Consul. Are you from Berlin?"

"Mother, look," Kurt interrupted, pointing to the massive structure in front of them.

"Ah, the Tour Eiffel. Everyone's lasting impression of Paris," Rolf recited, like a tour guide.

"Can we come back after lunch?" Kurt asked.

"Of course," Hertz replied. He turned back to Rolf. "No, we are from Vienna."

"I too am Austrian. From a small village in the Tyrol."

"How long have you been with the party?" Hertz asked.

"Since before the Anschluss. I was with the Austrian Party. We worked so hard to bring the reunification about. I was so delighted the day we became one Reich, one people. And you? How long have you been with the cause?"

Hertz was now certain von Hauptmann was behind this. His mind raced back to the Anschluss, his humiliation, scrubbing the street on his knees with a brush in front of his wife and son. He wanted to grab the wheel of the car and punch Rolf in the head, forcing him out of the car. This man's pride was the mirror of Hertz's disgrace. Instead, Hertz maintained his smile, and his role.

"Since the beginning. I joined the party just after the Great War. I fought the communists in Vienna in 1927." As Hertz said this, as he perpetrated this charade to save himself and his family, he felt the bile rise from his stomach. In some way, Hertz realized, to impersonate a Nazi was worse than to be the object of their hate.

"And you, young Kurt? Are you a member of the Hitler Youth?"

Kurt was in a state of confusion. His heart beat rapidly. Listening to his father lie about who they were, about being one of them, was surreal. He couldn't have imagined that he would have reacted this way. He wanted to shout, I am a Jew! Instead, Kurt lied. "I was the Gauleiter of my group. Last summer I attended training camp near Salzburg." Berta squeezed his hand.

"How old are you?"

"Sixteen"

"Perhaps you will join the SS when you turn eighteen?"

Kurt squeezed his mother's hand back. "That's my plan."

The car grew quiet. Rolf continued east. He slowed near a small bridge that crossed the Seine. "There, you see that monument?" he said. "That is the Place d' la Republic. To the right is the Louvre. It was the Royal Palace before the revolution. The guillotines were there. We will proceed to Notre Dame. You can have some lunch. There are many fine cafes. Then I would suggest you see the Cathedral. There is a fine view from the top. We can climb it together. Afterward, we can return to the Tour Eiffel."

"As you wish," replied Hertz. Hertz knew tension would preclude any desire to eat on anyone's part. Lunch though, would provide a break from Rolf's endless chatter.

"I know of an excellent bistro a few blocks from here."

"That will do fine."

"It's restricted. Germans only."

Hertz smiled and nodded. "Of course."

Rolf pulled around the block and slowed the car. He jumped out to open the doors.

"What's that going on there?" Kurt asked, pointing toward a commotion farther down the street. They watched as a German in uniform struck an old man across the face with his gloved hand.

Rolf chuckled. "Just some Jews. They probably got caught without their stars. We began enforcing that regulation more strenuously a few days ago."

Kurt felt his father's hand on his upper arm. "Come, son." The image of the soldier striking the old man was burned into Kurt's mind forever.

试找

The Commandant's residence was an 18th-century townhouse on a quiet, elegant street, in the Fifth Arrondisement. Uniformed guards stood in front of the house. One of them approached the car. "Welcome," came a voice from behind the guard. "Deputy Consul Berlin?"

"Yes. Heil Hitler." Hertz stifled a shudder, realizing he became a little more comfortable with the phrase each time he used it.

"Heil Hitler. Please, follow me."

Hertz stepped onto the sidewalk, Berta and Kurt following him. "Be careful what you say. And stay calm," he whispered to Kurt.

"Yes, father."

The interior of the townhouse was elegantly furnished. Crystal chandeliers hung from ornate plaster ceilings reflecting off the polished marble floor. They climbed the carpeted stairway to the second floor. "May I present, Ambassador Otto Abetz."

A tall, blond, middle-aged man dressed in formal evening clothes stepped forward. "It is my great pleasure to have you in my home. May I present my wife, Suzanne de Bruyker-Abetz."

Hertz took the Ambassador's wife's hand and kissed it. He thanked himself for his Viennese manners. "My pleasure."

"Thank you for having us to your beautiful home," Berta said.

"The pleasure is ours," replied Madame Abetz.

Hertz noted the wife's German. It was good, but it wasn't native.

Suzanne Abetz approached Kurt. She devoured him with her eyes. "You have a very handsome son."

Madame Abetz's gaze made Kurt uncomfortable. "Thank you, ma'am," he replied, took her hand and kissed it, imitating his father.

"And well mannered." Madame Abetz gestured toward the dining room. "Please come in. I know you've had a very long and active day. You must be exhausted. Come meet our other guests."

They followed Madame Abetz into the dining room. The table was exquisitely set with fine, silver-rimmed china, sterling silver cutlery and etched crystal stemware. Two men in tuxedoes and a young woman in a black, shoulderless evening gown, her long, blond hair styled atop her head exposing her long neck, stood at the table. There was an empty place in between each of them and one at the foot of the table.

Suzanne Abetz gestured toward the empty chair at the end. "Deputy Consul Berlin, please do us the honor of sitting opposite my husband. And you, young Kurt, please take that spot there, next to my niece. Madame Berlin if you would sit here, next to me."

"Of course," replied Berta.

"May I present my niece, Colette de Bruyker and two members of my husband's staff, Günter Brinks and Milo de Ruthiers. It's my pleasure to introduce Deputy Consul Berlin, his lovely wife Madame Berlin, and their son Kurt."

"A pleasure to meet you," both Brinks and de Ruthiers said, bowing.

"Please, be seated. Francois." Abetz called to the butler. "Serve some of that fine burgundy we brought up for the occasion. I must apologize, Deputy Consul Berlin, or may I call you Hertz?"

"Hertz, of course, and no apology is needed?"

The butler returned with the bottle of wine and poured it into Abetz's glass. Abetz swirled the wine, checked its bouquet then tasted it. He nodded to the butler, who then poured the wine around the table

Abetz raised his glass. "To Deputy Consul Berlin and his family."

"Prost," the assembled guests cheered, raising their glasses."

"Normally we would have assembled a larger group to welcome you," said Abetz. "And have begun with cocktails in the study. We didn't know you were coming and sadly, you have only tonight."

"The fault is mine," Hertz said, he sipped the wine again. It was excellent but had no effect on the level of his stress. "I should have notified you. We didn't want to be a bother, as we are here for such a short time."

Abetz tasted his wine. He swirled it in his glass again and held it up to the light to check its hue. "Don't be foolish, you're no bother." He was nonchalant. "Frankly, I'm surprised I didn't receive a cable from the Reich Ministry for Foreign Affairs. They usually notify me when a janitor is passing through, much less a Deputy Consul. It's very curious."

Hertz swallowed hard. He considered again whether von Hauptmann was behind this and chose his words carefully. "It is curious. One would think our ministry would be more efficient. In any event, I have to thank someone for notifying you. Travel is so arduous these days."

"You can thank that young officer in Brussels who helped you at the station," Madame Abetz said.

Hertz considered the possibilities. It could have been the young officer, or it could be von Hauptmann manipulating or impersonating that young officer.

"He sent us a cable to make sure someone would be at the station. He saw that you had tickets only as far as Paris and wanted someone here to assist in case of a problem," said Abetz.

"We will send him a note," Berta said.

Madame Abetz touched Berta's hand gently. "I will have his name forwarded to you before you leave. When is that again?"

"At 6:00 tomorrow evening."

Abetz raised his glass again. "Here, here. To the Fuehrer, the Fatherland, your posting in Santo Domingo and that fine young officer in Brussels."

After the toast, servants entered the dining room, eight of them in line, each carrying a plate of foie gras, which they placed in front of the dinner guests in perfect unison.

"Enjoy your first course," Abetz said. "Directly from Bordeaux." Abetz sampled the foie gras and pronounced it excellent. He smiled at Hertz. "And where are you from?"

"Vienna," Hertz replied.

"A lovely city. I spent some time there, after the war, in the early 20's."

"We miss it already," Hertz said. "But our assignment is only for two years."

"By then the war should be over. Too bad for you, young man, you'll miss all the fun. How old are you?"

Kurt smiled. "I am sixteen. I will be seventeen in March."

"You look so much older," Madame Abetz said.

"I think it's the dinner jacket," Berta said. Kurt blushed, the redness on his face evident in the glow of the candlelight.

"I think you look very handsome in your dinner jacket," Colette Bruyker said. "I'm sorry you won't be staying longer. I'd like to know you better."

"Thank you," Kurt said. He felt the blush intensify.

"Perhaps when young Kurt returns," said Abetz, "he will help us build a new Europe. He can spend some days with us here in Paris. You can show him around, Colette."

"I would love that," Colette replied. She placed her hand on top of Kurt's. "We can write to each other in the meantime. It's exciting to hear about life in an exotic place. Where is it again that you are going?"

"Santo Domingo." Madame Abetz said.

Collette looked directly at her. Suzanne Abetz shifted her gaze, eyebrows arched, from Colette's eyes to her hand on Kurt's. Colette withdrew her hand and placed it in her lap. "Writing would be a wonderful idea," Madame Abetz agreed. "And we would love to have you back when you return to Europe."

The head butler approached Abetz. He leaned into him from behind and whispered something in his ear. "Yes, yes," Abetz said aloud. "Of course."

The butler signaled to the staff to enter the room. They removed the plates from the first course and returned with the second, a salad of lobster and haricot vert. The sommelier followed, pouring a pale white wine into new glasses.

"Oh my," said Berta. "That looks exquisite."

Abetz raised his glass. "From Brittany. To you Madame. Please enjoy."

Hertz raised his glass. "To our host."

"To our host," replied everyone at the table.

"I have to say I'm a bit surprised," Hertz said.

"By what?" Abetz asked.

"The availability of such rare things. We heard there were terrible shortages here."

Abetz chuckled. "For the French, that's true. But for us…well…you know, to the conquerors go the spoils." He cut a large piece off the tail of the lobster, popped it in his mouth and savored it. "Delicious," he mused, then cut another. "I'm surprised at you, Berlin. As a diplomat, you must know what our plan is for those we have conquered."

Hertz glanced at Berta. He wasn't sure how to respond to Abetz's statement.

"What a beautiful home this is," Berta said.

"Thank you, Madame Berlin, or may I address you as Berta?" Abetz raised his glass to her once again.

"Berta is fine."

"It was the home of a wealthy Jew," Abetz said.

Hertz's skin crawled. He thought of von Hauptmann living in Halevy's townhouse in Brussels. Hertz gazed around the room, filled with paintings and fine objets d'art.

"He claims his family lived here since the time just after Napoleon," Abetz said. "I believe he mentioned sometime in the 1820's. He's living in a small flat in the Marais now." Abetz laughed. "With the rest of the vermin."

"We began enforcing the Nuremberg laws here just the other day," said de Ruthiers, who had been silent up until then.

"We will be enforcing them rigorously," Abetz added. "De Ruthiers here is in charge of that program. He is the party's representative on matters of racial purity."

"We can't make these changes soon enough," interjected Günter Brinks. "They are like vermin. If we are ever to win over the French, we need to separate them from the Jews. Can you imagine, some French help them."

"Really," Madame Abetz said. "I am French, and I don't understand some of my countrymen. Let the Jews go elsewhere, America, Britain, Africa, though no one seems to want them." The guests chuckled. Suzanne Abetz raised her glass to her lips covering the smile that had crept up around them.

Kurt felt rancor rise in his chest, but kept one eye on his parents, mimicking their behavior. He wanted to run from the room. The scene in the street earlier today, the old man abused by the soldier, filled his mind.

"Why just today I had a situation where a Frenchman was caught applying for an additional ration card to be used by a Jew," de Ruthiers said. "He claimed his brother had arrived from the countryside and that ration cards hadn't been issued there yet." De Ruthiers put down his glass and leaned forward over the table. "Do they think we are fools? We know where we have issued rations. It turns out the Jew was his former business partner."

"It's curious how these Jews have such control over others that they can get them to break the law," de Ruthiers continued. "I'm beginning to believe the theory that the Jew can control our minds if we aren't careful of them."

Hertz began to perspire. He dabbed his napkin at his lips then his forehead. His predicament was beyond surreal. He was a Jew parading around as a Nazi, in the company of Nazi officers, in the home of a Jew, who had been stripped of his possessions by the Nazis.

"And you Hertz. What do you think of this mess with the Jews?" asked Abetz. He continued to devour his lobster, sucking the meat out of the knuckles. "What shall we do with them? Everywhere we go we encounter more of them. In Germany, we had what, 250,000-300,000. Our programs convinced many to leave, but wherever we go we get more. And some of them are the same Jews!"

"And you should see the looks on their faces," said Brinks, laughing, "when they find themselves in our hands again."

"Did they really think we would stop at the old borders?" de Ruthiers asked.

"So, tell us Berlin, what do you think we should do with them?" Abetz asked again.

Hertz avoided Berta and Kurt's eyes. He took a deep breath and smiled. He wanted to rise slowly from his seat and walk around the table, wrap his hands around Abetz's neck and choke him till his eyeballs popped out of his head. Hertz told himself again, I am no longer Hertz Berlin, refugee Jew fleeing the Nazis. I am Hertz Berlin, member of the Party, just another dedicated servant of the German Reich.

"We should round up every last one of them and send them to America," Hertz replied. "The Americans love them so much, let them have them. There are rumors that their President is one of them, you know."

"Here, here," Abetz said, raising his glass once again. "I'll drink to that."

"Because," Hertz continued, "I believe de Ruthiers here might be right. They seem to have some kind of power over us."

Abetz smiled. "It's good to see you are a thinking man, Berlin." Abetz drained his glass and signaled to the butler to bring the next course.

CHAPTER 31

Outskirts of Mechelen, Belgium - June 1945

Kurt picked up the pail of water Saul hauled from the well and threw it on von Hauptmann. The icy liquid caused the Nazi's body to strain against the ropes holding him to the chair. His eyes showed both surprise and fear. Kurt felt a momentary pang of pity and pulled the gag from von Hauptmann's mouth.

"Is there anything you want to say?"

Von Hauptmann flexed his jaw. "A little water, please," he mumbled, squirming in the chair. "I need to relieve myself."

Kurt gestured to Saul, who dipped a metal cup into a pail of water and brought it to von Hauptmann. Von Hauptmann sipped tentatively, the water not quite reaching his lips. Saul tipped the cup at a sharper angle. The water flowed into von Hauptmann's mouth, some of it dribbling down his chin to his naked chest.

"Thank you," von Hauptmann said.

Kurt was astounded. The Nazi thanked Saul? He wasn't Superman after all. "Go ahead, relieve yourself," Kurt said.

Von Hauptmann let himself go. When he finished, Kurt grabbed the pants he had torn off him the night before and threw them over von Hauptmann. The Nazi's chest, arms, and legs were covered with bites from the insects that lived in the hay. He hoped the rats had come to nibble on him as well.

Saul sat on a chair about ten feet behind Kurt. He pointed his rifle at von Hauptmann even though there was no way the Nazi could escape. "Let's get started," he said.

Kurt put his hands behind his back and paced from side to

side. He stopped in front of von Hauptmann. "You said the other day during your interrogation by Captain McClain, that you were ordered to round up non-Belgian Jews in July of 1943 and send them to Mechelen from where they were sent to the camps. Is that true?"

"Yes."

Von Hauptmann's response was so weak Kurt could barely hear him. "Why? Explain to me why only non-Belgian Jews?"

Von Hauptmann attempted to shift his position is the chair. He winced as he turned his midsection, raised his head and looked directly at Kurt. "Because that was our policy. To rid Europe of Jews." He managed a defiant half-smile.

Kurt noticed that one of von Hauptmann's front teeth had chipped. He hoped it was from his fist and considered breaking the rest.

"We would have sent the whole bunch then, but your Queen appealed to the Fuehrer to let Belgian nationals remain, and for some unknown reason the Fuehrer deferred to her. We began by taking non-Belgian Jews only. People like yourself."

Kurt caught himself. He knew von Hauptmann was baiting him, to throw him off balance. Kurt pulled his revolver from its holster and stuck it in von Hauptmann's open mouth. Power overwhelmed him. "Be careful how you speak to me, because I will kill you. If you cooperate, I may not. If you are disrespectful I will, almost certainly." Kurt withdrew his gun.

"Are you willing to throw away your life? McClain will put you in prison for this, or worse."

Kurt pushed the pistol back into von Hauptmann's mouth. "I told you don't ask me any questions," he growled. Kurt smirked, "Perhaps I should have Saul break another finger?"

At hearing this, Saul got up from his chair and approached von Hauptmann with the hammer. At the third tap, von Hauptmann screamed, "No, no, stop!"

Kurt laughed. "How quickly you turn into a crying old woman. You crumble pretty easily. Like those communists you described to McClain. Let's continue. Why did you seek out children from Kindertransports?

Von Hauptmann thought for a moment. "You are talking

about that group of children that disappeared?"

"Yes."

Von Hauptmann coughed, then winced in pain. "It was simply a matter of accounting. We were to account for every Jew in the country. It didn't matter if they were children or adults, Belgian or refugee. They were still Jews, and some had disappeared."

Kurt was furious. He wanted to bash von Hauptmann's head in, but he still needed to know what von Hauptmann knew about Elsa. He thought to ask him about Elsa directly, but doubted von Hauptmann would know what or who he was asking about. Kurt thought it better to lead von Hauptmann to her, to make von Hauptmann admit the crimes he committed in his search for her. "What do you mean they disappeared?"

"There were no records of exit visas issued by the Belgian government for these children, yet we couldn't locate them."

"And what did you do when you failed to locate these children, or the records?"

Von Hauptmann again tried to shift in the chair. "This is very uncomfortable. It's hard for me to speak in this position."

Kurt enjoyed von Hauptmann's squirming. "I'm waiting."

Saul came out of the darkness. He went over to von Hauptmann and shifted him in the chair. "This treatment is too good for you." He pulled the Nazi's head back by his hair. Von Hauptmann screamed. "Funny," said Saul with a broad smile. "You seemed to enjoy doing that to others." He gave another tug then let go, returning to his perch behind Kurt.

"Now, answer me!" screamed Kurt. "What did you do to find these children!"

"We went to their school, and we interrogated the headmaster. And it wasn't the first time. We looked for that group of children in the summer of 1940."

Kurt recalled the frenzy when the SS came looking for the children that July but kept his counsel and instead focused on questioning Von Hauptmann. "The headmaster? Do you know his name?"

Von Hauptmann sighed. "How can I be expected to remember the name of one single Jew?"

Kurt charged him and slapped him across the face with the back of his hand. "That Jew had a name!" He grabbed von Hauptmann's throat. "It was Isaac Wolfson!" Kurt stepped aside, releasing von Hauptmann. He pushed out his chest and took a deep breath to calm himself. "He brought me out of Vienna!" Kurt's fury reverberated through him. He slapped von Hauptmann across the face again, this time twice. "He saved my life!" Kurt raged. "Now tell me what you did to him!"

Von Hauptmann recoiled.

"Tell me, or I'll have my friend over there break your hand!"

Von Hauptmann averted his eyes from Kurt's. "We beat him," he mumbled.

Kurt grabbed von Hauptmann's chin. He pulled him up from the chair, the ropes restraining von Hauptmann's movement. The legs of the chair tipped backward. Kurt's anger amplified his strength, holding the chair precariously upright on its two back legs. "What did you say?"

Von Hauptmann summoned whatever strength he still had. "We beat him," von Hauptmann stated, slowly and audibly, iterating each word.

Kurt lowered his grip from von Hauptmann's chin to his neck and tightened it. "Really? How does it feel to be beaten? Do you like it?" Kurt's anger swelled, which could just as well have resulted in von Hauptmann's execution now, rather than later. His words escaped his mouth with venom. "Should we beat you to death, the way you did Wolfson!" Kurt let go of von Hauptmann's throat and stepped back, the chair jerking forward.

Von Hauptmann gasped, drawing in as much breath as he could. Despite the cold air and his nakedness, the sweat poured from him. "You don't understand. It was my job."

"Your job!" Kurt screamed, inches from von Hauptmann's face. "You made it clear how much you hate the Jews to McClain!" Kurt paced in front of von Hauptmann. "Don't try to change your story. I was in the room. Now, how did you find the list of the children and the host families?"

"It was in the headmaster's possession. He hid it inside the wall in a strong box."

"Did he crack? Did he tell you where the list was?"

Von Hauptmann spit, his saliva was tinged with blood. "No," he croaked. "He was quite brave, for a Jew. There was unevenness to the wall, marks in the plaster. We found the strongbox hidden there after we finished him off."

Kurt strutted back and forth in front of von Hauptmann.

"Do you know why you never found those children in 1940, the first time you went looking for them?" Saul said, appearing from the darkness that hid the recesses of the barn.

Von Hauptmann looked up. "What would you know about that?"

Saul laughed. "Because I was there. And now I have put all the pieces back together. We hid them, all of them, right under your eyes, Wolfson and Halevy and my father and his, and us."

"I was one of those children you sought. We outsmarted you," said Kurt. "We were spying on your men in the park listening to them chatter at the ice cream stand. It was me selling the ice cream. I was listening and reporting back to the Jewish Council."

Von Hauptmann's head slumped to his chest.

"We knew what you were about to do with that first roundup in the spring of 1940," said Saul. He was standing over von Hauptmann now, a hunting knife at the German's throat. We took the children away to a farm not far from Oostende, run by monks. We brought them back later, right under your nose."

Von Hauptmann began to laugh, each chuckle excruciating for his broken ribs.

"What's funny?" Kurt asked. He pointed the pistol at von Hauptmann's head.

"I thought that was you. I wasn't sure. But now that you mention Halevy, I am sure. You're Hertz Berlin's son, or should I say, Hirsch Katz. As cunning as him, perhaps more so."

The mention of his father caught Kurt off guard, his mind now in disarray. "How could you know that?"

"Because I've known your father in several lives. He's like a cat. He keeps landing on his feet and escaping, despite my best efforts to the contrary." Von Hauptmann strained against the rope, blood seeping from his wrists where the twine cut into them. "I thought I had killed him in Budapest some twenty-five years ago, but then he showed up again in Brussels." Von Hauptmann chuckled, his teeth covered with blood and saliva. "You know young Berlin, we wouldn't be here like this together, if I hadn't sold him those passports, the diplomatic forgeries. You'd all have ended up in Auschwitz. Seems I did myself a disservice. And how are they, your father and your lovely mother? I imagine they are safe, in America? Perhaps I will see him again when I get there."

The mention of his parents pushed Kurt over the edge. He took his revolver from its holster and struck von Hauptmann across the temple. The force of the blow knocked the German unconscious onto the earthen, hay-covered floor. Kurt felt satiated.

Several hours later Von Hauptmann regained consciousness. He winced in pain as he opened his eyes. Something deep inside Kurt nagged at him as he watched von Hauptmann regain consciousness. Kurt was ashamed of the hate that had taken over his mind. He felt entitled to that hate but was disgusted by what it had done to him. Von Hauptmann was a murderer, but he was still, somehow, human.

Kurt nudged Saul, dozing on the pile of hay behind them. "He's awake."

Saul opened his eyes and yawned. "Good, let's finish this."

"Wait," Kurt said, holding Saul back. "I want to say something."

"What?"

"I've been thinking about what we've done. We came with a mission. To find out what happened to Elsa, your family, and the Mandelbaum's."

"And to punish him for his crimes."

"We're not going to kill him."

"No? Then what do you propose we do? Return him? They will kill us for what we've done. We have to finish him off and get rid of the body. He's responsible."

Kurt put his hands on Saul's shoulders. "I have an idea."

"What?"

"Sam."

"What about him?"

"I left the transcripts and the tapes in his apartment. He has the truth. He was away for a couple of nights. They sent him to Frankfurt. I figured his apartment would be the safest place to leave everything. When he sees what Rosenthaller and McClain have done, the way they altered the testimony, he'll take it to his superior officers."

"Go on."

"We'll make this pig sign a confession, then give him to Sam. That will discredit Rosenthaller and McClain too. The British want Von Hauptmann."

Tear tracks lined Saul's face. "Perhaps. Let's see. I'm not done with him yet."

Kurt averted his eyes. He hesitated. "Neither am I," he replied. "But we can't kill him. That makes us him."

Saul nodded. They understood each other in a way only brothers do.

"Help me right him, and the chair."

It was clear how severely injured von Hauptmann was. A lump and a purple bruise had formed where Kurt pistol-whipped him. "Bitte," he said, weakly. "I will tell you whatever you want to know, but please either kill me or let me go. No more torture."

Saul and Kurt picked up the chair from the floor of the barn with von Hauptmann in it. Kurt picked up Saul's rifle and pointed it toward von Hauptmann. "Untie him."

Saul looked at Kurt. "Are you sure?"

Kurt switched to French. "Yes. Think about what we are doing. Would your father, or mine, or Wolfson or Mandelbaum have condoned this?"

Saul caught himself at the thought of his father and his teachers. He had strayed so far from what they taught him. He felt as if the Nazis had turned him into something less than human. That's what they wanted. Saul felt the tears rise. He wanted his revenge, but more than anything he wanted to feel human again. He untied von Hauptmann.

"Put on your pants," Kurt said.

"I can't walk," von Hauptmann replied.

Kurt looked at von Hauptmann's legs and feet. They were black and blue from the beating. Perhaps they had broken a bone or two. "Saul, go in the house please, bring some blankets."

Saul ran off. Kurt kept the rifle aimed at von Hauptmann's head. "We're not going to kill you. But you are going to sign a confession. You're going to admit to what you've done. You're not going to America. I don't care what they do to me. I'll go to prison happily, as long as you do too."

Von Hauptmann remained silent. Saul ran back into the barn with two heavy blankets, one in each hand. Kurt threw a pair of handcuffs over to Saul. "Cuff one arm to the back of the chair and cover him." Von Hauptmann disappeared under the grey wool blankets. "We have a few more questions."

"May I have some water?"

Kurt looked over to Saul, who nodded and brought a cup of water to von Hauptmann. The Nazi took the cup with his left hand, as yet unbroken, and sipped at it. He breathed deeply after he finished the water.

"Why were you so intent on locating Elsa Graz?" Kurt demanded.

Von Hauptmann looked up at Kurt. He grimaced. "Is that what this is about? That half-breed?"

Kurt had to control himself. He felt the anger rising again. Von Hauptmann was unrepentant. "Is that what you call her?"

Von Hauptmann became agitated. "I told you, it was an accounting exercise. We lost track of some of the children. The reason for that is obvious now. Her name didn't appear on any lists of those who had left Brussels, nor on the lists we found in the headmaster's possession. It was clear she was still in Brussels. She was the daughter of a troublemaker. I wasn't about to let her get away. I had lost track of too many. It was my responsibility to deliver her."

"Why did you go looking for her at the Mandelbaums?"

"The old Jewish couple?"

"Yes."

"Because that's the only lead we had. Her Belgian documents mentioned them."

Saul stepped from the shadows. "Why did you beat them?

They clearly were no threat. I was there, I saw what you did."

Von Hauptmann shook his head from side to side. "You were the boy who escaped over the rooftops?"

"Yes."

"And the two of you think for the beating of an old man and his wife I will be sent to prison?"

Saul stepped closer to the Nazi. Only the thought of his father restrained his fists. "No, I think you will be sent to prison, or perhaps executed, for sending tens of thousands to their deaths."

Hate and the desire for revenge overwhelmed Saul, regardless of what his father would have thought. This was for his father and mother, Mandelbaum and Wolfson, and most importantly, his sister. Saul took two more steps toward von Hauptmann and grabbed his hair again, pulling back his head violently. Von Hauptmann shrieked. Kurt came up behind Saul and tried to pull him back. Saul released von Hauptmann and turned. "I've got to do this," he said to Kurt. "I won't kill him."

"Saul, stop!" Kurt pleaded.

Saul pushed Kurt back, a knife in his hand. "No, brother, don't even try!" Nothing could stop Saul now. An image of himself as a boy, tzitzit dangling from his pants, appeared before his own eyes. Then that innocent Jewish boy walked away into the barn's darkness. Saul turned back to von Hauptmann and grabbed his hair for the third time, pulling it back even more tightly. He slipped a dagger under von Hauptmann's throat. "I could butcher you now like a kosher chicken." He dragged out the word kosher as if it were an incantation. "That old Jew was my teacher. He taught me to read and to pray. He put a piece of candy in my mouth the first time I correctly said the Shema. He taught me to love my Jewishness. You made me hate it, and myself. Now it's my time. I stood there on those steps listening to their pleas, an old man, an old woman, and a screaming child. You laughed like a madman. I won't kill you. I promised my brother over there I wouldn't. But I will take a souvenir."

Saul yanked back von Hauptmann's head, and with one quick motion he sliced off half of the Nazi's left ear. Von Hauptmann shrieked in pain. "This was no use to you anyway, as you apparently couldn't hear their screams! I hear those screams every moment of every day!"

Kurt came up from behind Saul and grabbed his arm. Saul turned. He opened his right hand, the knife falling to the ground. In his left, Saul held the piece of flesh shorn from von Hauptmann. "He's all yours," Saul said and disappeared into the same shadows as his boyhood phantom moments earlier.

Kurt picked up the remnants of the shirt he ripped off of von Hauptmann's body the night before. He tied it around von Hauptmann's head to cover the wound and absorb the bleeding. He was sickened by what he had just seen, but at the same time, he understood the deep pain that drove Saul to do what he had done.

CHAPTER 32

Lyon, Vichy France - October 1940

The mood in Lyon was surreal, different than in Paris or Brussels; which were occupied outright. Vichy France felt more like Vienna just before the Anschluss. There was something amiss, something running just under the surface. Nothing was exactly as it seemed, but unless one was aware of it, unless one knew the signs, one would never know.

The Gare de Lyon rail station was built in the same grand style as every belle epoch station in Europe. Soaring spaces designed to impress the masses. "Bon jour," Hertz said to the clerk behind the brass bars at the ticket window.

"How can I help you, sir?" the clerk asked.

Hertz followed the clerk's eyes to the Nazi party pin on his lapel. "I need three tickets in a sleeper car to Madrid."

"I have a cabin for three on the 21st, two days from now. It's in first class."

"That will be fine."

"May I have your documents monsieur?"

Hertz handed his leather folio to the clerk. "You will find everything you need in here."

"Merci," said the clerk. "I'll need a few minutes."

"Where might we go for a coffee while you prepare the tickets?"

"There is a café in the main hall."

Hertz and Kurt walked to the Great Hall and found a small café at the far end beyond the passenger waiting area. They strolled to it and sat at a table at the front. A waiter arrived a moment later. "Only coffee for me, thanks," Hertz said in French.

"And for the young man?"

"Orangina, si'l vous plait."

Hertz surveyed the seated travelers in the waiting area, men mostly, a few with women, one family with two small children, an elderly couple. "You see," he whispered to Kurt, trying to convince himself as much as his son, "It's as I've told you. We look and sound the part. No one suspects anything."

The waiter returned with their drinks. "Anything with that? The waiter nodded in the direction of the kitchen. "The croissants are fresh."

"I'll take one, please," Kurt replied.

The rich scent of coffee wafted to Hertz's nose. A voice, amplified through a megaphone, drew both Hertz's and Kurt's attention.

"This is the Municipal Police. We are conducting a check of identification. Please have your papers out and ready for review."

Hertz caught the look of terror in Kurt's eyes. "Stay calm."

The Vichy police swarmed into the cavernous waiting area. The pigeons that made the soaring interior of the station home, scattered. Those caught in the action appeared to wish they could do the same. They nervously reached into pockets and bags to produce their documents. Behind the Vichy police, were three men, all in suites.

"You see those men there?" Hertz said.

"Yes," replied Kurt.

"They're SS."

The SS men sauntered into the Great Hall. Two followed the police. The third approached the café.

"Remember, act as if you belong here." Hertz sipped his coffee. Kurt followed Hertz's lead with his Orangina, then took a bite of the croissant. He was so frightened he wasn't sure he could swallow what was in his mouth. The SS officer swaggered into the café and looked around. Smiling broadly, he nodded his head to the customers and the proprietor. "I'll take an espresso," he said in German, too loudly.

"Ja wohl," replied the proprietor, running off to the kitchen.

The Nazi was tall by Hertz's estimate, at least his own height. He was elegantly dressed in a dark gray, double-breasted suit with a black, wide-rimmed fedora. He scanned the crowd and nodded at Hertz and Kurt.

"Your espresso, sir" the waiter said, returning with the coffee in a small cup and saucer. The German sipped without paying. He nodded at Hertz. "A guten morgen."

"Good morning," Hertz replied.

Kurt followed his example. "Good morning, sir."

"May I join you?" the SS officer said, approaching their table.

"Of course," Hertz said.

The croissant and orangina crept back up into Kurt's mouth. He thought he might vomit. Shouting came from the center of the Great Hall. Kurt eyes locked onto the scene. The Vichy police demanded the papers of a young woman with a small child. The woman fumbled with her bag, the little girl hiding in the folds of her dress. The police shouted at her. Now the child was crying. Kurt felt beads of sweat forming on his forehead.

"My name is Willy Krantz," the large Nazi said, distracting Kurt from the developing drama. Krantz pulled up his trousers at the knee as he sat down. Once seated, he extended his hand to Hertz.

"Hertz Berlin. This is my son, Kurt." Krantz reached out over the table. Kurt rose from the chair and shook Krantz's hand. Shouting from the passenger area continued.

Krantz pointed toward the pin on Hertz's lapel. "Party members."

"Yes. I'm a diplomat." Butterflies fluttered in Hertz's stomach and chest. He was testing the limits of his new persona. "We're on our way to Santo Domingo for two years."

"Very nice." Krantz sipped the espresso. "Is the croissant good?"

The question caught Kurt off guard. He was engrossed by the spectacle in the Great Hall. "Yes."

"Bring me one of those," Krantz called out to the waiter. The pastry appeared within seconds.

Kurt re-focused on the waiting area. The contents of the woman's bag were now strewn on the floor, but she finally produced her papers. She was crying, and the child, hysterical. The police pushed her away. They proceeded on to their next victim, a man of about his father's age. He cut a forlorn picture in worn clothing, holding his hat in his hand, his eyes cast down to the floor, a single, frayed suitcase at his side.

Krantz consumed the croissant in two bites. He wiped his hands clumsily on his napkin then brushed his fingers against his pants, leaving the remaining crumbs there. Hertz was astounded at how so many members of Hitler's elite clearly lacked social grooming, manners, and polish.

"Care to have a little fun?" Krantz asked? Let's go over there. See what the Frenchman does with that Jew."

Hertz hesitated for a moment. It was hard enough to maintain this charade to begin with. Participating in terror he could only too easily be caught up in himself, was something else altogether. He didn't think he was capable. "How do you know he's a Jew?" Hertz said.

Krantz laughed and slurped up the last of his espresso. "Look at him. He's so nervous he's about to piss himself. That can only mean one thing."

"Normally I'd love to," Hertz said. "But we have to pick up our tickets. We leave for Madrid tomorrow."

"Nonsense," said Krantz. "Send the boy for the tickets. Let's teach this Jew a lesson."

Hertz took a deep breath. "That's a fine idea." At least he could spare Kurt. He reached into his pocket and produced a wad of Francs. "Pay the man and go back to the window. I'll meet you there in a few minutes."

Krantz put his hand over Hertz's before Kurt could take the banknote. "Nonsense. Put that away. We don't pay for anything here."

Hertz looked at Kurt. "Go," he said.

"Of course, father." Kurt picked up his hat from the table and walked off quickly toward the ticket window. He looked back as he walked across the hall to where the police were harassing the unfortunate soul Krantz had selected for his entertainment.

Rage and fear rose from Hertz's stomach into his chest as he watched Kurt disappear from view. Fear reached the finish line first.

"Come, let's have our fun," Krantz said.

"All right, let's go," he said, following Krantz.

"We'll take over from here," Krantz said, to the policeman.

The policeman saluted. "Of course, sir."

Krantz looked at his victim then back to the police. "Does he have his papers?"

"No, monsieur."

"I didn't expect so." Krantz slapped the terrified man across his cheek with his leather gloves, leaving a welt and knocking off the victim's hat. "Look at me, Jew!" Krantz shouted.

The man, trembling, lifted his head. For a second Hertz wasn't sure. The face was familiar, but thinner and now bearded, though poorly coiffed. The man's eyes were sunken into his skull and expressed deep fear. Krantz's prey looked up and caught Hertz's gaze. Hertz was now certain. It was Benny Offenberg. Offenberg looked back at Hertz. Hertz knew Offenberg recognized him as well.

"Jew! Where are your papers?" shouted Krantz again.

Offenberg opened his mouth to speak. Nothing came out. Krantz slapped him across the face again, this time bare handed and even harder, knocking him off balance. Offenberg stumbled but righted himself. A small trickle of blood escaped from the corner of his mouth. He reached into his pocket and pulled out a passport and some other papers, handing them to Krantz.

Krantz examined them. Offenberg shifted his gaze back to Hertz. Hertz realized the image of him in a suit and wearing a Nazi party pin in the company of Krantz was so incongruous that Offenberg couldn't react. He merely looked at Hertz and furled his brow in confusion.

Krantz threw the passport and papers on the floor. "Pierre Moulin? Bullshit! These aren't even good forgeries! Who are you Jew, and where do you think you're going?"

Hertz watched as Offenberg crumbled. He wanted to reach out to him, to keep him on his feet like a man, but Hertz knew

Offenberg was finished. Offenberg looked directly at Hertz. Hertz mouthed the words *no*, and *I will help you,* from behind Krantz. Offenberg closed his eyes and spoke softly. "My name is Benjamin Offenberg. I am a Jew."

Krantz swung his hand downward toward Offenberg's face slapping him hard again, this time opening a cut on the left side of his mouth, knocking him down. "Stand up you swine! Where are you coming from!"

Offenberg struggled to his feet. His face contorted. "Paris. Do what you want with me." His voice cracked, and his face contorted. "I can't run anymore."

"I should kill you right here," Krantz said, "but we have a bigger problem. There are too many like you. We need to know where you got those papers."

Offenberg's tears slid silently down his cheeks onto the tiled floor of the station's waiting area. Hertz's breath caught in his chest. He knew he had to maintain his calm, his cover. If he broke now, he would not only end his own life, but Berta's and Kurt's as well. Offenberg looked at him again. Hertz saw the confusion in Offenberg's eyes. Hertz mouthed silently, again. *Don't betray me. I will help you.*

"You, there," Krantz screamed at the policeman standing about two meters to the left. "Take this man into custody. Deliver him to the station for interrogation."

The policeman handcuffed Offenberg and dragged him away. Krantz turned to Hertz, smiling. "Too much for you, Berlin? You look a little gray."

Hertz paced about the suite in the hotel. The curtains were drawn against the window behind them. "What do you expect me to do?"

Berta leaned against the back of the couch. She put her hand over her eyes but said nothing.

"I can't just leave him there."

Kurt looked at Hertz. He wanted to scream but knew better. The endless stress of the past two years taught him to bottle his anger, save it for the appropriate moment, a moment when he would use it to give him strength rather than to sap him of it.

"Father, it's too dangerous."

Hertz placed his hands behind his back and stuck out his chin. "Really? You think so? It seems to me that this little pin on my lapel has turned me into some kind of superman. They think I'm one of them. They'll never know."

Berta took her hand from her forehead. She feared their success to this point had gone to Hertz's head. "Unless they suspect something and interrogate you, and if they really want proof, you know what, they'll pull down your pants."

Kurt was shocked. He'd never heard his mother speak so foully. Kurt felt a mixture of dread and panic. What would they do if his father were caught? "Please," Kurt pleaded, "mother is right."

Berta stood up. She took two steps toward Hertz. "This man is nothing to us!" she shouted. Her hands balled into fists. "You cannot take a chance like this!"

Hertz stepped back. He looked at Berta and understood that she was frightened, but also knew he could never live with himself if he did nothing. "Nothing to us? He was my friend in a place where there are no friends. I can't stand by and watch this."

"So, you would risk our safety for his freedom?" Berta pleaded.

"Yes."

"Why, father?"

"Because despite all of this, despite everything we have been through, I need to show you, my son, what is right and what is wrong."

�

Hertz waited till late in the evening to go to the police station. He walked into the lobby directly to the duty officer sitting at the desk. Hertz addressed him loudly, rudely, and in German. "I am with the Foreign Ministry! I have orders to speak with one of your prisoners, immediately!"

The duty officer jumped out of his chair. He answered in broken German. "Please sir, could you wait here?"

"Why should I wait here!" Hertz shouted at him. "I have business to conduct, and it's quite late!"

"Please, let me get my superior officer. His German is much better than mine," the duty officer replied, then ran off to the back of the station.

Hertz breathed a sigh of relief. Had he been convincing enough, or perhaps he was merely aggressive enough? Maybe they were the same thing in this situation. The duty officer returned a moment later with another officer, a man in his middle forties whose uniform was just a bit too tight.

"Captain Jean-Marie Coupelle. May I help you?" the officer said in passable German.

"I am Hertz Berlin, with the Foreign Ministry. I need to speak with one of your prisoners. We received a call from Commandant Abetz earlier this evening. You have a Jew in custody by the name of Offenberg. I am to interrogate him. We believe he has information about a forger we have been hunting in Paris."

"This is very unusual, especially at this hour. Perhaps I should contact Captain Krantz."

Hertz stiffened and took a step toward Coupelle. "I was just with him!" he shouted. "Who do you think sent me! Perhaps you would like to contact Commandant Abetz in Paris himself!"

The Frenchman took a step back. He glanced at the clock on the wall behind him. It was past 11. "The prisoners are asleep."

"Then wake him and get to it. I don't have all night."

Offenberg stared at Hertz, his mouth agape. "Berlin?" he whispered, "I thought that was you. But how could it be?"

Hertz walked toward him. He put a finger over his mouth. "Be careful what you say. Follow my leads. I'm sure they're listening. What happened? I thought you were going somewhere in the Caribbean?" Hertz whispered.

Offenberg looked at him, still in disbelief. "They found out I lied on my application about being single. They rejected me. I was trying to get to Spain, so that I might get to England."

"Where did you get those documents!" Hertz shouted at him. "Tell me Jew, or I will kill you here!"

"I told your associate this afternoon," Offenberg replied loudly. "I bought them from a man in the market in Paris. I don't know his name."

Hertz approached him and whispered, "I'm going to strike you." Then Hertz shouted, "You're lying!" and slapped Offenberg across the face, knocking him off the chair and onto the floor. Hertz turned and flung open the door. Coupelle and the duty officer were standing directly in front of it, as he suspected. "Do you have some handcuffs and a nightstick?"

The two men looked at each other. "Yes," Coupelle replied.

"Fetch them. And be quick about it." Hertz turned quickly and slammed the door to the interrogation room. He rushed to Offenberg and helped him up from the floor. "Forgive me, friend. I had no choice."

"I understand, that's alright." Offenberg rubbed his chin and cheek where Hertz struck him.

Hertz helped him back into the chair. "We don't have much time. What are you doing in Lyon?"

"I was in Paris when the Germans invaded. I've been living on forged papers. These were only the most recent."

There was a loud knock on the door. "I have what you've asked for," called Coupelle though the door.

Hertz opened the door and took the cuffs and baton from Coupelle. "Give me fifteen minutes." He slammed the door again.

"I'm going to have to put these on you."

"I understand." Hertz cuffed Offenberg's hands behind the chair.

"How is it that you are impersonating a Nazi? Is your family here with you?"

"Yes. We got stuck in Brussels waiting to leave for the United States. I bought passports from a corrupt SS Captain. Turns out they are diplomatic passports. I am to be the cultural attaché to our embassy in Santo Domingo."

Offenberg smiled through his pain and despite his terror. "That would be really funny if not for the situation."

Hertz looked at Offenberg then nodded. "Yes, it would, wouldn't it? I am going to try to help you." He stuck his hand in his pocket and pulled out three one-karat diamonds. "I am going to have to beat you a little to make this look real. I am leaving tomorrow on the train for Madrid. Use these to bribe the guards after I leave."

Offenberg looked at Hertz with tears in his eyes. Hertz slipped the stones into Offenberg's pocket. "Thank you, I'm ready. Do what you must. And God protect you."

"Tell me who sold you those papers!" Hertz shouted, then struck Offenberg in the chest. Offenberg screamed in pain. They continued this charade for a few minutes. Hertz opened the door of the cell and shouted to Coupelle. "I have the forger's name. Where is the bathroom? I need to clean myself up before I call Paris." Hertz took a handkerchief from inside his pants pocket and wiped Offenberg's blood off his hands.

"Down the hall, sir."

"Clean that prisoner up!"

Hertz walked briskly to the bathroom. He vomited into the sink. Every blow to Offenberg was excruciating for him. Hertz wanted to sink to his knees and cry. He had no choice, and he knew Offenberg forgave him, but nonetheless Hertz was devastated by what he had done. He hoped only that the diamonds would help Offenberg to escape.

Hertz washed his face and hands and fastened his cufflinks. He put his jacket back on and slipped out of the bathroom. He walked down the hall and out of the police station. Hertz hurried down the street and stopped in the shadows. He leaned against a wall, took a cigarette out of his pocket and lit it, his heartbeat pounding. He took a long drag on the cigarette, held it a moment in his lungs then exhaled.

"Turn around, Berlin," Hertz heard from behind him. It was Krantz. He had a gun pointed at Hertz. "If that's really your name."

Hertz backed up a few steps. If he could get to the corner, he would make a break for it.

"Stop right there. I got a call earlier from that cockroach Coupelle. That's when I knew for certain that you were a fraud. I did some checking. I contacted the Foreign Ministry. They have no record of you at all. I called Abetz. He suspected something was off when he met you. He checked with Brussels, a Captain von Hauptmann. This von Hauptmann told us who you really are."

The mention of von Hauptmann made it clear to Hertz what he needed to do. "It's not what you think," he said, moving back a few more steps.

Krantz laughed. "I'd say it's exactly what I think. You're a Jew."

Hertz laughed as well. "If I were a Jew would I have beat up the prisoner?"

"You're a sly one, sharper than most," Krantz said. "Then where did the prisoner get these?" He held the diamonds in his open palm. "We searched him this afternoon. He had nothing. He could have gotten these only from you."

Hertz turned the corner and ran. Krantz was right behind him. He saw an alley on his left and ducked into its inky darkness. Hertz stuck his foot out just enough to trip Krantz. A moment later he grabbed the Nazi by his arm as Krantz tripped and began to fall, punching him in the jaw. Hertz dragged the big man into the alleyway, covering Krantz's mouth with his hand to stifle his shouts. Hertz didn't know where his strength to overpower Krantz was coming from.

They struggled in the darkness. Hertz slammed Krantz's arm against the wall to knock the gun out of his hand. Krantz was strong, but Hertz was desperate. On the third attempt, the pistol fell to the pavement. Krantz bit down on Hertz's palm. Hertz stifled his own scream then slammed his knee into Krantz's groin. The German doubled over. Hertz twisted Krantz's arm backward. With his other hand, he grabbed Krantz's chin and jerked it in the opposite direction snapping his neck. The Nazi's body went limp. Hertz let Krantz slip to the ground.

Hertz dry-heaved. He knew he had very little time. He reached into Krantz's pants pocket and removed the diamonds. There was nothing more he could do for Offenberg.

He had to dispose of Krantz's body. There was a large garbage tin at the rear of the alley. Hertz dragged the body to it, opened it, dug down through the garbage to create a hole, tossed in the body and covered it. By the time anyone found Krantz,

Hertz and his family would be long gone.

CHAPTER 33

Brussels, Belgium - June 1945

S am closed the briefcase containing the files on Joachim von Hauptmann. He found it with a note from Kurt at the bottom of his closet in his apartment when he'd returned to Brussels the day before. He shuttered when he read Kurt's note. Kurt had crossed a line. Sam would do whatever he could to help him, but he knew they were navigating in unchartered waters.

Clearly, there was enough here to hold von Hauptmann for trial. He was in charge of the deportations of Jews from Brussels and other major cities in Belgium. That alone would preclude recruiting him for intelligence work, according to the agreements made between the Allied commands. All that was evident from the documents Kurt had left for him, confirmed by the reports on von Hauptmann he'd gotten from British army intelligence.

Yet Sam knew there was more, and he was certain Hertz knew what that more was. He checked his watch. It was past midnight. That would work in his favor on two counts. The telephone exchange would be empty, and it was six hours earlier in Washington, D.C. Hertz would likely be at home.

Sam took the files and locked them into the top drawer of his file cabinet then locked his office and walked down the two flights to the switchboard. A single operator, a woman in her mid 20's, was on duty. She was reading a book, the boards dark for lack of activity.

"Excuse me, sorry to bother you," Sam said.

The young woman looked up. She appeared to be in her mid-twenties. Short, brown hair framed her pretty face. "No, bother. Did you need to place a call?" She had the accent of a Londoner from the East End.

"Yes." Sam handed her the number.

"Please, go into the booth."

Sam entered and turned on the light. A moment later the operator signaled to him to pick up the phone. It rang twice.

"Halo," said the voice at the other end.

"Hertz, it's Sam."

Hertz hesitated a moment. "What's wrong?"

"Nothing."

"Something has happened to Kurt?"

"No." Sam's stomach turned.

"Why are you calling? It's the middle of the night there."

"I need to ask you some questions. About this SS Officer you mentioned to me, von Hauptmann. I've come across him."

Hertz paused. "He's very dangerous."

"I'm aware of that. It's worse." Sam threw caution to the wind. He knew the operator was listening and he knew he was exposing both himself and Kurt. "The Americans have him. Kurt is the translator for his interrogation." He knew better than to tell his brother the whole truth.

Hertz screamed into the phone. "Get my son away from him!"

Sam breathed deeply. "Calm down, brother. I intend to do just that. I need to know his secrets. The Americans want to play with him. They're recruiting him to work for them."

Sam heard Berta screaming in the background. She wanted to know what was wrong, who was on the phone. "You can't tell her, brother," Sam said.

"It's nothing Berta, nothing. It's Sam. The connection is terrible, I misunderstood something he said and got frightened."

"Hertz, what do I need to know?"

"For starters, he's a murderer going all the way back to the first war. Second, he's not who he says he is. He parades around as an aristocrat. His father was a commoner and a Hungarian. And he's corrupt. He was in league with officials at a dozen embassies in Brussels to produce false papers, which he then sold to wealthy Jews. And he stole your father-in-law's house and the cottage at Oostende. And most importantly, he's very dangerous. He's a born killer. He enjoys it. Get my son away from him."

"I promise brother, I will. Stay calm."

"Said like a true Englishman. That's not going to help me." The line clicked off.

Sam looked at the operator. He signaled to her to stay in her seat.

"Yes, Colonel?" she said as he approached.

"Can I trust that this conversation will remain between us, at least for the time being?"

"It was highly irregular," the operator said.

"My nephew's life may depend on your discretion."

She smiled. "Of course, Colonel," she said. "We have to look after each other. Especially after what's happened to our people."

Sam smiled. "Thank you…"

"Miriam, Miriam White," she said, offering her hand. It used to be Weiss. I was born in Frankfurt."

试戈

Sam sat opposite Rosenthaller in his office. McClain hovered behind Rosenthaller, pacing.

"Colonel Berlin, your nephew has kidnapped a future asset of the OSS," McClain said.

"He's facing a Court Marshall," Rosenthaller added. "If you want to be of any help to him, you must help us find him. If he's killed von Hauptmann, he'll be tried for murder. If found guilty, he'll face a firing squad."

Sam waited a moment before responding. He commanded his best British accent. Sam didn't want to sound at all Viennese, or worse, Jewish. "Gentleman, from what I've learned, you're protecting, and worse recruiting a Nazi who is both unrepentant and has confessed to mass murder. I fail to see how that can be acceptable to your superiors?"

McClain stepped around the desk. "American policy isn't really your business, is it Colonel Berlin? In addition, I am unaware of the prisoner's confession to mass murder. Where did you come across that information?"

"We have our sources, Colonel. And we trust them. We know in great detail what von Hauptmann has done. I believe my government would be extremely unhappy to learn of your callous disregard for this man's intentional actions. He belongs in prison, or worse, speaking of firing squads, in front of one."

Rosenthaller smirked. "Do you think His Majesty's government and fighting forces aren't fully aware of our work, and that they aren't participating in the same themselves?"

"His recruitment by the OSS is contrary to your agreements with the French and us."

McClain and Rosenthaller looked at each other, both holding back their breaths. "Let's not fool ourselves, Berlin. We have mutual interests here. We need von Hauptmann back alive, and you want your nephew back. Help us to find them, and we can see what can be done. Do you have any idea where he might have taken him?" said McClain.

Sam smiled. "Yes."

"Do you plan on telling us?" asked Rosenthaller.

Sam looked directly at Rosenthaller mirroring his smirk. "Perhaps. I have a very personal, quite vested interest in this matter."

"Of course, your nephew," McClain said.

"Yes, but more than that. When we locate them, I want assurances in writing, that I may interrogate the prisoner myself."

Rosenthaller looked at McClain. "I'm sorry Colonel, we couldn't possibly agree to that without knowing why. Is the MI-5 interested in him? Or the High Command, for prosecution?"

"I'd rather not discuss that," Sam replied.

"What if we agreed to provide you with all the transcripts in both German and English from his interrogations?"

Sam had to stifle a laugh. He had all the transcripts he would ever need. And they were the real thing, not the doctored ones McClain would give him.

"I assure you, your nephew's translations are incredibly

accurate, and we have covered everything you could possibly want to ask him."

Sam smiled. "Sorry gents, that won't quite do it." Sam got up to leave.

"Stop," said McClain. "What is it you want to know?"

"I'm not at liberty to say."

"Does this have anything to do with the girl your nephew was searching for?" asked Rosenthaller. "I'm sure we could help in that department as well."

"I already have access to whatever information you have or can access in that area."

"I'm afraid this isn't a negotiation, Colonel Berlin."

"Then I'm afraid you will have to find my nephew without my help.

McClain pursed his lips. He walked back to the window and peered outside. "All right, you can interrogate him. But only with me present."

"I don't think so, Colonel."

McClain kicked the wall under the window. "Don't you understand how important this program is, Colonel?"

"I'm not sure I agree with your analysis McClain, but for my nephew's sake I am willing to look past my objections."

McClain turned. "All right then. But your nephew is going to pay for what he's done."

"I will need some assurances on that subject as well," said Sam. "In writing."

Rosenthaller picked up the phone. "Bring two jeeps around to the front of the building, pronto!" he screamed. "And six soldiers. I want two sharpshooters among them!"

"Cancel the sharpshooters," Sam said.

"No!"

"I won't take you."

"Colonel Berlin, I will throw you in the brig!"

"I don't think so, Captain. I outrank you, and I'm not under the command of U.S. forces."

Rosenthaller glanced at McClain.

"I think he's got you there, Johnny."

Rosenthaller picked up the phone and redialed the motor

pool. "Cancel the sharpshooters!" He slammed down the phone. "You'd better be right, Berlin."

CHAPTER 34

Hendaye, Border of Vichy France and Spain - October 1940

The train slowed and pulled quietly into the station at Hendaye. Spain. Relative freedom lay on the other side, a few hundred meters away. Hertz took Berta's hand in his. She squeezed it and smiled. "Almost there." Hertz kissed Berta gently on the cheek. "Yes, but not quite yet."

The memory of Hertz's encounter with Krantz tortured him. While he did what was necessary to save himself and his family, Hertz abhorred that he had taken a life, any life, even that of a hateful, vicious Nazi. One is never prepared for how the act of taking another man's life changes you, forever. Hertz disguised his distress and smiled at Berta. "We'll celebrate when we pass the border. Kurt, it's time to get our things together."

"Of course." Kurt smiled broadly. "May I remove this from my jacket now?" he asked pointing to the Nazi pin on its lapel.

"No, not until we reach Portugal. Franco is Hitler's ally. We have to keep up the charade." He reached out to Kurt. "Just a little longer, son."

Kurt placed the few remaining items from his sleeping compartment into his suitcase. His perspective on life as a Nazi diplomat's son weighed on him. While Kurt understood the feeling of fear he had learned as the object of Nazi hatred, he despised the feeling of fear he saw in the eyes of others when they looked at him now. This experience changed him. There were moments in the past when he wanted to be them, to be Aryan. Now Kurt knew he could never be them. He could only fight to defeat them.

"Good morning Monsieur Berlin," came a voice from the corridor.

"Good morning," Hertz said, opening the door. The conductor stood in front of him in a freshly pressed and starched uniform.

"I will need your documents please."

"Will we be de-boarding?" Hertz asked.

The conductor smiled. "I'm not certain. But I would wait before stretching my legs."

Hertz casually handed the conductor their documents. The feeling of anxiety he had every time he gave the papers to an official had lessened. They were close to freedom; it was almost over. A few more meters and they would be out of the Nazi vise. A few more days and they would be safe. Hertz was beginning to believe his plan had worked.

"I will be back shortly," said the conductor. "Would you like some coffee and breakfast?"

Hertz looked at Berta and Kurt. They nodded yes.

"Please," Hertz said. "And thank you."

"Do you think he forgot about the coffee?" Berta said. "It's been quite a while since he left."

Kurt looked at his watch. "Nearly an hour."

Hertz paced between the cabin door and the window. Vehicles with Nazi flags were parked on the other side of the tracks. Guards with rifles patrolled the platform. Hertz had a bad feeling. He was too close to freedom to take chances. Hertz jumped when he heard his name from the corridor, but it wasn't the conductor's voice. "Yes?"

"May we speak?" someone said in German.

Hertz opened the door. In front of him stood an SS Captain. "Heil Hitler. I am Lieutenant Albrecht Heimler."

Hertz saluted. "Heil Hitler."

Heimler returned the salute. "Please, could you come outside, bitte?"

Hertz shot a glance at Berta and Kurt. "Of course." Hertz stepped out and closed the door. He felt extremely uneasy. "How can I help you?"

"You are Hertz Berlin, the Deputy Consul designate on your way to Santo Domingo?"

"Yes." Hertz heart pounded.

The Captain looked at a sheet of paper in his left hand. "And your wife and son are in your cabin?"

"Yes." A lump formed in Hertz's throat. Had he come this far to fail? Was he still within von Hauptmann's grasp? "Is there a problem?"

"No, not at all, why would there be?" The Captain leaned into Hertz putting his gloved hand on Hertz's shoulder, appearing giddy. "We apologize for the delay. Confidentially," the SS Captain whispered, "the Fuehrer is less than 100 meters from here. He is meeting with Franco right…over…there!" The SS Captain pointed with his index finger in the direction of the opposite track for emphasis. His expression was ecstatic. "We expect the Fuehrer will be finished by midday. He has requested to meet with all military and diplomatic personnel in the area before he returns to Paris. We thought, in light of your future service to the Reich, that you and your family would want to meet the Fuehrer before you leave for your post."

Hertz felt his knees buckle. He stiffened and smiled. There was no way out of this. "What a great honor," Hertz said. "But I'm afraid we are undeserving of this. Neither my son nor I have rendered military service to the Reich."

"Nonsense," said the SS Captain. "You are on your way to serve the Reich now. We will be back shortly to collect you."

A quick "Heil Hitler" followed the knock. Hertz turned the knob and opened the door. "Heil Hitler," he replied, saluting.

"You are ready?" Heimler asked.

Hertz turned to Berta and Kurt. They followed Heimler and two armed guards to the exit at the far end of the second car. Hertz breathed deeply to calm himself, but worried about Kurt. He had maintained his composure through situations that most eighteen-year-olds couldn't have handled, but this was completely different. Even the idea of meeting Hitler was terrifying.

Kurt took a deep breath. He had been cooped up in the tiny cabin for hours. He felt sick to his stomach. How was he going to do this? It was said Hitler could sense a Jew once he laid eyes on him.

"Wait here," Heimler said.

"Of course, as you wish," Hertz replied, speaking loudly enough for the guards to hear. He turned to Kurt and Berta and smiled. "How fortunate we are."

"Yes," Berta replied. "A great honor." She took Kurt's hand in hers and squeezed it. "I am so excited my head is spinning."

"Mine, too," Kurt said.

Hertz looked at Kurt then touched his shoulder. "Do as we do," he whispered, then in a loud voice said, "Consider how fortunate we are. You will tell your grandchildren about this."

"I hope so," Kurt replied, smiling.

Heimler returned with two other men and a woman. They nodded at Hertz, Berta, and Kurt. "All right then, we are ready. Please board that car there," he said pointing toward a large black German Army staff car.

The limo had three rows of seats. Kurt climbed into the back row with Berta and Hertz. The car rolled past the platform and about 100 meters down the road. The driver turned right, crossed the tracks and turned right again, driving back to the stationhouse on the other side of the tracks.

"Please follow me!" Heimler shouted. There were several other groups of civilians, perhaps twenty people and another twenty military officers assembled. They followed Heimler into the building in almost complete silence.

Kurt searched their faces. They smiled wildly, ecstatically. He hoped the fear he felt in his gut wasn't evident in his eyes. To calm himself, Kurt thought of Elsa, of her smile, of how she would laugh if she knew what he was doing. It was funny in a way, this Jewish boy who had been hounded out of Vienna, shaking hands with Hitler.

"Please find a spot along the walls!" shouted Heimler as they filed into the main waiting area in the station house. "There is more than enough room, you will all be able to personally thank the Fuehrer for his dedication and sacrifice for the Reich."

"Go toward the corner at the far end," Hertz whispered. "He will likely enter where we did and hopefully will tire of greeting a crowd before he gets to us."

Kurt grabbed Berta's hand and followed Hertz. "Remember," she said slightly above a whisper. "Let us greet him first. Stand behind us. If he speaks to you, respond with concise answers. Yes or no, if possible."

"Yes, mother." Thoughts of Elsa quickly slipped away as reality closed in on Kurt.

They found a spot between two Wehrmacht officers in full uniform and the couple that had been in the car with them. The couple wore civilian clothes with Nazi party pins on their lapels. "I'm so excited," the woman said. "Have you met the Fuehrer before?"

Berta smiled. "No, I'm afraid we haven't. We are so fortunate to be here today. And you?"

"Once before," replied the woman, giddily. "In Munich, at a rally. My husband had a friend high up in the party, he arranged for us to meet the Fuehrer in a private audience. I'm so...."

"Achtung!" shouted Heimler. "Everyone! Quiet, please! The Fuehrer will be with us in a moment!" As he finished his sentence, he shot his arm into the air and snapped to attention along with the guards standing next to him. "Heil Hitler!" they shouted.

Hitler entered the room surrounded by an entourage of uniformed soldiers, SS officers, and a few diplomats and lifted his arm in salute. His entourage saluted and shouted back, "Heil Hitler!"

The entire room exploded, first in a shout of, "Heil Hitler!" then in applause. Kurt was spellbound and petrified at the same time. He caught the beginnings of the mass salute a moment late then raised his hand and his voice as all the others did. A terror swept through him. He began to sweat. These people would construe the slightest gesture or lack thereof as an indication of disloyalty. "Heil Hitler!" Kurt shouted a second time while applauding, just for good measure.

As the applause receded Hitler bowed his head slightly in several directions. Kurt studied him as he shook hands with Heimler and another high-ranking officer. Kurt was surprised. Hitler was shorter and less formidable looking than in newsreels. He looked a bit older and more worn. His double-breasted suit was perfectly tailored as it always appeared in photos, but Hitler's persona was significantly less than what Kurt expected. Kurt thought perhaps he would be able to do this. Then Hitler spoke.

"My people, my soldiers, thank you!" Hitler shouted in that same bellicose, exaggerated tone, and with that same booming voice he always used. Hitler's face changed, and that evil fire appeared in his eyes. Fear consumed Kurt's mind and body.

"Today is a great day," Hitler continued. The room was silent, the eyes of every person there riveted on the Fuehrer. "Today, I have brought the forces of our ally, Generalissimo Franco, and Spain into our orbit. When the time is right, they will enter the fight on our side. Gibraltar will be ours!"

A scream went up from the crowd followed by shouts of Heil Hitler! and Deutschland Uber Alles! Kurt looked about the room at the hypnotized crowd. His skin went cold. He thought he might faint. Kurt realized at that moment, more than ever before, that Germany would follow this madman anywhere, even to its own destruction.

The shouting subsided, and Hitler spoke again. "I owe everything to you, meine Volk," he said. "You are my strength and the future of our fatherland."

The shouts came for the third time. Kurt looked at his parents. Their arms were raised. "Heil Hitler! Heil Hitler! Heil Hitler!" Berta's left hand trembled behind her. Kurt followed their lead, saluted and shouted. When the salute ended, Kurt took Berta's hand in his own. "Stay calm," he whispered. He breathed deeply again to try to do just that himself.

Hitler made his way around the edges of the room. Kurt felt as if he were not actually in his body, but watching from somewhere else, far away. He noticed that Hitler rarely spoke to the person whose hand he was shaking, rather to someone on either side. Kurt prayed he would bypass them all altogether. The Fuehrer neared them. Kurt's legs began to shake. "I can't do this, father," he whispered.

"You have to, son. It will be over shortly. He's only a man."

As Hitler approached, Hertz moved in front of Kurt. Berta

did the same. Perhaps Hitler would move along quickly, missing him. Hitler stopped directly in front of Hertz. Kurt was stunned by how short he appeared next to his father. Kurt himself was taller than Hitler by several inches. This real perspective was a revelation. Hitler was a little man, not the giant he was made out to be. He wasn't a god, to the contrary he was quite ordinary. Then it happened again. Hitler spoke. "And you are?" he said directly to Hertz.

The voice. Kurt realized, it was Hitler's voice that mesmerized and generated fear. There was something about it that drew and repelled at the same time, that insinuated terror and obedience into every pronouncement.

Hertz bowed his head slightly and averted his eyes from Hitler's gaze. "Hertz Berlin," he said, "Deputy Consul to your Embassy in Santo Domingo."

"You are on your way there, or returning?" Hitler asked.

"We are on our way there to serve you, meine Fuehrer."

Hitler was silent for a moment. He turned to Berta. "And this is your wife?"

Berta curtsied. Hitler took her hand and held it in his. "How lovely you are, such pure Aryan beauty. Where are you from?"

"Thank you, meine Fuehrer," Berta replied. She blushed. "Vienna."

Hitler looked directly at Kurt and smiled. "Austrians, like me."

"Yes, meine Fuehrer," Hertz said.

"And is this your son?"

"Yes," said Hertz.

Kurt locked his knees so as not to collapse from fear. This evil man had brought nothing but disaster to his family. Kurt prayed that the blush that rose from his neck to his face when he was frightened wouldn't betray him. He opened his mouth to speak. Nothing came out.

"This is our son, Kurt." He heard his father's voice but didn't quite know where it was coming from. Kurt's mind was on fire. He had to say something. He forced the words through his dry mouth, his tongue nearly sticking to its roof. "I am so honored, meine Fuehrer."

Hitler looked him over. "How old are you, young man?"

Kurt's heart beat so hard he thought Hitler could see it moving under his shirt. "Sixteen," he lied.

Hitler looked him over again. "How long is your posting to Santo Domingo?" he said to Hertz, while still staring at Kurt.

"Two years," Hertz said.

"You will be back in time for your son to serve the Reich, as all young Aryan men should."

"I look forward to it," Kurt said. He bowed his head slightly to avoid eye contact. Hitler turned and continued down the line. Kurt felt the acid in his stomach move up into his mouth. He swallowed hard to keep it down and touched the fingers of his left hand to the wall behind him to steady himself. Yes, he would serve, not to fight for the Reich, but rather to defeat it.

CHAPTER 35

Outskirts of Mechelen, Belgium - June 1945

It took a couple of hours for the bleeding from von Haupt-mann's ear to stop. Saul hadn't said a word since exploding in rage. He watched from the shadows as Kurt changed the bandage on the Nazi's head several times. Kurt understood. Von Hauptmann's was responsible for Saul's suffering.

Von Hauptmann seemed to regain some level of alertness. Kurt pulled a chair directly in front of him and sat down. "Why did you destroy the convent?"

Von Hauptmann was barely able to speak above a whisper. "I told you, it was our policy."

"It wasn't an order?"

"No."

"Did you find Elsa Graz there?"

"I did."

Kurt nearly choked before the next words came from his mouth. "Did she die there?"

"No," Von Hauptmann swooned from pain. "I took her with me. She was to be accounted for and sent east."

"But she was mischling."

Von Hauptmann lifted his chin. Speaking was difficult. Blood seeped both from his head wounds and his mouth. "She was a different case. Her father was an enemy of the Reich. He had caused us too much trouble. She was to be made an example."

"An example to who?" Kurt didn't understand.

"It didn't matter. She was the daughter of an enemy of the

state."

"Was she sent east?"

"No."

Kurt was relieved in some way. At least Elsa hadn't ended up in a death camp, though he feared what had happened to her might be worse. "You said you took her with you. What did you do with her?"

Von Hauptmann attempted a smile, vindictive right to the end. "The same thing I did to her mother."

Rage rushed back at Kurt, even more deadly than before. He didn't know how to process this information, but it all fell into place. Kurt knew what had happened to Veronica Graz. Now this monster had admitted to killing Elsa as well. Saul was right. Kurt didn't feel anything for von Hauptmann except hate. He put his hand on his revolver ready to pull it from its holster. "What did you do to her?" He kept his anger in check waiting for an answer.

"I took her, the same way I did her mother," von Hauptmann wheezed. "Then I beat her. She screamed a bit more than her mother did."

Kurt catapulted out of the chair and pulled the revolver from his hip placing it against von Hauptmann's temple. The thought of von Hauptmann touching Elsa was too much for him.

"Kill him!" Saul shouted from behind him, walking out of the shadows. "Kill him!"

"Is she dead?"

"Yes."

Kurt moved back a step. He cocked the gun. "I promised myself I wouldn't do this. I was wrong to make that promise." Kurt took a deep breath and mumbled, "for you, Elsa."

A shot rang out. Kurt turned to the left to the dark recesses of the barn now filled with blinding sunlight. "Drop the gun!" came a voice from the doorway.

Kurt looked for Saul. He saw him on the ground, held down by a soldier.

"I said drop the gun!" shouted Rosenthaller.

Kurt moved closer to von Hauptmann. "I'll kill him!"

"Berlin, if you kill him you will face a firing squad!"

McClain screamed.

Kurt laughed, pushing the gun even deeper into von Hauptmann's temple. "Really, Colonel? Do you think I care! Fuck
you, you Jew-hating bastard! I'm not afraid of you. You're no
better than him. As a matter of fact, you're worse. You would
cover for what this murderer did."

McClain stepped out of the shadows. He pulled his gun from
his hip and pointed it at Kurt. "I don't know why we let you
scum into the country, to begin with. I should take you out right
now."

Sam jumped out of the shadows and grabbed McClain. He
pulled him to the dirt floor and placed him in a neck hold, his
pistol against McClain's head. "Make one move toward me
gentleman, and I'll shoot him!"

"You kill him, and we'll kill you, Berlin!" screamed Rosenthaller.

"Uncle!" Kurt shouted.

"Kurt, let him go!"

"You brought them here?" Kurt shouted. He pressed the gun
harder into von Hauptmann's head. "I never should have told
you! What's important to you! He killed Elsa!"

"You're what's important to me! Don't kill him. I won't let
them free him. I promise."

"You can't stop us, Colonel. Let McClain go, or we'll kill
you."

"Try," said Sam. "You think I haven't left details of what
you've done with my superiors, along with the originals of your
doctored interrogations?"

"Shit!" screamed Rosenthaller.

"I told you we couldn't trust this bastard kid," shouted
McClain from under Sam's hold.

"I won't let them have him!" Kurt, shouted. "I'll kill him
then I'll take you out, Rosenthaller!"

Rosenthaller redirected his revolver toward Kurt. "Release
him, now!"

"Kurt, don't do anything you will regret!" Sam shouted. He
turned to Rosenthaller, shifting his body on McClain to keep
him pinned down. "And you Captain, do you feel anything for

our people? When your friend here referred to us as scum, he was talking about you too!"

Rosenthaller's nostrils flared. He kept his gunned fixed on Kurt. He knew he was trapped. "All right let's bring this down a notch. Colonel Berlin, let McClain go!"

"Tell your men to lower their guns first!" shouted Sam.

"At ease, men," Rosenthaller said.

"Now," Sam said, "release that boy."

Rosenthaller nodded to the soldier holding Saul.

"Saul, go over there by the hay bales," Sam said.

"Let McClain go!" Rosenthaller shouted.

Sam carefully removed himself from McClain. McClain lifted himself from the dirt floor. He limped back into the shadows behind Rosenthaller.

"I'll handle this now," Sam said. "And don't think I won't be filing a complaint with your command about your clearly anti-Semitic remarks."

McClain laughed. "Yeah, right. Now, get me my prisoner back, or I'll order my men to shoot the lot of you."

"Please nephew, let me come talk to you," Sam said in German, slowly approaching Kurt, the light at his back. "Please, Kurt."

Kurt saw Sam clearly now. "He killed her, uncle. He killed her." Kurt began to weep, his pistol still at von Hauptmann's temple. "I loved her. She was so gentle, so fragile." Kurt's lowered his arm. "He killed her."

Sam watched as Kurt's body deflated. "I killed her," he said.

For a moment, Sam thought Kurt was turning the pistol on himself. Sam reached out for Kurt's hand. "Give me the gun."

"If I had stayed, I could have protected her."

Sam touched Kurt's shoulder. "Nothing could have saved her."

Kurt looked up at Sam, his face covered with tears. "They'll let him go, Uncle," he wept.

"No, they won't. I won't let them. Give me the gun."

"I can't." Kurt cocked the trigger and pointed it at his own temple.

"Please, Kurt. We've lost enough. We can't lose you too."

Kurt pulled the gun back slowly and handed it to Sam, who threw it behind them. He reached for Kurt and pulled him close. Kurt wept, his face buried in Sam's jacket.

"It's all right nephew," Sam said through his own tears. "There is only so much we can bear. You've been asked to bear too much."

CHAPTER 36

Spanish Portuguese Frontier - November 1940

The Spanish border control lay behind them. Hertz removed his jacket and lay it on top of one of the bags. Freedom, real freedom, the ability to get to America, lay one hundred meters away. Hertz felt tears well up in his eyes. There were so many moments when he thought it was over, in Paris, at Hendeya, especially when he killed Krantz. Hertz wouldn't have cared so much if it had been only him, if Berta and Kurt had been safe in America.

They walked down the dusty road through the no man's land to the Portuguese border station. Several other groups of people were already waiting. An armed border guard stopped them about ten meters behind the last group. As they waited, several cars passed and were ushered through the crossing.

The sun grew hotter as they inched toward the checkpoint. Two groups passed through, but the group ahead of them appeared to be having a problem. The group consisted of a man and a woman accompanied by two teenage children and an older woman. By their dress, it was apparent they were refugees. Hertz couldn't hear any of the exchange, though it was clear it was becoming agitated. The border guard was pointing to the Spanish checkpoint. The man had his head down and pointed to the papers with one hand, his other open-palmed, imploring the guard to listen to him.

The woman dropped to her knees. She was crying and begging. The guard raised his arm as if to strike her, but then the man and one of the children picked her up and pulled her back and to her feet. The older woman embraced her as she wept. The group, now clearly recognizable as a family, began walking back to the Spanish checkpoint.

"Father, do you think they aren't admitting Jews?" Kurt asked.

"We're not Jews, we're German diplomats," Hertz snapped. "Remember that."

The rejected family passed them on their way back to the Spanish checkpoint. Hertz avoided any eye contact with them. The last thing he needed was to be connected to them in any way. "Berta, do you still have the pins?"

"Yes," she said, looking at him. "Why?"

"They might serve us well right about now."

Berta reached into her handbag and pulled the Nazi party pins from the inside pocket, handing one to Hertz and one to Kurt.

"Put your coat back on," Hertz said.

"Father, it's so hot."

Hertz looked directly at Kurt. The elation of his earlier mood was gone. "Just do as I say."

"I just don't…"

"Just do as I say!" Hertz snapped back.

One of the guards waved Hertz forward to the makeshift desk set up outside the border gate. Hertz approached the official standing behind it and handed him their papers. The guard looked at the documents and passports and scrutinized each.

"Herr Berlin."

"Yes," replied Hertz. He tried to appear calm.

The guard held up one of the documents and reread it. "You are to be the Deputy Consul for Economic Development for the Reich to Santo Domingo?"

"Yes, we leave by ship in three days from Lisbon."

"This is very curious."

"How so," Hertz looked at the official's epaulets and guessed, "Lieutenant?"

"Thank you, but that's Captain. Herr Berlin, you are the third Deputy Consul for Economic Development for the Reich to Santo Domingo to pass through the border here in the past two weeks."

Hertz felt as if he had been punched in the stomach. "I assure you as to who I am. Our documents are real and official."

The lieutenant straightened up and puffed out his chest. "Shall I contact the German Embassy in Lisbon? I'm sure they must be expecting you."

Hertz glanced at Berta then at Kurt. The fear in their eyes was evident. "No need for that."

"Then I think you should return to the Spanish side. We can't let you into Portugal Herr Berlin, or whoever you are. Your papers and passports are obvious forgeries."

"I assure you, I am Herr Berlin, that much is true." Hertz looked around the checkpoint. There was a fenced off area about one-hundred meters up the road. Men lingered on the other side of the fence. By their clothing and beards, it was apparent they were orthodox Jews. "You let them in," Hertz said, gesturing in the direction of the camp.

The guard stopped writing in his notebook and looked up at Hertz. "Perhaps they were more persuasive. Please begin moving back." He pointed with his pen in the direction of the Spanish checkpoint.

"I can make it worth your while," Hertz said.

The guard looked up from his pad. "Let's walk over here and discuss that."

Hertz followed the guard toward the crossing station and behind a half wall. He pulled the sock from his pocket with the last of the diamonds, the currency with which he would have set himself up in America. But first, he had to get to America.

"You may put your hand into this sock lieutenant, and whatever your hand can hold is yours, but first you must let us cross."

The guard raised his eyebrow. "What is it, gold or diamonds?"

"Diamonds, of the highest quality, cut in Brussels." Hertz opened the top of the sock and let the sunlight catch the brilliance of the stones as the guard peeked in.

"Give me the sock."

"No," Hertz said, pulling it back. Hertz knew the guard could betray him. He could grab the sock and send them back, or worse, shoot him.

The guard placed his hand on his pistol and withdrew it slightly from its holster, thought a moment, then replaced it. "Grab your bags," he said. Hertz, Berta and Kurt followed the guard to the gate through the crossing. When they were through the gate, the guard grabbed Hertz's arm. "Drop the bags."

They did as instructed. The guard pulled Hertz behind the wall of the crossing station. "Now, the sock."

Hertz pulled the sock from his pants pocket. He held it open and out to the guard. The guard shoved his hand inside and struggled to wrap his palm around as many stones as he could. He grabbed and released several times before finally pulling his fist out, some of the stones tumbling to the ground. "Now, go," he said.

Hertz bent to retrieve some of the fallen stones.

"I said go, now!" He cocked his gun. "Or I'll kill you."

Hertz stood up and shoved the sock with the remaining stones back into his pocket. It was much lighter than before. He grabbed two bags and looked at Berta and Kurt, both of them with their mouths wide open. "Come, now, while we can. We are free."

试战

Kurt rose early as he did every day, to get use of the bathroom facilities before they became overrun. After that, he would head for the kitchen to make coffee for his parents and himself. The family Berlin occupied a corner of one of the barracks buildings of a former Portuguese Army school, separated from other refugees by sheets strung hastily and sloppily on clothesline.

Kurt sectioned off a small area for himself within their space by stacking their suitcases on top of a dresser he had found in one of the unused barracks. It afforded all of them the tiniest bit of privacy, particularly for his mother. The walk to the latrines was too distant in the middle of the night.

Kurt walked out into the cold morning. The dust that had covered everything when they arrived at the end of October had become a thin, muddy film that stuck to everything as the winter rains pelted the camp almost daily. Dampness pervaded every corner. What little his father had left after the Portuguese border guard dipped his fist into the sock was whittled down to nearly nothing by the constant need to bribe the guards to get virtually anything they needed from outside the camp.

Hertz thought their American visas would get them to Lisbon and on a ship in a matter of weeks. He hadn't known how wrong he was. Their American visas had expired long before they arrived in Portugal, and the American government was not feeling friendly or forgiving. Kurt's Aunt Lena, in America, was doing everything she could to have the visas reinstated. Since they were in a neutral country, the American government didn't consider them to be in imminent danger.

Hertz had changed much since their arrival. Kurt noticed it almost immediately. He was like a machine that had been operating continuously for too long and suddenly couldn't maintain its former speed. As time passed, one week, then two, a month then two, and then finally a visit from a Jewish aid worker handling their case from Lisbon, Hertz became more and more morose and depressed.

Kurt placed the coffee-filled thermos on the concrete floor along with his bag and peeked around the curtain. Berta, awake, smiled at him from their bed, his father still asleep. Kurt pulled back the curtain and entered, placing the thermos on the wooden crate that served as a table.

"Hertz," his mother said, her hand on his father's shoulder.

Hertz opened his eyes slowly and looked around the room. "Good morning, son," he said. He sat up on the bed. "What delicacy have you brought us?"

Kurt placed three cups on the crate next to the thermos. "The finest Viennese coffee, father."

Hertz smiled. "Let's have a taste then."

Kurt poured two cups and passed them to his parents then poured one for himself. The warm cup felt good in his hands against the cold air. His parents stayed in bed under the covers.

"You're getting quite good at this," Berta said.

"Yes, even with this poor blend of the cheapest beans and

sawdust," Hertz added.

Kurt laughed. "Thanks,"

They sipped at their coffee in silence. Kurt went to their cabinet and pulled out a box. "Would you like some crackers?"

"No, no," they both said. "You go ahead."

Kurt knew they were avoiding eating so that there would be more for him. "Are you sure?" he said.

"Yes," his mother answered. "We will wait until lunch."

He bit into one of the crackers. It was stale and bland. Elsa's face flashed into his mind. It's time to talk to them, she told him. He looked up at them. "My birthday is next week," he said.

"We know," Berta replied. Hertz turned away. Berta looked at Kurt, imploring him with her eyes not to continue."

"I'll be nineteen."

"Kurt, please," Berta said.

Hertz turned toward him and put down the cup. "I won't have this discussion again."

"Father, please, I can't stay here. I can't do this anymore."

"I will not permit it."

"I'm a man," Kurt said. He stood up and puffed out his chest.

"No, you're our son!" Hertz shouted.

"I'm nineteen. You're out of danger...!"

"Far from it!"

Kurt stomped around the space. He didn't care who heard. "They've stolen everything from me! I have to fight! All we do is sit!" As these words escaped his mouth, he regretted it. Kurt knew the quick thinking and maneuvering his father and mother had done from the day the Nazis marched into Austria almost three years earlier had saved their lives. They had lived in constant danger. The simple act of escape was defiance, and they had done that more times than Kurt could count.

"Sit!" Hertz shouted rushing toward him. His arm was extended above his head as if to slap Kurt for his insolence. "How dare you, after all that your mother has been through?"

Kurt backed off a few steps. "I'm sorry, papa. I didn't mean that."

"Then what did you mean?"

"It's just that I feel I have to do something to stop them. To show them they can't destroy us. In Sam's letter, he said…"

"Forget Sam's letter. My younger brother often says more than he should, particularly to you."

"But if I volunteer, they will let you go to Britain."

"So that your mother and I can work as domestic servants and worry day and night if our only son is alive or dead fighting for a country that wouldn't admit us to begin with?"

"But Sam…"

"But Sam, nothing," Berta said, breaking her silence. "Sam forgets that you're still a boy, and all we have."

Kurt squatted against the wall. "You don't understand."

"We understand well enough," Hertz said. "You are angry, you want to fight, and that's good, but that's not why we risked everything to get to America."

Kurt chuckled and rolled his eyes. "We're not going to America."

"That remains to be seen. Your aunt…"

"My aunt?" interrupted Kurt. "She knows no one, and our money, what little there is left as you told mother when you thought I was asleep last night, goes to pay for a lawyer in Washington while we rot here." Kurt stood up. "You think I don't hear you talking at night when you think I'm sleeping? I'm lying right there." He picked up one of his schoolbooks, useless as they were, and threw it at the curtain. It flew past and landed somewhere outside with a heavy thump.

Hertz sat down on the edge of the bed and began to cry. "We have lost everything. We have no idea where your grandparents are. My mother and sisters have been missing for more than two years. You are all we have. I won't permit it. I won't lose you too."

"I want to kill Nazis!" Kurt screamed. "I want to go back to Brussels and save Elsa, before they kill her!" With that, he stomped out of the room.

试戋

A few weeks later at the beginning of March, almost two years to the day on which he left for Brussels alone, Kurt moved out of their small space and into a barracks where single men who had straggled across the border individually were housed. It seemed that there was nothing in Europe but refugees desperate to go anywhere where there weren't men in German uniforms.

Hertz and Berta agreed to the move begrudgingly. They were determined to keep Kurt here. If moving to an adult barracks would make him feel more in control of his life, then so be it. Kurt still brought them their coffee every morning, but he spent the rest of the day talking with the other men.

They each had a story as harrowing as his own, sometimes even more so. The overall effect was that he came to understand how much his parents had done to save his life. He regretted his anger toward them, but still felt driven to do something.

Kurt continued to correspond with his uncle. Having escaped via Dunkirk in June of 1940, Sam was in London now, working for the British Army as a translator in an intelligence unit. He expected to be sent into the field shortly. The British were mounting a campaign against the Germans in North Africa. They needed native German speakers.

Kurt missed Sam. Sam had been a counterpoint to his parents. When he needed someone to talk to and his parents didn't understand, there was Sam. When Kurt arrived in Brussels, there was Sam. When he needed to talk about Elsa, there was Sam. And then, Sam was gone.

Kurt took his cigarettes and went out of the barracks to get some air. His parents weren't aware of his smoking. Living in a large room with two dozen men, all of whom smoked, made the likelihood of him smoking inevitable. He sat down against the wall of the barracks and lit up, then took the latest letter from Sam and reread it. Sam would be deploying imminently. Sending letters would be difficult. He understood how Kurt felt, but please, Sam pleaded, respect your parents' wishes.

Kurt folded the letter and put it back into his pocket. He took out another cigarette and lit it off the previous one. Kurt would do as his uncle asked for a little while longer. He couldn't promise more than that. If they were still here in June, Kurt would sneak out of the camp and get back to France to join the resistance. One of the men here in the barrack had a contact in Marseille.

试戈

Kurt was writing a letter to his parents to apologize for what he was about to do when Hertz came into the barracks nearly running. Kurt slipped the piece of paper off the table and stood up. "What is it, father?"

"We are going!" Hertz shouted, his arms spread wide.

Kurt was startled. "To where?"

"To the United States of America!" Hertz grabbed him, nearly in tears. "We leave tomorrow."

Kurt pulled back. He wasn't sure what to say. Kurt had his plan. He was going to save Elsa. America would have to wait. "Are you sure?"

"Yes, it's certain. We just received a letter from your aunt. Our visas have been reinstated."

Kurt sat down on the edge of his bed. "No, father, I can't go."

Hertz sat down beside him. "What are you talking about?"

Kurt pointed to the sheet of paper on the floor. Hertz picked it up and read it. After a moment, he put it down on the bed. Hertz took a deep breath. "You will break your mother's heart. I can't allow you to do this. It's suicide."

"Father, I can't leave her there."

Hertz put his arm around Kurt and drew him to him. "I understand what you want to do and it's honorable, but it's futile. Even if you made it back to Brussels and you found her, where would you go?"

Kurt began to cry. "I should be full of happiness," he said. "But I can't leave her."

Hertz lifted Kurt's head from his shoulder. "You say you've become a man and I believe that. Now you must act like a man and think through what your plan is. You can't save her by doing this. You will only get yourself killed. We will go to America. They will take you soon enough. It's only a matter of time before they enter the war."

"And you and mother will let me go? You won't try to stop me?"

"No, we won't. Now let's pack. We are leaving today for Lisbon."

Kurt wrapped his arms around Hertz. "Thank you, papa."

"For what?"

"For everything."

Three days later they were on a ship to New York. Kurt looked back at the shoreline as it disappeared. He never wanted to see Europe again. A week later they docked in New York Harbor. New York City hung at the edge of the water like a giant cliff. The weather was warm and pleasant. The air was slightly thick with humidity. As they waited to disembark at Ellis Island, a man from the Hebrew Immigrant Aid Society boarded the boat to interview them. He wore a light-colored tan suit and a straw Panama hat and was carrying a newspaper.

"May I see that?" asked Kurt.

"Can you read English?"

"Pretty well," Kurt replied. "I've been studying for some time."

The man handed him the paper. Kurt looked at the headline and read it to himself. "Germany invades Russia." The date was June 22, 1941. They had been running for twenty-seven months.

"Look, father," Kurt said. He handed the paper to Hertz and read the headline to him in German.

Hertz looked up and smiled. "The war is over. Hitler has lost. He has awakened a sleeping giant."

CHAPTER 37

Brussels, Belgium - July 1945

In the month that passed since Kurt's abduction of von Hauptmann, the weather turned quite warm. Kurt sat in the little park with Sam where he and Elsa had had their first ice cream together some six years earlier. Children ran on the grass playing a game of tag, laughing carelessly with glee. To Kurt, it felt like a lifetime had passed. "Why did you bring me here, Uncle?"

"I thought this would be a good place to talk."

"It's mired in the past. Too many memories."

"That's why it's a good place to talk about the future."

"I'm not sure I have much of a future."

"You do, but you have to open your eyes to it."

Kurt kicked at pebbles with the toe of his shoe. "Where am I going? I'm to be court-marshaled."

"I've made a deal for you."

Kurt looked at Sam. "Uncle, I have to face what I did. I nearly killed a man."

"You nearly killed a man who was responsible for monstrous acts, some of them directly affecting you and our family."

Kurt contemplated what Sam said. "What's the deal?"

"You agree to sign a document swearing you to secrecy about von Hauptmann. He gets a new identity. He goes to the United States to work for the OSS . Your rank is reduced to Private. You get a clean discharge. If you ever break your silence, you will be arrested and charged with attempted murder and treason in a closed military court…"

"...which would mean a firing squad."

"Correct. Can you live with this?"

"And what about McClain, and Rosenthaller?"

Sam took a deep breath, then exhaled slowly. "Rosenthaller will be disciplined for what he did, altering documents, ordering you to lie. He will be demoted to private, then discharged."

Kurt nodded. He took a drag on his cigarette. "And McClain?"

Sam put his hand on Kurt's shoulder. "He's OSS, there's nothing I can do. He's a spook, untouchable."

"And Saul?"

"I'm still working on that."

"You have to get him released and out of here. He has no one, save me. If they let him come to the States with me, I will agree to whatever they want."

"It might be easier for me to get him to London. We can work on the U. S. from there."

"I'll consider that."

Sam laughed. "You've become a real tough guy."

Kurt looked at Sam, his face expressionless. "Did I have a choice?"

Sam put his arm around Kurt's shoulder. "You've had a terrible time of it. You were so sweet when you were a boy. I'm sorry for you, nephew. We put you through too much, but then we really didn't, couldn't, wouldn't let ourselves see the maelstrom that was approaching. We always thought that one step ahead was enough. You have to forgive us for that."

"I'm not angry with you, or my parents."

"Then what is it?"

"There's no price for their actions. It's not von Hauptmann. He's a hateful animal. He would have been a killer, regardless. Hitler gave him a license. The only reason they disciplined Rosenthaller is because he's a Jew, though he doesn't want to admit it. It's McClain and all the people like him. It's our neighbors who turned against us. It's my teacher who led the crowds on Kristallnacht. It's that woman who lives in the Mandelbaum's apartment, ignoring their ghosts. No one cares."

Sam sighed. "But there were those who did help us. Would

we have escaped if not for Bauer and the Winklers? You were too young. You never had the time or the luxury to learn how good or how cruel people could be. If you let this consume you, they will have won. They will have murdered your heart and your soul."

"I'm not sure I still have either."

"You do." Sam pulled Kurt closer to him. Let them heal."

Kurt fought back the tears. "I miss her uncle. I failed her."

"You made promises you couldn't possibly keep."

Kurt took the pack of cigarettes from his shirt pocket. He offered one to Sam.

"No, thank you."

Kurt lit the cigarette and took a long drag, letting it out slowly. "She was so alone. And now I'm letting her killer go free, for my own sake."

"If she wasn't dead, if she were here, what would you say to her?"

Kurt took another long drag and frowned. "What kind of nonsense is this? Who are you now? Freud?"

"I have something to tell you."

Kurt dropped the butt of the cigarette on the ground and crushed it. "What?"

"Elsa's alive."

Chaos rose from Kurt's stomach into his chest. He thought he might explode. He jumped up from the bench and away from Sam. "What are you talking about? How long have you known this?"

"I confirmed it a couple days ago."

"How?"

"After you told me what von Hauptmann said about Elsa, I did a little investigating. I arranged to speak with him myself. It was part of the deal I made with McClain to help them find you. Your father knew von Hauptmann and told me he sold my father-in-law his papers. It turns out von Hauptmann set him up. Von Hauptmann had Jacques intercepted shortly after he left Brussels for Paris and killed him himself. He admitted it to me."

"And you will let the murderer of your wife's father walk free."

"I traded him for you."

"And what does this have to do with Elsa?"

"After von Hauptmann murdered my father-in-law, he had all of Jacques' property transferred to him. Jacques had a summer residence at Oostende. We spent our honeymoon there. I asked him where he took Elsa. He laughed at me and refused to tell me, but I had a hunch. I went to Oostende. The house was still there. It sustained little damage during the war. Halevy's household staff had moved in and was maintaining it. They recognized me from my visits before the war. I showed them this picture you had of Elsa and asked if they had ever seen her. They said yes."

Kurt was speechless for a moment. "He said when he left her, she was dead."

"He thought so. The other Sister, the older woman who protected her was dead, but they found Elsa barely alive."

Kurt thought he might faint. He put his hand on the back of the bench to steady himself. "I have to see her."

誽㦎

Sam pulled the British Army jeep into the gates of the convent in Oostende. The salty smell of the North Sea was in the air. "Are you ready to do this?" he asked Kurt.

"Yes." Kurt stepped out of the jeep and reached for a cigarette. He thought better of it and put the pack of Gauloise back into his pocket. Sam took the tulips wrapped in brown paper they had purchased in town from the rear of the jeep and handed them to Kurt. "I'll wait here."

Kurt walked up the steps to the door of the convent. He turned the knob. The door was open. He pushed it inward and stood in the anteroom. A nun appeared. "May I help you?" she asked.

"Yes. I'm Kurt Berlin. I am here to see Sister Cecilia Agnes." Kurt's voice shook, he felt his hands trembling, the tulips shaking with them.

"This way, please. She is in the garden making her daily devotions."

Kurt followed the Sister through the silent, whitewashed halls of the convent. She gestured toward a heavy wood door then left him. He pushed it open, tentatively. A brilliant light filled the cloister beyond. By the fountain in the middle of the garden sat a small, fragile woman in a nun's habit. As Kurt's eyes adjusted to the light, he recognized Elsa's face, though in some way it was changed. He smiled and walked toward her slowly, his heart pounding as if it were about to pop out of his chest and run away.

Elsa rose to greet him. Kurt drew closer. Elsa's face became clearer, her expression tranquil. Kurt reached out for her, dropping the tulips. Elsa opened her arms and embraced him, both of them silent. The scent of Elsa's skin, so familiar to Kurt's memory, tickled his nostrils. They held each other for a long time. Kurt felt as if he would weep but willed his mind to maintain his composure. Finally, after what seemed like a lifetime, Elsa whispered in his ear. "How I have missed you."

Kurt released her embrace. Unable to speak, he picked up the tulips and handed them to her.

"Thank you, how beautiful they are. Please, sit down," Elsa said, gesturing to the stone bench next to them.

Kurt took her hand. He looked into her eyes. They were as beautiful as he remembered, the vibrant green of new leaves in the early spring. "I've missed you too," Kurt whispered. "More than you can know."

"Are you well?" Elsa asked. She stroked his hand.

"Well enough. And you."

"I am at peace."

Kurt hesitated for a moment. "Elsa. May I still call you that?"

"I call myself Cecilia Agnes now, but yes, you may call me Elsa. That was my name. The name my parents gave me."

Kurt felt the tears well up in his eyes.

"Why do you cry, Kurt? We are both alive. So many aren't."

"I need to say something. To apologize."

"For what?"

"For failing you. For not keeping my promise."

Elsa smiled and looked directly into Kurt's eyes. "We were

children. You made a promise you could never keep. I should never have asked you for that."

"I made it because I loved you. I still do."

"I know that. I loved you too. I always will."

"Then come with me. Marry me. We can have a life together, children. Come to America with me."

Elsa tightened her grip on Kurt's hand with both of hers. "I can't, my darling. I am not the same. I have made a vow to God. For those who died."

"But we made a vow to each other."

"I know, but too much has happened."

Kurt pulled his hand back from hers. "Elsa, can I ask, I have to know."

"Can you ask what?"

"What happened?"

Elsa got up from the bench. She reached for Kurt's hand again. "I was living in the convent. He came looking for me. The sisters tried to protect me."

"I know that part. He beat Sister Jeanine Josef, and you offered yourself to him."

"Yes."

"Then he took both of you and destroyed the convent."

"If you know, then why are you asking?"

"What happened afterward? I'm sorry. I have to know the truth."

Elsa let go of Kurt's hand. She thought for a moment and then continued. "He kept us at SS headquarters in Brussels for a few days. We were in separate cells. He told me I would be sent to Mechelen for deportation east and that Sister Jeanine Joseph would go with me. I asked him to spare her. He said I could do something to save her life." Elsa stopped for a moment, then crossed herself and mumbled a short prayer. "He told me if I let him use me, he would free her."

Kurt's stomach began to churn. He wanted to scream. He couldn't agree to let von Hauptmann go free. Not knowing this.

"I let him do what he wanted. He came to me every night, and sometimes during the day as well. I closed my eyes and sent my mind elsewhere. After some days, I don't know how many, he told me he was taking me someplace else. He would keep me there. I was supposed to be sent east, but he had falsified the records to make me disappear. He would have to bring Sister Jeanine with us as well, as he made her disappear too."

"Where did he take you?"

"Here, to Oostende. He had a house. Well it was a house he had stolen from somebody. I found out later it was Halevy's. He locked us in a large room on the second floor. It was the first time I had seen Sister Jeanine alone since he took us from the convent. She looked at me, and she knew. She was devastated. We prayed to the Virgin to help us. She wept for me, and sometime later, she said she had to commit a terrible sin to save my life. She would kill him. She searched the room for a weapon. She found a long, sharp, letter opener in the dresser. When he came back, she lunged at him and stabbed him. The letter opener pierced his uniform and lodged here." Elsa indicated the area between her shoulder and her collarbone.

"It wasn't strong enough. It drew some blood, but otherwise all it did was anger him. He grabbed Sister Jeanine by her shoulder and struck her. He continued beating her. I couldn't watch. She was like a mother to me. I don't know how, but suddenly I found strength I never imagined I had. I picked up a chair that stood in the corner of the room and struck him over the head. He stumbled, then pulled his gun and shot Sister Jeanine Josef."

Elsa stopped for a moment and wiped a tear from her eye.

"You don't have to continue," Kurt said.

"No, I must." Elsa steadied herself. "He grabbed me and tore off my clothes. He raped me again. Then he beat me. Then he called me a whore, like my mother. I didn't understand then how he knew my mother. Now I understand, I know what he did. Von Hauptmann murdered my mother. Sam explained everything to me. Von Hauptmann said he would finish me off the same way he had her. I was in a fog. I couldn't process what he was saying. He raped me a second time then choked me till I was unconscious. He left me for dead. Sometime later that day the servants came. They found me there. They told me later that he had told them to dispose of our bodies. They buried Sister Jeanine here at the convent. They nursed me in the basement of the house in secret for a few days, till I could be moved. Then they brought me here. The sisters hid me and brought me back to health and to life."

Kurt reached for Elsa's hand. The tears streamed down his cheeks. He felt as if a part of him had died. "How do you go on?" he asked.

"I have faith, and I bear witness."

"Come with me. We can forget all this together."

"I can't," Elsa said. "What we had was beautiful. I will carry it with me always, but my place is here with my sisters, remembering. I pray for their souls so that they can forgive their tormentors."

Kurt watched as Elsa's eyes shifted from him to something behind him. He turned his head. Sam stood in the doorway.

"Go with Sam," Elsa said. "Go to America. Remember me. I will always carry you here in my heart and in my prayers. I have prayed for you every day since you left."

Kurt felt Sam's hand on his arm pulling him away, gently. Sister Cecilia Agnes turned and knelt before the statue of the Virgin. Kurt watched as the rosary beads slipped through her fingers.

EPILOGUE

Washington D.C, United States, September 1949

Kurt approached the librarian's desk. An attractive woman with dark hair and an intense expression carefully checked the bindings of some ancient volumes. She dusted them off lightly with her white-gloved hands before putting them on the cart to return them to the stacks. She looked up at him and smiled. "Would you like to check those out?" She tipped her head to the heavy books in Kurt's arms.

"Yes. I would." Kurt placed the books with his student ID on the counter.

The young woman looked at his card. "Kurt, well now that's a name one doesn't hear much in this country."

Kurt smiled. He detected a slight accent in the woman's speech.

"Where are you from?" the librarian asked.

"Vienna," Kurt said. "And you?"

"A small town in Slovakia. Does my accent betray me?"

"A little."

The woman extended her hand to Kurt. "Susan Reichmann," she said. "Please excuse my gloves. We wear them to protect the books from the oils on our fingers."

"Not at all," Kurt said. "Nice to meet you. How long have you been here?"

"Since 1939. And you?"

"1941. Seems like a lifetime ago, doesn't it?

"Yes, it certainly does." Susan handed him the books. "They're due back in two weeks."

"What if I'd like to see you again before that?"

"Come by. I'm here every Monday, Wednesday, and Friday at this time."

"I will," Kurt said.

Susan offered her hand again. Kurt took it, bowed politely and kissed it like a Viennese gentleman, the fuzzy cotton fabric soft against his lips. "I hope to see you soon." He smiled and turned, walking toward the exit. At the door, Kurt turned back. Susan waved and smiled. Kurt saw the blush on her cheeks. He left the building and strolled the two blocks to a small café. Saul was seated at a small table outside.

"How goes it, brother?"

"Very well," Kurt replied.

"What's that smile on your face?"

"I think I just met the woman I will marry."

"And how do you know that, Romeo?"

"She was wearing white gloves."

THE END

About the Author

A J Sidransky has published three novels since 2013. The National Jewish Book Awards selected his first novel *Forgiving Maximo Rothman* as a finalist in Outstanding Debut Fiction in 2013. Next Generation Indie Book Awards selected *Stealing a Summer's Afternoon,* his second book, as a finalist for Best Second Novel in 2015. *Forgiving Mariela Camacho*, his third work, received the David Award, awarded by Deadly Ink! Writer's Conference for Best Mystery of 2016. His next work, *The Interpreter*, will be released March 28, 2020. *Forgiving Stephen Redmond*, the final chapter in the Forgiving Series, will be released December 5, 2020.

He has published the following stories, *La Libreta,* (The Notebook) in Small Axe Salon (on-line) and was also selected as the winner of the Institute of Caribbean Studies short story contest in 2014. *Mother Knows Best,* was published as part of an invitation only collection, Noir Nation 5, and *The Glint of Metal* which appears in Crime Café Short Story Anthology, will also appear in the upcoming Fictional Café Anthology, both by invitation. *El Ladron* (The Thief) was published by Spinetingler Magazine in summer 2017. *The Just Men of Bennett Avenue* will appear in Jewish Noir II, a major short story anthology to be released in 2021.

A J is a staff writer for *The Cooperator Magazines,* which publishes seven monthly magazines to the condominium and cooperative apartment industry. He was a contributing writer to *#News*, a daily news satire that appeared on YouTube, and is a frequent contributor to *UptownCollective.com* a blog about life in Upper Manhattan. He has also taught writing classes for the Bronx Council on the Arts.

He is currently at work on *The Investigator*, the second installment in the Interpreter series. *The King of Arroyo Hondo*, a novella that will anchor a collection of short stories about life in the Dominican Republic today titled ***Becoming Bachata***, will be published sometime in late 2021

A J Sidransky lives in Washington Heights in Upper Manhattan with his wife. He is a dyed in the wool New Yorker, born in the Bronx, and a life-long Yankees fan.

Contact info:
A.J. Sidransky
917-282-5553
www.ajsidransky.com
ajsidransky@berwickcourt.com
alan.sidransky@yahoo.com
@AJSidransky